Paper
Roses

by

Patricia Rice

A TOPAZ BOOK

TOPAZ
Published by the Penguin Group
Penguin Books USA Inc., 375 Hudson Street,
New York, New York 10014, U.S.A.
Penguin Books Ltd, 27 Wrights Lane,
London W8 5TZ, England
Penguin Books Australia Ltd, Ringwood,
Victoria, Australia
Penguin Books Canada Ltd, 10 Alcorn Avenue,
Toronto, Ontario, Canada M4V 3B2
Penguin Books (N.Z.) Ltd, 182–190 Wairau Road,
Auckland 10, New Zealand

Penguin Books Ltd, Registered Offices:
Harmondsworth, Middlesex, England

First published by Topaz, an imprint of Dutton Signet,
a division of Penguin Books USA Inc.

First Printing, March, 1995
10 9 8 7 6 5 4 3 2 1

Topaz is a trademark of Dutton Signet,
a division of Penguin Books USA Inc.

Printed in the United States of America

HE KISSED HER SOUNDLY— WITHOUT WARNING

The total unexpectedness of it caught Evie off guard. She had grabbed his shoulders for support when he swept her off the floor. Now she clung to them as Tyler's kiss did what no other man's ever had. She felt the heat of his lips clear to her toes.

Tyler seemed to feel something of the fire, too, because what had started out as an exuberant salute gradually became something more. His lips softened and slid along hers and left Evie gasping for more. He took the advantage to part her lips, and she felt a sudden rush of something totally foreign as his tongue intimately entwined with her own. She was burning in places that shouldn't be burning, and her head bent backward to more thoroughly accept his deepening kiss.

But when Tyler's hand came up to caress the curve of her breast, Evie stepped away. Glaring at him, she crossed her arms protectively across her chest. "Don't you dare, Tyler Monteigne. You're not really Pecos Martin and I'm not one of those kind of women. . . ."

ANNOUNCING THE

TOPAZ FREQUENT READERS CLUB
COMMEMORATING TOPAZ'S
I YEAR ANNIVERSARY!

THE MORE YOU BUY, THE MORE YOU GET

Redeem coupons found here and in the back of all new Topaz titles for FREE Topaz gifts:

Send in:

 2 coupons for a free TOPAZ novel (choose from the list below);
- ☐ THE KISSING BANDIT, Margaret Brownley
- ☐ BY LOVE UNVEILED, Deborah Martin
- ☐ TOUCH THE DAWN, Chelley Kitzmiller
- ☐ WILD EMBRACE, Cassie Edwards

 4 coupons for an "I Love the Topaz Man" on-board sign

 6 coupons for a TOPAZ compact mirror

 8 coupons for a Topaz Man T-shirt

Just fill out this certificate and send with original sales receipts to:

TOPAZ FREQUENT READERS CLUB-1ST ANNIVERSARY
Penguin USA • Mass Market Promotion; Dept. H.U.G.
375 Hudson St., NY, NY 10014

Name_____

Address_____

City_____State_____Zip_____
Offer expires 5/31/1995
This certificate must accompany your request. No duplicates accepted. Void where prohibited, taxed or restricted. Allow 4-6 weeks for receipt of merchandise. Offer good only in U.S., its territories, and Canada.

Chapter 1

"Excuse me, gentlemen. I am looking for Pecos Martin. Is he here?"

The drawn shutters of the gambling hall turned the late afternoon sun into dusk. Smoke from dozens of cigars curled into the murky air, giving the room an atmosphere resembling the first circle of hell. Engrossed in their various card games, few of the occupants paid much attention to the vision in the open door.

And there was no doubt that she was a vision. With the sunlight for a backdrop, her chestnut hair glowed almost auburn. Arranged in thick, loose folds at the back of her head and topped by an incongruously tiny green velvet and lace hat, her hair rivaled the setting sun outside. The features beneath the thick waves of chestnut were not distinguishable in the gloom, but they appeared to be of the delicate cream and evenness that were fashionable. Perhaps the eyes were larger and darker than customary, having a certain exotic slant, but the clientele in this room weren't connoisseurs of fashion.

So the exquisite walking gown of green foulard and adorned with yards of ruching and topped with a darker green fitted tunic adorned in matching ruching went unrewarded by her audience. Only one head lifted in this sea of male attire, and the vision breathed an almost audible sigh of relief as her glance found him.

Surrounded by men in dark top coats, grubby sack coats, and black hats, this one man alone wore buff linen. The frock coat fitted snugly to wide shoulders, and his starched white collar contrasted nicely with the golden-brown of his coloring.

He seemed golden-brown all over, and Evie felt a swell

of reassurance at his appearance. This had to be the man she was looking for. Of course, he was much younger than she had expected. A man who had done everything that Pecos Martin had done should be older and grizzled and weather-beaten. She had expected one of the derelicts in shirtsleeves and vest with three-day's growth of beard to be the man Daniel had told her about. But this man was obviously accustomed to sun, more so than anyone else in here.

His hair lay in smooth, thick lengths of sun-licked gold and brown. From what she could see through the gloom, his features were regular and probably quite handsome. She hesitated to call a cold-blooded killer handsome. But he was definitely remarkable-looking.

Reassured by those looks, certain she was in the place described by Daniel, Evie approached the gambler without hesitation. It was all just as she had imagined it.

"Mr. Martin?" she inquired softly as she approached, her petticoats rustling slightly in the silence. She didn't want to disturb anyone's concentration. The men in the card game with the golden gambler scarcely noticed her presence. She wasn't accustomed to that, but she wasn't accustomed to frequenting dens of vice, either.

The gambler grinned as his gaze slowly raked over her new walking gown. Evie hoped he noticed the clever way she had cut the gussets so the tunic fit her waist neatly before flaring out over the full skirt and modified bustle. He certainly seemed to be appreciating some aspect of her attire, anyway. She smiled tentatively.

"Deal me out, boys," the man murmured, laying down his cards and scooping up the coins and greenbacks littering the table in front of him. He crushed his cheroot against the table and rose without a word of protest from the other players. They almost seemed relieved to see him go.

"How may I help you, my dear?" he inquired genially as he boldly took her hand and placed it on his linen-covered arm. When she seemed prepared to withdraw her fingers, he held them and started toward the door. "Let us go outside. This is no place for a lovely lady such as yourself."

Deciding there was no harm in holding a man's arm even though it was dangerously more muscular than she had ever dreamed, Evie followed him through the gloom to the brilliant Natchez sunshine outside.

She was perfectly aware that this was not the kind of place where ladies strayed, but she knew of no other way to obtain her goal, and she wasn't known for giving up. Don Quixote wouldn't have given up at the sight of a few cigars and the smell of unwashed bodies. The blacksmith and buggy shops of Under-the-Hill might harbor men of the lower orders, but Evie had full confidence that they wouldn't be interested in harming her. It was broad daylight, after all, and the street was filled with horses and wagons and buggies. She realized the shuttered buildings like the one she had just been in and other establishments of even less repute down the back streets and alleys were dens of iniquity, but she wasn't exactly certain how iniquity could affect her if she simply walked by it.

So Evie smiled up at the gentleman holding her hand with full confidence of her power to appeal and launched into her prepared story. "Daniel told me all about you, and I knew you were the gentleman who could help us out. I am Maryellen Peyton, Mr. Martin. I'm pleased to meet you."

Tyler Monteigne smiled slowly as his gaze took in the full glory of this creature he had only dimly assessed earlier. She wasn't so young as to be innocent, but young enough not to be a hardened case. Her face was an exquisite cream and rose accented by eyes so dark and heavily lashed that they scarcely seemed to belong to her. Full lips of a vibrant rose came to a natural pout that begged to be kissed, and sun-warmed hair gave off an enticing scent of cinnamon and roses that stirred all his senses at once. He wanted to eat her and bed her at the same time.

He didn't know who in hell Pecos Martin was, but he was willing to be Robert E. Lee if she wanted. "Pleased to meet you, ma'am. It's a pure honor to be called upon by such a vision of loveliness." Tyler made a slight bow, then securely tucked her hand into the crook of his elbow as he turned their direction up the hill. "Let us speak somewhere less public. My hotel is just up the street . . ."

"So is mine, and my brother would be delighted to meet you, Mr. Martin. If you would prefer to get in out of the sun, we could go there."

He had not foreseen a brother in the picture. Images of an idle afternoon spent in white, shapely arms rapidly faded. Tyler hesitated beside the barred windows of a tavern as he gave his companion a second look. "Perhaps you had best give me some hint as to what this is about, Miss Peyton. I am a busy man, after all, and I don't wish to waste your time or mine."

Evie sensed his reservations at once, and she gave him the full benefit of her smile. "I wouldn't dream of wasting your time, sir. I'm fully prepared to pay for your services. I suppose expenses and a daily salary are required, but we can discuss that later when you hear my story. I really need your help, Mr. Martin. Surely you couldn't refuse a lady in distress."

Ladies in distress were the first people he would refuse. They pouted and cried and clung and made a general nuisance of themselves. But this one seemed all shimmering copper and light, and Tyler couldn't resist a tentative questioning at the mention of pay.

"Best tell me what you need now, ma'am. I don't rightly know that I've time to book many more good deeds in my schedule."

That brought a brief frown and a quick look from dark eyes. But finding nothing ominous in his bland expression, she hurried on. "It's my sister, sir. We haven't heard from her in months, and her last letter sounded terribly desperate. We've got to find her, and we may have to rescue her from that brute of a husband of hers. I shouldn't be telling you things like this, but I'm certain you're a man who can keep a confidence. Daniel tells me you know all about Texas. I just know you're the man who can help us."

"Texas?" With regret, Tyler disengaged her hand. He sure as hell wasn't going to Texas even for the Queen of England. And from the corner of his eye, he had spotted another reason for sending this little temptress

on her way. "I'm afraid not, ma'am. I'll not be going to
Texas again anytime real soon. There's too much to be
done here. Now if you'll excuse me ..."

Evie grabbed his coat sleeve with determination. "It
shouldn't take long, I promise. And we'll pay you well.
I don't know of anyone else who can help us. Please,
come back and listen—"

"There you are! And who is this? Tyler Monteigne, if
you've been two-timing me, I'll pull every slick piece of
hair out of your gorgeous head. Let go of my betrothed,
you slut!"

The virago in shimmering red silk cut to expose a generous expanse of equally generous breasts placed her
hands on her hips and glared at her supposed rival. Evie
instantly released the coat of the man she had called
Pecos Martin. Her questioning look, however, had more
to do with this new appellation than the woman's
presence.

"Betrothed?" Looking slightly startled, Tyler tried to
extricate himself from one woman while soothing the
other. "Now, Bessie, why would I be two-timing the love-
liest girl in all Natchez? The lady was just asking directions, and I was trying to be helpful. Miss, do you know
the way now?" He smiled with disconcerting reassurance
at his new acquaintance.

Evie sent him a furious glare as she lifted her skirt. "I
most certainly do, *Mister Monteigne*. I'm sorry to have
troubled you."

With a swish of her heavy petticoats, Evie swirled
away in the direction of her hotel and Daniel. Humiliation crept up to color her cheeks, but fury followed close
behind. She should have known he was too good-looking
to be Pecos Martin. A darned rascal, that was what he
was. She should have guessed when he offered to take
her back to his hotel.

She could hear Bessie's loud voice carrying up the
street after her. The woman seemed to be alternately
berating the cad and cooing at him. Evie walked faster,
but she couldn't lose the sound. The Monteigne man
seemed to be placating her with pretty murmurs. Even
a loose woman ought to know a cad when she heard

one. The man didn't mean a word he said; she would wager on that.

The fact that *she* had been lying to *him* from the very first word didn't stem Evie's wrath in the least.

She cursed as she ran up the hotel steps and heard the loving couple come in the door after her. Apparently Monteigne had sweet-talked his lady out of her temper. It was just her luck that the lying rascal would have rooms in the same hotel. Just because it was the only decent hotel in the area shouldn't matter. The lying cad belonged in the lowest den of iniquity in this terrible town. Villains weren't supposed to look like heroes.

As Evie stormed up to the first landing, a black man popped out of one of the rooms down the first-floor hallway. Leaning over the balustrade, he cursed at the sight in the lobby and took the stairs in a long-legged stride, scarcely noticing as he swept by her.

Startled, Evie glanced over the balustrade. The sight of a black man in a white hotel didn't startle her that much. This was Mississippi, after all, and the Freedmen's Bureau had given all sorts of freedoms that would take some getting used to. She supposed it was perfectly all right for him to have rooms here. But since she had just come through the lobby, she knew the only sights to be seen down there were Mr. Monteigne and Bessie. The situation had some similarity to one in that novel Daniel had insisted she read, where the hero was actually a secret agent of the government. Perhaps Mr. Monteigne had a hidden identity.

The black man was speaking even before he hit the bottom step. His voice was too low-pitched for Evie to discern the words, but she was quite certain that the gambler wasn't any too pleased. Bessie's carrying voice made the problem a little clearer.

"But Tyler, honey, I've just told you, I'm ready to give up the sporting life and get hitched. I thought we could celebrate. We need to make plans. I want the whole town there when I walk down that aisle. Can't Ben wait just a while longer?"

The black man and the gambler were gradually leading Bessie to the door. The fool ought to know better than to think a man like that would be pleased about getting married. It was rather obvious it wasn't Bessie's brains that had captured Mr. Monteigne's interest. But didn't Daniel's secret agent have lots of women? Perhaps if he wasn't Pecos Martin, he was leading a double life. That would be vastly more interesting.

A rustle of silk on the floor above captured Evie's attention. Not wishing to be caught spying, she returned to the stairs and started upward as the door below closed on Bessie. Glancing down the hall as she passed it on the way to the next floor, Evie saw a woman in a walking dress more elegant than her own just leaving one of the rooms.

Behind her, she heard the unmistakable tread of a man's feet on the stairs. Curiosity was a terrible thing, right up there next to imagination. Evie hesitated on the landing, almost certain now of the next scene about to unfold. Amusement danced around her lips as she heard the soft, coaxing voice of the woman in the hall as the man approached. If this were a dime novel, she knew what would happen next.

"There you are, Tyler! I was so worried. I've left Timothy. I know you told me it would be foolish, but I can't help it. I want to go with you when you go to St. Louis. I'll hire a lawyer and see about a divorce as soon as we're there, and then we can be together as much as we like. Tell me you're happy for me, Tyler."

Unaware of his audience just around the corner, Tyler ran his hand through his hair, groaned inwardly, and stuffed his fist into his pocket. He hid his dismay as he looked down on the petite female in elegant silks before him holding out a beseeching palm. Bessie was a problem, but Marjorie Anne was a lady with a rather volatile husband. She was a fiery asset to any man's bed, but she was a loose cannon if ever there was one. Two such in one day was more than a man should have to bear.

Looking hastily around for any avenue of retreat, Tyler's gaze caught on the laughing dark eyes of the temptress in green as she demurely placed her dainty feet on the landing and proceeded to sail down the hallway in his direction. At this moment, salvation had the face of one Maryellen Peyton.

"Why, Mr. Monteigne! I didn't know you were married. I thought I heard something about you being betrothed ..." She let the sentence dangle insinuatingly before turning to the lady. "I am so sorry, Mrs. Monteigne. I had no idea I would be taking your husband away like this. Travel to Texas is so uncertain in these times, you know, and he offered to escort my brother and myself. You see, my brother is only eighteen and his leg was dreadfully maimed in a carriage accident, and he tries so hard to be responsible for me, but we both felt we would be much safer in Mr. Monteigne's care. You do understand, don't you? I wouldn't want you to be too hard on your husband for his generous ways."

Evie flashed a winning smile in Tyler's direction. "I'll let you two lovebirds have this chance alone. Just ask the clerk for my direction when you have a chance. We need to discuss details."

Triumphantly, Evie swept down the hall and toward the stairs. Tyler Monteigne was not only a rotten cad, he was a two-timing son-of-a-female dog, but she would have the last word yet. Daniel wanted an escort to Texas, and he was going to have one. Bessie and Miss Priss back there would see to that for her. If she were writing this adventure, she would have provided a more honorable hero, someone more like Ivanhoe, but a spurious Pecos Martin would have to do. She didn't have the time or resources to locate anyone else.

Miss Priss was talking almost as loudly as Bessie by the time Evie reached her room. She would almost predict absolutely for certain that Mr. Tyler Monteigne would be pounding up here sometime in the very near future. Unless, of course, he persuaded Miss Priss into some compromising situation before he sent her home to her husband. There was always that possibility. He was an indecently good-looking man, and secret agents did that kind of thing.

That thought brought a frown to her brow, but Evie wiped it away before she entered the room.

The boy resting against the bed headboard looked up

from his book and sprouted an eager grin at her appearance. "Did you find him? Was he at the Green Door like the books said?"

Evangeline Peyton Howell casually swept off her lacy fragment of a hat and tossed it to the dresser. "Of course. Did you have any doubt?" she asked airily.

"Tee-rrific! What's he like? Is he like the book? Does he have narrowed eyes and a lantern jaw and a hand that lingers near his holster?"

"Daniel Mulloney! Do you think I would get within ten miles of a man like that? Why didn't you tell me that was what he was supposed to look like before I went out there? Good grief! I could have fainted if my inquiries had produced such a creature."

Daniel didn't look the least bit abashed. "If I'd told you, you wouldn't have gone. He's supposed to be a real softy underneath that rough exterior. I knew he'd fall for you the instant he saw you. He did, didn't he?"

"Nanny should have been harder on you, I swear. You're incorrigible." Trailing the green foulard to the window, Evie checked the street below. There wasn't any sign of Miss Priss emerging. The nameless cad had no doubt sweet-talked her after all. Disgusting. She wasn't at all certain that they wouldn't need protection from their protector if they took Tyler Monteigne with them, but beggars couldn't be choosers. She would have preferred Sancho Panza to Tyler Monteigne, but this adventure required a guide of some sort, and they didn't have time to look for another.

Evie plumped down in the over-size chair and poured herself a glass of water from the pitcher. "Pecos Martin is every inch a gentleman. I'm not at all certain that he was even wearing a gun. He said he would be stopping by later this evening. We'll discuss the details with him then. You'll remember our story, won't you?"

Daniel grinned. "One of these days, Evie, someone's going to call you out on one of these tales of yours, and I wouldn't be at all surprised if Pecos Martin won't be the one. He's likely to whale the tar out of you when we get to Mineral Springs and he finds out you lied."

"I told you, he's a gentleman. He'll understand that

we can't trust anyone just yet. We'll tell him what he needs to know when the time comes."

Daniel shook his head at his older "sister." "I haven't met the gentleman yet who didn't want to tan your hide when he discovered he was the victim of your tall tales. You'll not have Nanny here to protect you this time."

Evie smiled serenely. "Don't worry. This is one time when the gentleman won't be able to say a thing. You just practice on calling me Maryellen."

Chapter 2

"Don't you dare try to kiss me, Tyler Monteigne! You're lying, and don't tell me different." Marjorie Anne tugged out of his placating embrace and strode for the door.

"Honest, darling, I wouldn't lie to you. She's an old friend of the family and is in desperate need of help. I would be revealing confidences to say any more."

"I'm going home to tell John Allen all about you. My friends warned me that you were no good, but I wouldn't believe them. John Allen will put an end to your lying tongue."

Marjorie Anne threw open the bedroom door and with a swish of rich silk, hurried out to the corridor she had been persuaded to abandon not minutes before. Fury colored her powdered cheeks and spurred her small feet into a rapid patter down the stairs.

Tyler leaned against the doorjamb, arms crossed, waiting resolutely for the next scene to follow.

It wasn't long in coming. With long, unhurried strides, Benjamin Wilkerson the Third approached from the back stairs. His narrow black face was singularly unexpressive as he noted Tyler waiting for him.

"You're heading for big-time trouble, boy," he said as he ambled closer. "That woman's got fireworks where her heart should be. She'll be bringing that troublemaking husband of hers down here for certain. And Bessie's gone off to find Dancer. She don't no more believe a word you said than the other. You're losing your touch."

Since Dancer was more or less Bessie's "employer" and had a reputation for testiness when it came to his girls, Tyler grimaced and allowed Ben into the room before closing the door behind him.

"The moon must be full or something. Why in hell do even the best of women get it into their heads to feather nests? There couldn't be two less likely females to take holy matrimony into consideration—particularly with an unemployed bastard like me—but they both have to do it on the same day. Must be something in the air."

"Spring, I reckon. All the animals are doing it. Want to hole up at the Ridge for a while?"

Tyler poured himself a whiskey and stared out the hotel window. He knew why Benjamin wanted to go back to the Ridge. He had family and friends there. But going home to Tyler only meant facing failure and defeat. He had spent these last five years avoiding that. He didn't see any particularly good reason why he should face it now.

"You know you're free to go anytime you want, Ben, but I'm thinking of moving on. I hear the railroads are finally starting to build toward Texas, and the price of cattle is going up. There ought to be money there to go around now. Maybe I'll pick me up some."

The lanky negro stared at his friend as if Tyler had suddenly announced he was going into the priesthood. "Texas? Have you lost your mind, boy? Way I heard, they're practically shooting at each other in the halls of guv-mint. We got enough of that kind of trouble right here. You just asking for trouble to stick your nose in with all those wild men over there."

"Well, I'm not much interested in wild men, but there's a certain little temptress who just might make it worth my while. She's got eyes on her that would make a man melt, and a tongue swifter than a whip. I think maybe it's time to come to a little understanding with her."

Ben rolled his eyes heavenward. "Boy, you got brains in the wrong part of your anatomy. Let's go back to the Ridge and do a little fishing, and I'll find you some nice quiet girl to fool around with. A roll in the hay ain't worth a trip to Texas."

Tyler's hand stilled as he raised the glass to his lips. With a soft curse, he set the glass back down again and turned to face the man who had taught him to fish and ride and had been his companion more certainly than his own brothers.

"I'm not taking any more Ridge girls, Ben. I'll stick to the kind who like a little fun and nothing more. I'll see you after a while."

With that, he walked out. Ben frowned and finished off the whiskey Tyler had left behind. That old story had eaten at them both. He'd thought it was behind them, but it looked like the past would dog their shadows into the future. Hell, maybe Texas was where they ought to be.

"Why, Mr. Martin, how good to see you so soon. Do come in. Daniel, find Mr. Martin a seat."

Since the room had little more than two twin beds, one chair, and a dresser, finding a seat presented certain difficulties in choice but nothing else. The skinny adolescent wryly drew out the one chair and gestured for their guest to take it.

Tyler noted that the boy walked with a decided limp that required balancing himself on the rickety furniture. A dashing gold-handled cane rested against the wall in one corner. His gaze took in the boy's pale brown hair and gray eyes, then traveled back to the vision still in green. There was no family resemblance whatsoever, but their familiarity with each other was marked. Maryellen handed her brother his writing desk as he returned to prop himself against the headboard of one bed, and she poured him a glass of water before he could ask for it. Daniel pulled out a bundle of letters and a small dime novel, and handed them to Maryellen as she spread her skirts carefully across the second bed. Neither of them needed to speak for the other to know what he or she wanted. It was quite a cozy tableau.

"Mr. Martin, this is my brother Daniel. We've come down here from St. Louis to find you because of this book. The reporter seems to think you know all there is to know about Texas. We understand the interior isn't particularly civilized yet, and we'd like your help in getting to Mineral Springs. We're willing to pay whatever fees you charge."

Judging by the costliness of their clothing, Tyler could see that their pockets weren't empty, but he had to wonder at their staying in a hotel in Under-the-Hill and sharing a room. Such economies spoke of a lack of cash flow. He caught Maryellen's knowing gaze as he glanced around and grinned.

"Well, you're fortunate that something has just recently come up that requires my attention in that direction." Tyler hadn't failed to notice the woman's continuance of the pretense that he was this Pecos fellow. She couldn't be more than a couple of years older than her brother, but it was obvious that the maturity was all on her side. She was cosseting a dreamer, and in a more cynical fashion than Tyler had expected. Her angelic expression gave away nothing of the lie.

"Teee-rrific." Daniel beamed happily. "I knew you would come. Maryellen thinks we can do everything ourselves, but she doesn't read about Texas like I do. If someone offered her an insult, all I could do is smite them with my cane. And if it came to stagecoach robbers, we'd be at their mercy."

Tyler sprawled back in his chair and fastened his gaze on the nonchalant female smiling through this pretense. If it came to stagecoach robbers, he'd be as much at their mercies as they, but she didn't seem in the least bit concerned.

"Tell me more about your sister in Mineral Springs. Are those her letters?" He nodded toward the bundle in Maryellen's hands.

"Sister?" Daniel looked momentarily confused, but Maryellen answered quickly enough.

"Yes. She always wrote regularly until just these last few months. We're terribly worried about her." Evie sent Daniel a fixed look, but he was already turning his eyes toward the ceiling and admiring the cobwebs there.

The little witch was lying. Intrigued, Tyler let her continue weaving her web of deceit.

"As I told you earlier, her marriage didn't seem to be working out. She seemed to be afraid of her husband. And then there was mention of attacks on their ranch. And then there was nothing. It is all very frightening, and we're determined to go to Mineral Springs and rescue her, if necessary. Evelyn always was delicate, and Mama cried her heart out when she left St. Louis for Texas. We have to find out what's wrong, you see."

Daniel was smiling oddly at the ceiling, and Tyler wondered how much of that fairy tale he might find between the covers of the cheap novel she was holding in her hands. Or perhaps she was always so inventive. He liked inventive women. He smiled lazily and stretched his legs across the narrow floor.

"Well, now, ma'am, I don't rightly know how much help I can be in your family matter, but I'd be happy to escort you to Mineral Springs. I'll need my salary and expenses on a daily basis, you understand, and I'm to have the last word in our travel arrangements. You're paying me for my experience, so I expect you to accept my decisions."

Maryellen began to look a little nervous, but Daniel was nodding his head seriously.

"We thought . . . Well, I think it would be better if we waited until the end of our journey to pay you, Mr. Martin. We don't know you, after all,' and . . ." Maryellen halted when Tyler raised his brows, and Daniel hurriedly interfered.

"We'll pay him half. That's what the book says. Then when we get to Mineral Springs safe and sound, we'll give him the rest, and he can decide whether or not to stay and help us."

Tyler hid his grin. His estimated fee of ten dollars a day just went to twenty. If they somehow managed to get to Mineral Springs all in one piece, he'd consider what to do about the excess.

Rising, he made a curt bow. "I trust you can be ready to travel by morning. I have a piece of business to take care of up the river a spell, and we'll be catching the boat from there. It's been a pleasure meeting you both, and I'm sure we'll have a safe and enjoyable journey. Good day."

Maryellen stared after him, openmouthed, as Tyler walked out of the room without so much as a by-your-leave. She might not have been raised in the best circles, but even she knew a gentleman should behave better than that. Who in Hades did the man think he was? He acted as if he really were Pecos Martin instead of a two-timing cur with two women after his hide. Maybe she ought to persuade Daniel out of this.

But Daniel was too enthralled to be tackled easily. "Did you see that? Lord, I wish I could be a man like that someday. Did you see the gun he kept in his waist-coat pocket? I wonder if he had another in his boot? I wager other people will think twice before taking him on."

Evie sighed and checked her hair in the mirror. Daniel had never had a man to look up to before, and she had to admit that Tyler Monteigne was certainly worth look-ing at, if not up to. She could still smell the spicy scent of his cologne, and something in her middle did a jig at the thought of the way he had looked at her. Men looked at her all the time, but none had ever looked at her as if he could see right through her and know her every thought, not to mention how she looked under her dress. Even his eyes had been a kind of golden-brown. His good looks were quite disgusting. She supposed they would have to endure women chasing after him wherever they went.

But that was just fine. She was going to be the heroine of this particular adventure. She really didn't think they needed Pecos Martin or a secret agent; that was Daniel's fantasy, not hers. She was quite certain she could handle this all on her own. But it would be rather exciting to have a handsome man along for the ride.

"How's your leg? Would you like to go downstairs to eat, or shall I bring something back?" she asked Daniel over her shoulder.

"Evie, you know perfectly well you can't be wandering those streets out there after dark by yourself. I'm coming with you."

Evie frowned, but she supposed he was right. That was one of the reasons she had agreed to Daniel's nonsense about finding Pecos Martin. As much as she would like to do everything herself, she couldn't bear to see Daniel hurting while he tried to protect her, and his pride wouldn't allow for anything else. She just hoped this Tyler Monteigne was at least a portion of the gentleman he appeared to be.

She turned and watched with concern as Daniel consulted their tiny bag of cash. "He didn't say how much he was going to charge. Do you think there will be enough?"

"We've been careful. We still have almost the whole month's allowance, and I suppose we can always sell some of our stuff if necessary. I understand people in Texas are eager for anything from back East. We'll manage."

Evie frowned as Daniel stood and grimaced in pain. "Are you sure you want to do this, Danny? After all, you've got your own family you could go to."

The boy's serious young face grew suddenly tighter and more mature. "You're my family, Evie. Do you really think I want to meet the bastards who didn't want to keep a cripple? Now come on, I'm starved."

He was right, of course. Daniel usually was. Reflecting on that thought, Evie felt a tremor of premonition as she remembered his warnings about Mr. Pecos Martin. She didn't know what Mr. Martin/Monteigne would do when he discovered the full extent of her lies, but there was no sense in worrying about it now.

She'd worry about it when she found out who she really was.

Chapter 3

"This is such lovely country. I can't imagine anyone ever wanting to leave." Evie glanced up at the towering magnolias along the lane they were traversing, then at a field seemingly inundated with wild redbuds and dogwoods in full bloom. St. Louis was a beautiful city, but this countryside was like nothing she had ever known. She had been raised on the English classics and thought adventures ought to begin in the mists of Cornwall or the rugged wilderness of Northumberland, but if anyone should ever write an American classic, it ought to start right here on the Mississippi. This was a magnificent beginning for any adventure.

Tyler urged the wagon horses to a greater speed. "It was a lovely country until the carpetbaggers and scalawags took over. Now its just the same as every other place. Some of the finest homes in the South used to be right along here."

Remembering the crumbling mansion they had just passed farther back, Evie bit her lip and kept quiet. She tried not to glance at Tyler too often. He was good to look at and the prospect was tempting, but his face had been gradually growing harder the farther along the road they went. She hadn't much thought of the man beside her except as a means to an end. His quietly growing anger and sorrow were beginning to unnerve her. Heroes weren't supposed to be sad.

As they approached another white-columned mansion, this one in slightly better condition than the last, Benjamin rode up to block their view. Tyler had never made any explanations or introductions when they had set out this morning with the black man in tow, and Evie had assumed the man was a servant. As the morning trailed into afternoon, she began to understand that the man was something a little more than that.

"I'm goin' to ride ahead and make certain they got rooms for all of us. I'll see about the boat tickets while I'm there."

Tyler gave him a look that should have left him flat and bleeding in the road, but Benjamin appeared impervious to the injury. Taking the small purse of coins that Tyler handed him, he made a grinning bow and danced his horse off down the road. Even Evie could tell he was an expert horseman, and she wondered at that. Surely the man had been a slave not too long ago. How could he have learned to ride a horse that well? If he weren't so skinny, she could liken him to one of the genies from the *Arabian Nights*.

Directing his words to the boy in the wagon bed behind them, Tyler announced, "You'll need to call me Tyler Monteigne from here on. 'Monteigne' is Martin in French. That's how I'm known up here, and that's how I travel."

Evie raised her brows but didn't question as she continued to look straight ahead. The mansion that Ben had distracted them from was already behind them, and Tyler hadn't given it a second look. Her overactive imagination was getting ahead of her again. There was no reason to connect this gambler with the lovely home they had just passed.

She deliberately moved on to other thoughts. Had the cur answered to "Martin" yesterday when she called because some people used the Anglicized form of his name? She didn't know French. He could be lying about that, too. It gave her something else to wonder about.

Daniel asked some question, and the desultory conversation between the two men continued as they traveled into a weather-beaten town that seemed to have only the river as an asset. Evie knew well the vagaries of the Mississippi River. It never stayed in its bed. To build along it was the work of fools. But to take advantage of its commercial opportunities was always a temptation some fool couldn't resist.

Obviously the fool behind this particular town had thought that building an inn on pilings and placing it behind a levee would keep it safe. A dock had been built out into the water to service the steamboats that came by on the way to Natchez. A few houses had popped up around the dock to house the laborers and their families. At one time it might have bustled with men hauling bales of cotton to market and goods back upstream for the plantations along the way. At the moment, it looked as if the whole town might blow away in the first good wind. If there had ever been paint or whitewash on the timber sidings, there was no evidence of it now.

Tyler said nothing as he reined the rented wagon into the inn yard. A man coming out of the stable greeted him with surprise, but Tyler made no more than a courteous salute before handing Evie down from the wagon and managing to put himself in Danny's way so the boy could borrow his shoulder as he climbed out. He had the manners of a gentleman even if something in his eyes said he no longer belonged to that class.

Having led a reasonably protected life, Evie wasn't familiar with the hard light shining behind Tyler's golden-brown eyes, but instinct told her to be wary of it. She was growing accustomed to his casual manner of appropriating her hand, and she didn't flinch now as he led her toward the rickety inn. She felt oddly secure with him walking beside her, even though the building they approached was one she would certainly have avoided on her own. Tyler wasn't a tall man or a heavy one, but he stood a head taller than she and walked with a muscular fluidity that somehow reassured.

He was in immaculate brown today, his linen freshly starched and pressed, his boots polished to a brilliant gleam. He had the arrogant air of confidence only the very wealthy could afford, and Evie felt a tingle of anticipation as they entered the building. She had never encountered a man quite so masculine as this one. He was almost frightening in his assurance, but at the same time, she found him exciting. She wasn't particularly inclined to timidity herself. She certainly couldn't fault it in a man.

"Monteigne! Haven't seen you around in a dog's age. That is you, isn't it? Last time I recollect seeing you, you weren't no more than a scraggly rag of a boy."

The speaker was slumped in a wooden chair with his feet propped on the front desk, his chair tilted on its back legs. He didn't bother to rise as they entered. Tyler frowned and shoved his boot beneath the tilted feet of the chair, unbalancing it enough to send the man leaping for safety.

"You haven't changed any, either, O'Ryan. The lady would like a room to rest from our journey. I trust you've cleaned one since Benjamin came by?"

Of average height and skinny build except for the belly hanging over his belt, the proprietor looked aggrieved. "That boy didn't mention nothing about no lady. He just said to set up some rooms. This ain't no fancy parlor, you know."

Before Tyler could take out any more of his anger on the innkeeper, Evie smiled and interrupted gently. "Why, I think this is a perfectly enchanting situation, Mr. O'Ryan. If you would just be so kind as to show us our rooms, I'll take care of everything. My nanny taught me all about traveling, and I'm prepared for just about anything."

Since she had along enough trunks to furnish a small house, Tyler didn't doubt that. He'd had to hire a wagon instead of a carriage to carry them all. He probably should have made her leave them at the warehouse in Natchez, but she had insisted that they needed them while they traveled. For all he knew, they contained gold bullion. Who was he to argue when she was paying the way?

With increasing impatience, Tyler assisted her in sorting out the trunks she wanted carried upstairs. He finally left her contentedly spreading fresh linens on the beds she and Daniel were using. The boy was entitled to a room of his own, but his sister was insistent that he not be forced to use the third floor attic that Ben had reserved for him. Since Daniel was sitting in the lobby with his head buried in a book, Tyler didn't question her decision.

He left them to their own devices and set out to put a few of his own into action.

"This is a public accommodation. I see no reason why we should have to stay in this miserable little room while they're downstairs having fun. Even Benjamin is in there. I heard him. What if they gamble away our tickets? I think we ought to go down and watch."

Daniel watched as Evie paced the length of their room—which was considerably larger than their hole-in-the-wall in Natchez despite her description. Ever since Nanny had died and they had discovered the letters, Evie had been restless, increasingly so with every passing day. She had always been the kind of person who never sat still. Even when she was little and came down sick and had to stay in bed, she would spend the time writing wild tales and drawing pictures to go with them. Until Nanny died, Evie had taught a room full of young girls their lessons every day and spent her spare time turning Nanny's garden into a palette of colors in the warm months and her walls into murals in the winter. It was a good thing Nanny had the patience of a saint.

But Nanny was no longer here to calm Evie's fits and starts, as she called them, and Daniel was in no position to do so. He lived life vicariously through her escapades and was usually in the position of encouraging her rather than otherwise. But descending into the saloon of drinking, smoking, gambling strangers probably wasn't the wisest of choices for a little fun.

But Evie had already made up her mind and was gathering up her little reticule and shawl as if she were going to an afternoon tea party. Hiding a grimace, Daniel reckoned he better accompany her on this particular escapade. He didn't think Pecos Martin was going to appreciate the presence of a female at this showdown.

For Daniel was quite certain it was a showdown of sorts from things the men had let slip when they thought he wasn't listening. There was a man by the name of Dorset who had acquired something valuable whom Ben and Pecos were determined to fleece, one way or another. Daniel hoped Pecos Martin wasn't a cheat, but he and Ben had sounded mighty certain of themselves when they set up this game.

The men in the saloon scarcely noticed when Daniel and Evie entered. The man they were supposed to call Tyler looked up and scowled briefly, but then he returned to his cards and his wager. The growing stack of coins in the table's center caused Daniel's eyes to widen. They weren't even using greenbacks, but real money. This was serious.

Evie was enchanted. This was just the way Daniel had described it from the Pecos Martin books. She looked around and was disappointed not to see any saloon girls to liven the action. Well, then, she'd just have to see what she could do herself. Perhaps she could catch a cheat.

There were more onlookers than participants in this game, but Evie managed to wedge her way through to watch the action. Daniel wished for a chair, but evidently saloons didn't believe in allowing people to sit for long. The only chairs were the ones the cardplayers were using at the table. He leaned against the bar and accepted the beer the bartender shoved in his direction. Nanny had never allowed him to drink beer, but it was high time he learned if he was going to Texas.

Tyler was perfectly aware when Maryellen pushed her way through the crowd across the table from him, but he didn't allow her to break his concentration. He was fairly certain Dorset was cheating, but he had expected that. The other men at the table didn't have enough brains to cheat with any degree of success, and he disregarded them as opponents. It was Dorset he wanted to break.

He cursed as the hand went to Dorset, but he didn't allow any of his fury to show. Taking this opportunity to look up and enjoy the beauty of his unexpected companion, Tyler surprised a frown on her clever little face.

It hadn't taken a day of traveling together for Tyler to recognize that Maryellen Peyton's stunning beauty held a quick and altogether too-clever mind, although she occasionally seemed to inhabit a world of her own. He wondered what fantasy she had entered into now. She was smiling, whispering eager questions to Benjamin and enlisting the interest of every man around her, but she was up to something. His glance casually swerved to Daniel. The boy was easier to read than his sister, and his face usually reflected everything that went on in his sister's head.

Daniel was well employed bending his elbow at the bar, but the frown that moments before had been on Maryellen's face was now on the boy's. Tyler returned his attention to the dealer, but his concentration was now divided. He caught Maryellen's ingenuous smile as she looked at Dorset's cards, and he noticed Benjamin had forsaken his place to her. That wasn't at all according to plan.

Dorset threw out a pair of low cards of unmatched suits and drew two more. Maryellen frowned. Tyler folded. A few minutes later Dorset took the pot with a pair of knaves. Tyler ordered the lady a lemonade.

"Hell, Monteigne, I thought you was a gambler." Dorset threw back a shot of whiskey, and turned slightly to wink at the pretty lady over his shoulder before turning back to the table and accepting the deck of cards. "Looks to me as if you're as piss-poor at gambling as you are at farming."

Tyler merely grunted and picked up his cards, disregarding Dorset's insults. He knew more about the psychology of gambling than the other man would ever learn in a lifetime. He didn't look at Maryellen as he scanned his cards and lay them facedown on the table.

Dorset lost the next round to one of the other players, and he complained about Benjamin's presence. Maryellen patted him on the back sympathetically and whispered some joke in his ear that ended his complaint before Benjamin could be thrown out. Daniel limped over and put a beer at Dorset's fingertips.

Dorset appeared thoroughly appeased. In his thirties with thick raven black hair that the ladies adored and a jaw that stuck out and dared anyone to defy him, Dorset was accustomed to being pampered. He chucked Maryellen under the chin, and Tyler ground his teeth together.

The little pestilence was going to hear about this later, but now wasn't the time. He needed to keep Dorset in this game.

Maryellen smiled at every card that Dorset drew in the next hand. She told jokes to the men around them, evidently enjoying herself. Mostly her listeners were dirt farmers, and their limited means didn't allow them much entertainment. Maryellen took the haunted look of desperation out of their eyes and made them grin. They offered her more lemonade. One with a little more beer in him than sense offered her a cigar. She stuck it in her mouth and chomped on it like a licorice stick. Tyler won the round.

Dorset was still enjoying himself. Tyler took the deal, and Maryellen continued smiling when Dorset picked up his cards, a sure sign that the man's cards were bad. Tyler wondered if she knew what she was doing. He tipped her a wink, and she stuck up her nose at him. The men around her laughed and Tyler pretended to frown, but elation soared through his veins. The witch was damned good at this game. Benjamin had taken the sidelines for good reason.

The next hand was long and drawn-out, and money began to build again in the table's center. Benjamin gave him the signal that a card was floating in the game that shouldn't be there, but Tyler hadn't seen Dorset pull it. He ventured a quick look up and found Daniel leaning drunkenly on Maryellen's shoulder. Two beers didn't make even an eighteen-year old drunk. Tyler was beginning to feel as if this particular scenario was getting out of control.

Maryellen patted her brother's hand and sent Daniel back to the bar. But when she turned her attention back to the table, she spilled her drink down Dorset's coat. The planter roared and leapt to his feet. Benjamin grabbed him before he could swing, and Maryellen chirped and patted his vest with her lace hanky while Benjamin deprived him of his coat as neatly as any valet. Daniel brought the irate man another beer.

As the source of Dorset's spare cards was neatly removed by the actions of a couple of striplings, Tyler wanted to laugh. He wanted to roll on the floor and hold his sides until he ached. He wanted to kiss Maryellen Peyton and even her brother if necessary. Instead, he growled and ordered everyone to get back to the game.

It was easy after that. Without the assistance of his coat pockets, Dorset's cards went steadily downhill. Maryellen's cheerful smiles and reassurances kept Tyler betting for as long as Dorset would hold out. Dorset lost every hand. Maryellen's frowns seemed to signal bad hands for Tyler, for he folded every time she did so. Dorset won those rounds, but the pot was much smaller.

The stack of money around Tyler grew larger and began to include greenbacks as Dorset emptied out his pockets and ordered more whiskey. Several of the other men at the table dropped out to go home with their small winnings. Others stepped in to take their places. Their audience grew tenser as Dorset grew angrier.

Daniel hiccuped and slid from the bar to the floor. Benjamin lifted him up and carried him out. Tyler didn't miss either of them. Maryellen was yawning and glancing at her nails. Tyler let the pot go to the man beside him. Dorset threw down a pair of deuces and swore.

"Monteigne, if I didn't have a man watching you, I'd swear you were cheating. Take off your coat for insurance, and I'll go you one more round."

Tyler gave his opponent a look that should have shriveled him in his seat. "Those are fighting words, Dorset. Gentlemen don't cheat. But since I'm winning this game, I'm prepared to be generous." He shrugged off his tailored frock coat and threw it at one of the men standing near him. The man instantly searched it for hidden cards or devices and shrugged when he found none.

"Now, put your money where your mouth is, Dorset." Tyler picked up the deck of cards and began shuffling. The mound of money in front of him was enormous, sufficient to pay off almost every grudge he had against the man. But he wanted one thing more.

"I want a new deck of cards. Henry, have you got a clean deck?" Dorset shouted to the bartender.

The bartender obligingly threw an unopened pack. Someone caught it and passed it to the men at the table.

Tyler caught Maryellen's eye as Dorset's man took the old deck. She glanced thoughtfully in the man's direction, then nodded almost imperceptibly.

While the men at the table broke open the new pack, Maryellen called sweetly, "Could I have those old cards, gentlemen? I'd like them for a souvenir of one of the most exciting nights of my life. Maybe you could autograph the aces for me when you're done playing?"

Tyler hid his laughter as Dorset's accomplice scowled and surrendered the cards. The farmers were willingly scribbling their names across deuces and treys as he dealt the new cards. Tyler now knew where the spy was in the crowd, although he'd harbored the suspicion all along. And Dorset wouldn't have the advantage of the extra deck as he had hoped. Deprived of whatever was left in his coat, the planter would have to play an honest game.

"What are you wagering, Dorset?" Tyler called as he examined his hand without allowing a glimpse of it to anyone.

"You'll have to take my marker, Monteigne. You know I'm good for it. After all, you ought to be more aware than anyone of what my crop brings."

The room fell silent. Maryellen looked thoughtful as she placed another beer beside Dorset and glanced at the hand that he so carelessly displayed. This time she gave no evidence of laughter or frowns.

Not high cards then. Reading Maryellen's deliberate expression, Tyler ignored Dorset's jibe and discarded one card and drew another. "I'll not be here long enough to collect your marker, Dorset. Wager that watch you're wearing."

Feeling the currents of tension, the other men in the game quickly folded. Dorset frowned and put the intricately engraved gold watch on the table and took two more cards.

Tyler dropped a stack of coins on the table. "I call."

Dorset spread out a pair of tens. Tyler had two knaves.

"Damn it, Monteigne, I know you cheated." Dorset reached to take back the watch.

A click from Tyler's revolver halted Dorset's hand in midair. Tyler pocketed the watch without looking at it, then began filling his pockets with cash. "I wasn't the one with cards in my coat, sir. Now, if you'll excuse me, I have an early appointment tomorrow." Tyler rose and made a slight bow to their audience. "Gentlemen." He swung around and started for the door.

"Now, that's not nice," Maryellen's voice scolded at the same time one of the farmers shouted. Tyler heard a slap, then the sound of a shot.

Swinging around, he noted the imprint of a hand on Dorset's thick jaw. A new hole gaped in the ceiling and a smoking gun lay on the floor. With a look of fire in her eyes, Maryellen stalked through the crowd. Tyler offered his arm. She gave him a pithy look and took it, gathering her full skirts gracefully in her free hand as she did so. A small grin played at a corner of her lips as she whispered, "Do I make a good sidekick for Pecos Martin?"

As they left the fury of the argument behind them, Tyler gave her an incredulous look, but her disarming grin swept through him on the wings of elation. He leaned over to whisper in her ear, "I think it's time Pecos and his partner gets the hell out of here."

And Maryellen nodded a wide-eyed agreement as they raced up the stairs before the fight in the saloon could spill into the lobby.

Chapter 4

Benjamin looked up as they flew into the room and slapped the bar across the door. Daniel was sound asleep, fully clothed, in one of the beds.

"Party's breaking up," Benjamin ruminated laconically at a crash from below.

"Is the boat in yet?" Shrugging his coat back on, Tyler grabbed one of the carpetbags he'd carried up for his traveling companion and threw it to Maryellen.

"Heard the whistle coming 'round the bend not too far back."

"Maryellen, pack whatever you need for tonight. Ben, you can get the trunks on the boat in the morning. I don't think they'll come looking for the two of you, but you might wait until the last minute before you head out so they don't follow you. Use your own judgment."

Caught up in this amazing adventure, Maryellen came down from her cloud abruptly with the staccato exchange between the two men. She didn't mind riding triumphantly into the sunset, but she wasn't doing it without her luggage. Holding her bag, Maryellen stared at Tyler as if he'd taken leave of his senses. "Pack what I need? I'll have to strip the beds and crush the gown I took out for pressing and ..."

Impatiently, Tyler pulled the garments she had left hanging on a hook and grabbing her bag, stuffed them in. There wasn't any room left for anything else. He held out his hand to Benjamin. "Give us our tickets."

Ben handed them over. "I'll keep an eye on the stairs. You take the back way."

Clutching Maryellen's bag in one hand, Tyler grabbed

her arm with the other and called to Ben, "See you in the morning."

Before she had any idea what was going on, Tyler dragged her out of the room and toward the kitchen stairs. Maryellen dug in her heels, but he didn't notice. He went down the stairs first as a gentleman should, but it wasn't a gentleman's hold that he had on her arm as he practically jerked her after him.

"Tyler, let go of me! Where do you think you're going?" she whispered furiously. "I can't leave Daniel."

"Hush." Tyler stopped at the bottom of the stairs and listened to the drunken roars from the front of the inn. If he judged his man right, after the brawl there would be a brief respite while he slept it off. In the cold clear air of morning, Dorset would come to realize what Maryellen had done. Tyler wasn't taking any chances between now and then, however.

There was no sound of pursuit as yet. Throwing open the back door, he pulled Maryellen down the path toward the privy. He could hear her gasp of surprise, but she was keeping her mouth shut. He'd give her a few more points for cleverness.

He wasn't giving her any chance to argue. Triumph rocketing through his veins, Tyler raced down the path, towing the creative little witch behind him.

Maryellen jerked her hand away from him to hike her skirts up as far as she could as she ran after him. Nanny had taught her that ladies never cursed, but the epithets coming to mind as tree branches grabbed at her flounces weren't precisely euphemisms. Laughter bubbled up as the success of their venture mixed with the reality of torn flounces. Heroes didn't wear skirts.

The paddle wheeler at the dock spilled light and music across the dark river, but the plank wasn't in place. Tyler cursed and hallooed the guard until the man came to the railing and leaned over.

"You've got to help us out, man!" Tyler caught Maryellen by the waist and held her close. "We just got married, and they're trying to chivaree us. We've got tickets for the morning. Could you let us on now?"

The guard looked down at the handsome couple and

chuckled. The bride looked bewildered and lost, and the groom had the air of a man on his last rope. The guard called for help in lowering the plank.

Tyler swept Maryellen up to the boat and pulled the tickets from his pocket along with a handful of greenbacks. "They might come looking for us here. Is there a stateroom vacant? You can handle the exchange with the purser in the morning and keep the change for your trouble."

"I do believe you're in luck, sir." The guard continued chuckling as he pocketed the cash. "Just follow me."

Coming down from her euphoric cloud, Evie hesitated at the sound of this, but she wasn't yet ready to create a scene. Tyler might conceivably be honorable in his intentions. And from the sounds of the brawl they had just left behind, he was undoubtedly correct in making their escape. Remembering her part in this, she grinned. She'd never done anything remotely like that before, and she had enjoyed herself thoroughly.

Tyler's exuberance matched her own as they entered the room they were shown to and the door closed behind them. With a whoop of triumph, he flung her bag to the floor and caught the heroine of the hour up in his arms, swinging her around the small space left between bed and door.

"You're a treasure and a joy to behold, Maryellen Peyton. I've been waiting for this day for years!"

And without any further warning than that, Tyler's mouth swooped down on hers, and he kissed her soundly.

The total unexpectedness of it caught Evie off guard. She had grabbed his shoulders for support when he swept her off the floor. Now she clung to them as Tyler's kiss did what no other man's ever had. She felt the heat of his lips clear to her toes.

Tyler seemed to feel something of the fire, too, because what had started out as an exuberant salute gradually became something more. His lips softened and slid along hers and plied the corners of her mouth with subtle pecks that left Evie gasping for more. He took the advantage to part her lips, and she felt a sudden rush of something totally foreign as his tongue intimately entwined with her own. She was burning in places that shouldn't be burning, and her head bent backward to more thoroughly accept his deepening kiss.

But when Tyler's hand came up to caress the curve of her breast, Evie stepped away. She knew the point where reality met fantasy, and this was it. Glaring at him, she crossed her arms protectively across her chest. "Don't you dare, Tyler Monteigne. You're not really Pecos Martin, and I'm not one of those kind of women."

Lit by the lantern, the devil danced in Tyler's eyes as his gaze swept over her. "Come now, Maryellen, don't tell me you've never been kissed. You're too beautiful for a man to resist, and you know it."

"Kissing is one thing. What you were trying to do was quite another. Nanny warned me about men like you. Now remove yourself from here at once. Sharing a room with you wasn't part of our agreement."

Quite content with the night's work, Tyler shrugged and tugged his coat off. "It hadn't been part of my original intention, either. You were the one who disobeyed orders and came down and got involved."

Scandalized, Evie stared as Tyler threw his coat over a chair and began to tug at his cravat. His shoulders seemed to grow wider as he stood there in shirtsleeves and satin waistcoat. The light glinted off his golden hair, and the square outline of his jaw suddenly possessed a dangerous tilt. Making princes out of frogs was one thing. This was quite another. She panicked. "If you won't leave, then I will. I'll find room in the ladies' cabin." Evie swung around to make her escape.

Before she could open the door, Tyler was in front of her. He leaned against the panel and crossed his arms over his chest in imitation of her earlier stance. "You're employing me to take care of you, Miss Peyton. I would be lax in my duties if I left you open to attack by those bullies. There are no bars on the ladies' cabin doors."

"I didn't do anything," she answered defensively, backing away from Tyler's rather overtly masculine pose.

He smiled. "Let us come to an understanding now, Miss Peyton. You can lie to your brother. You can lie to every Tom, Dick, and Harry who crosses your path. But you can't lie to me."

Evie studied this problem, which entailed studying the man who blocked the door. He was too cocky by far, and the laughter in his dancing eyes was sorely irritating. But she remembered the heat of his kiss and the press of his body against hers altogether too well. She hadn't lived this long by being a total fool.

"What makes you think I'm lying?" she asked evasively.

"Let's just say a little bird told me. And that same little bird will tell me again. You lie beautifully, Miss Peyton. That lovely little face of yours never reveals a thing—when you don't want it to. That was quite a masterful performance you put on tonight. You wouldn't happen to be an actress by any chance, would you?"

"Nanny wouldn't let me even perform with the girls at school. She said acting isn't for ladies." Evie straightened her skirts and took the room's only chair. With a graceful move that kept her petticoats covering her, she lifted her foot to examine her ruined shoe.

She was good, very good. Not even a protest. Tyler removed his shoulders from the door and checked the bolt. "Well, I wouldn't recommend what you did tonight as being healthy for your career, either. From now on, I'd prefer you'd stay in your room when I tell you."

"But he was cheating. Even Daniel noticed it. I couldn't let him keep on cheating. You might have lost our tickets or worse."

"I make my living by gambling, Miss Peyton. I had no intention of losing. You just made a long night shorter. And much more entertaining." This last Tyler added as an afterthought. He would have skinned Dorset of his last dollar if it had taken him all night and day, but it would never have been as much fun as watching Maryellen Peyton at work.

"Why did you take his watch?" Evie didn't consider what they had done cheating, but she didn't like robbing a man of his last possession. Removing her shoes, she cast the room's lone bed a furtive look. Now that the rush of excitement was dying down, she was feeling bone weary. But she wasn't about to let this disturbing man know that.

Tyler stepped to the lantern and drew out the watch, snapping it open and examining the contents with satisfaction. "Because it was my daddy's watch. This is my mother's portrait." He handed it to her so she could see. "It's all I've got left. Vandals destroyed the family portraits after she died. This is the only one that survived."

Evie examined the miniature of a lovely blond woman in pink satin. She was the picture of delicate Southern womanhood. She threw Tyler a glance as she returned the watch. "She's beautiful. Did she die during the war?"

"They all died during the war. My father, my brothers, most of my neighbors. There are times when I think I died with them. But that's another story. You can have the bed. I'll go down to the main cabin and see if there's any interesting games going on. I'll lock the door from the outside. That way you'll be safe until I'm back."

He was already combing his hair in the mirror and reaching for his coat. Evie shook her head and tried to put everything together, but she was too tired to think. Tyler Monteigne was turning out to be a man of more facets than she had imagined, even putting secret agents and Pecos Martin aside. But if he thought his sad story would persuade her to allow him to stay with her, he picked the wrong woman.

"I'm sorry about your family, Tyler. Will you be safe in the cabin? Dorset won't come looking for you there?"

Tyler examined his crumpled cravat and threw it aside. His mouth wore a wry grin as he turned to her. "Your brother's inadvertent brilliance of feeding beer to a man drinking whiskey ought to keep Dorset sleeping it off for a few more hours. I'll be most discreet when I return. You needn't worry."

Evie didn't know whether she blushed at Tyler's words or at the sight of his open shirt. Tugging on his coat had loosened the linen, and she could see a portion of his chest and a slight curl of brown hair there. The sight did strange things to her insides, and she looked away.

"If we had my luggage, there would be blankets and things you could use. How will you sleep?"

"The same way I always do. Lightly." Taking advantage of her averted gaze, Tyler leaned over and kissed her hair.

She jumped, startled, but he was on the way out the door before she could do anything.

Evie woke to the sound of furious shouts and soft snores. Since the latter were closest, she glanced around in search of the source.

She found Tyler rolled up in the spare blanket on the floor, the other pillow from her bed beneath his head. His hair was rumpled for a change, and she was quite certain he had no shirt on. She could see a glimpse of bare shoulders and back where the blanket fell off. He was as golden-brown there as he was everywhere else. She wondered what it would be like to touch him. The thought was very tempting. He had such wide shoulders, and they bulged intriguingly. Her gaze drifted down to his blanket-covered hips and stopped. What if . . . ?

She wasn't given a chance to wonder long. As the noise outside got rowdier, Tyler stirred, wiping the hair out of his eyes with the back of his arm as his hand reached beneath his pillow. The blanket fell back, and he was on his feet with revolver in hand before Evie could follow his movement.

He wore trousers. Stifling an irrepressible giggle of disappointment, Evie reached for the robe that had been shoved into her valise last night. Tyler Monteigne without his shirt was more man than she could deal with at this hour of the morning.

Without a word, he grabbed the shirt he had flung over the chair and pulled it on. Without bothering to fasten it, he eased open the door, taking in as much of the scene below as he could from this angle. Evie could see the tension in the muscles of his back as they stiffened against the linen. She wished she'd had more time to see the other side of him.

To her surprise, Tyler gave a piercing whistle. A moment later, he stepped back and Benjamin pushed Daniel through the door. They slammed it and threw the bar while the commotion continued out on the dock.

"Evie!" Daniel glanced in horror from his sister's state of undress to Tyler in his unfastened shirt.

He missed the other man's lifted eyebrows at this new name, but Evie didn't. Her gaze fell briefly to the soft *V* of curly hair on Tyler's chest, then it shifted to her shocked brother. "Don't be silly, Daniel. Now look what you've done." She tightened her robe and swung her feet out of bed. "Benjamin, I hope you brought Mr. Monteigne a clean shirt. Maybe then he can be persuaded to put it on properly."

Benjamin grinned and leaned against the door as he watched Daniel square off against the man eyeing him askance. Keeping a cautious gaze on Daniel, Tyler aimed his words at the woman on the bed. Her loose braids were down around her shoulders this morning, but she still seemed to be wearing half a dozen petticoats beneath her morning robe.

"Evie, is it? Have you any more secrets to unveil before the boat moves out, Miss Peyton? Or is it Peyton? I thought we'd reached an agreement last night."

That took some of the wind out of Daniel's sails. He threw Evie an apologetic glance. Accustomed to seeing her in dishabille, he noted only the determined thrust of her jaw.

"The name is Peyton, and you may continue to call me Maryellen, Mr. *Monteigne*." She drew out the word tauntingly. "Now if you will all excuse me, I would like to get dressed. No thanks to a certain someone, I'm going to look rumpled enough as it is."

Daniel put his fists down and shoved them in his pockets. He knew Evie well enough to know when she was about to rake someone over the coals. He didn't think there was anything lover-like between these two this morning. Tyler looked as if he might scalp her.

Ignoring her command, Tyler turned to Ben. "I take it that's Dorset out on the dock."

"He turned the inn upside down at daybreak. Me and the boy here came down the back way." Benjamin turned to Evie. "Your trunks are all loaded, ma'am. You'll just need to tell a porter which ones you want in the room." He turned an inquiring look to Tyler. "Shall

I have your bags sent up here, too? Dorset's telling the captain he can't leave until the sheriff has searched the boat."

"The captain will throw him overboard before he allows that. I can hear the boiler warming up now." Tyler threw Daniel a quick look. The boy was following the discussion closely. It wouldn't do to get his hackles up this early in the game. Knowing when to walk away, he shrugged his shoulders. "I'll join the two of you downstairs, and we can leave the lady to her ablutions."

Before Evie had time to release a sigh of relief, Tyler turned in her direction. "You and I are going to have a long talk as soon as we get some food in us. Don't take too long."

Evie threw the pillow after him as he closed the door.

Chapter 5

She was smiling brighter than the Mississippi sun when Tyler saw her next. He stopped to watch in fascination as Evie maneuvered the ruffled train of her totally inappropriate pink gown along the promenade deck, alternately entertaining Daniel who sat in a chair near the cabin, and the male passengers who stopped to hear her sparkling conversation—or watch her bustle as she paced the deck.

Not liking the way several of the sharks were looking at her, Tyler sauntered up and appropriated her arm with a casual possessiveness that caused several men to stand back out of range and brought "Maryellen's" attention on him with a frown.

"There you are, my dear. I'd wondered where you'd got to. Daniel, if you'll excuse us, I'd like a minute or two alone with your sister." Without waiting for anyone's consent, Tyler led the way to the Texas deck.

"Mr. Monteigne, you're determined to be rude this morning," Evie commented airily, guiding her gown and petticoats carefully up the narrow stairway.

"Since we're supposedly newlyweds, no one should object to my wanting to be alone with my bride." Tyler found a place out of the wind where they could watch the scenery go by. New spring leaves made a hazy glow of green along the riverbanks, and sunlight danced over the muddy waters.

"Well, now, that was an embarrassing tale to tell that man last night. Daniel isn't at all pleased with these arrangements." Evie popped open her matching parasol with secret delight. She'd always dreamed of traveling on a paddle wheeler with a handsome man at her side. This had to be the epitome of all her dreams. That the man was probably madder than two wet hornets didn't concern her in the least. The thought of sharing a room with him did make her quake slightly, but she was bound and determined not to let him know. She turned her best devastating smile on him.

Tyler turned his on in return, flashing a healthy set of white teeth. "You're asking to be kissed, Miss Peyton. I'll be happy to oblige, but you must be aware that we have an audience."

Miffed that her best weapon was neatly parried by his equally formidable one, Evie blithely turned to watch the scenery. "This is a business arrangement, Mr. Monteigne. Let's keep it that way. What did you wish to see me about? Did Daniel not pay you adequately for your services yesterday?"

Tyler chuckled and leaned against the upper cabin wall, shoving his coattails back as he put his hands in his pockets to keep them away from the slender back presented to him. "On the contrary, I paid him a percentage of my take for last night's performance. You two were very convincing. Have you been working together long?"

Evie swung around in puzzlement. "Working together?"

Tyler wished he had Daniel here. The boy's face was much more easily read than this little witch's. She could be putting on an act, but he had no real proof. "As shills, my dear. There isn't a con man or a gambler in the business that wouldn't pay good money for your services. I can't think why else the two of you would be traveling without benefit of family or servants."

Evie's smile was sour as she looked him up and down, assessing the gold chain displayed prominently across his discreet chocolate brocade vest, acknowledging the well-tailored fit of his fawn frock coat and trousers. Today he even wore a light-colored Stetson to keep the sun from his eyes. He looked every inch the professional gambler that traveled these rivers.

"I can't think why it would matter to you. I've told you all you need to know."

"You've told me a bunch of faradiddle, Miss Peyton. Shall I call you Evie?"

"I told you, you shall call me Maryellen. I have reason to hide my identity. If my brother-in-law should learn I was coming, he might do something desperate. I'll thank you to remember that."

"I shouldn't think your mother would be too happy to send her children into the wilds of Texas. I can't imagine any parent allowing the two of you out on your own. This isn't an afternoon jaunt, Miss Peyton. I'd suggest you tell me the truth before I take you home again."

"My mother is dead, sir. Evelyn's marriage killed her. Do you have any more silly questions, or may I return to see if Daniel needs anything? If you haven't noticed, the dampness pains his leg."

"Where's Daniel's mother?"

That caught her by surprise. She lifted exquisitely arched auburn brows and studied Tyler's pleasant expression carefully. "She died giving birth to Daniel. Our father was heartbroken. Does that answer your question?"

"I thought you said your mother died when Evelyn was married. Are you telling me you're younger than Daniel?"

A glint of mischief sparkled briefly in her eyes before she insouciantly replied, "Evelyn's mother was the only mother we ever knew. Evelyn was only fifteen when she married."

Without waiting to see how this outrageous lie went down, Evie turned her feet toward the stairs and Daniel. She had no obligation to tell Tyler Monteigne anything. Heaven only knew, he was as much a liar as she was, more so for all she knew. Her stories didn't harm anyone. His story landed her in the same bedroom with him.

Tyler was clutching her elbow before she could make the first step. "What does Evie stand for?"

"Evergreen." Snatching her elbow away, she descended in front of him, leaving Tyler to hang over the railing and watch her go rather than be put in the position of running after her.

What difference did it make to him if she lied through her pretty white teeth? He'd said he'd escort her to Mineral Springs. That task didn't require that he know anything at all about Maryellen Evie Peyton.

But instinct told Tyler she was big trouble.

His instincts were rewarded in New Orleans when one of the passengers decided Evie would make an excellent addition to his bordello and attempted to carry her off. Tyler arrived in time to watch Evie feign a dramatic faint, trip the cad, and push him off the gangplank into the filthy waters of the river, to the cheers of everyone on the dock. He almost considered cheering himself, if he didn't feel quite so sorry for the idiot who had fallen for Miss Peyton's all too obvious allures.

Before Evie could sing a song and pass the hat to her audience, Tyler grabbed her arm and ushered her out of harm's way. Even Daniel managed to look relieved when he saw his sister firmly taken in hand.

"Your concern for my well-being overwhelms me, Mr. Monteigne," Evie murmured sweetly as he dragged her off. "Where were you when that son of a female dog was trying to press chloroform over my face?" She tried not to show her relief as Tyler's strong arm caught her waist and carried her away. Her legs were trembling too much to be relied on. She had thought that nice man was the director of an acting troupe. Sometimes reality conflicted a little harshly with fantasy. She was going to have to watch herself.

"Son of a female dog?" Tyler couldn't help his lips from twitching as he figured out the reference. Maryellen Peyton might be a liar par none, but she was a lady right down to the point of her little tongue. And speaking of tongues, he very much wanted to taste hers, and he saw no reason why he shouldn't. He'd stayed out every night since they had left Mississippi so she could have her beauty rest undisturbed. It was her own damned fault that he'd been asleep when the boat docked.

Jerking her into the nearest doorway out of sight of the crowd hurrying to disembark, Tyler pulled Maryellen into his arms and bent his head to taste her sweet lying lips again. She fit perfectly into his embrace, her breasts pressing just where they ought to against his chest, her waist neatly cinched by his hands. Her lips were soft and inviting when he found them, and he drank deeply of their heady nectar until he pressed too far and she bit his lip and pulled away.

"I don't need to be molested by the man who is supposed to protect me from such attacks. If you can't do any better than this, sir, you may stay here in New Orleans and we'll go on without you."

Evie brushed past him and stalked down the deck with Tyler following close behind, cursing every sway of her cute little rump.

"Damnation, Daniel, if you don't keep her under lock and key, I will," Tyler shouted when the lad limped into his path, cutting off his access to Evie.

Daniel watched his sister's irate back as she kept on going, then turned back to the self-assured gambler who had seemingly kept her so well in control until now. "If I could keep her under lock and key, we wouldn't be here now. That's your job."

"Fine, if that's my job, don't complain when I do it." Inexplicably as irritated with himself as he was with the impossible Peytons, Tyler skirted around Daniel and went after Evie.

When he caught up with her, he dragged her kicking and protesting into the stateroom, slammed the door, and trapped her against the wall with a hand on either side of her head.

"It's time for another little talk, Miss Peyton."

Evie bit her tongue and forced her fury and fear back into their cages. She hoped her eyes weren't as wild as Tyler's right now. She had never been so frightened in her life. She was doing everything she could to keep from shaking with fear so as not to frighten Daniel. And this bully was trying to terrorize her more.

To be fair, she had wanted Tyler's arms around her earlier. She had wanted to curl up against his broad chest and weep hysterically, as if he really were the hero of her dreams. She had even welcomed his kiss as a balm to her shattered defenses. But she had quickly realized it wasn't comfort Tyler Monteigne was offering.

She clenched her fingers behind her back and glared

back at him. She had learned long ago that letting people see her fear gave them an advantage over her. She wasn't about to admit that she had just been scared half out of her mind. She was quite certain that wasn't fear in Tyler's eyes now. It was just plain male frustration. She knew how to handle that.

"I should have thought a little faster action would have been called for, but you're the expert," she answered sweetly.

She was quite certain if she had been a man, he would have socked her one. To his credit, Tyler only pounded the wall.

"I'm not going one inch farther with you until you learn a few ground rules, Miss Peyton, a few things your 'mother' should have told you. Or your nanny. Or whoever was responsible for bringing up an undisciplined brat like you."

He was still too close for comfort. Evie could see the shining pearl buttons on his shirt. His hips were pressed uncomfortably close to hers. The crinoline that went with her new dresses only had a hoop in the rear. That made it much too easy for a man to get close to her front. And it was nigh on impossible to press backward against the wall any more.

"I'm certain it was my fault that whelp of an unmarried mother tried to abduct me. Won't you please tell me where I went wrong?"

The good Lord in heaven above, she was doing it again. Whelp of an unmarried mother. Tyler had an irresistible urge to smile, but as soon as he did, she would be on top again. He couldn't keep letting her get away with it.

He wasn't at all certain what "it" was, but Maryellen Peyton had plenty of it.

"You're damned right I'm going to tell you," he replied forcefully.

"Your language, sir," she admonished with a sweet smile.

"Bitch, bastard, hell, and damn!" he shouted in frustration at his inability to get through to her. "They're words, Evie, not weapons. They won't kill anyone. Now shut up and let me finish."

She regarded him with those sloe eyes, and Tyler felt himself going under. Shoving away from the wall, he paced the room, carefully keeping his gaze away.

"Men outnumber women three to one in Texas, and they're not the type to politely carry you off when they take a fancy to your pretty ass." He heard her gasp but ignored it. "They're tough, undisciplined men, and they carry guns. They'll respect a lady, but damn it, Evie, they're men. You go flaunting that swinging rear end of yours and winking those big dark eyes, and they're going to do what men naturally do. And you're not going to like it one bit."

He swung around to see how she was taking this. She looked pale enough to faint. Pushing her down in the chair, Tyler poured a glass of his bourbon, mixed it with some water, and shoved it in her hand. "Drink it slow."

Evie sipped and grimaced, then handed it back. "Poisoning me won't help."

Tyler emptied the contents and immediately felt better. "Knocking you out until we get there would," he replied as he set aside the glass.

"I didn't do anything. I was just standing there. Why are you blaming me?"

"Damn it, Evie, you know perfectly well what you do to men when you pout those little lips of yours. I've watched you do it on purpose. It's going to get you in even bigger trouble than this one of these days. You're going to have to promise me you'll stop it, or I refuse to take responsibility for you any longer."

She pouted. Her little chin trembled. Lashes fluttered over her big blue-black eyes and he could swear he saw a tear trickle down her cheek. But Tyler knew damned well that was laughter behind those lashes.

With a swift jerk, he pulled her out of the chair and threw her down on the bed. Obviously the devil had created this hell just to make him burn right here on earth. He fell on top of her and began to scatter kisses across her cheeks.

"I'm going to do this every time you do that," he warned.

Evie struggled against Tyler's greater weight. Since she had never been in close contact with a man, she had never thought of them in terms of their greater weight or strength before. She didn't like the overpowering feeling of vulnerability created by his heavy weight pinning her from the waist down. She was used to men dancing to her tune, but force was beyond her circle of knowledge. She didn't like the feeling one bit, but she couldn't keep her gaze from straying to the firm lips that now hovered tantalizingly above hers right now.

"You're going to crush my dress!" she responded, ignoring the instinct demanding she throw her arms around him and pull his head down and kiss him until both their heads were spinning. Tyler worked on a woman's instincts like that. She wouldn't let herself be one of the many women who fell into his wicked trap. Tyler Monteigne definitely wasn't Ivanhoe, or even a Pecos Martin. She'd have to keep remembering that.

"I'm going to crush a damned sight more than your dress if I don't have your promise, Evie. I'll put you in sackcloth from head to toe. I want your word, Evie. I want you to swear on whatever in hell it is that you respect the most. No more flirting."

Tyler lowered his head and bestowed one of his kisses dangerously near her mouth, and one of his hands developed a tendency to wander. Evie caught her breath as his thumb stroked lightly at the side of her breast. This was why ladies weren't supposed to be alone with men. What was keeping Daniel?

She had forgotten what she was supposed to say as Tyler's mouth moved inexorably closer to her own. She wanted to feel his lips again. She wanted to taste his tongue, feel it probing for hers. The place where his hips were pressed against hers was beginning to burn, and she even had the urge to turn so his thumb would do more than just caress the curve of her bodice.

"Promise, Evie." Tyler's voice was soft and coaxing.

"I promise," she managed to repeat, just before his mouth closed over hers.

He was supposed to get up now, Tyler thought mindlessly as his tongue did a slow exploration of forbidden passages. He was supposed to get up and leave the brat lying there feeling like he did every time she teased him and left him hot and bothered. Instead, he feathered kisses across her delectable mouth and felt her breathe a sigh of relief. She wanted this as much as he did, he told himself. There was no reason why he should stop.

But a pounding on the door warned Tyler there were at least two very prominent reasons why he had to stop. No doubt both of them were standing outside the door right now.

Reluctantly, Tyler stood and pulled Evie up with him. She wasn't laughing at him now. She was staring at him with bewilderment. Lord, she was as innocent as she looked. If his mother were here, she would smack him silly.

Running his hand through his hair, Tyler shouted at the door, "What do you want?"

"The captain wants to apologize to Evie, to Maryellen, that is." Daniel's voice stuttered through the door.

Tyler grimaced, glanced once more to the stunned girl in the pink confection, and reached for the door.

If he had any sense at all, he'd get off right here in New Orleans and never look back.

Sunlight glistened through the open draperies, sparkling off the silver lamp base and throwing rainbows through the polished crystals dangling from the shade. The colors danced across a desk covered with scattered papers, but none of the men in the room were aware of them.

"I'm sorry about your ma's death. She was a good woman." The man behind the desk nervously ran his hand through hair already going thin, though he was no older than the two men facing him.

The oldest of the two paced the cluttered office as if the confinement of being inside was more than he could tolerate. He was a tall, well-built man with thick dark hair and a dent in his chin that women sighed over. His features weren't so much handsome as they were strong and determined, and his eyes as they focused on the lawyer were no less so.

"You don't have to tell us that. If it weren't for her, me and Kyle would no doubt be wilder than Indians by now. It's been a long day, Hale. We appreciate your sentiments, but let's get this over with. I didn't even know ma had a will."

The younger man sat slumped in a leather chair, his hands shoved in the pockets of his dark suit. He looked as out of place in a suit as a donkey would, and his fidgeting reflected his discomfort. "Why don't you two handle this? I'm going to go down and see to the horses."

He started to rise until his older brother gave him a steely glare that sent him slouching back into the chair. He muttered a curse and stared out the window, watching a fat cumulus cloud float past on a blue sky. If it hadn't been for the funeral, they'd be starting the roundup by now. It was the perfect day for it.

"You both need to hear this." Hale confirmed the older man's conjectures. "You know your father didn't buy the ranch until your real mother died?"

Jason Harding nodded curtly. "Pa earned every cent he ever made. We've heard the tale before."

"And your stepmother, Louise, you knew she came from a wealthy family before she married your father?"

Kyle groaned and rolled his eyes heavenward. Jason merely stopped his pacing and stared out the window.

At their silence, the lawyer continued nervously, polishing his unrimmed glasses as he glanced over the papers on the desk. "You have to understand that Louise made this will out when her father died leaving her all that money. At the time, your father was already doing very well for himself. The two of you were young men with promising futures and didn't need more than you already had."

Jason threw him a look of disgust. "She showered us with everything money could buy and taught us how to behave at the same time. Quit making excuses. We loved her just like she was our own ma. Get on with it."

Hale sighed and picked up the yellowed pages in front of him. "Well, there's something that you don't know, and I don't know how I'm going to tell you this. Louise's father always did business with my father, and he's the one who drew up this will and the trust agreement for Louise. I never looked at it until your father died in that accident and it looked as if your stepmother wouldn't survive. I knew about the payments leaving the estate, but I never looked into the reason. I didn't think I would find anything. My father was a very closemouthed man, he kept everything in his head, and his files went with him. I just honored the agreement. It wasn't until I found this will that I understood."

Kyle's attention had wandered to the dancing prisms, but Jason was watching the lawyer more intently now. His eyes narrowed as the lawyer hesitated, but Jason didn't speak up. Except for the fact that Hale had gone back East to school, they had grown up with him and knew all his pretensions and weaknesses. Talking would only delay the story. Silence forced him to get on with it.

Hale lifted his head, noted the angry twitch of Jason's jaw, and hurriedly returned his attention to the aging papers. "Your mother, your stepmother, that is, left her entire estate to a child by the name of Evangeline Peyton Howell."

Both Jason and Kyle were staring at him now, and Hale ran his finger between his stiff collar and his neck. Both men were larger than he, and they were notorious for their quick tempers. He counted on the fact that they still didn't grasp the legal implications.

"Who in hell is Evangeline Peyton Howell?" Jason asked quietly.

Hale shrugged. "Your guess is as good as mine. All I know is that there have been payments going out of a trust set up by your mother in this girl's name for the last seventeen years, since her daddy died. The payments are sent to a woman in St. Louis for the girl's maintenance. I had always assumed that the woman was some retired servant of her father's." Or his mistress, but Hale didn't say that. Cyrus Howell had been an important man in Mineral Springs. One didn't cast wild aspersions on a man of consequence, even after he was dead.

Jason watched Hale with a dangerous calm. "All right.

So ma's money goes to some female in St. Louis we've never met. Pa never let her use the money on the ranch, so it's not as if we'll miss it. She used it for foofaraws and gimcracks around the house, and we have more of those than we need. We'll not suffer for it. If her money is all that this Evangeline person has for support, I daresay she needs it more than we do."

Hale took a deep breath and polished his glasses again. "That's mighty open-minded of you. According to the trust agreement, the child inherits the bulk of the trust when she turns twenty-one, which should be roughly six months from now. I wouldn't have concerned you in the matter at all if it weren't for one thing."

Jason leaned both hands on the desk and waited. Hale glanced down at his paperwork.

"Your father's will left half his estate to you and Kyle. The other half went to Louise, as his wife. I don't believe he was any more aware of Louise's will than I was. Like I said, when she drew it up, you two had everything. She had no need to leave you anything. She was just recently wed to your father. I don't think it occurred to her that your father would leave half the ranch to her."

Jason lifted his hands from the desk and clenched them into fists. Even Kyle was listening now, and his glance went worriedly to his older brother for confirmation of what he was thinking. The look on Jason's face sent his stomach into spiraling knots.

"You're saying that because pa died instantly in that accident, half the ranch went to ma, even though she was dying, too. And now her half of the ranch is going to this mysterious Evangeline Peyton Howell."

Hale cleared his throat and nodded.

A whistle of shock issued from between Kyle's lips, and Jason's face crumpled into a blank wall of disbelief.

Chapter 6

Tyler's conviction that he should have stayed in New Orleans hadn't changed by the time the steamboat reached Houston. He'd managed to secure a second stateroom on their new boat to prevent the certain insanity of staying any longer than necessary in Evie's company, but there was an inevitability to their continuing encounters that made Tyler curse the fates.

Since returning from the federal prison where he had languished the better part of the war, Tyler had made it a point not to get involved with any so-called "good" women. The ties that bind weren't for him. For seventeen years he had been tied up in a cocoon of love that had burst with the onslaught of war. Now he was free and damned certain to stay that way.

But he had never anticipated a free spirit like Evie Peyton. In a manner of speaking, she was the kind of innocent miss he avoided at all cost. When he had taken up the gambling life, he had left behind the genteel society of his youth. He meant to take no part in the polite world of courtship that kind of innocence entailed. He wanted his women hot and willing and with no strings attached. Evie Peyton, however, seemed to fall into some category between the two.

In the constant company of her or her brother, he couldn't indulge himself as he would like in the charms of the other women on the boat. And with Evie constantly in sight, her big eyes flashing laughter, her slender waist wagging that enticing tail, Tyler couldn't find the urge to deliberately stake out another woman. He didn't look too closely into his reasoning. He just assumed the momentary aberration would disappear the minute he dumped Evie and her brother in Mineral Springs.

As Tyler stared now at the garrulous man in bowler hat in the Houston stagecoach office, he had to wonder if he was going to ever get rid of the troublesome pair, however.

"Only one stage a week? What am I supposed to do, put the lady and her trunks on a mule and send them in the general direction of Mineral Springs?"

The ticket seller shrugged. "There's still two seats available on tomorrow's stage. You could send her ahead with her brother and take the next one yourself the following week."

If only he could. The temptation was strong. He could just put them on the stage and wave his hat good-bye and walk away. What could happen to them on a stage going to nowhere?

Contemplating all the things that had happened between here and Natchez, Tyler cursed. Evie would no doubt convince the driver to allow her to ride on top, and they would have red Indians chasing after them to capture a piece of her tempting scalp. He had never disliked being in the company of an attractive woman before, but most attractive women didn't have the propensity for trouble that Evie Peyton did. The combination was deadly. He almost wished she had a hooked nose and a pointed chin.

Allowing Evie and Daniel to travel alone just wouldn't sit well with his conscience. Besides, Tyler was quite convinced they wouldn't let him out of their sight until they reached their destination. There was a certain tenacity in their innocence that he respected.

The alternative of waiting a week for the next stage, however, was equally reprehensible from his own standpoint. Another week and he would no doubt either bed the brat or strangle her.

Leaning over the counter, Tyler began counting out his money. "Give me the two tickets for tomorrow and tell me where I can find the nearest livery."

Daniel and Evie took the news of his purchase of two horses with questioning looks but no overt objections.

Tyler charged them only one half the cost of the horses, but they didn't even seem aware of that. They were damned babes in the wood and lucky he'd found them instead of someone less scrupulous, but he wasn't feeling particularly lucky when they set out the next day.

A wagon had to be hired to haul Evie's numerous trunks since the coach could only carry limited baggage. She had taken that news with casual aplomb, selecting her most important valise as the one she wished with her and admonishing the wagon driver to be careful with her mothers' "best linens" destined for her "sister" in Mineral Springs. The wagon driver might buy that story, but Tyler had seen mountains of feminine fripperies in some of those trunks, and although at least one carried linens, the others weighed too much to be either clothing or sheets. He was secretly harboring the gold bullion theory himself.

Both Evie and Daniel were bubbling with excitement as the stage set out, but Tyler and Benjamin looked forward to the dusty trip following the stage with a great deal less pleasure. By mid-morning the hot Texas sun had confirmed their expectations, and they were covering the bottom half of their faces with the crude neckerchiefs they had bought back in Houston to keep the dust out of their lungs.

Although out of the sun inside the stage, Evie was feeling the heat just the same. The leather shades on the windows kept out the light, but kept out any breath of fresh air, also. Since the stout man across from her was busily puffing on a cigar while inspecting her bodice waist with unnatural interest, Evie felt certain the queasiness in her stomach would soon lead to further unpleasantness.

"Sir, if you wouldn't mind, I am feeling quite faint. The smoke is beginning to make my head spin. If you could just put out the cigar until the air clears . . ."

He tapped the cigar end out the window and blew a long spiral of smoke into the thickened air. "You'd best get accustomed to it, little lady. We Texans like our tobacco and whiskey strong. If you don't like it, just go back where you came from."

So saying, he drew out a flask of whiskey and began to imbibe.

The sales drummer next to him looked disgusted, but half the other man's girth and height, he didn't make any attempt to interfere. The faded farmer's wife in the other corner looked resigned, and the child across from her was asleep. That left only Daniel and Evie to protest the man's rudeness.

They exchanged glances. What would Pecos Martin do in a situation like this? Daniel gripped his gold-knobbed cane in the middle and grabbed for the strap overhead as the stage swayed when it hit a rut. The cane swayed with him.

The flask the fat man had been about to cap encountered the cane and flew out of his hand, spewing its contents over his lap until the entire interior reeked of whiskey. Even the farmer's wife watched with a degree of interest as the man shrieked his rage, until the child woke and began to cry.

"So sorry, sir. It's this deuced leg of mine. Doesn't support me even sitting. I'll buy you a fresh supply in the nearest town." Daniel apologetically produced his large handkerchief to dab at the damage.

Evie sweetly reached over and removed the cigar from the astonished man's hand, flinging it out the window. "You'll catch fire if that falls on your trousers. Why, I had a neighbor once who spilled some brandy all over his best jacket, and he was so surprised that he dropped his cigar, and before anyone knew it, he went up in flames. Rather like a dessert flambé, only not so amusing."

The drummer chuckled, and the child quit wailing as it watched the fat man slowly turn purple. Blithely ignoring his fury, Evie pulled back the shade and waved at the two men laconically riding alongside the lumbering stagecoach. Benjamin tipped his hat, but Tyler pretended to ignore her. The distraction worked, however, and Evie smiled as the fat man took a look at the rifle tied to Tyler's saddle and held his tongue.

"Are y'all going to Mineral Springs, too?" Evie asked the quiet woman in the corner. The silence inside the coach was too intimidating, and she sought the sound of another voice.

"We went to see after my sister in Houston. She's been down ill, but she's better now. Are you the new schoolteacher?"

Schoolteacher. Evie didn't glance at Daniel. She knew the look on his face without seeing it.

"I'm interviewing for the position. Will your young one be attending?" She cast the grubby youngster a dubious glance, but the child had gone back to sucking his thumb with his eyes closed.

"He's the baby. He's only four. But the others ought to go. I've only got one what's eager, but the others ought to know something of their letters. I don't want them to grow up as ignorant as their mother."

"There's all kinds of knowledge besides letters in this world, and I'm sure you possess a lot of it, Mrs.—" Evie left the sentence dangling while she waited to be supplied a name.

"Dabney. Mrs. Otis Dabney."

"I'm Maryellen Peyton, Mrs. Dabney, and this here is my brother Daniel. We're happy to meet you."

Daniel rolled his eyes upward as Evie dived feet first into this new adventure. He didn't want to think what Pecos Martin would say when he learned he was escorting the new teacher to Mineral Springs. Men of his caliber generally didn't appreciate lies. The tension in the gunfighter's eyes every time he looked at Evie was more than evident. She had a tendency to ride a fellow's nerves like that.

Daniel took his book from his pocket and began to read. There wasn't a thing he could do to keep Evie from doing just what she wanted, and there wasn't any sense in trying. She lived in a world all her own. He was just an occasional participant in it.

They stopped at a way station to rest and water the horses. Evie produced fried chicken and biscuits and fried apple pies from the huge sack she had insisted on carrying into the coach with her. The woman she had befriended brought out some bread and jam and boiled eggs, and they happily exchanged their various fares as if this were a family picnic.

Tyler appreciated the food, but he kept an eye on the fat man with the whiskey stains down his front. The man was watching the Peytons with a belligerent look that bespoke one of their more rebellious escapades, but Tyler knew it was worse than useless to question either one of them. Daniel would merely look surprised and tell him everything was just fine, and Evie would produce some outrageous lie or another. He'd decided some time back if he didn't want to hear lies, he shouldn't ask questions. So he didn't.

The sun was even worse as they set out again. The terrain was growing steadily less forested and more shrubby, and the dirt beneath the horse's hooves flew up in a fine dust that coated everything in sight. Years in a Yankee prison camp had taught him to endure many things, but Tyler wasn't well pleased with having to suffer for the sake of a capricious brat and her brother.

But it was his own damned fault for continuing with this journey against his better judgment, so he would pay the price. He was beginning to realize that curiosity was as strong a factor as anything else in his pursuit of this insanity. He wanted to see what really awaited them in Mineral Springs.

So Tyler allowed the sun to lull him into a stupor as they rode steadily westward. He pulled his hat brim over his eyes to shade his face and pulled his neckerchief more securely around his nose until he looked like a Mexican bandit. His newly acquired horse had learned the gait of the stage and followed it obediently without much direction. A man could almost take a nap through this country and not notice the difference when he woke up.

That was the excuse he gave himself later when the thieves rode out of a stand of oaks, and he didn't see them until it was too late.

The horses screamed their fear as shots rang over their head. The stage swerved perilously, and the passengers grabbed the straps over their heads to try to hang on. Evie searched for some sign of Tyler out the window, but he had been lagging behind these last few miles and she saw no sign of him now.

The two male passengers grabbed for small weapons hidden in the various folds of their coats and waistcoats, and Daniel gripped his cane like a sword as the coach gradually rumbled to a halt. The shouts of the thieves could be heard ahead, and terror laced the driver's reply.

Making certain none of the robbers had come around to their side, Daniel flung open the stage door and pushed Evie out. "There's a dry riverbed down there. Run for it. They won't shoot a woman, and Pecos won't have to worry about you when the shooting starts."

Too frightened to argue, Evie grabbed her skirts and began to run. She and Daniel had discussed what they would do if they were set upon by thieves, but neither of them had ever really believed such things would happen. Daniel had read her the newspaper accounts of rape and robbery, and tried to impress upon her that she was in more danger than he, but it had never seemed so real before. She knew he couldn't run. She knew he could be hurt if she stayed here and he had to defend her honor. But it still didn't seem right to be running.

She almost stopped and turned around, but she heard the pounding hoofbeats of Tyler's horse coming up the road just as the dry riverbed loomed ahead. She hurriedly slid down into it. What Daniel said made sense. Heroes were always much more likely to go after the thieves if the heroines weren't around needing protection.

Tyler saw her sliding down the embankment and cursed, but it was too late to stop her now. If she preferred to take her chances with rattlesnakes instead of with him, that was just fine.

He had never thought to raise a weapon again, but instinct was stronger than any vow a man could make. He shifted his rifle to take aim at the bastard holding his gun on the driver.

Tyler was aware of Benjamin riding up on the other side of the coach. He saw one gunman go down as he aimed at the next. There were half a dozen of the outlaws, but they hadn't been expecting resistance. Two of them turned tail and ran as Benjamin got off three neat shots with his repeating rifle. Tyler took careful aim at one of the two left fighting.

That was when one of the idiots in the coach decided to come to his own defense. Even as a third gunman toppled from his horse and the last one galloped off after his comrades, a thin swirl of smoke and a sharp bark issued from within the stage, and Benjamin fell.

Tyler was in hot pursuit of the man riding in the same direction as Evie when the scream reached him. He turned in time to see Benjamin hit the dirt. But then the other two thieves were riding out of the bushes, and the only thing Tyler could do was spur his horse after Evie.

His heart screamed its rage and fear as the stagecoach abruptly jolted into motion, but it was too late for anything: too late to stop them, too late for Benjamin, and too late for himself and Evie if he didn't act soon.

Chapter 7

Evie screamed as the horse practically flew over her head and into the dust of the dry riverbed. Before she could recover her senses, Tyler was upon her, jerking her from her feet and throwing her over his knees like a sack of flour. She scrabbled for handholds as the horse took off down the gully without so much as a by-your-leave from its rider.

She had never been inclined to hysteria, but it took a great deal of effort to keep from mindlessly screaming now as her fingers dug into Tyler's leg and she felt her position slipping with the jarring gait of the horse. Tyler caught her bodice waist and pulled her more forcefully across his lap, but now her head hung over his knee and she had a terrifying view of the landscape flying by beneath her.

She closed her eyes as shots rang over their heads. The steady stream of curses Tyler had been emitting when he first grabbed her now ceased as he turned his entire attention to forcing his tired horse to outpacing the thieves. Evie clung to his nankeen trousers and attempted prayer. It was a trifle difficult when her corset was bouncing off Tyler's knee.

The shots eventually grew farther away. As the horse stumbled and heaved, Tyler let up the pace, slowing to a walk while listening for any sign of pursuit. Finally, satisfied that their pursuers had given up the chase, Tyler halted and lowered Evie to the ground.

She grabbed the saddle as her legs collapsed under her. Then with an air of surrender, she slowly settled into the dust and bent her head to her knees, taking in great heaving gasps of air as she tried to quiet her shaken insides.

Tyler climbed down and watched her, but he was already cutting off the pain by closing off his emotions. The stagecoach rumbling off without them caused a moment's fury, but he refused to think of Benjamin crumpling to the ground, lying still in the roadway without anyone stopping to help. To the occupants of the stagecoach, Benjamin was only a black man, less than an animal, and possibly one of the thieves to their bigoted minds. Tyler swore at himself for not going back to see to his friend instead of going after this miserable brat who hadn't the sense God gave a goose. But his damnable sense of Southern chivalry had reared its ugly head, and he had gone to rescue the lady rather than help the friend who had stood beside him since childhood.

It didn't make sense. But life would never make sense. He knew that; he just had to remember it at times like these. Watching Evie gulping back tears and terror, Tyler let his mind travel to the next thing to be done if they were to survive this situation. The sun was sinking slowly toward the horizon. They would have to find shelter and water. His horse couldn't travel much farther, particularly with two riders.

He wanted to go back to look for Benjamin, but practicality told him he had to get Evie settled and his horse watered before he could do anything. He scanned the horizon in all directions, seeing nothing habitable. But a stand of trees toward the west spoke of water.

He held a hand out to Evie. "Come on, we've got to get going."

She didn't look at him. She didn't take his hand, either. She merely caught up her skirts and rose, somewhat shakily perhaps, but she hid that well as she dusted herself off.

Without a word of question, she followed as Tyler led the horse toward the trees. She knew he was furious with her. She didn't even need to see the set lines of his jaw to know that. She could see the knots of tension in his shoulders, the way he strode with his back straight and turned to her. She had learned to read other people by watching the way they moved. Tyler was bordering on irrational, and she tried not to be afraid. Heroines were never afraid. The heroes always got them out of these situations. Hadn't Tyler just saved her from the outlaws? Who was going to save her from Tyler?

A dilapidated cabin sat among the skinny trunks of oaks someone had obviously planted to keep the house cool. No smoke came from its one chimney. No reply came after Tyler's yell of greeting.

They found a crude well in the side yard and drew up water for the horse. With no dipper in sight, Tyler cupped his hands and dipped some of the muddy liquid for himself. Evie watched him and attempted to repeat the motion, but she succeeded mostly in splattering her gabardine bodice. Getting enough water to quench her parched lips, she gave up the attempt and walked toward the cabin.

Tyler was ahead of her, holding her back with his hand as he knocked, then threw open the door. The interior smelled musty and unused, and a rustle in the darkness warned the inhabitants weren't human.

Stamping his boots to scare off any other intruders, Tyler entered and glanced around. Whoever had left the cabin had meant to return. In the light of the dying sun through the room's one window, he could discern a crude table and chair, and a bed nailed to the corner walls and supported by one post. A faded quilt covered the thin mattress, and an iron skillet still hung beside the fireplace. Dust covered everything, but dust always did. It was impossible to tell how long the owner had been away.

Evie swept by him and immediately began scanning the cabin's meager supplies. "Can you start a fire? I can cook these beans. It looked like there was a bit of a garden out there. There might be some root vegetables for a stew."

Tyler watched her for a minute, hating her for her cool behavior, wishing she would behave like any hysterical female so he could despise her even more. His best friend was dead or dying in the middle of a road to nowhere, and she was discussing beans and stew. In the room's crude interior her trailing gabardine gown and ruffled ruching were as out of place as a ghost in daylight. She ought to be cursing the fates and yelling at him to do something.

Instead, she turned and waited patiently for him to light a fire in the ghastly heat of this day.

Tyler turned around and walked out, returning shortly later with an armload of tinder. He carefully set the fire, went back out for some larger limbs, and fed them into the blaze until they caught. Then he stood and stared down into her pale face.

"I'm going back out to look for Ben."

Her blue-black eyes widened into shadowed circles. "Ben? What happened to Ben?"

Of course. She hadn't seen him fall. She was too busy running like a scared goose in the opposite direction. Tyler wanted to ask her what the hell she had thought she was doing, but he was too tired to care anymore.

"One of the passengers shot him," Tyler replied with a hint of scorn, the only emotion he could summon at the moment. When she seemed at a loss for words for once, he turned and walked out. There was still enough daylight left to ride back to the road. He didn't give a damn what happened to Miss Evie Peyton while he was gone.

By the time Tyler returned, without any sign of Ben or his horse, the sun had long since gone down. Tyler was weary clear down to the marrow of his bones, and the contents of the flask of whiskey in his saddlebag was the only thing keeping him going.

He could smell the smoke from the fire as he brushed down his horse and the stray he had found, watered them, and fed them some hay from the ramshackle stall beside the house. He threw the saddle over the gate when he was done, picked up his bags, and headed for the cabin and Evie.

He hadn't come home to a woman since he was seventeen years old. The eight years since then might not have been long in terms of time, but they were decades in terms of experience. Tyler felt nothing now at the thought of the woman waiting for him, supper on the table, her lovely face lined with worry. He wanted to feel nothing.

Evie always caught him by surprise. He walked in and found her hanging her newly washed petticoats beside the fire. In the fire's light, her wet hair gleamed with a dull red against chestnut. She looked up at him without surprise or criticism, and his glance instantly went to her slim figure silhouetted against the fire. To his disappointment, she had apparently donned a corset and all the other proper accoutrements of a lady after her bath, all except the heavy petticoats.

"There's a vegetable stew in the pot. Help yourself."

Evie went back to adjusting her petticoat so the wetter side faced the fire. For a moment, she had glimpsed something in Tyler's eyes that she didn't want to see. He was grieving. She could feel his grief. It shouted from the depths of his amber eyes. It displayed itself in his hostility. It rolled through him with every jerky motion of his muscles as he approached the fire and helped himself to the stew. She didn't want to feel his grief, and she didn't want to know what he was thinking. Her own emotions were a turmoil she could just barely handle without becoming embroiled in someone else's.

But even though she tried not to, Evie knew Tyler's thoughts. He was thinking it was all her fault that his friend was dead. She knew Ben had to be dead or Tyler would have carried him back here. The thought was terrifying. The people who died in books weren't real, but Ben was. Had been. She wanted to grieve with Tyler, to show him she cared, but that would be presumptuous of her. He obviously wanted nothing from her. It would be better to stay out of his way.

Tyler watched through hooded eyes as Evie played the part of homemaker. She was always playing some part or another. He ate his stew while she shook out the bedcovers and inspected the mattress for insects. He sipped his whiskey while she scoured the plates and pot. She was beautiful, efficient, and eerily silent. He liked it that way. They had nothing to say to each other.

But when Evie left the cabin to avail herself of the privy before retiring for the night, other ideas began to stir from somewhere in the pits of Tyler's insides. He knew he was halfway to being drunk. He didn't often indulge, but the occasion seemed worth the effort. Still, even knowing he was drunk, he couldn't keep the visions from forming in his head.

Evie came back with a length of rope from his saddle, and Tyler watched in bemusement as she looped it around a peg in the wall and carried it across the room to loop it to another. He waited in drunken anticipation for the whole thing to come tumbling down when she proceeded to knot a sheet over the makeshift line, but she evidently had some experience in creating cloth walls. She was now effectively hidden behind the sheet. All he could see of her was her trim ankles when she removed her shoes.

Tyler contemplated Evie's bare toes beneath the sheet when she sat on the bed and pulled off her stockings. Just looking at her toes made his loins ache. They curled sweetly against the rough wooden floor while she worked at the rest of her clothing. He wanted to take those toes and cup them in his hands to keep them from the splintery wood floor. He would rub their softness until she sighed with pleasure. In his imagination Tyler slid his hands from those soft feet to slender ankles. The alcohol rushing through his brain pushed his hands farther, up the long curves of shapely legs. From there, he could only close his eyes and imagine the satisfaction to be achieved when his fingers reached the place where her legs came together.

He'd gone too long without a woman. It couldn't be good for a man's health to abstain this long. Tyler took another swig of whiskey as he surmised the movements behind the sheet represented the removing of her corset. He summoned a vision of that willow slim waist free of steel encumbrances, curving into full hips, rising to firm breasts, and his trousers were suddenly too tight. He took another drink and hoped the heated sensation would go away.

Still wearing chemise, drawers, and her under-petticoat, Evie climbed into bed. Fear tickled at her insides and edged along her skin, but she forced herself to remain calm. Tyler was a gentleman. The heroes in Daniel's dime novels were always gentlemen at heart. She would rely on that. She could do nothing else. She couldn't stay awake all night and watch him drink himself into a stupor. One of them had to have a clear head in the morning.

She lay quietly, listening to any movement from the other side of the sheet. The fire was dying, but they didn't need the warmth. She could hear the crackle of a branch breaking and crumbling into ash. The faint scent of cooked turnips hung in the air. The paper over the window had been torn in several places, letting in a draft of clear air but also letting in a mosquito. She could hear the whine somewhere overhead. Evie listened to the drone and tried to talk herself into sleep.

She couldn't relax. The cornhusks in the mattress rustled with her every movement. She heard Tyler get up and go outside, and she held her breath. Maybe he was going to sleep in the barn. She heard him splashing in the pail from the well. An animal howled somewhere in the distance, and she shivered. She had imagined adventures when coming to Texas, but this wasn't the kind she had imagined. Pecos Martin never touched women, but Tyler did.

All she had wanted to do was find her parents. She wanted to know why they never came back for her. The lawyer's letters had explained nothing. She couldn't believe they had abandoned her on purpose. Something had to have happened to them. And she meant to find out what.

She had imagined many things in her pursuit of the truth, but she had never imagined Tyler Monteigne. Even as she heard the door open again, her heart beat faster. There weren't any extra blankets for him to lie on. She knew what he meant to do, but still she lay there, hoping she was wrong.

She had been wrong to run from the stagecoach; she knew that now. But there was no turning back the hands of time. Perhaps she was wrong in coming to Texas, but she couldn't imagine spending the rest of her life wondering. Everyone in St. Louis knew she didn't have parents.

She could dress herself in the finest gowns and do all sorts of charitable works, but without family, she was nothing, nobody. So she had to come to Texas. It was inevitable.

Just as Tyler's pulling back the sheet wall now was inevitable. The dying light of the fire illuminated the golden-brown expanse of his bare shoulders as he stood there for a moment, holding the sheet back from his head. Light glimmered briefly in his hair, and Evie could still see water droplets glistening on his skin from his hasty washing. She pushed to the far side of the bed, leaving him plenty of room. This could still work, if he would just be reasonable. It wasn't quite like the prince coming to rescue Rapunzel, but he looked like a prince. She could pretend he was one for just one night. It wasn't at all difficult to do.

Tyler sat down on the bed's edge and began pulling off his boots. Evie could feel the heat emanating from his naked back, and she had the overwhelming urge to stroke that wide expanse of smooth flesh. She could see how his broad chest tapered to slim hips and flat, muscled stomach, but she didn't want to know any more than that. Just the glimpse of his bare front as he kept his back to her caused sensations she didn't want to describe.

She attempted to draw the quilt up around her as she sat up, but Tyler was sitting on it. Abandoning this last thread of protection, Evie started for the bottom of the bed. Pretend as she might, she could put only so much trust in Tyler's gentlemanly instincts. His silence lacked the reassurance she needed.

He turned and caught her with one strong arm, hauling her back down to the bed. He leaned over her briefly, pinning her with his unwavering gaze. "Stay," he ordered.

She almost obeyed, until he stood up and began unfastening the buttons of his trousers. She had no desire to become that well acquainted with male anatomy, no matter how curious she was. She grabbed the quilt and tried to escape around him.

Tyler caught her and tossed her back to the bed as if she were no more than a sack of grain. Evie stared as he peeled off his trousers, revealing the white knit of his drawers. Even in this dim light she could see the mysterious male bulge that had so fascinated her peers in school when they talked of men. The bulge seemed to grow even as she looked at it, and she hastily looked away.

"Let me up, Tyler," she said quietly. "I'll take the quilt and sleep by the fire."

She ought to be panicking. She could feel the grief in him, feel the black gulfs of anguish swirling in his soul, and knew he wasn't in his right senses. Heroes didn't feel like that; villains did. But Tyler had never hurt her. Even now, when he tossed her back to the bed and came down beside her, he was gentle in his touches. He was abrupt, demanding, sometimes irritable, and often furious with her, but he had never raised a hand to her. The one he raised now merely caressed her cheek.

Evie held herself still as Tyler's lips feathered across hers. Maybe this was all he wanted—a little comfort in his time of sorrow. Her heart went out to him. She knew what it was like to be all alone. Tentatively, she touched his hard jaw. She could feel the stubble of whiskers and the way the muscles tensed beneath her fingers.

And then Tyler's mouth was closing more forcefully against hers, and panic finally began replacing her need to hold and comfort. Evie tried to shove his shoulders away as he moved over her, but Tyler was bigger and heavier and there was nothing she could do to budge him. Her fingers bit into his biceps as he nipped at her lips and parted them until his tongue could find entrance. She cried out a protest at the invasion, but something warm and wonderful was happening to her insides at the same time.

She wasn't really frightened. She ought to be. This was the last thing in the world that she wanted to happen if she thought about it, but there was a sense of inevitability to it if she didn't think. If she let Tyler's kisses drug her into insensibility, she could almost enjoy the masculine musk surrounding her, the sense of power and security his large body held for her. She liked the way his muscles tensed beneath her touch. She craved the pure sensuality of his tongue exploring the recesses of her mouth, his lips possessing hers with a hunger that she suddenly recognized matched her own. She wanted to be held and loved, and she wanted to make this man hold and love her. She could feel the power of the forces drawing them together, and she craved the sensation.

But she knew the instant Tyler's hand reached between them to caress her breast that he didn't mean to stop with kisses and hugs. Evie cried out a harsh protest as his hand cupped her through the chemise, but Tyler merely covered her mouth with his own again, suffocating her cries with his kiss.

"Tyler, no!" she whispered frantically as his mouth moved to nibble at her throat. But she made no effort to stop his hands when they unfastened the buttons of her chemise.

Her breasts felt like they were swelling upward, ripe and ready to pop as he uncovered them. Tyler moaned low in his throat as he reached to take one in his mouth, and Evie lost herself in the sensation of his lips and tongue teasing her into a white hot heat that she didn't understand.

She held him to her, ran her hands through the rich thickness of his hair, offered herself to his anxious kiss as she felt the grief and sorrow rush through him. She felt Tyler's back heave as he bent his head and finally gave vent to a drunken sob of sorrow against her breast. Caught up in her compassion and desire, she placed kisses along the harsh plane of his jaw everywhere she could reach.

In return, Tyler jerked her chemise back until her arms were practically pinned by the material. Evie struggled out of the hampering cloth while he pressed and stroked her breasts into tingling mounds of sensation. His touch created ribbons of desire that crept through her middle and down to her toes. She wanted his kiss on her mouth again, and he gladly obliged, but this time she could taste his tears, and she cried with him.

The light mat of hair on Tyler's chest brushed her breasts, and Evie lifted against him to feel more. She was as terrified of herself as she was of him, but she didn't seem able to stop. It was as if this was meant to be, as if some unseen hand wrote her actions on the page.

Oblivious to where he was or who he was with, Tyler gave into the comfort of a woman's welcoming body washing away his pain. Another woman had taught him how he could drown his sorrow in this physical joining, and he had never forgotten the lesson.

The momentary closeness, the sense of oblivion, the physical release—all rendered the pain to a distance that he could deal with later. He was very successful at distancing himself once he overcame the immediate shock. That was all he needed now, the brief physical pleasure to separate him from the beast within tearing him apart. He pushed up the flimsy piece of clothing protecting her and untied his drawers.

Tyler knew his error the instant his body thrust into hers. A woman's cry of pain and disappointment echoed in his ear, but it was too late now. Closing his eyes, he lunged forward and took possession of the satin haven that would save him from the beast.

He didn't need to know who she was. He only needed the temporary shelter she offered.

Her newly opened body quivered as he filled her completely, but she was wet and he was ready. He moved out and slid deeper until she was crying and heaving in tandem with his exertions. That was all he needed to know.

He came quickly, immersing himself in multiple explosions that buried him deep within her heat. He accepted the solace of this physical release and her hands braiding through his hair with relief and refused to think of what he had done.

That would come on the morrow, when the beast was back in his cage again.

Chapter 8

Evie held herself still as she curled near the wall as far as she could get from the large man lying beside her. She had never thought Tyler particularly large before until confronted with the obstacle of his body between herself and the door to safety. His bare shoulders loomed immense, blocking out all view of the room but the ceiling. She was grateful he was turned away from her. She didn't think she could tolerate the sight of his broad chest without jumping out of her skin. Fantasy had met reality last night, and fantasy had lost. Stripped of the protective shelter of her dreamworld, Evie shivered in her nakedness.

The early morning sun cast a sliver of light across the log joists she could see above Tyler's arm. The light glimmered golden against the hair of his skin, but Evie tried not to think about that. She tried to concentrate on what she had to do, but her mind was useless while she was totally aware of the naked man not inches away. She could feel the heat emanating from him in the early morning coolness. She now had full awareness of the strength behind the deceptive suppleness of his lean frame. And she was terrified of what would happen should he turn over and use his powerful maleness against her once again.

She still ached from last night's encounter. There was an unpleasant stickiness between her legs where he had been, and the feeling of invasion was still strong within her. She despised him for what he had done, but she despised herself worse.

She had sworn this would never happen to her. Even though she had painted pretty pictures of her parents in

her head, she knew what she was—a bastard. Everyone
knew it. That was why she could never hold her head
up in St. Louis society despite her wealth and beauty.
She had sworn never to allow a man to do to her what
one had done to her mother. And now look at her.

Clenching her lips shut, Evie sought some means of
escape. Because of her birth, she had studied the subject
of bastards as carefully as it was possible for a gentle
lady of means in society. She knew how children were
created, and she fully meant to be married before she
had any. She knew there were ways of preventing children and ways of getting rid of them. She knew very
little about those ways, but common logic told her where
to find the answer when she needed it. She prayed she
wouldn't need it, but the chances were far better if she
got out of Tyler's bed right now.

She tried to pull the quilt over her breasts as she sat
up, but Tyler had it wrapped around his hips and was
lying on it. She struggled to find her chemise in the tangled debris of the bedding, but he seemed to be lying on
that, too. Her toes grazed his leg, and she jumped backward from the contact, but it was already too late.

He turned on his back and stared at her. Stricken, Evie
couldn't look away from his eyes. They weren't amber
any longer but a deep, festering brown that had none of
the laughter and charm she associated with him. She
couldn't look away even when she knew his gaze had
gone from her face to her breasts. She merely struggled
to pull the quilt around her.

Tyler looked at the pale, rosy perfection of two firm
young breasts hovering just inches from his nose and
cursed. His head pounded, and he could feel his loins
rising to the occasion, but he was no longer lost in the
oblivion of whiskey and desire. He damned well knew
where he was and why and what he had to do about it.

Jerking the quilt away from Evie, he wrapped it
around himself and got up. She instantly tugged the tangle of her petticoats back around her legs, but not before
he caught a glimpse of the dark stain marring them. Still
cursing, he tore away the sheet wall and throwing it at
her, stalked out. Now wasn't the time to plead insanity.

Evie watched him go with a mixture of relief and disappointment that quickly gave way to outrage. Keeping the cotton wrapped around her, she hobbled over to the hot ashes and the pot of water she had left hanging there. Thank goodness she'd had the forethought to set out water for their morning ablutions.

She scrubbed herself viciously with the old cake of lye soap she had found the night before, all the while contemplating with pleasure the image of Tyler washing in the icy cold well water. That should take some of the starch out of him.

She dressed hastily in fear of his return. It was obvious that whiskey and grief had been the influence the night before, but she couldn't be sure that he wouldn't decide to come back for more now that the damage was done. She was rather uncertain about how a man's mind functioned. Or his body. She knew men liked to look at her. She knew they often wanted to do more than look at her. But except for those few stolen kisses at times of excitement over other things, Tyler had done a very good job of ignoring her. She wasn't at all certain that he really desired her in the way a man does a woman.

And she had no wish to find out. She buttoned up her bodice waist as far as it would go despite the fact that the air was already growing warm as the sun reached higher in the sky. She dragged on all her petticoats and ignored her rumbling stomach.

She was just finishing fastening the buttons of her shoes when Tyler walked back in.

He had slicked back his hair with well water and found fresh clothes in his saddlebags. He evidently didn't possess any of the colorful shirts Evie had seen on some of the men here in Texas. The one he wore now was of the same respectable white linen he wore in town, although he didn't bother fastening a collar or cravat to it. She tried to keep her gaze from straying to the tight crotch of his fawn-colored trousers, but she was aware of it, just the same. She pulled her skirt down farther and returned to buttoning her shoes.

"If you're ready, I've got the horses saddled."

Evie's head went up quickly, but she didn't say a word.

What did one say to a man who had just taken one's innocence? Judging from Tyler's behavior, it wasn't "Good morning, darling." Her book reading and imagination failed her.

She followed him out to the brightness of a Texas morning and watched as he brought the two horses forward. The one she recognized as his, but the other wasn't the one Ben had ridden. She turned him a questioning glance.

"I reckon it belonged to one of the thieves. I found it wandering out by the road last night. You can ride, can't you?"

"No." She glanced again at the tall horse, the western saddle, and down to her gabardine traveling skirt with its heavy train draped over the bustle at her back. She knew what ladies wore when riding, and she was definitely not wearing it.

"Then you'll just have to sit in the saddle and hang on while I lead you. I don't have any idea how far away we are from civilization, but we'll get there faster on two horses."

Without waiting for argument, Tyler grasped her by the waist and deposited her in the saddle sideways. Even he could see the foolishness of trying to put her on properly in that getup. He tried not to think about how she would feel if she had to straddle a horse after last night. Her careful steps had already reminded him that he hadn't been precisely delicate with her.

When Tyler was certain Evie was grasping the horse's saddle and wouldn't fall off, he swung into his saddle and took her reins in hand.

Before they could leave, he had to say something. He'd been brought up right, even if he had fallen on evil days since then. Tyler turned in his saddle and caught himself looking at Evie's haughty profile. She was doing her best not to look at him, and he had to smile slightly at this response. Did she think ignoring him would make what happened go away? Knowing Evie, she probably did.

"When we find town, I'll look for a preacher. I'll make things right," he assured her.

Evie nearly fell off her horse. She jerked, startled at

his words, then turned carefully to assess Tyler's degree of sincerity. Or insanity. He was already gathering up their reins and kicking his horse into motion as if the matter of marriage was a foregone conclusion.

"If that was a proposal, I refuse it," she replied with as much steadiness as she could summon. Her grip on the saddle left her knuckles white.

It was Tyler's turn to look startled. He glanced back at her frozen face but as usual, he couldn't read the thoughts behind it. "Despite what you might think, my mother brought me up to be a gentleman. What I did last night was unforgivable, and I'm ready to pay the consequences. Marriage is the only way I can repay you for what I took away."

Evie compressed her lips until they almost turned as white as her knuckles. "I'll call myself Mrs. Peyton and say I'm a widow before I'll marry you, Tyler Monteigne."

Evie caught the glimmer of relief in Tyler's eyes at her words and wished she had something to throw at him. He could at least look disappointed. She wasn't exactly ugly, and she had displayed more than adequate housekeeping skills. Obviously the only thing that interested him was what happened in bed, and she certainly wasn't very good at that. That settled the matter, then. She had no intention of repeating last night's performance for any man.

"We'll see about that," was Tyler's laconic response as he turned his back on her and forced the horses to a faster pace.

Relief swept through him that he wouldn't have to tie himself down with a wife and all the complications that ensued, but there was a certain amount of insult in her refusal. Tyler wasn't used to women turning him down. He had to admit that he hadn't performed as he ought last night. She deserved better than to be the recipient of one of his worst rages. But aside from marrying her, he couldn't see any means of correcting the situation. From the sour look on her face, she certainly wouldn't be amenable to a little dalliance to show her his better talents.

Besides, she knew nothing of protecting herself, and

he wasn't about to get himself caught up in that situation again. Remembering the child he had fathered when he was no more than a boy, Tyler set his jaw and proceeded onward without any further objection to her refusal. He had lost a child and a friend that last time. He'd stick to experienced women from now on.

They rode in silence except for the rumble of their empty stomachs. As the morning wore on, the sun beat mercilessly on their heads. Evie had lost her hat in yesterday's escape, but it had never been adequate for protection in the first place. She felt her nose begin to blister but didn't dare lift her hand from the saddle to cover it.

At some point, Tyler turned to check on her. A silent woman was an unnatural one in his experience. He could see the pink forming on her fair skin and cursed his own stupidity.

Stopping his horse, Tyler waited until Evie's was beside him, then removed his hat and set it on her head. She had not attempted her usual fashionable coiffure but wore her hair in a loose chignon at the back of her neck. The hat slid over her forehead and down to the chignon, but it shaded her face.

Evie tried to give him a haughty look, but the desperation of their situation kept her from succeeding. Trying not to sound pitiful, she asked, "Do you think it is much farther?"

"Can't rightly say, but if there isn't a town soon, there's bound to be a way station where we can inquire. I need to find you a hat that fits better when we get to town. That looks kind of cute on you."

Evie offered a small smile and tilted the Stetson to a jaunty angle. "I suspect it looks better on you, but thank you for the kind words."

Tyler felt a jolt of something electric at her bravado and quickly kicked his horse back into motion. Most women would have harangued him until he died for what he had done and was doing. He could imagine Bessie's endless complaints about the dust, the horse, the lack of food, the sun, the destruction of her clothing, and that without even the insult of the night before. Yet this female sat there looking beautiful and brave without a word against him. He didn't want to admire her. He didn't even want to like her. But he damned well wanted her in his bed again.

That was a puzzle he would have to work on. He'd liked Bessie and all the other women in his life well enough as long as they kept their places to his bed and nothing more. But Evie was a liar he couldn't trust for ten seconds, and a rebellious nuisance who demanded his entire attention. He couldn't like her, but he had bedded her.

Well, he would get her to Mineral Springs and leave her and not concern himself any longer. Except now that Ben was gone, he really had no place to go. Ben would have wanted to return to Natchez, but Tyler had no desire to return to the place of his humiliation and defeat. The card game hadn't changed that any. And there was still the matter of what he had done to Evie. If a child came of it, he wanted to know. He wasn't sending any more women out into this world carrying his bastard.

By the time the buildings of Mineral Springs wavered into view, Tyler was resigned to spending some time there. Waves of heat made the town appear to be an oasis amid the desert, but as they rode on, Tyler could see the river running on the far side that provided the reason for the town's existence. It wasn't a bad-size little town, he admitted grudgingly as they rode closer. And it certainly couldn't be much worse than Under-the-Hill.

"Would you like your hat back?" Evie called from behind him.

Tyler turned and watched hope light her sunburned face as she scanned the town ahead. He still didn't know why in hell she wanted to come here, but just one look at her face right now belied the story of a lost sister and her rotten husband. Tyler shook his head in disgust but couldn't help smiling at her eagerness.

"I like the outfit just the way it is. Stay out here very long and you'll make a great lady cowboy."

The smile she threw him was devastating. He ought to be immune to them by now, but for some reason this one went straight to his gut. Tyler ached to reach and touch her, to seek solace in the same generous willing-

ness she had offered before, but he had caged the beast
this morning. He didn't need anyone, would never need
anyone again. He would see that Ben was found and
given his last respects, he owed him that much, but he
had no intention of grieving any more than that.

Evie was disappointed when he turned away and determinedly headed to town without another word, but she
was resigned to his taciturnity. Tyler could be as charming as the next man when he wanted, but that charm hid
a mean streak. She would do well to stay away from it—
and from him.

The first person she saw when they rode into town was
Daniel leaning against the rickety stagecoach office. She
screamed in delight, and he dropped the stick he was
whittling. With a look of wonder, relief, and joy, he ran
jerkily into the street to greet them, forgetting his cane,
forgetting his self-consciousness, forgetting everything
but the welcome sight of Evie riding into town on a horse
with a Stetson perched over her eyes.

"Evie! My word, they've sent search parties after you!
Are you all right? Did Pecos rescue you?" At Evie's
admonishing look, he covered his mouth with his hand
and sent Tyler an apologetic glance. "I'm sorry, sir. We
were just so worried . . ."

"We?" Tyler asked caustically, throwing his leg over
the saddle and climbing down. His glance went around
the near-empty street. A few matrons had wandered
from the general store, but there didn't seem to be any
outbreak of excitement.

"Ben and me. He swore you'd outride those bandits,
but their horses looked awful fresh to—" Daniel looked
startled as Tyler halted in mid-stride and interrupted
him.

"Ben? Ben is here? Where?" Tyler grabbed Evie by
the waist and hauled her down, but his mind was quite
evidently elsewhere.

"Upstairs in the hotel. He took a pistol ball in the side
but the doc says he'll be all right if he'll just rest awhile.
He rode in by himself, and we had a devil of a time
persuading those bigots at the hotel that he was entitled

to a room, but when I told them he worked with Pecos Martin, they came around."

Tyler barely stood still for all of this explanation. He was on the way to the impressive edifice with the sign proclaiming "HOTEL" before Daniel had all the words out. Evie heard it, however, and she gave Daniel a fulsome look.

"Now everybody in town will know he's Pecos Martin. How are we going to explain that?"

Daniel looked defensive. "I couldn't leave Ben to sleep in the stable, and I'm not as good at making up stories as you are. What can it hurt if they know who he is?"

Because that wasn't who he was, but Evie couldn't tell Daniel that. She just prayed that Tyler Monteigne had the swiftness and accuracy with a gun that Pecos Martin was proclaimed to have. She'd read enough dime novels to know what happened to notorious gunslingers, and she threw the man walking away an anxious glance.

She really didn't want to see a showdown.

Chapter 9

By the time Daniel and Evie reached Ben's room, Tyler was already there. They could hear his shouts even as they hurried down the hall.

"Who the damn hell did you think you were? General Sherman? You could have got yourself killed back there, and for what? A bunch of rednecks who can't tell the difference between a fox and a hen?"

They couldn't hear Ben's reply, but it wasn't necessary. All Evie's feathers were bristling, and she shoved into the room without invitation, nearly knocking Tyler from his feet with the swing of the door.

She didn't apologize as he jumped clear of the door. She launched into him with all flags flying. "Ben was trying to save us and maybe even you, you stupid fool! If you can't appreciate that, then get out and leave him to someone who can."

Black eyes danced with laughter as they swept over the lady's masculine chapeau and dust-covered attire, then back to a bareheaded Tyler with fury mounting in his face. It had been a long time since he'd seen Tyler with anything in his eyes besides that deceptive smile of his. Ben grinned and winked at Daniel.

"Now, Miss Evie, lay off the boy. Anybody can see he can't be both pretty and smart. Besides, the sun always bakes his brains when he leaves his hat off."

Daniel snickered, and Evie had to grin back at the man in the bed as Tyler glared at them all and stalked out. He didn't bother slamming the door, but the echo of his boots carried all the way down the stairs.

Ben stopped laughing. "You'd better go see to him, Miss Evie, or he's likely to ride right out of here and not look back. He's got a burr up his rump you don't know nothin' about."

"That isn't all he's going to have up his rump if I have anything to say about it." Gathering up her sadly disheveled skirt, Evie swung out of the room with the determination of a soldier marching off to war.

Daniel and Ben exchanged glances and shook their heads, although Daniel's gesture indicated confusion while Ben's reflected his doubt as to the wisdom of what was happening here. Still, neither of them had much to say about it.

Evie caught Tyler leading the horses to a building with a falling sign on which the word "LIVERY" could still be distinguished. Ben had been wrong about Tyler riding out without looking back. No doubt he meant to water the horses first.

"What was the meaning of that scene back there?" she demanded as she caught up with him.

Tyler sent her a stony look and reappropriated his hat. Jamming it back on his head, he replied curtly, "It's none of your business."

"Well, it seems to me if we're paying you by the day to act like a donkey, we ought to be entitled to some explanation."

"Jackass. The word is jackass. Did you have to look these things up in the dictionary and memorize them?" Tyler handed the man coming out of the livery a greenback and started unfastening his saddlebags.

"I can say donkey if I choose. It's no skin off your nose if I choose to speak like a lady. And you're evading the point." Evie was aware the stable hand was giving her odd looks, but she could survive odd looks. She wasn't at all certain that she could survive Tyler Monteigne. The sight of those broad shoulders easily taking the weight of the saddlebags as he swung them over was giving her heart palpitations.

"You sound like a schoolteacher, and you're damned right I'm evading the point." Tyler headed back toward the hotel with Evie trailing right behind. From the corner of his eye he could see a tall man walking their way, and it didn't take even his half-baked brain to figure this was

the law in town. Idly, he wondered if he got Evie angry
enough if she would turn him in for rape. He supposed
she had that right.

"Pecos Martin?"

Evie stopped in her tracks and swung around at this
question coming from a stranger. The man coming up to
them was tall and heavy enough to make two of Tyler.
She stepped protectively to Tyler's side.

Tyler extended his hand. "Tyler Monteigne, sir. What
can I do for you?"

The man with a tarnished star dangling from his vest
eyed his outstretched palm doubtfully, then with a glimmer of understanding, accepted it. He looked Tyler
straight in the face when he replied. "I don't hold with
gunslingers in this town, but if you're staying incognito,
then I'll do what I can to keep trouble out of your way.
This the lady the boy was raising such hell about?" He
nodded in Evie's direction.

Evie was staring at both men with astonishment and
didn't react immediately. She let Tyler reply for her.

"She means to be a schoolteacher," he replied
maliciously.

Realizing he had no knowledge that was just what she
intended to claim, Evie recovered her equanimity suffi-
ciently to smile sweetly. "I'm Maryellen Peyton, sheriff.
I understand Mineral Springs is in need of a teacher, and
I'm here to apply. Mr. Monteigne here has been generous enough to escort Daniel and myself. I don't know
what would have happened had he not been available
when those robbers struck."

"I heard about that. I've got men out now searching
for those thieves. That gang has struck once too often
lately. When you've had a chance to settle in, I'd like to
talk to both of you about what happened. But for now,
it's good to meet you, Miss Peyton. My name is Alan
Powell."

"It's Mrs. Peyton, sheriff. I'm a widow. It's a pleasure
to meet you, too. But if you don't mind, I simply must
find a room and rest. It's been quite an ordeal."

Tyler watched as the hard-bitten sheriff melted into a
puddle of butter before Evie's smallest smile. He didn't

want to imagine what would have happened to the man
had she turned the full force of those devastating lips on
him. He could see the devilment in sloe eyes as she
glanced up at him through those long lashes, and he
wanted to wring her neck. Mrs. Peyton, indeed. She was
going to rub it in until it hurt.

"I'll be back to talk to you in a bit, Powell. I'll see
the lady gets settled in first." Appropriating Evie's elbow,
Tyler steered her toward the comparative safety of the
hotel. He was either going to have to get out of here
fast or poke the eyes out of every man in the damned
town. It might be easier if he just pulled a sack over
Evie's head.

Once they were in the dim light of the lobby, Evie
halted and removed her arm from Tyler's possession. She
gave him a thoroughly quenching look that he took with
a threatening frown.

"You may talk to the sheriff as long as you like, Mr.
Monteigne, but unless you explain that scene upstairs,
you're now formally off my payroll. I'll not have anything
to do with a man who can treat an injured friend so
callously."

In the dusky gloom she was a shimmering candle of
indignation. Light from the dirty window caught on her
chestnut tresses, capturing the strands of auburn he'd
noticed that first day. Her sunburned cheeks glowed with
ire, and there were even sparks in her eyes. Tyler found
it hard to believe that she was the woman he had taken
so crudely last night. She was right. He was a jackass.

"As of now, I formally offer my resignation, *Miss* Peyton." He swung the saddle off his shoulder and dropped
it to the floor. "But if you would care to join me wherever they serve food in this godforsaken hole, then I'll
be happy to enlighten you."

Evie jumped at the sound of the saddle hitting the
floor. Or maybe it was at the light in Tyler's eyes as he
offered this offhand invitation. She had been ignoring
what had happened between them, but it was obvious he
didn't mean to be gentleman enough to forget it. He
would never meet the standards of an Ivanhoe.

But the hotel clerk entered then. Evie was starving,

and there didn't seem to be anything else she could say while Tyler made arrangements for their rooms and learned the location of the nearest café. She had to eat, and ladies didn't go to public places alone.

There was time to have second thoughts when the clerk led her to a room with a single large bed and she realized that she wouldn't have Daniel's protection at night. But her trunk was already in here, the warm water was tempting, and her stomach demanded instant satisfaction. She washed and changed and answered the door when Tyler knocked some time later.

She could feel his eyes assessing the ecru crepe de chine skirt with the lace sacque she had chosen to wear. It was the coolest thing she could find in her trunk, and the lace didn't wrinkle as much as some of her other bodices. As long as she had to wear long sleeves and loads of fripperies in this weather, she might as well look cool and comfortable. Besides, she liked the blue rosettes at the waist and the blue sash that went with it. She gave him a haughty smile when he said nothing.

"Have you no insult to offer over my attire, Mr. Monteigne? Or would you care to throw in a few threats and curses first before we eat? Or perhaps what you need is a good game of cards and a bottle of whiskey. Shall we go in search of them?"

Since they were indoors, Tyler had been holding his hat politely in his hands. Now he jammed it on his head and offered his arm. He was determined to charm this little witch right off her broom if it took a magic spell and a love potion to do it.

"It's good to see you again, too, Miss Peyton. Shall we dine?" He noticed her hand trembling as it took his arm, and Tyler instantly regretted his sarcasm. He truly was turning into a sardonic bastard. With a sigh, he patted her fingers and whispered, "I'm not wearing my gun, Evie. If you so much as smile at a man while wearing that outfit, they're going to be all over you. You don't really want my blood on that pretty lace, do you?"

Evie sent him an uncertain look, but when she saw the laughter in his eyes, she relaxed. Tyler the Charmer was back. She knew how to handle charmers. It was the man behind the charm who terrified her. As long as she didn't have to deal with him, she would do all right.

"Red with blue is vulgar, sir. I'll thank you to keep your fists to yourself, if you would. And I'll more than thank you if you would just feed me. I'm about to expire of hunger."

"More than thank me? I like the sound of that. Let's go."

Laughing, chatting as if they were truly a courting couple, they made their way down the stairs and out into the hot sun. No one looking at them would realize that he was a gambler with an itchy trigger finger and a reputation for winning and that she was a liar and a bastard that no one wanted. They appeared a gentleman and a lady made for each other.

Evie's fashionable gown was altogether too elegant for the bare café where Tyler led her. A pane of flyspecked glass gave the room light. A glass pitcher of warm beer on the counter added a touch of hospitality. They took seats in wooden chairs at a bare table and were waited on by a youngster in dirty apron and bare feet. The food, however, when it came, was steaming hot and plentiful.

Sometime later, with appetites nearly satiated, they negotiated the uneasy path of conversation.

"You promised explanations," Evie reminded Tyler as he refilled his glass with warm beer.

Tyler sipped the liquid and contemplated the persistent woman seated across from him. He knew she couldn't be much more than twenty, but at that age he had been a man grown. The war did that to people. He wondered what it was that had turned this beautiful child into a woman at twenty. He'd certainly had a hand in it, but he had only stolen the last vestige of innocence. Evie Peyton hadn't been a true innocent for a long time.

"I have a foul temper," he answered casually.

"I noticed." Evie waited.

Tyler set the glass down and frowned. "What do you want me to say? Ben's my best and only friend. We grew up together. He taught me to fish and ride. He was supposed to be my slave, but he was closer to me than my brothers. They were a lot older and always about their own business. Ben's only business was me."

"So you yell at him when he gets shot?"

Tyler moved uncomfortably in his chair. "He had no business risking his life for anyone. He doesn't even want to be here. He has family back in Natchez."

The door opened and shut behind them, but neither noticed until someone kicked the chair between them. Daniel stumbled over a loose floorboard as Ben draped his long form into the chair.

"Saw the two of you go out. Took you so long to come back, thought maybe we ought to come pry one of you off the ceiling. Pardon us if we're intruding." Ben helped himself to the pitcher and Tyler's glass while Daniel maneuvered into a chair across from him.

Daniel sent Evie a nervous glance, but she was daintily wiping her fingers on her handkerchief since there seemed a dire dearth of table linens.

"Not at all, Mr. Benjamin." Evie sent Tyler a cold glance. "Since we've never been properly introduced, I assume that's the appropriate address?"

"Benjamin Wilkerson the Third, spelled out and not with Roman numerals," Tyler intoned with years of practice. "If there ever was one born to be an upstart darky, you found him."

Ben grinned and folded his arms across his chest. "My ma believed I was meant for better things."

Tyler shouted for another pitcher of beer and more glasses. Since they were the only patrons in the place, it shouldn't have been a difficult request, but no one came to answer his call. With a wry look to Ben, he shrugged and rose. "Excuse me, ladies, gentlemen. I have a bad habit that I'm about to indulge in. Go on without me."

Ben rolled his eyes and looked resigned. Understanding that smoking a cheroot wasn't the habit he had in mind, Evie watched Tyler head for the rear of the café with a certain degree of nervousness. She didn't like the way his muscles rolled with feline intensity as he strolled around the counter. She was beginning to learn a few things about Tyler Monteigne, and one of them was the error of considering his casual grace as laziness.

He disappeared into the kitchen, and a moment later there was a loud outburst having to do with "damned niggers" and "not in my place," followed by a slamming noise, the tinkle of broken glassware, and a thump.

A few minutes later Tyler emerged dusting off his frock coat. The young boy who had served them earlier came rushing after him with a tray of beer and glasses. The look on his face was more astonishment than anger, and he set the tray out without a hint of resentment. Giving the table's occupants a look of curiosity, he hurried away without a word.

Tyler settled back into his chair and helped himself to a fresh glass. "Benjamin was his mother's third boy. The other two died early, and both were named Benjamin. She was a damned persistent woman, just like some others I know."

He smiled beatifically at Evie's astounded expression. He'd finally got through to her. Not the way he wanted, perhaps, but still, it was good to know that he could wipe the dreamy mask from her face upon occasion.

She recovered rapidly. Picking up her water glass, she answered his smug expression serenely. "Tyler Monteigne, you are not only a liar, a cheat, and a donkey, but a man of rare perception. You were telling me why you were yelling at Mr. Wilkerson."

Daniel spluttered in his first drink of beer and set it down to watch the response to Evie's famous two-pronged thrust.

Tyler shrugged and held his gaze steadily on her. "I spent three years in a Yankee prison, Miss Peyton. I was seventeen years old when I went in and twenty when I came out. They would have carried me out in a wooden box if it hadn't been for Ben. He found me, joined the Union army, and got himself stationed at the prison until the war was over. He told them he couldn't see well enough to shoot a gun, but he was real good with his fists, and they believed him and put him where he requested. Do you have any idea how difficult that was?"

"And to this day the damned fool thinks I did it for him," Ben grumped as he sipped his beer. "I told you he was real pretty but not too bright."

Tyler grinned. "I'm not so dumb that I don't know you were after my plantation. Thought you almost had it, didn't you?"

Ben shrugged. "Worked well for a while. You were the only one left to inherit and if you had to sell it for back taxes, can't rightly see why it couldn't go to me. That Yankee captain thought it damned funny when I offered to buy it. Wouldn't have worked if you'd been dead. The government would have sold it to the highest bidder then."

Daniel interrupted this obviously rehearsed routine. "You're saying that Tyler had to sell his plantation because of back taxes and Ben bought it? I knew the Freedman's Bureau was saying they were going to give every slave forty acres and forty dollars or some such idiocy, but they never did. How can a slave buy a plantation?"

"Ben's a bigger card cheat than I ever was. He cleaned those Yankees out for nigh on to three years. The taxes weren't all that much but I didn't have a red cent, and they wouldn't give me time to earn any. The Ridge was too tempting a prize."

"All right. I give up. So what happened? Why isn't Ben running the plantation right now and making you work in the kitchen or something?" Caught up in the story and the interplay between the two men, Evie momentarily forgot her grievances. Ben and Tyler were unlikely companions, but they were as close to friends as she and Daniel had out here. It suddenly struck her that in the dime novels, Pecos Martin always had a sidekick.

It was Ben's turn to shrug. "I didn't have all that much money. All the people who worked the plantation pooled their resources, so we all owned it. That was our downfall: too many chiefs and not any Indians. Everybody wanted to move into the big house and sip lemonade, and nobody wanted to work the fields. It was like givin' a bunch of children a chance to play dress up. Some of us tried, but the times were against us. I don't know nothin' about cotton. I'm a horse trainer. We didn't keep the cotton clean. It got picked too late. And nobody wanted to buy it when we got it to town. Even the Yankee carpetbaggers wouldn't buy from darkies. Not that the crop was much good, but they could have given us something. Tyler had to take it down to New Orleans to unload it. By the time he got back, Dorset had forced the place into auction and bought it himself. He was the military commander by then, and we were still under martial law. There wasn't nothing nobody could do."

"So Ben and I duded ourselves up in fine clothes with the proceeds and went to Natchez. End of story."

Tyler shoved his chair back and rose from the table, offering his arm to Evie as he did so. It was evident he didn't mean to express his feelings about the whole situation, and Evie was beginning to think she really didn't want to know. She had evidence enough of what happened when Tyler Monteigne gave vent to his feelings. She wasn't prepared to experience that holocaust again. She took his arm as coolly as he offered it and nodded to Ben.

"It's been a pleasure, Mr. Wilkerson. Don't tell Daniel too many tales; he tends to believe them." As she strolled out on Tyler's arm, she could hear Ben chuckling behind them. She liked to leave men laughing.

She threw Tyler an anxious look. He wasn't laughing. He wasn't even smiling. And he hadn't said anything about going away.

Her stomach knotted nervously as she realized she wasn't certain whether she was better off having him stay and help her find out what happened to her parents or having him go away and never reminding her again of what had happened between them. Both alternatives had an element of danger—was she better off with him or without him?

As they entered the hotel lobby and she disengaged her hand to properly return to her room alone, Tyler answered her questions without their being asked. Catching her hand in a firm grip and fastening her with a steely gaze, he said, "It's your turn, Miss Peyton. I'll have the truth from you before I leave this town. Would you prefer to do it in your room or mine?"

Chapter 10

He wanted her to tell him a story. Evie loved to tell stories, although she occasionally had difficulty separating truth from fiction. Fiction was so much more entertaining, but she had a niggling feeling this man wouldn't appreciate the difference.

She wasn't wearing gloves, and Tyler's fingers were smooth against hers where they touched. But when she tried to draw away, their pressure was strong and inescapable. Evie felt a shiver of something warm flowing through her veins as she met Tyler's gaze while his hand clasped hers, but she refused to give in to his easy attraction. She had more character than the floozies he was accustomed to. She knew what he was, and she refused to become another one of his women.

"Does this mean you're still on my payroll?" she asked sweetly.

"No, ma'am, it doesn't. It means you still owe me the truth, and I mean to collect." Tyler circled his thumb in her palm and watched the color rise in her cheeks. He wasn't playing fair, but then, neither had she.

Sensing his looser grip, Evie jerked her hand away and tucked it under her arm. "Under the circumstances, I don't believe I owe you anything, Mr. Monteigne." Her disdainful glare spoke what her words could not. She thought she managed the royal princess look rather well, although she didn't think it would work in a Pecos Martin book. "Unless you mean to help us, I don't see any reason why we should see each other again."

She caught up her skirt and regally started up the stairway. Tyler stared after her, momentarily struck by the realization that she could just walk away like that.

Women didn't walk away from him. It was a fact of life he had taken for granted. And women he had taken to bed not only didn't walk away, but clung like thorny roses. It had never occurred to him that she could just turn around and walk away and he would have absolutely no claim to say anything about it.

He didn't like the feeling one little bit. Reason told him that he ought to let the spoiled brat go. He had better things to do than to baby-sit a pair of greenhorns with trouble up their sleeves. And she was the kind of woman he had sworn long ago not to touch. She was doing him a favor by walking out. But reason had nothing to do with the fury steaming out his ears. He hit the steps running.

Tyler grabbed the edge of her door as she opened it, standing with his back against it so she had to brush by him to enter her room. Evie threw him a wary glance and remained standing in the hallway.

"I never said I wouldn't help. You've just never told me what you needed done." Smiling at her wouldn't do any good, Tyler reflected. He had smiled at her before, and she had all but slapped him in the face. If he couldn't get under her skin with his looks and charm, what in hell would it take?

Evie contemplated the man holding her door open so that she couldn't shut him out. There was more to Tyler Monteigne than his looks, but he obviously wasn't the type to put his talents to use. He seemed perfectly satisfied frittering his time away at the gambling table. She didn't need him for this next step of her plan, but she couldn't be certain that she wouldn't need him later. Frowning, she crossed her arms over her chest.

"I am not one of your women, Tyler Monteigne. I want that perfectly understood."

Tyler relaxed and leaned against the door jamb, mockingly crossing his arms in imitation of her stance. "Yes, ma'am. I prefer a little experience on my women, anyway."

That struck where it hurt, but Evie's didn't flinch. "Fine, then you can wait until Daniel comes back to hear

our story, if that's what you like. But unless you mean
to help us, I don't see any purpose in it."

She was offering him another chance to walk away—
and he wasn't going to take it. Tyler wasn't exactly certain why. It could have something to do with the delectable curve of her waist beneath all that lace. Or the
indignant swell of her bosom when she realized he was
staring at it. But mostly he thought it was boredom and
curiosity and the need to know more of what went on
in that strange mind behind those deceptive dark eyes.

"I don't rob banks for anyone," Tyler replied calmly.

"I wouldn't ask you to." Evie felt a slight quiver of
relief. He was going to stay. She offered a tentative smile.
"It could be very simple, and I won't need you at all."

"Or it could be so dangerous that you need a gunslinger like Pecos Martin to protect you," he offered
solemnly.

"That was Daniel's idea. I'm not certain if he thought
he needed a gunslinger to keep me in line or my
relatives."

"If they're anything like you, I suspect both reasons.
Daniel is a very astute young man."

He was doing it again. He was smiling and being
charming and Evie wanted to touch his hand and feel
him touch her. On the brink of a discovery she had
sought all her life, she was as nervous as a mama cat. It
would be comforting to have the shelter of Tyler's reassuring embrace. But reassurance wasn't what he meant
to offer.

Steeling herself, Evie drew her back up straight. "It
isn't proper for us to linger here like this. The whole
town will be talking, and I won't get that job as schoolteacher. If this takes very long, I might very well need
the money. Let me know when Daniel returns. We can
talk then."

He had thought she was beginning to soften. Well, at
least she wasn't slamming the door on him or walking
away. Knowing when it was time to fold, Tyler made a
slight bow of acquiescence and moved out of her way.
"I'm looking forward to it. And Evie?"

She halted in closing the door on him and gave him a questioning look.

Tyler smiled down into her delicious eyes. "Wear something blue tomorrow, will you? That blue sash really looks good on you."

Her eyes widened, and then realizing what he was doing, Evie very carefully shut the door in his face. She heard his chuckle as he walked off, and she wanted to throw and smash things, but that would only give her away. Tyler had years more experience at charming the opposite sex than she did. She would have to learn from him if they were going to work together.

But those very sensible thoughts didn't keep her body from tingling in unexpected places as she imagined what it could be like if she let Tyler Monteigne charm her into his arms again. Not his bed. She hadn't liked that. Just his arms. She wanted his arms holding her and his mouth on hers, and she wanted to know that he wanted the same thing. But then, he wanted that with any woman he saw.

Cursing to herself, Evie went to the window and watched as Tyler stepped down from the hotel veranda and headed for the café. He was going to go get Daniel and Ben and eventually drag the story out of her. She wasn't at all certain that she was prepared to give it to him. Would Tyler's eyes light quite so nicely when he discovered she was a bastard instead of a lady?

She watched as the sheriff came out and intercepted Tyler's determined path. She breathed a sigh of relief as the two men wandered back to the sheriff's office. Maybe they would get caught up in men's talk and leave her alone. There was time to look into a few things on her own.

Chin set in determination, Evie consulted the distorted hotel mirror, adjusted her hat, found her gloves, and checking the window again to make certain Tyler wasn't in sight, set out on her own.

By the time she returned, Daniel was sprawled across her bed reading a book, waiting for her. He looked up at her entrance and set the book aside when he saw the carefully blank expression upon her face.

"I thought you were with Tyler," he accused.

Evie removed her hat and gently lay it upon the dresser. "All this time? Shame on you."

There wasn't the usual note of banter in her voice, and Daniel felt his insides tighten. "You went looking for that lawyer, didn't you?" His eyes widened. "You didn't try talking to him yet, did you?"

"He wasn't there." Evie sat down on the padded seat of a wooden chair and began to unbutton her gloves.

"It's kind of late in the day. I suppose he went home. But you found his office, didn't you? We can go back tomorrow."

"He won't be back tomorrow." Evie peeled off the gloves and examined a chipped fingernail. Perhaps she ought to cut her nails back. It was hard to write on a chalkboard without scratching them against it.

"What do you mean he won't be back tomorrow? Is he dead?" Daniel sat up and stared at her with horror. Evie in a silent mood was a strange and dangerous thing.

That summoned a small smile as she looked up to him. "I certainly hope not. After coming all this way, it would be terrible if he were, wouldn't it? I hadn't thought of that. But he's not dead. He's just away on business. They don't expect him back for weeks, maybe months. It's just so terribly disappointing to come this far to sit and wait again."

Daniel didn't exactly express relief. "Months? I don't think our funds will hold out for months. Pecos gave us as much for our help in that game as he's charged us, but even so, this hotel isn't cheap, and neither is food. What happens if our families find out that Nanny is dead and stop sending our monthly allotments?"

"I've thought about that. Knowing Nanny, I should think she must have sent them some report on how we fared, so the chances are very likely they'll get nervous if they don't hear anything from her. On the other hand, since they didn't want anything to do with us, just cashing their checks might be enough notice. If we keep on forging her signature, they might never know. But we can't take that chance."

Daniel waited for the inspiration he knew she would provide.

Evie smiled. "I'm going to get that job as school-teacher. I found out who to apply to, and I'm going there tomorrow. I'm sure the pay will be very small, but we don't need any clothes. You know that. And surely they'll pay enough for room and board. We'll just have to find a less expensive place to stay than this hotel."

Daniel's face reflected his misgivings. "We can't keep paying Pecos for months. What if the lawyer won't tell you anything?"

Evie shrugged. "Tyler resigned. I can't imagine what he could do in any case." Her eyes brightened. "Maybe you could get a job in the lawyer's office as his clerk! We wouldn't even have to tell him who I am that way. You could go through his files and find out everything. I'm certain there's more money where my checks come from. Maybe we can get our hands on some of that, and then we can go looking for my parents on our own."

"That's probably about the craziest thing you've ever dreamed up." Daniel collapsed against the pillows he had propped against the wall. "The chances of anybody hiring me are about nil. I imagine a law clerk has to run all over town doing errands and things. If I thought I could do that, I'd hire on at the newspaper. I've always wanted to work on a newspaper."

"Have you really?" Evie contemplated that idea for a while, her head cocked at a thoughtful angle. "Well, I don't see any reason why you shouldn't. Tomorrow, we'll set out to become self-supporting workers. We're quite old enough now to be on our own anyway."

A thumping on the door caused Evie to frown. She hadn't kept watch, but she could imagine who the intruder was. She sent Daniel a thoughtful glance, then nonchalantly began to file her nails as she called for their visitor to come in.

Tyler entered, hat in hand. His gaze went first to the boy lounging across the bed, then to Evie sitting innocently in the corner making herself beautiful. He wasn't entirely fooled by her display. Many beautiful women

were so vain that they thought of nothing but themselves.
This beautiful woman had too devious a mind for that.

"The sheriff's posse just came back in. They didn't find
any trace of the thieves. I told him I'd go back out with
them again tomorrow. If we're going to have that little
talk, it had best be tonight."

Evie set her file aside and made a graceful gesture at
the other chair in the room. "Won't you have a seat,
Mr. Monteigne? That's mighty kind of you to offer your
services to the local sheriff. I do trust he isn't expecting
you to single-handedly catch the outlaws, is he? He
seems to be under the impression that you are someone
that you aren't."

Tyler sent Daniel another look. The boy still believed
he was his hero, Pecos Martin. And it looked like the
sheriff had read the same silly novels. He could guess
where the sheriff had got the notion.

Shrugging, he set his hat on the table and crossed his
legs. "I know how to shoot a gun as well as the next man,
I reckon. Southerners learn to shoot and ride before they
can walk. Don't worry your pretty little head about me,
Miss Peyton."

Evie gritted her teeth as she pretended to be the sim-
pering idiot he was playing up to. She smiled and batted
her eyelashes. "Why, Mr. Monteigne, how could I not?
I'll say a prayer for you tonight before I go to bed."

"You do that." Tyler's smoldering look spoke of what
he would prefer she do in that bed, but he played the
part of gallant for the boy's sake. "Now, you were going
to tell me how I could help you here in Mineral Springs."

"I thought Evie said . . ."

Evie sent Daniel a quenching look. When he'd shut
up, she turned a smile to Tyler. "I'm afraid you won't
be able to help, after all, Mr. Monteigne. It appears we're
going to have to stay here for some little while, and we
wouldn't wish to delay your return to Natchez."

Tyler swept his frock coat back and shoved his hands
in his trouser pockets as he considered the evasive little
witch across from him. He had no reason to demand that
she assuage his curiosity other than that she had dragged
him all the way out here and he wanted to know why.

But he was damned tired of hearing her lies, and he could tell by the set expression on her face that was all he was going to get right now.

So he rolled his shoulders and shrugged. "I'm not planning on returning to Natchez anytime soon. There's no profit in reaching a new territory without exploring it first. I mean to look into a few business enterprises while I'm here. You just let me know if I can be of any help, you hear?"

Evie thought she might just throw up when Tyler donned that bright Southern gentleman smile and syrupy drawl. Maybe the Yankees didn't hang on to him long enough. A few more years in a federal prison might work wonders. She smiled sweetly in mocking reply. "Why, of course, Mr. Monteigne, I wouldn't hear of anything else. Now you take care tomorrow, won't you?"

Tyler slowly unfolded himself from the chair and rested his hand on the doorknob. His gaze fell thoughtfully on the lovely bird of paradise perched on the worn bedroom chair, then flickered in the direction of the boy on the bed. Daniel was tense and upset, but he was keeping his mouth shut.

Tyler nodded at the kid. "You tell me when your sister gets herself in too deep. And if there's anything else you want to tell me, I'll be keeping rooms here for a while. You just come find me."

Daniel looked cautiously relieved. Satisfied, Tyler bowed a polite farewell and walked out.

Evie kicked the washstand. "Who does he think he is? I didn't hire him for a nanny. Why doesn't he just go away and leave us alone?"

Daniel sent his "sister" a look of curiosity and slowly raised himself from the bed. "I don't know what you've got against the man, Ev. He's only trying to help. Maybe he could be looking around for you while he's here. It's a lot easier for a man to snoop and ask questions than for a lady."

"Don't be ridiculous." Evie rose and helped Daniel find his cane. She wasn't at all certain that she liked the idea of sleeping in a strange hotel room without Daniel nearby, but she supposed if they were going to stay here,

she was going to have to get used to the idea. They had
used to share rooms when they were little, and it had
seemed natural enough when they started out on this
journey, but Daniel was close to being a grown man now.
She couldn't continue to pretend he was a little boy. "I'm
perfectly capable of asking all the questions I need."

Daniel took the cane and limped to the door. "And
getting your nose bit off doing so. Let's just wait until
that lawyer gets back. It could all be very simple."

Evie didn't think so, but she let Daniel leave with her
reassurances. Nothing was ever simple in her experience,
and Tyler Monteigne's decision to stay in Mineral
Springs was only just one example.

Closing the door after Daniel and staring at her empty
room, she tried not to think of how Tyler had looked
when he sat in that chair, or the way his eyes had all but
undressed her. She knew why he had stayed all right. A
man like Tyler couldn't stand rejection.

Like a dog after 'coon, he had his nose to the scent—
and she was his prey.

Chapter 11

Evie clasped her gloved hands in the lap of her blue serge skirt. She hadn't worn blue for Tyler's benefit. This just happened to be the most schoolmarmish outfit she could find. And it seemed to be working very well. She smiled meekly for the benefit of the stout, graying man across the desk from her.

"I had references from the school where I taught in St. Louis, but they seemed to have been lost in the confusion of the robbery. I can give you their address, and you are free to write and confirm them." She spoke with just enough soft Southern charm that she would be believed without making her seem like a meek-mannered Milquetoast who couldn't handle a schoolroom full of children.

The man across from her folded his hands over his ample belly. He wore a gold watch chain across his vest, but he hadn't consulted his watch as yet. Evie thought that might be a point in her favor.

"I understand you arrived here in the company of a gunslinger, Mrs. Peyton." Disapproval rippled through him as he spoke these words.

Evie widened her eyes and touched a gloved hand to the discreet cameo at her throat. "A gunslinger?"

The school board chairman shifted uncomfortably in his wooden chair. "I wasn't born yesterday, Mrs. Peyton. My brother Alan is the sheriff here. He told me you rode in with Pecos Martin."

Evie scrambled for the man's name. Powell. He'd said his name was Powell. And the sheriff was Alan Powell. She was going to have to remember that this was a small town and everybody was related to everybody else. She gave a small smile that should indicate something vaguely embarrassing but amusing.

"Oh, dear. Since you have a brother, perhaps you'll understand. Daniel wanted to impress the hotel manager, so he made up that story about Pecos Martin. He's been reading those penny-dreadfuls, I fear. As far as I know, there is no such person as Pecos Martin. Tyler Monteigne is an old friend of the family from Natchez. I'm sure you can write and confirm that. He had business here and offered to escort Daniel and myself. After you meet my brother, you'll see that there is some concern for his health, and the physicians thought this climate might be more salubrious to his recovery. I certainly hope it doesn't lead to encouraging his imagination."

David Powell nodded understandingly. "Well, we'll see that doesn't happen. You are orphans, I think?"

Evie summoned a sad smile. "My husband and I tried to be parents to Daniel for some years now. But since my husband's death— Well, his family has been more than kind, but it is time we stand on our own. Daniel has expressed some interest in studying law, but I fear his health wouldn't allow him to go back East to study. I don't suppose there is a lawyer in town who might be interested in a clerk?"

He took it hook, line, and sinker. Evie could tell the moment he swallowed the whole story. In a little while, it would be fully digested and all over town. She sank back in her chair with a feeling of satisfaction for a job well-done.

"Jonathan Hale is our local attorney. I'll mention the matter to him when he comes back. You have come at a timely moment, Mrs. Peyton. It hasn't been easy to establish a school in these parts. The money and support just hasn't been there. But the late Louise Harding saw the need and established a fund before she died. We've been functioning since last fall. Unfortunately, the young man we recruited to teach our children decided to take a more lucrative position last month, and we haven't found another candidate until now. To be truthful, Mrs. Peyton, we had hoped to hire another man. A young and pretty woman isn't likely to remain single for long around here."

Evie smiled understandingly. "I am dedicated to my teaching, Mr. Powell. I continued to teach after I married. And I imagine the salary you are offering would be difficult for a man to support a family on, but I won't have that problem. So perhaps this is the best way for everyone concerned."

The salary being offered was positively miniscule, but it was better than nothing at all. Had she wished, she could have taken room and board with the families of the children she would be teaching and saved that expense, but Daniel's presence made that awkward even had she wished to live with strangers. Which she didn't.

Gathering up her reticule, shaking Powell's hand, agreeing on the day she would begin, Evie escaped the musty office with the school board chairman at her side. She didn't escape his presence, however. As they gained the street, Powell noticed a tall man walking in their direction, and he caught Evie's shoulder and halted her escape.

"Here comes Jace Harding now. His mother's the lady who set up the trust fund. He's on the board. Might as well meet him now while you have the chance. He's one of those single young men I've been warning you about."

Evie took all this in as she watched the man coming toward her. From the way he carried himself, she had assumed Jason Harding would be older, but as he approached, it appeared he couldn't be more than in his early thirties. Beneath dark curly hair, his eyes were a serious gray and his jaw a stubborn square, but there was the same familiar light of inquiry in his expression that Evie had seen in many another man. She offered a small smile and was rewarded with a quickness in his step as he came forward.

"Howdy, Jace, this here's Mrs. Maryellen Peyton, our new schoolteacher. Mrs. Peyton, let me introduce Jason Harding, owner of one of the biggest spreads in the area."

The only spread she knew of covered a bed, and Evie couldn't imagine a big bed something to be bragged about, but she surmised the word had a different meaning in Texas, and she offered her hand. Harding took it in his large one and grinned blindingly at her.

"Pleased to meet you, Mrs. Peyton. The sheriff's been telling me about your little incident. I hope your introduction to Texas doesn't put you off none. It would be a pure shame to lose you before we had a chance to get acquainted."

"I have a little more spirit than that, Mr. Harding. I understand there's a posse out now tracking down the culprits. I'm sure we'll all be safe once they're caught."

Evie was beginning to feel a little bad about deceiving all these nice people. She hadn't come here to deceive anyone. She had only wanted to protect herself—and her family, if it came down to it. But now one lie was topping another, and the lie of being a widow seemed to be the worst one of all. Darn Tyler Monteigne, anyway. If it hadn't been for him, she could face this nice man in all innocence and accept his attentions just as if she were the kind of young lady he might be interested in.

But she wasn't, so what was one lie on top of another? Being a slightly soiled widow certainly wasn't worse than being the bastard she really was. She didn't know why she had adopted the married title in the first place. She wasn't going to be around long enough to allow a little flirting to develop into courtship and certainly not marriage. So no one would have ever known she wasn't anything but what she seemed had she not continued the lie.

But it was too late to take it back now. She was a virgin no longer, so she might as well act the part of experienced woman. Harding was telling her something about his days as his mother's student, but her mind had wandered. Now she smiled at the right moment, made reassuring noises, and was about to move on when a movement down the street caught her eye. Tyler.

He was supposed to be doing posse duty. Couldn't she do anything without him interfering? Ignoring the man rapidly approaching, she turned a brilliant smile on the older man who had evidently fallen for her vapid Southern belle pose.

"I can't wait to meet my new students, Mr. Harding.

I wish I could learn something about them before class begins. Will many of them be attending Sunday services?"

"I'd be more than happy to introduce a few of them to you now, Mrs. Peyton." He took her arm and gave Powell a nod, which the other man returned with a wink. "I'm certain the ladies in town are dying to meet you, too. We could ..."

He halted as Tyler stepped up on the stair in front of them. Sweeping his hat off the golden glory of his hair, he made a formal bow. "Mrs. Peyton." He lifted a questioning brow, forcing her into introductions.

As Evie seethed, Tyler ingratiated himself with the two men, calling himself a plantation owner looking for new ventures and all but patting Evie on the head since she had introduced him as an old family friend. When Jason seemed more interested in leading Tyler off to discuss a new herd-breeding theory that Tyler mentioned, she nearly put her foot through the floor.

Instead, she smiled her most saccharine smile and turned to Mr. Powell. "Well, I can see that my services aren't needed immediately, sir, so I'll bid you adieu for the moment. I must see how Daniel fares."

Jason recovered rapidly, catching her arm before she could escape. "I meant that, Mrs. Peyton. I'll introduce you around if you would like."

Tyler replaced his hat and neatly drew Evie's hand into the crook of his elbow. "The lady has a prior appointment, but I'm certain she'll be happy to take up your offer at a later date. Gentlemen." He doffed his hat in farewell, then swung Evie out into the street.

She wanted to dig her heels in and screech, but she knew as well as he that such a scene would ruin her chances. As it was, it was going to look mighty odd that an "old family friend" would behave so proprietarily. She followed at his side in hostile silence.

"You can't keep from flirting with every damn man who crosses your path, can you?" Tyler asked from between clenched teeth. The sight of Evie batting those long lashes at a good-looking man who reeked of respectability and wealth had given him a few bad moments, and he meant to make her pay for them. Until now, he had thought they had something in common. Seeing her with Jace Harding was making him think twice. She might be a liar, but she gave every evidence of being a lady of means. And until he had ruined her, she had been an innocent whether he wanted to believe it or not. Just because she had fallen into his company didn't mean she was accustomed to low life. So they really had nothing in common at all. She looked quite in place with that damned rancher.

Evie sent Tyler a look of incredulity. "Flirting? Is that what I was doing? How absolutely criminal of me. I should be taken out and flogged. Or perhaps you have found a card game where you have some use for me?"

He could throttle her. He didn't think there was a man in this town who would condemn him once he heard the whole tale. But she wasn't worth the explanations. Tyler stopped in mid-stride and glared at her. "Do you want to discuss this privately or publicly?"

"I don't wish to discuss anything with a man who cannot see reason. You are no longer in my employ, Tyler Monteigne. You have no call to act like this."

She was wearing blue. It brought out the blue in her eyes as he had known it would. Damn, but she shouldn't have lashes like that. Any other woman with hair that color would have skinny red lashes and freckles. She ought to dye her hair black if she was going to look like that. Tyler tried to unclench his teeth before he made a scene.

"Did it ever occur to you, Miss Peyton, that you could already be carrying my child? Aside from protecting her reputation, that is the reason a gentleman marries a lady if he dishonors her. If we should have to get married, I don't want a wife who's going to flirt with every damned man between the ages of fourteen and ninety."

Evie went pale as she stared into the furious brown of his eyes. The Tyler she didn't know was back, and she didn't know what to do with him. As long as they were standing in the middle of the street she was probably safe, but she could hear a wagon approaching. She tried to shake off his hold, but he wouldn't release her.

She gathered up her skirt and hurried toward the boardwalk. "You have nothing to worry about, Mr. Monteigne. I have no intention of being your wife under any circumstances. And you're a fine one to talk about flirting. Haven't you found the local bar girl yet? I'm sure there must be one. Why don't you go ply your charms on her and leave me alone?"

He had her hand trapped on his arm, but she was practically dragging him. Tyler had the uncomfortable feeling she had been dragging him around since the day they met. He didn't know himself anymore. He had never forced a woman in his life. He certainly never had any intention of even seducing a woman like Evie. And marriage was the last thing on his mind. So why in hell was he behaving like a jealous lover?

Shaking his head to clear it from whatever webs she had woven in it, Tyler released her hand when they reached the boardwalk. "Fine, I'll do just that. At least bar girls manage to be honest about what they want."

He stalked off, leaving Evie to dart into the hotel without him. She hoped the men from the school board hadn't been watching all of that. She didn't know what they would make of it. She didn't know what to make of it. She would never understand Tyler Monteigne if she lived a million years.

Daniel was waiting for her when she came in. She was going to have to find something for him to do besides sitting in his room and reading all day. Nanny had forced him to accompany her on all her rounds, but Evie wouldn't be in a position to do that if she spent her time in a schoolroom. But for now, it was good to have a friendly face to come back to.

"What happened? Did you get the job? What did they say?" Daniel threw his book aside and waited eagerly for her response.

"I've got the job. Don't crow yet. I was the only applicant." Evie threw off her hat and glanced out the window. Tyler was heading into the saloon. Tightening her lips, she turned her back on the window. "And I inquired about a law clerk position for you, so when Mr. Hale returns you can apply without anyone thinking anything of it. And I met the nicest man, a Mr. Jason Harding. He's on the school board. He would have taken me to meet some of the ladies, but Tyler interfered. I thought he was supposed to be riding a posse or something."

"Ben came by and said the posse caught up with the thieves. They're down in the jail now. He says they're part of a notorious gang the sheriff's been trying to stop for some time now. Pecos apparently killed two of them, and one they brought in is raging mad because one of them was his brother. This is just like reading a novel, Evie. Do you think they've got a father out there who will ride in to save his son and get revenge?"

Evie sighed and pulled off a glove. "Tyler isn't Pecos Martin anymore than I am, Daniel. He's just a Natchez gambler with time on his hands. He's probably over at the saloon fleecing some poor farmer right now. I'm sorry I ever let you think he was anything else."

Daniel looked momentarily deflated, then threw Evie a shrewd look. "You wouldn't be saying that just because you're mad at him, would you? I know he doesn't look like the description in the book, but you've got to admit he's awful handy with his guns. Did you find him at the Green Door like I said?"

"I found him at the Green Door, yes, but I suspect he was just looking for an excuse to get out of a card game before the other players caught on to what he was doing."

"Tyler doesn't cheat, Evie." Daniel swung his legs over the side of the bed. "I watched him play. You cheated by giving away Dorset's hand, but Tyler was playing it straight. And Monteigne means Martin in French. What makes you think he isn't Pecos?"

"Because the minute he walked out of the Green Door he was accosted by women who called him Tyler. Not just one woman. Two. He was known in that town we went to, too. They all called him Tyler. And if he isn't known as Pecos in Texas, then where does the name come from?"

Daniel studied that for a moment. "Well, I suppose it doesn't matter what he's called. He got us here safe and sound. But if you don't start being nicer to him, he's going to leave before that lawyer gets back, and we might never find out who your parents are."

"Nicer to him?" Evie realized she was practically screeching when Daniel gave her an odd look, and she lowered her voice. "I'd sooner be nice to a rattlesnake. You're not a woman, and you don't understand these things, Daniel. Just take my word for it: being nice to Tyler Monteigne would be the biggest mistake of my life. We can find out about my parents without him."

"Somebody was awful careful to keep your identity hidden, Evie. How do you know they weren't trying to hide you from something dangerous?" Daniel limped toward the doorway, cane in hand.

"Have you seen anything dangerous in this town? A person could fall asleep in the road, and horses would just step over him. They're just hiding the fact that they weren't married. I'm old enough to face the truth. It's time we both did."

Daniel frowned. "People don't keep paying that much money to hide a mistake. I'm perfectly legitimate, for heaven's sake, and my parents don't pay that much to hide me. Be careful, Evie. Don't start going honest yet."

Don't go honest yet. Evie threw her gaze heavenward as Daniel walked out. She wasn't even certain what honest was anymore. But then, neither did that scoundrel, Tyler Monteigne.

She wondered how scandalized the town would be if the new schoolmarm visited a saloon.

Chapter 12

Jason Harding stretched his long legs beneath the wooden table and desultorily threw a card at the stack in the middle. "Cotton prices ain't what they were before the war, I agree. And I can't argue that we've been benefiting from the demand for beef."

Tyler gave the cards in his hand a cursory glance and threw a coin on the table. "With all that free government range out here, feeding cattle should be relatively inexpensive. Looks like a promising business to me."

The man in the bowler hat on Tyler's right raised the ante and checked the pocket watch in his red-plaid waistcoat. Tyler mildly pushed the man's coins back to him.

At the man's surprised look, Tyler merely waved his hand for a second round of beers and said casually, "You might want to check that top card you have there. I don't believe it belongs to this deck. I'm ready to call this game, boys. How about you?"

Jason raised heavy black eyebrows at this mild suggestion that the drummer was cheating, but he threw his cards over face up and raised no objection to ending the game. The fourth party in the game took the hand and added the few coins on the table to his meager winnings. He tipped his hat at the offered beer and wandered off with the mug. The red-faced drummer pocketed his coins and left his beer behind. Tyler pocketed the large stack of greenbacks in front of him.

Before any comment could be made on the game, the saloon door bounced open and a younger version of Jason strode in, a grin a mile wide on his face showing the main difference between the brothers' characters.

Kyle was wide-open and easygoing. Jason was the serious one.

"Jace, why in hell didn't you tell me about the new schoolmarm? A fellow could trip over his own feet meeting her without warning like that. Whooee! Reckon I can go back to school?"

Jason noted the frown tugging at Tyler's brow but kept his own expression clear. "I know a better way to teach you manners than sending you back to school. This here's a friend of Mrs. Peyton's. He might want to straighten you out on the proper way of speaking about a lady."

The reprimand didn't reduce Kyle's enthusiasm. He held out his hand to the stranger. "Kyle Harding. Any friend of the lady's is bound to be a friend of mine. She ain't already taken, is she?"

"Tyler Monteigne, Mr. Harding. And the lady does her own choosing. I'll warn you she comes in a package with an eighteen-year-old brother, though. You can't court her without courting him."

Kyle straddled a chair and took the untouched beer in front of him. "Brothers are easier than kids. That the boy with the gimp? Heard he raised hell when Phil tried to throw the nigger out. Phil's one of those hotheads convinced the niggers are planning to take over the government. The boy better get his friend out of there before Phil decides a bit of arson will speed his progress."

"It's the white men behind the niggers that you gotta watch out for. Personally, I think all politicians ought to be taken out and shot on general principles. What do you say, Monteigne? Want to come out and look the ranch over and stay a spell? As soon as we get railroads in here, the cattle business is really going to boom."

Tyler relaxed and decided he really didn't need to punch out Kyle's teeth. Both Hardings wore the stamp of that rare breed of Western generosity that made it impossible not to like them, even if their references to Evie and Ben were less than polite. He might want to kick their teeth in, but he would like them the whole damned time he was doing it. He saw no reason not to accept Jason's offer.

"I've heard about those cattle drives to Abilene. Is that the closest station, then?"

"There's Santa Fe if you want to ship them west. We drive ours to Abilene. Hang around, and you can go with Kyle. I rode that trip once and decided I was getting too old too fast to do it again."

Tyler grinned and drained his mug. "Might take you up on that. If I come out to stay, you'll have to give me some chores. I'm not used to a life of leisure."

"He can have mine, and I'll stay here and court the beautiful Mrs. Peyton. It'd be nice to have a woman around the place again."

Jason leaned over and gently cuffed his younger brother. "You'll do your own chores and leave the lady to hers. Saturdays are good enough for courting. Have you got that bag of feed we came in for?"

Tyler felt his good humor eroding fast. He wanted this opportunity to investigate cattle ranching, but he was going to have a hard time holding his temper while he watched the Hardings court Evie. They were no doubt good, honest, upright citizens, but Evie came from a different world that they would never appreciate. They shouldn't be allowed to touch her.

The deputy sheriff leaning against the bar picked the wrong moment to open his mouth.

"Hey, Kyle, did you get a good look at the bazooms on that new schoolmarm?" The man made a curving gesture outward from the front of his shirt.

Tyler was already up and ready to follow the Hardings out the door. It didn't take any extra effort to swing his fist upward and carry the loudmouth from the floor with a blow under the chin. As the man slithered down the bar, Tyler looked regretfully at his bruised knuckles, shrugged, and donned his Stetson. He really had his job cut out for him if he meant to defend Maryellen Evie Peyton from her admirers.

The Hardings watched him with a mixture of admiration and wariness as they left the saloon. Tyler reckoned for certain he wouldn't be hearing anything more about Evie from their mouths. That was a relief. The Harding men were both older and broader than he was.

From her window on the third floor of the hotel, Evie watched the three tall men walk down the dirt street in the direction of the livery. The thought that Tyler was leaving town made her ache, but it was the best thing for both of them. Playing cards and traveling on steamboats with a handsome gambler made for exciting novels, but real life had just slapped her in the face.

Turning her back on Tyler, she contemplated real life, and seeing Daniel sprawled as always on the bed, she tightened her lips in decision.

"Come on, Danny boy. We're going to find the newspaper office. Where are those articles you had printed in the *Dispatch*? You can show them to the editor here. He ought to be glad to have someone who can read, write, and spell to call on."

Some time later, after getting directions and telling the Hardings he would catch up to them, Tyler took the hotel stairs two at a time and walked in on Benjamin. Ben had already tired of lying about in bed and was oiling his gun by the window when Tyler came in.

Ben threw his friend an enigmatic look. "Appears you've found some acquaintances already. You planning on heading out?"

"They've got a cattle ranch. I'm going to check out their operation. Feel well enough to come along?"

Ben gave him a look of disdain. "I don't need no redneck farmers around me, thank you. What in hell would I want with cows?"

Tyler casually twirled his hat on his hand. "They've just brought in a herd of wild mustangs they mean to tame. Thought you might be interested."

Ben started piecing the gun back together. "And what about them kids you brought out here?"

"Evie's already got a job as the new schoolteacher. I don't see anything dangerous around here that they need protecting from. I'll go tell them where to find us while you pack."

Ben gave a disapproving grunt and watched with suspicion as Tyler sauntered out. The boy only sauntered when he had a female on the mind. But Miss Evie was not the kind of woman Tyler usually stalked. Miss Evie was the marrying kind. Ben would like to know how Tyler's resolve to never get tied down was going to survive this encounter.

Evie answered the door, and Tyler felt the shock of her proximity as if this were his first time with a woman. She was still wearing the dark blue gown that made her eyes look warm and sultry, and his gaze involuntarily drifted to the curve of her breasts. They were as beautifully proportioned as the rest of her, and he hadn't even taken the time to enjoy them. Lord, but he had been a jackass.

He suddenly became aware that they weren't alone. Giggles issued from the room behind her, and he looked over Evie's shoulder to a pair of young girls in short skirts and loose hair streaming down their backs. He silently cursed and returned his gaze to Evie, who was now smiling mockingly.

At his questioning glance, she replied, "Philly and Delphia, the daughters of Mr. Averill, the newspaper editor. They will be two of my students."

"I suppose I could make a wild stab at where Mr. Averill hails from." Tyler remained in the hallway, though Evie had stepped aside to allow him in.

"Wouldn't you like to meet them?" Slightly puzzled at his unusual taciturnity, Evie tried her best smile.

Tyler took a step backward, as if she had just offered to introduce him to the devil. "Not particularly. I just came to tell you I'll be staying out at the Harding ranch for a while, in case you need anything." His gaze drifted past the giggling girls to an easel by the window. The canvas was turned so he couldn't see the picture. He had the urge to walk in, make himself at home, and examine it, but their audience made him nervous. He didn't know Evie painted. Taking a breath, he returned his gaze to her.

She was watching him with a certain degree of puzzlement. "Don't you like children, Mr. Monteigne?"

"I wouldn't know. I've never had any. Well, if you don't need me for anything, I'll be off then."

Feeling like a fly escaping a sticky ointment, Tyler made a sketchy bow and practically ran for the stairs. Evie's laughter chimed with the giggles of the children as she closed the door, and Tyler closed his eyes and clutched the wall for a brief moment before descending. Echoes of similar sounds rocked his memory, and he fought them off, banishing the joyful noise to the dark recesses of his mind where it belonged.

Summoning his usual demeanor, he clattered down the wooden stairs to find Daniel limping through the doorway, a smile wider than the horizon on his face. At sight of Tyler, his eyes lit.

"I've got a job! Mr. Averill said I could start out proofreading his work and learn typesetting when things were slow. I'll be learning all about the newspaper business. Have you ever seen printing presses? They're . . ."

Tyler interrupted the monologue with a wave of his hand. Remembering the giggling girls in Evie's room, he asked wryly, "Does she always get her way?"

Daniel didn't have to think twice to know what he was talking about. He grinned. "Usually."

"Thanks for the warning." Holding out his hand, he offered, "Congratulations on your new job. I just told Evie that Ben and I are heading out for the Harding ranch for a while. If you should need anything, you just send someone out there."

The smile disappeared from Daniel's face as he shook Tyler's hand. "Are you going to stay around awhile? It could be weeks before that lawyer comes back." He stopped, as if realizing he had said too much.

Tyler pretended not to notice. "I'm not making any promises. The Hardings seem to be influential men around here. Should I be trying to find out anything from them?"

Daniel hesitated and scanned Tyler's face anxiously. Making a decision, he answered, "We can't do anything until Mr. Hale returns. He's on some business trip, and no one seems to know for certain when he'll be back."

Tyler nodded knowledgeably. "I'll see what I can find out about Mr. Hale. Look after your sister, and keep in touch."

Daniel watched as the gambler walked off. This adventure had remained exciting while Tyler Monteigne stayed with them. Now that they were on their own, he felt the first stirring of doubt and worry. He knew Evie better than anyone. She was beautiful and charming and had a way of twisting people around her little finger. She was also running as scared as he was. Daniel could understand why people didn't see that right off, but he'd thought Tyler was a little more perceptive. Maybe he was, and he just didn't want the responsibility of looking after two young people old enough to take care of themselves.

That meant they were really on their own. Squaring his shoulders, Daniel began the painful maneuver of ascending the stairs.

At almost this same time, Jonathan Hale was standing before the unobtrusive brick town house of one Delilah "Nanny" Witherspoon. Large shade trees up and down the street indicated the length of time this neighborhood had been established. The substantial homes, well-kept yards, and the scattering of carriage houses in the rear of many of the houses gave some indication of the quiet wealth of the area. It was not precisely the kind of area Hale had expected to find a former mistress and her illegitimate child living in.

Revising that theory but not having a new one to put in its place, Hale attempted the discreet door knocker one more time. He had been here three days in a row at various times and had never caught anyone at home. There should at least be servants, he thought. But as in the previous days, no one answered the summons.

Much as he disliked the idea, he was going to have to start making inquiries. Glancing at the substantial home next door, he straightened his frock coat and set out in that direction. Someone, somewhere, had to know where to find Delilah Witherspoon. And he hoped that Mrs. Witherspoon would swiftly lead him to one Evangeline Peyton Howell. The Hardings were generously financing this expedition to St. Louis, but Hale had his own interest in the matter.

With a certain amount of eagerness, he pounded on the massive knocker of the house next door.

On the other side of the country, in a boardinghouse in San Francisco, a dark-haired gentleman contemplated a portrait hanging near the woodstove that heated the room. At one time the portrait had hung over a massive marble fireplace in the parlor downstairs, but the house had seen better days, and so had he.

His gaze returned to the crudely scratched letter in his hand. Angelina had always been a poor student, and the years spent raising that brood of children had not improved her handwriting any. He had helped her when her husband was alive, when the money had been easy and plentiful. He felt a deep regret that he could do so little now that she was a widow. He felt a small rush of homesickness, but it had been a long, long time since he had been home. There had been no place for him back there. He had found a life here, but it was almost over. Perhaps this letter meant it was time to go home again.

Tears rimmed his eyes as he read the words over. He had been betrayed all those years ago, but he still couldn't help feeling the pain of the love he had carried with him ever since. Perhaps she had been right to betray him. Look at where he was now.

His fingers trembled as he read about the carriage accident that had sent his beloved into a river that wouldn't be considered a puddle anywhere else in the world. What kind of incompetent fool was her husband to allow the accident to happen? The man deserved to die, and he was glad to know he'd received his fitting punishment.

But she was still alive. She was ill and injured, but alive. Was it a sign? Was there some promise in it for him? Could he dare let himself hope after all these years?

He was being foolish. He was over forty and had spent nearly half his life out here. He had earned a certain amount of respect in this town. His talent had faded with his eyesight, but he lived comfortably enough. People accepted him for what he was here. He didn't have to endure the insults, the cold stares, the hatred that his ancestry earned back in Texas. Why should he ever return?

Because she was alive and her husband was dead. Because he had promised to return. Because he wanted to see her again, if only just one more time before he died. The longing was too strong to be denied. He had to see her.

Then his soul would rest in peace.

Chapter 13

Evie listened to her beginning students sing-songing the alphabet and almost felt contentment. She never felt better than when she looked over a sea of clean-scrubbed young faces and knew she was making a difference in their lives, however small that difference might be.

Glancing at the recalcitrant scowl on young José's face as he mouthed gibberish, she had to smile at how small a difference she made in some of her students. José apparently had the impression that real men didn't need book learning. The only reason he was here today was because his oldest sister threatened to beat him into sour mash if he didn't come.

Evie glanced to her older students who were supposed to be diligently composing an essay on why arithmetic was important in a modern world. Carmen had already completed her essay and was neatly penning it into perfect script on a clean sheet of paper. Most of the others were using the elbows of their shirtsleeves to erase the chalk on their slates for the first draft. It was amazing how two children from the same family could be so different.

The middle child from the Rodriguez family, Manuel, was nodding off behind a book he had carefully propped in front of him. He was a bright child and could do his work without help, he just seemed to have other interests that deprived him of his rest. She would have to look into that situation soon.

There was another situation she would have to look into soon, also, but it wasn't the kind of thing Evie wanted to think about on a beautiful spring day with the faces of innocent children turned on her. Her stomach tightened nervously at just the thought, and the pain lodged somewhere around her heart began to act up again. She couldn't think about it now. Wouldn't think about it.

As she dismissed the children for recess and began straightening up the room to the sounds of their cheerful cries, she let herself dwell on the few times she had seen Tyler recently.

She had scarcely seen him at all in these weeks since he had gone to stay with the Hardings. If she did, it was by accident. One time, she had been in the feed store inquiring about loose kernels of corn for an art project when Tyler walked in. He had been his usual charming self, offering to carry her parcels, walking her to the hotel, inviting her for coffee. But Mr. Averill's twins had been sitting on the hotel steps waiting for Evie, and the invitation had mysteriously disappeared.

Another time she had been in the company of Carmen and her baby sister, and Tyler had merely made polite noises and wandered off. She would never understand the man, and she didn't mean to try. It was the third time Evie had seen him that made her stick to her decision. He had been coming out of the saloon with one of the saloon girls on his arm. Evie knew the woman was a saloon girl even though she was wearing a dress a hundred times more respectable than the one Bessie had worn back in Natchez. Evie had made a point of getting to know the saloon girls, but Tyler didn't have to know that.

It had been impossible to disregard the look of satisfaction on Tyler's handsome face as he smiled down at the woman. He certainly hadn't looked like that when he'd jumped up and left Evie the morning after that disastrous night. Evie didn't even try to dissect her feelings on seeing that look. She had just walked up to greet Starr, said hello to Tyler, and watched surprise replace his smug satisfaction. It hadn't felt as good as she had hoped, but it was better than going back to her room and crying her eyes out.

There were hundreds of men in this town besides Tyler Monteigne. All she had to do was decide among them. None of them seemed particularly concerned about who her parents were or if they even existed. It wasn't the same as St. Louis society at all.

But knowing that she could literally pick and choose among all the single men in town left Evie thoroughly disinterested in the process. It had been a challenge before, forcing men to look at her and acknowledge she was just as good as every other woman in the room. She had enjoyed the challenge, but she had never wanted the prize that had to be won in such a manner. Now she didn't even have the challenge to look forward to. It was perverse of her, she knew, but she couldn't figure out what she would do with any of the men if she caught them.

Perhaps when Mr. Hale returned and she found out who her parents were, she would feel more secure and everything would change. She might even return to St. Louis. That thought brought a frown to Evie's face as the children obediently trampled back in at the sound of the bell she was ringing.

There wouldn't be money to return to St. Louis unless something happened soon. The hotel was eating into their funds, and there didn't seem to be an inexpensive place to rent anywhere in town. People didn't leave Mineral Springs. They built their houses and moved in to stay.

She would check at the general store after school and see if the mail had arrived yet. She and Daniel had arranged for their mail and Nanny's to be forwarded here, but so far there hadn't been anything. The month was up. There ought to be another check. She prayed that no one had heard of Nanny's death yet. Without those monthly allowances, they could be starving shortly.

The day had grown warm by the time classes were dismissed. Evie cleaned up the room and straightened the desks. Assured everything was in its proper order for the morrow, she hurried out into the bright Texas sun. She might never get used to the seemingly endless parade of sunshine, even in spring. A wind caught her skirt and whipped it around her ankles, and Evie glanced at the horizon. Perhaps some end to the sun was in sight. A dark cloud spread across the distant sky.

The clerk at the general store shook his head when Evie inquired about mail, and dispirited, she started back to the hotel. Dust swirled up out of the street, and she stayed on the boardwalk to keep her petticoat clean. Even laundering their clothes had become an expensive proposition. They were going to have to do something soon.

Evie visited the privy first, ascertained that her time of month still hadn't come, and feeling even more depressed, climbed the stairs to wash in the lukewarm water in the stand beside her bed.

Perhaps she ought to check and see if Mr. Hale had returned yet. She looked hopefully toward the window, but she could only see the cloud moving closer. It looked as if it were raining farther up the river. That's just what she needed when she was feeling like this—rain.

She couldn't visit the lawyer's office so soon after last time. People would begin to grow suspicious. Maybe Daniel would have heard something. All the news went to the paper office eventually.

If only she had some means of cooking meals, they wouldn't have to spend so much money at the café. Checking the coins in their private hoard, Evie calculated how many they would need to eat for the next week. If they just had soup until Friday, there would be sufficient means to pay another week's rent on their rooms.

They were gong to have to go back to sharing a room, or Evie was going to have to start staying with the parents of her students. Putting the purse back in the drawer, she heard Daniel's limping footsteps coming down the hall. They had discussed the question before, but neither of them could agree on the solution. This time, they would have to come up with some answers.

"We're in for a downpour Mr. Averill says," Daniel announced as he entered without knocking. "My leg aches like hell, so he's most likely right."

"Daniel!" Evie frowned at this use of a word for which Nanny would have washed out his mouth with soap.

Daniel shrugged and sprawled in the chair beside the bed. "Everyone says it. You don't want people to think I'm a girl, do you?"

Daniel's rebellion was just one more headache added to the list of headaches Evie was already dealing with. She wasn't used to everything going wrong at once. Actu-

ally, she wasn't used to anything going wrong, ever.
Nanny had always seen that everything in their lives went
smoothly. There hadn't been much she could do about
Evie's parentage or Daniel's limp, but beyond that they
had lived relatively uneventful lives.

And now they were almost broke, she might be pregnant, and Daniel—her best friend—was turning rebellious. The simplest thing to do would be to break down
and cry.

Before she could do so, the heavens did it for her.
Rain crashed against the hotel's tin roof, and they both
ran to the window to see their first Texas storm.

"My word, it moved in fast." Evie watched the thick
clouds scudding across the sky. Rain plastered the windows and sent gullies down the dirt streets, falling faster
than the ruts could carry it off.

"We're going to get wet if we go to the café to eat,"
Daniel said gloomily.

"I don't suppose you've heard any word about a place
to live, have you?" Unable to bear the gray gloom, Evie
turned away and picked up one of the books from her
trunk. She'd had all the trunks carried up, and they now
filled an entire corner of the room, spilling books and
paints and all the accoutrements of fine living.

"Mr. Averill says I can make a bed in the back of the
shop if I want. That will give us enough money for you
to stay here for a couple more weeks. Maybe the lawyer
will be back by then."

"If you stay there, then I'll stay with my students. That
will give us enough to scrape by on for a month, if we
can stand a month of soup and crackers. I wish there
were some discreet way of selling some of my clothes,
but there isn't even a dressmaker in town." Actually,
Evie did have an idea about how to sell some of her
evening gowns, but she wasn't about to mention it to
Daniel.

"Maybe you can persuade the school board to pay
your salary monthly instead of quarterly. With free
rooms, we could managed to eat a little better, and you
wouldn't have to sell anything."

Evie had contemplated that idea, but she suspected it

would lead to talking to Jace Harding and then word would get to Tyler that they were short of cash, and she wasn't about to have that happen. She would sell all her clothes first.

"We'll see," she replied evasively.

They read quietly until the rain let up enough to venture out. By that time it was almost dark. Evie offered to bring soup back for Daniel, but he insisted on accompanying her. He couldn't offer much protection, but Nanny had brought him up to behave like a gentleman, even if he never could be a whole one. And gentlemen didn't allow ladies to walk the streets at night unescorted.

The boardwalk was wet and slippery as they started out for the café. Oil lamps flickered in several windows along the way, but the hotel was in the town's business district, and most everyone had gone home. The saloon in the other direction was conducting a noisy business, but the rain had kept even their customers home to a great extent. The music was loud but the laughter was not.

The early gloom depressed their spirits as much as the bowls of potato soup that constituted their supper. Evie tried to keep their spirits up by commenting it was good that they didn't have beans again, but Daniel growled that it could at least have been beef, and the conversation died after that.

Rain had begun to fall again when they left the café. Daniel's cane slipped on the slick surface of bare wood, but he caught himself and remained upright. Evie could have gone to the hotel twice as fast on her own, but Daniel's mood was so bad that she couldn't do that to him. She expressed fear of the shadows and clutched his arm when a drunk down the road staggered out of the saloon cursing someone still inside. Daniel straightened and walked a little faster.

Perhaps it was her fault then, that he slipped on the steps going down to the cross street. He was hurrying to impress her, and this time when the cane slipped and his foot went out from under him, he couldn't make the adjustment. Daniel staggered, grabbed for support, and went stumbling sideways down the stairs into the mud.

Evie screamed as he pitched forward, but she

screamed even louder a moment later at the sound of
something snapping. Daniels' moan of pain brought her
down on her knees in the mud without any regard to
petticoats or skirt.

Her first scream was sufficient to alert John in the café
and the drunk in the street, and before long people came
tumbling out of both buildings to investigate the source.
Someone pulled Evie out of the mud and away from
Daniel. There was a scuffle as some of the more sober
men pushed the drunk and his friends away from the
boy in the street. Daniel stoically tried to stifle any further groans, but when the men lifted him, he gave a cry
and passed out.

Evie didn't even know she was crying until someone
handed her a handkerchief as they entered the hotel. She
had been wondering how anything could get worse, and
now she knew. White-faced, she watched as the men carried an unconscious Daniel up to his room. If anything
happened to Daniel, she would never forgive herself. She
should never have griped about his recent contrariness.
He had a right to be contrary once in a while. He was
the best thing that had ever happened to her, better than
having her own brother. She couldn't let him suffer for
her sins.

She knew she was being hysterical, but she couldn't
stop crying. Someone sent for a doctor, but Evie refused
to go change into dry clothes while they waited for him
to appear. She sat beside Daniel's bed, sponging off his
muddy face, tears streaming down her cheeks as she
wished he would wake and grin at her again.

Men shuffled around her. The town was full of men.
Men operated the hotel and café. Men frequented the
saloon. Only men would be out on a night like this. Only
men stayed in a hotel. The women were safely behind
closed doors in lighted rooms serving supper to their
children. Evie wished Nanny were here.

A slight figure in faded black skirts rustled in, scolding
the men in Spanish and English. Evie looked up without
interest and recognized Carmen's mother. They had
never been introduced, but she had seen the woman with
her children shopping in the general store. Dully, Evie

realized this was the one woman who would hear of the accident immediately. Her late husband had owned the livery, and the family lived in a small house somewhere near it, according to Carmen.

"You will go and change your clothes before you catch cold," she scolded Evie, literally pulling her from the chair although she was no taller than Evie. "I will clean him up, and the doctor will be here soon. Vamoose." She pushed Evie toward the door.

Having another woman to give orders seemed to work wonders. Evie stumbled to her room and stripped off all her clothes. Mud had seeped through the cotton of her gown to the petticoat beneath and from there, to her ruffled pantalets. She was a sodden mess from skin out, but she didn't feel any better after she toweled off and found dry clothes. She felt worse knowing Daniel wasn't feeling better.

The crowd had thinned out considerably by the time she returned. Someone had helped Carmen's mother to undress Daniel and put him in a dry nightshirt. He was still unconscious, and his lame leg lay at an awkward angle. Evie felt the pain just looking at it.

The doctor arrived, and Evie retreated to a corner while he examined Daniel's leg. Carmen's mother took Evie's hand and patted it.

"He will be fine," she whispered as Daniel uttered a whimper when the physician twisted his leg slightly.

"Thank you, Mrs. Rodriguez." Evie managed to remember enough of her manners to speak that much.

"You must call me Angelina. No one calls me Mrs. Rodriguez." She winced as Evie's hand crushed hers when the physician tugged Daniel's leg into place, and Daniel's screams echoed to the rafters.

It would be very strange to call a woman almost old enough to be her mother by her given name. Evie merely nodded her agreement and kept her gaze focused on Daniel.

At last, the doctor had the leg straightened and wrapped, and Daniel was mercifully unconscious once more. Evie hurried to the bed, and the doctor moved aside so she could sit in the chair.

"I imagine he'll be out for a while. You can give him laudanum when he complains of the pain. Sleep will be good for him. His leg was malformed at birth, wasn't it?"

Evie didn't look up but nodded as she held Daniel's hand. His hand was warm, and his breathing was even. Those had to be good signs.

"Thought so." Satisfied, the doctor began to repack his bag. "I daresay it was broken then and some misinformed idiot didn't set it. It probably always gave him pain, and he learned to compensate by limping. The muscles on that side are slightly atrophied. When he fell, he broke it along the old fracture. I'd say, unless he wants to be permanently disabled, he'd better learn to exercise that leg while it heals."

Something in the doctor's voice jerked Evie from her reverie, and she turned to look at the man. "You mean if they'd set his leg at birth, he would be whole today?"

The doctor nodded. "Probably. Now the bone's grown crooked, and there isn't a lot I can do to straighten it. I've set it the best I can, and he's young; that's in his favor. But his muscles in that leg aren't strong enough to support a growing young man. In a week or so, I'd say he needs to start lifting that leg up and down. That will build the muscle. He can start slowly, but he'll have to keep increasing the exercise. He won't be able to get out of bed for some time. I don't want him walking on that leg until it's completely healed. But he can do various exercises while he's in bed. I'll be back to show him when the time comes."

The doctor scribbled out his bill, left it with Evie, and bustled out. The men who had carried Daniel had been slowly departing. The last one tugged his hat and left now. Angelina Rodriguez offered to sit with Daniel for a while, but Evie thanked her and sent her home to her children. Daniel would expect to see her here when he woke.

Not until the room cleared did Evie glance at the piece of paper in her hand. The bill was for almost exactly the same amount of coins remaining in her purse.

Chapter 14

She had to pay the hotel bill. There wasn't any way Daniel could be moved to the back of the newspaper office now.

Evie's stomach churned as she stared out at the leaden sky the next evening. She had given Daniel some laudanum, and he slept peacefully for the moment. She put her hand to her abdomen and stared at the rain-drenched streets. She knew what she had to do, but she was so scared that she couldn't think straight.

Crying hadn't helped. She had cried herself to sleep last night, but all she'd had to show for it this morning was reddened eyes. She had sent word that she wouldn't be able to teach today. It was Friday. That gave her two more days to come up with a few solutions. If she was going to do it, she had to start tonight. She had to be back in class on Monday or risk losing what little income they had. If Daniel couldn't work, their wages were practically cut in half.

She felt the pain in her insides, and she closed her eyes. She had sworn this would never happen to her. How could she have let Tyler do what he had done? She knew what it was to be a bastard. She had never meant to bear one. She couldn't. It was simply unthinkable, so she wouldn't think about it.

But as darkness settled over the scene below and lamplights began to twinkle up and down the street, Evie had visions of showing up in the classroom with rounded stomach, of whispers of horror as she walked through town, of people crossing the street to avoid her. She'd had enough of whispers and speculations in her lifetime. She couldn't endure it again. She wanted people to like her. She needed people to like her. To be an outcast was anathema to her soul.

She would be out of a job as soon as the school board discovered she was pregnant. There would be only one way left for her to support herself and Daniel if she lost that job. The horror of that squalid occupation almost brought up the lump of lead situated in her throat. She had hated it when Tyler had done that to her. How would it be to have countless men a night touching her like that?

Glancing over her shoulder at Daniel's sleeping form, Evie straightened her shoulders with renewed resolve. She would do what she had to do. There simply wasn't any choice.

She had already ordered the hotel management to carry her things to Daniel's room and set up a cot for her there. They could cut expenses immediately by sharing a room. So far, no one had moved the trunks, and Evie slipped out of one room to go to the next. She knew the perfect gown to sell. It seemed only fair that she should sell such extravagance for such a purpose as she had in mind right now. Maybe a fair exchange could be made.

She folded the gown carefully, wrapped it in a newspaper, and tied it securely with a string. She wouldn't let anyone know that she was resorting to selling her clothing.

Hiding her destination was another matter entirely. Everybody knew everybody's business in this town. It hadn't been easy meeting Starr and the other two saloon girls. Evie had had to wait until she had seen Starr going into the general store late one evening. She had hurried from the hotel in time to "accidentally" bump into the other woman as she left the store. The accident had started up a conversation, and before long Evie had wrested the information from Starr that she had never learned to read or write.

It was a daring act of defiance to stand in a public street talking to a fallen woman. It was even worse to offer to teach Starr the rudiments of education. Evie might never have done it had she not been desperate. But she had accomplished it with a smile and a flutter of eyelashes when confronted with David Powell's accusations, and he had fallen like a ton of bricks. The schoolteacher now had permission to lend grammar books to saloon girls.

Evie almost grinned at the thought of the stately Mr. Powell actually believing that she meant to teach Starr how to read and write and lead her to the path of righteousness. He obviously thought all women were idiots. Starr wanted to run her own bordello, and she needed the basic mechanics to do so. Evie wasn't about to stand in the way of ambition.

She looked in on Daniel one more time before slipping down the stairs. It was Friday night and the worst possible time to try to meet Starr, but she had little choice in the matter. It was early. The men from the farm and ranches surrounding the town hadn't had time to ride in yet. Starr knew Evie couldn't come at any regular times.

It might have been better if she could have sent word ahead, but Evie didn't want to give herself time to think about this. She refused to think of what was happening to her insides as anything more than an infection like gangrene that had to be stopped, but if she gave herself time to think . . .

She wouldn't. Slipping down an alley beside the general store, Evie clutched her package carefully under her arm. She didn't want to be a coward, but she could always fall back on the gown as her excuse for being there if she had to. But the visions of the future if she chickened out were not pleasant. Even in the books she read, women who found themselves in her condition ended up floating in the river for their sins.

Evie hurried up the rickety wooden stairs behind the saloon as Starr had instructed. Rain began to patter against the building as she did so. The rain was bound to be a good portent. It meant there weren't as many men wandering around outside the saloon as there might have been had it been a warm, dry night.

Her stomach knotted painfully as she knocked at the door at the top of the steps. Evie refused to acknowledge what she was doing, what she was going to do. She had

to see Starr. That was all she told herself as she waited
for someone to answer.

The youngest saloon girl opened the door, and her
face fell with disappointment at Evie's presence. But she
offered no complaint as she led Evie into the private
parlor that the three girls shared. It had once been the
bedroom of a fourth girl, but the bed was covered now
with a swath of wine-colored velvet to which someone
had sewn gold tassels and added matching bolsters. It
almost looked like a couch instead of a bed. Evie tried
not to think of what the piece of furniture had been used
for previously as she sat down on it now.

Starr was already dressed for her evening performance
when she hurried in. Evie suspected the other woman's
stack of golden tresses was not only artificially enhanced
with lemon juice, but plumped up with a roll of fake
hair. Nobody had that much hair.

Nobody should have that much bust, either, but the
revealing cut of Starr's gown made it obvious that portion of her anatomy was real. Evie tried not to think of
Tyler touching Starr there. She tried not to think of Tyler
at all. He was gone, out of her life. He had nothing to
do with anything.

"Evie! What on earth are you doing here tonight? The
school board would fall flat on their faces if they saw
you here now."

Every rustle of Starr's silk produced a heavy waft of
perfume. Evie tried to choke back her nausea, but something must have shown in her face. Starr hurried to pour
her a glass of brandy.

"Here, drink this. It will steady your nerves. I heard
about your little brother. Is there something I can do?"

Starr was tall and strong and older than Evie. She
would know what to do. Evie took the glass but the smell
of strong spirits made her even more nauseated. She set
it aside and offered up the package in her hand.

"I don't need this anymore. There's more where this
one came from. They were made by a couturier from
Paris. They probably won't suit you, but Rose and
Peachie might like them. I'm very good at alterations, if
they need any."

Starr looked suspiciously from the terrified woman sitting on the garish couch to the newspaper-wrapped package she held out. Evie was properly attired in a gray foulard walking dress with a matching hat perched atop her intricately looped and braided chignon. She looked the part of proper society matron, but her eyes were the frightened black of a little girl.

Starr opened the package and drew out the lovely pink foam of a silk evening gown dripping in lace and ruffles with a train that would sweep the floor. Starr wouldn't know a Paris design if she saw one, but she knew a gown that would floor any man that encountered it. This was such a gown. And it was obviously designed for the woman waiting nervously for her response.

"You wish to sell it?" Starr asked, perhaps a little too harshly.

Evie flinched but nodded. With an offhand gesture, she tried to recover her poise. "Daniel will need a lot of doctoring. And I won't be returning to St. Louis. What use has a schoolteacher for the likes of that?" She tried to sound contemptuous.

"You have others? I can't offer this to one of the girls without having something to offer the other. I'd have war."

Evie didn't relax but nodded stiffly. "I thought the green might look good on Rose, but I couldn't carry both at once."

Starr stroked the silk thoughtfully, then impulsively took a seat. They would be having a riot downstairs if she didn't show herself soon, but Evie had gone out of her way to be kind when there wasn't a woman in town who would even look at her. There was more here than readily met the eye.

"I'll take them both." Mentally, Starr made a calculation of how much Evie and her brother would need to live on for the next month. She might never have learned arithmetic, but she knew dollars and cents. She quoted a figure that made Evie's face light.

"Now tell me why you came here tonight instead of waiting for a proper hour when there aren't a dozen men standing in line downstairs."

Evie tried to calm herself, to look Starr in the eye, and make the announcement as one woman to another. Instead, her gaze drifted off to a square, claw-legged table with a vivid scarf draped across it. She clenched her fingers and let the words tumble out of their own accord.

"I'm pregnant. I need to know what to do about it."

She heard a harsh intake of breath, and the voice that replied was heavy with scorn. "I should have known. I should have known that a proper lady and a school-teacher wouldn't have made friends with the likes of me for nothing."

Starr rose and walked toward the door. "Bring the other dress tomorrow morning. I'll pay you then. But there'll be a charge for what you want done. I know how to do it, but you'd better think long and hard about it first. It isn't pretty, and it isn't pleasant, and you're going to regret it for a lifetime."

She slammed out.

It would have been simpler if she could have cried, but she couldn't. Dry-eyed, Evie touched her hand to the glass door knob, clenched it as if she could drain strength from it for a moment, then forced herself to open the door and walk out. She would go through with this. She had to go through with this. What difference did it make if a prostitute despised her for it?

She let herself out the side door and stumbled on the stairs in the darkness. She clutched the wooden railing and kept herself from falling, but it felt the same as if she had. She felt as if she had been delivered a solid blow to the stomach. She was going to be sick if she didn't get out of here soon.

She couldn't hurry. She had to catch up her long skirt and petticoat in one hand and maneuver the rain-slick steps while grasping the railing with the other. She was actually leaving a bordello in the dark of night after asking the inhabitants for a way to get rid of the child growing within her. She had come a long way down since leaving St. Louis and Nanny's protection. There wasn't any way her bubble of dreams could survive any longer.

But she would fall even farther if she kept the child. She didn't have the money to do what her own mother had apparently done. She couldn't pay someone to take her bastard and hide it. She couldn't afford to raise it. There simply wasn't any other choice.

As if stifling the one other solution made it appear in person, a familiar form loomed before Evie when she stepped off the bottom stair. He caught her shoulder and jerked her against him, wrapping his long canvas coat around her to keep her from the sudden cloudburst of rain.

"What in hell were you doing up there?" Tyler growled, hurrying Evie away from the sounds of a tinkling piano and male laughter and the sultry song of a woman coming from the lighted building behind them.

"None of your business," Evie managed to mutter through chattering teeth. Now that she had done it, set the clock in motion, she was going to fall apart. Even her knees were trembling. She was almost grateful that Tyler was holding her up. Almost. She wished he would shut up and go away. This was all his fault. If she never saw him again, it would be too soon. And she didn't like the way his arm felt wrapped around her waist. She didn't like the heat of him beneath the coat. She was going to be sick in a minute.

As if he sensed her impending collapse, Tyler pulled her into a darkened doorway. He blocked the rain with his back and let her lean against the wall. The night was too thick to see more than the paleness of her face. It had been so long since he had seen her this close that he had almost forgotten how fragile she was. She had taken the form of an unforgiving phoenix in his mind. But she was still Evie, the lovely liar who had released the beast in him.

"I can't think of any good reason for you to be coming out of that place, Miss Peyton. You'd better start talking fast." Tyler tried to be abrupt. He really didn't want to know what she was doing up there. But instinct had kept him alive more than once, and he was overcome by a powerful instinct now. Or premonition. He wanted to shake her.

Evie whipped her head back and forth. "Go away. It's none of your business. Just go away. I'm sure Starr is waiting for you. You wouldn't want to disappoint her now, would you?"

She was recovering some of her old self, but not fast enough. Tyler waited for the lies to begin. "Starr waits for any man with money in his pockets. That's got nothing to do with this. Are you going to tell me what you were doing up there or should I begin guessing?"

"You may guess all you like. Let me by, Mr. Monteigne, or I shall scream and tell everyone that you are molesting me." Evie bravely straightened her shoulders and stood firmly on her feet. Her knees were still shaking, but Tyler had given her another problem to confront. She could only manage one problem at a time, and he was the most immediate one. Men, she knew how to handle.

"Do that, Miss Peyton, and let everyone question what the new schoolmistress was doing outside a saloon on a Friday night. Since I know for a fact that you're not the type to sell your porcelain body, shall I offer a conjecture or two?"

Tyler's scorn was almost as hateful as Starr's. Evie shoved at his chest, but the gesture only served to galvanize them. The broad strength and heat of him through the thin shirt made her jerk her hand as if burned, but she couldn't pull it away entirely. Tyler caught her gloved fingers and pressed them tightly against his chest again.

"If I'm wrong about you selling your body, forgive my stupidity. I'd pay good money to have you back in my bed. Do you have any idea how many nights I've laid awake chastising myself for not at least enjoying what you gave to me? How many times I've tried to recall all the beauty that I held in my hands and threw away?" Tyler's fingers tightened around hers as he gazed down at her bent head. Admitting these things didn't make him happy, but there was something about Evie that made him do what he didn't mean to do. "Apologizing won't make things better. Tell me what's wrong, Evie."

"You're what's wrong. Get away from me, Tyler Monteigne. Get out of my life. You've ruined me. You've ruined everything. I don't ever want to see you again."

He could hear the choked tears in her voice, and he

knew instantly what was wrong. He had lived through this once before, when he had been much, much younger. A cold, clammy hand stole around Tyler's heart, but he jerked Evie into his arms and refused to let her go. She struggled, but she was a slender wraith against his greater strength. Her skirts wrapped around his legs as she tried to kick free, but he placed a hand around her bustled bottom and lifted her from the ground.

"You're pregnant, and you wanted Starr to get rid of the child." Tyler announced it firmly, as if he had been privy to the conversation that had taken place. To do anything else was to open the loopholes for her lies. He wasn't going to let her lie about this. He might kill her, but he wasn't going to let her lie.

"You don't know anything!" she wept against his chest, kicking futilely in search of his shins. "Let me go. Daniel is waiting for me."

"We can just go ask Starr now, can't we?" Tyler lowered her gently to the boardwalk, even though his first urge was to throttle her. He could feel the violence building inside of him.

Evie jerked from his grasp and tried to escape through the small space between Tyler and the wall. He stuck his arm out and trapped her, and she stared up at him with hatred. "Go ask Starr. See if I care. You can't stop me, Mr. Monteigne. You have no claim over me at all."

Tyler felt her words like a blow to the gut, and he nearly bent double with the pain. But this was Evie, the actress. He caught her shoulder and jerked her until she glared up at him. "Tell me yes or no. Are you carrying my child?"

She wanted to spit in his face. She wanted to scratch his eyes out. She wished she could see his eyes. But all she could see was the shadow of his face beneath the broad-brimmed hat. His fingers were digging cruelly into her shoulder, and she wanted to redirect the pain. She gave him what he wanted, hit him with the blow he deserved.

"I'm getting rid of your child, and you can't stop me."

The violence that had built to the point that could have crushed her shoulder suddenly dissipated, leaving

Tyler limp and inert. His fingers fell away as he scanned her face. "You would do that? You would kill an innocent child?"

The pain in his voice was even worse than the anger she had instigated earlier. It struck directly to the place in her heart that had been wounded the worst. Evie held her anger around her like a thorny shield, but she knew he had already breached it. "The child will suffer less this way. I know what it is to be an unwanted bastard."

She almost made it two steps past him before Tyler grabbed her arm. He spun her around, and silhouetted against the lights from the saloon, he was the image of a vengeful angel with his long coat flaring out behind him in the rain and his hat pulled down like a fallen halo.

"The child won't be a bastard. I'll marry you. You can do whatever the hell you like after the child is born, but the child is mine. I won't have you kill him."

And gripping her arm firmly, Tyler dragged her back in the direction of the hotel.

Chapter 15

The door slamming as Tyler threw Evie into the room woke Daniel. Wiping his eyes of a laudanum-induced haze, he watched in amazement as the usually charming gambler practically shook Evie as he pushed her into a chair. Daniel almost pretended he was still asleep when Tyler glared down at him.

"What in hell happened to you?" he demanded, sending his gaze over Daniel's heavily bandaged and propped leg.

"Broke it," Daniel answered succinctly. He was glad the question needed only a simple answer. He wasn't quite ready for a more complicated one.

Tyler threw off his hat and drew his hand through his hair. "Hell," he muttered, before rounding on Evie as she tried to sidle toward the door. "Get back in that chair. You're not going anywhere until I get the preacher."

"Preacher?" Daniel mouthed the word more than uttered it.

Evie came forward to lay a cool hand against his forehead. Raindrops sparkled in her hair, and Daniel could smell the freshness of the outdoors on her. He caught her hand and held it, ignoring the pain that was creeping up on him.

"Tyler has apparently suffered sunstroke or cracked his head on something. Just bear with him for a little while until Ben comes." She threw Tyler a cross look. "Where is Ben, anyway? Have you already driven him away?"

As if the wind had carried his name, a light knock sounded at the door, and Benjamin stuck his head

around as he opened it without waiting for a reply.
"Heard 'bout the fall. How you doin', boy?"

Before Daniel could muster an answer, Tyler gripped
Ben's collar and hauled him into the room. "Keep her
here until I get back. Use your gun, if you have to. A
bullet in the leg should slow her down."

He threw Evie a look to indicate who he was talking
about, as if she weren't the only woman in the room he
could mean. She smiled sweetly at him, and Tyler
scowled and stamped out.

Ben crossed his arms over his chest and took both of
the young people in with one gaze. "You got him mighty
riled about something. What happened, boy? Did Miss
Evie throw you down the stairs?"

"We've just had a minor disagreement over something
perfectly frivolous," Evie purred, doing her best Miss
Nightingale routine as she straightened Daniel's covers
and offered him a sip of water. She had always admired
Miss Nightingale's work. Perhaps she ought to study to
be a nurse. "You needn't bother staying. It's Friday
night, and I'm certain you have other plans."

Ben grinned and planted himself against the door. "My
plans include staying alive, and I won't be that for long
if I'm not here when Tyler comes back. How's that leg
feel, boy? Should we be hollering for someone to fetch
you a beer?"

Evie smoldered. She wasn't going to let Tyler get away
with this. Marriage was forever. She meant to marry a
man who would give her a good solid house and who
would love her no matter who she was and who would
have a steady job and come home to her every night.
She wanted security and respectability. She didn't want
Tyler Monteigne.

She wished the pain in her stomach would go away. It
would be much easier saying no if she wasn't constantly
reminded of why Tyler was doing this. He was taking
away her reason to get rid of the child. With Tyler's plan,
the child wouldn't have to be a bastard. But would having a rambling, gambling father be much better?

She didn't know. She just didn't know. She was too
tired and confused and desperate to know what to think.

She needed time, and Tyler wasn't giving her any. She didn't want a baby. She had never thought about having babies. She had scarcely thought about having a husband. She wanted to know who her parents were. She didn't even know who she was until she knew that, and now Tyler wanted to make her a wife.

No, he really didn't want to make her his wife. He didn't want a wife any more than she wanted a husband. She remembered very clearly the relief in his eyes when she had refused him that first time. She knew perfectly well that the only reason Tyler had agreed to accompany them to Texas was to get away from two women who wanted to shackle him. So he wasn't doing this for her sake. He was doing it for some mistaken ideal of what a gentleman was supposed to do.

Daniel was watching her worriedly, and Evie tried to smile and be reassuring. She would take Tyler into another room and speak to him quietly. She would make him see that her way was better for all concerned. But she had a sinking feeling in the pit of her stomach that Tyler wasn't open to reason on that point.

Well, if she had to have the child, that child was going to have a father. She would make certain clear on that point. Mr. Tyler Monteigne was going to have to settle down and get a job and be a proper respectable husband and father if he meant to go through with this. That ought to scare the pants off him.

She didn't want to think about Tyler with his pants off. Her face felt like fire already. She took a hasty sip of the water beside Daniel's bed. That was another aspect of this marriage business that she didn't want to face.

But the alternative was even more grim. Finding her hand shaking on the glass, Evie gently set it down and went to the window. The men behind her watched her with expressions of curiosity and grief.

"You don't have to do anything you don't want to, Evie." Daniel was the first to speak. "Ben can move me over to the newspaper office. I'll be up and about shortly, and I can read and write lying on the floor for all that matters. And something could come in the mail any day."

A ghost of a smile lifted Evie's lips as she stared at her reflection in the rain-drenched window. She wondered if Tyler had considered that he would be supporting Daniel as well as herself and a child. That much responsibility ought to drive the man berserk.

"You're not getting out of that bed until the doctor says you can. You could ruin your whole life if you got up too soon. And if you exercise the way he tells you, maybe your leg will be even better than before. Think what you could do if you could throw away that cane." Evie turned and gave him a smile. She was good at hiding her heart. Daniel was worth hiding it for.

"I could take care of you then, Evie," he replied eagerly. "I could own my own newspaper someday. Do you really think my leg could get better?"

"Not unless you take care of it." She unfastened her jacket and threw it over the chair. She wished she could open the window. It was growing warm in here. "How's the pain? Should I give you more laudanum?"

Daniel set his jaw stubbornly. "I'll wait until Tyler gets back."

Ben hummed and fished around in his pockets. Finding what he was looking for, he threw it in Daniel's direction. "Reckon you could use a bite to eat, but I can't fetch you nothing until Tyler gets here. Try some of that. It's like chewing rope, but it's got some flavor."

Daniel tried the beef jerky with curiosity. It gave his mouth something to do while Evie paced the floor.

"I need to change clothes," she decided firmly, in her best schoolteacher manner. She looked up at Ben as if daring him to defy her.

He did. He glanced over her white shirtwaist with its frilled sleeves and the gray skirt showing a telltale trace of mud at the hem and shook his head. "You look just fine. We'll wait for Tyler."

"I can't be married in a walking suit. I'm just going next door. It's not as if I could go anywhere else on a night like this." Evie stood defiantly in front of the tall black man, who looked down at her with bemusement.

The mention of marriage had both men staring at her, but Evie didn't dare let the knowledge scare her. She was shaking like a leaf on the inside, but she wouldn't let anyone know that.

"I don't reckon Tyler can produce a wedding at this hour of night. You'll have plenty of time to dress fancy when he gets back." Ben remained where he was, although his face showed a trace of discomfort now instead of amusement.

The room was so fraught with tension that none of the occupants noticed the sound of footsteps coming up the stairs until they walked on by. Evie breathed a sigh of relief and returned her concentration to her brother's reaction.

"You're going to marry Tyler?" Daniel asked with incredulity. "Why? He isn't a lawyer or a banker or any of those other things you said you wanted. He doesn't even have a house."

Ben grunted, and Evie sensed his disapproval. She turned her back on him and faced Daniel. "Well, you just tell him that when he gets back. It doesn't seem to make any difference to Tyler."

The man in question shoved against the door, sending Ben stumbling into the room. He carried with him the heavy humidity of the night as he shook out his hat and threw his canvas coat over Evie's. He also brought with him a man they all knew as the recently arrived circuit preacher.

Evie stared at the bearded stranger with dismay. She hadn't really thought Tyler would go through with this. She didn't think he would actually be able to carry this out so quickly. She thought there would be time to talk, to come to some other solution.

The bearded stranger took off his black homburg and made a polite bow as Tyler made curt introductions. "It's an honor and a pleasure, Mrs. Peyton. I've heard you've worked wonders with the children. I trust your young man's hasty change of plans doesn't mean you will be leaving this lovely town?"

Evie sent Tyler a nervous look. He wasn't wearing the light linen suit she had first seen him in, but he still managed to look the part of gambler in a dark frock coat and string tie and a slight ruffle on his shirt front. Gold glittered on his cuffs and in the embroidery of his waistcoat. Raindrops glittered on the gold of his hair. He was handsome enough to take her breath away. She wished she owned a gun.

"Our plans aren't certain yet. I've been looking into the cattle business. We might settle here, if the atmosphere is congenial," Tyler answered smoothly for her. Catching Evie's waist, he pulled her closer to his side, his gaze drifting possessively over the curve of her bosom beneath the lace-edged shirtwaist before coming to rest on the fury in her eyes. "If you'll say the words, Mr. Cleveland, I'd like to get this over with. She doesn't believe I'm a marrying man, and I intend to prove her wrong."

"This is all very improper," the preacher murmured with a show of distress. "I like to have a chance to talk with the bride and groom before the wedding. These things ought to be gone into with much consideration and planning, not with haste. I'm sure Mrs. Peyton agrees with me. Why don't we set the time as Sunday after church? Then I'd feel as if you'd had time—"

Tyler rudely cut him off. "Reverend, I don't mean to be impolite to a man of the cloth, but we want to be married now. Can you do that or do I need to find the judge?"

"Tyler!" Evie hissed. She turned to the red-faced preacher. "If you wouldn't mind, I'd like a moment to freshen myself. Perhaps Ben could fetch something for you to drink?"

Tyler caught her waist tighter. "You can freshen yourself later, after the reverend says his piece. Then we can all have a drink."

"Tyler," Evie looked up at him pleadingly. She couldn't think, not with him standing so close. That night returned to her with sudden clarity, and she remembered the solidity of his muscles as he held her. She remembered other things, too, and her cheeks flushed with color as she realized Tyler was thinking along much the same lines. His fingers dug into her corset, and his other hand came up to touch her cheek.

"Just say yes to the man, Evie. It doesn't require any more than that." Tyler's voice was soft, almost gentle as his hand trailed down her cheek, then lingered a moment to rest at the nape of her neck.

The golden flecks in his eyes held her captivated; she couldn't look away. He was mesmerizing her like a cat does a mouse. Evie wanted to protest, but she could only return his stare as the others in the room stirred restlessly.

"Start the ceremony, Reverend," Tyler ordered, never turning his gaze from Evie.

After harrumphing and sending another look around the room in an appeal for assistance, the preacher pulled out his book and began repeating the words to the wedding ceremony.

Rain clattered against the tin roof. The heat of the closed room caused Tyler's wet coat to steam. Daniel stirred with restless frustration as Evie appeared to consent to this impromptu marriage. The combination of wet and heat brought out the scent of cinnamon and roses in Evie's hair, and the smell wafted through the room as the preacher droned on.

Tyler pinched her when it came time for her response. The reverend didn't know her full name and thus called her Maryellen Peyton as the town knew her. Evie repeated the lie, wondering how that would affect the vows they were exchanging. She noticed there was no mention of Pecos or Martin when Tyler gave his vows. This whole ceremony seemed unreal, like some act put on by a traveling theater troupe. Surely it took more than this to seal her to one man into eternity.

But the ring Tyler pulled off his finger to put on hers was very real. And it was even more real when the reverend told Tyler he could kiss the bride and Tyler did so. He smelled of tobacco and leather and a faint scent of spicy shaving lotion. His lips were hard and firm and very decisive against hers as she clutched his loose ring in one hand and tried not to touch him with the other. He was making a point here, and Evie wasn't at all cer-

tain that she was ready to accept it. The pain in her
stomach had changed to swirls of something very like
anticipation.

The reality was even stronger when Mr. Cleveland produced a printed license with scrolls and flowers around
the sides and asked that everyone present sign it. Evie
was first, and she hesitated, wondering what she was
doing when she went to sign her name and knew she
couldn't use her real one. She put an "E" in front of the
Maryellen and told herself that the Peyton was real
enough. It just lacked the "Howell" to be complete.

Tyler signed his with a flourish. His middle name was
Douglas. He didn't look like a Douglas. Evie sent him a
surreptitious look from beneath lowered lashes, but he
was patiently handing the pen to the preacher.

Ben signed in a very distinct copperplate hand, then
carried the paper to Daniel. Daniel was still looking at
Evie with uncertainty, but when she stood without protesting beneath Tyler's hold, he slowly carved his name
across the final line.

The preacher rolled the paper up after the ink dried
and handed it with satisfaction to Tyler. "All right and
tight, sir. May I congratulate you on your fine choice of
wife? And Mrs. Monteigne, may I be the first to welcome
you to your new name? I hope you will settle here so I
might christen your first child."

The color that drained from Evie's cheeks at the mention of her new name flared briefly at the mention of the
child. She was married and going to have a baby. She
thought the appropriate thing to do would be to swoon.

But no matter how hard she concentrated on it, she
couldn't seem to manage a swoon. She clenched her
teeth as Tyler bade the preacher farewell. She walked
out of his presumptuous hold and toward the door as
soon as the man left. She didn't even turn around to
speak to the other men in the room. She walked out,
and they all stared after her, listening carefully to be
certain her footsteps went no farther than the room next
door. They didn't.

Tyler exhaled a heavy breath, ran his hand through
his hair, and turned an uncertain look to Ben and Daniel.

They were both waiting for him to give explanations. He didn't have any to give. He'd just gone and got himself shackled when he had only just decided it was time to find another woman. He'd been planning on finally taking Starr to her room tonight. Now look at him.

"She's carrying my baby," he finally admitted before following Evie out the door. Daniel's furious cry followed Tyler out, but the silence from Benjamin was equally ominous.

Benjamin knew his history, and it wasn't a good one. Walking slowly, Tyler came to face the panel separating him from his newly acquired wife. He could open the door and face the future with a ball and chain that he had spent years avoiding, or he could walk away and never look back.

He'd done the latter once. He had regretted it ever since. With calm resolution, Tyler opened the door.

Chapter 16

Evie stared at the flowers through tear-misted eyes. She wasn't much of a gardener and wasn't certain of the proper names for everything, but the riot of color struck her with sobs that could have been joy had the circumstances been different.

A bouquet of giant paper roses adorned the tall dresser. Entire branches of real lilac were strewn across the bed, filling the air with heavenly scents. Green stalks topped by dancing yellow heads filled the water pitcher. Branches covered in pink occupied her sitting chair. She hadn't thought the entire town had held that much color. Obviously, it didn't any longer. Tyler must have robbed every garden in the territory, and maybe a cemetery or two. She didn't know where he'd found the paper roses.

Tears were rolling down Evie's cheeks when Tyler came through the door. She didn't look at him, just stood there clasping her elbows and shaking with sobs. He glanced around to better examine his handiwork in the light of the one lamp he had lit earlier.

The easel and canvas he had glimpsed that one day were stored away, as were the books and other niceties that Evie liked to travel with. The towering stack of trunks told their story. She had meant to move out of this room.

He didn't want to know what that meant. He came up behind her, but he was afraid to touch her. He'd thought the flowers would add a festive touch for a less than festive occasion, but he hadn't expected floods of tears. Not from Evie. He was afraid she would crumble if he touched her.

"The stores were closed. I couldn't buy a wedding

gift," he offered tentatively. He'd never really had to court a woman before, and Tyler felt awkward at the business. Had she been anyone but Evie, he could have her out of her gown and on the bed within minutes. But Evie had every reason to despise him and what would happen on that bed. It put a man in a damned awkward position.

Evie dashed at her tears with the back of her hand. "They're lovely. I wish I knew what they were all called. I'd like to have a garden someday with all of them in it."

"Roses, lilacs, Easter flowers, and I don't know what they call the pink things, but I can find out. It's a good thing they don't hang a man for flower theft around here, or you'd be a widow tomorrow." He tried the light touch, but it didn't sound so light after he said it.

Evie nodded hesitantly. "It would be very confusing to be twice widowed and never married. I guess it's a good thing you won't hang."

The laughter wasn't there, but at least she was making jokes. Tyler allowed himself a small breath of relief as he loosened his tie. The Evie he knew wasn't overly inclined to tears. That must be the effect of pregnancy. Already, she was starting to bounce back. They were going to have to learn to make the best of a bad situation.

"I guess the live ones ought to go in water. I don't suppose that collection of trunks has vases?"

"The top one has the china," Evie answered vaguely, her gaze traveling to the flower-filled water pitcher and not to the trunks. She would have to wash and prepare herself for bed sometime. How was she going to do it with Tyler in the room? She didn't think stringing a sheet across the room would work with a husband.

Tyler reached for the trunk. "Take the Easter flowers out of the water pitcher. I've ordered up hot water. You can go behind the dressing screen to get ready while I dig out your china."

She glanced worriedly to Tyler as he lifted the smallest trunk from the stack, but he handled it with care. A knock at the door sent her scurrying for the screen. She didn't want anyone to see her right now. It was as if the

whole world knew she was newly married and could see
in their heads what was about to happen to her. Or she
thought would happen to her. Tyler hadn't touched her.
Maybe he would leave her alone.

She really didn't think he would, but Evie clung to the
notion as Tyler moved around in the room beyond the
dressing screen while she cautiously unfastened her shirtwaist. He handed her a pitcher of steaming water, and
it looked inviting enough to encourage her to do as he
said. She needed to wash. She had heard of marriages
of convenience. Perhaps that was what Tyler intended.
She felt better just imagining it.

As she washed, Evie threw a dubious look at the high-
necked linen nightgown she usually wore to bed. She
wasn't at all certain that she could step out from behind
the dressing screen wearing that. Perhaps she ought to
keep on her chemise and corset and pantalets. Sleeping
in a corset sounded highly uncomfortable, but to allow
herself to be unfettered beneath a thin piece of linen
seemed a wanton thing to do in Tyler's presence.

She compromised and wore just the chemise and pantalets beneath the gown. It was going to be infernally
warm that way, but she couldn't just go out there practically naked.

Tyler had stuck the flowers in china teapots and crystal
vases, and also laid them in gravy bowls. He had unfastened his tie and thrown off his coat and waited anxiously
in shirtsleeves with his hands characteristically shoved in
his pockets as he leaned against the door. When Evie
appeared, his gaze automatically drifted over the loose
linen of her long gown, then came back up to meet hers.

The disappointment she had first thought she'd seen
in his eyes was carefully replaced now by a neutral
expression.

"You're going to be warm in all that gear. I won't
object if you want to make yourself a little more comfortable while I wash." Unfastening his shirt as he went,
Tyler disappeared behind the screen.

He was good, too good. Without giving an order or
voicing a protest, he had told her that he didn't want her
wearing all these clothes. He had also shattered her brief

illusion. Cheeks flushing, Evie stood in the middle of the braided rug and tried to decide what to do next. She didn't want to wear all this gear, either, but she remembered all too clearly what Tyler could do her if she didn't. To take it off would make it seem as if she wanted him to do that to her again.

She didn't. What they had done had been dirty, painful, and embarrassing beyond recall. There had been blood and stickiness. They had behaved like animals. He needed to be reminded that she was a lady. And since she was already pregnant, what was the purpose of repeating the act? Perhaps she wouldn't have to.

Relieved by that thought, Evie climbed into bed. It wasn't exactly a romantic marriage bed. The iron bars had been painted a white that had yellowed with age. She had left her own linens on it, however, and she was grateful for that. It seemed more civilized to sleep on linens embroidered with her initials and edged in lace.

Her initials. Evie glanced worriedly at the EPH neatly scrolled in antique white embroidery thread on each pillowcase. What was she going to tell Tyler?

Her stomach tensed again as she heard the unmistakable sounds of water splashing from behind the screen. Was Tyler standing there with all his clothes off? What if an intruder came in and she screamed right now?

That irrepressible thought sent Evie off into a fit of giggles she tried to muffle in her pillow. This was the most awful night of her life, and she was laughing at the thought of the grand Tyler Monteigne rushing into the room stark naked and carrying a six-gun. She must be losing her mind.

Tyler heard her giggles and felt a sudden quenching of his ardor. The sound of giggles in the boudoir could have that effect on a man, he reflected as he scrubbed at his face and wished he had his razor. What in hell could the little witch find to laugh about at this hour? He half expected to walk out of here and find her waiting with a shotgun.

The thought of walking out of here presented certain other problems. Whatever else she might be, Evie was a lady who knew nothing of the physical side of men except what little he had forced on her. She would most likely go into shock should he walk out of here in his birthday suit as he was inclined to do. If she was already waxing hysterical, he couldn't afford to send her over the brink.

There was no doubt in Tyler's mind what he meant to do with his wedding night. A man had only one wedding night, and he was meant to enjoy it. He wasn't accustomed to the long drought from feminine companionship he had endured since being dragged here, and he was looking forward to a little relief. On the morrow he would be confronted with the responsibilities he had shackled himself to, but not tonight. Tonight he meant to teach one Evie Maryellen Peyton Monteigne what it meant to make love. With any luck, there would be a permanent end to that drought. Marriage had at least one advantage.

Remembering the glimpses he'd had of firm white breasts and slender curves and long legs, Tyler felt a surge of desire so strong that he stared at himself with incredulity. Evie would jump out of her skin if he entered their bed looking like this. Regretfully, he reached for the lamp and blew it out. He would have to save the looking part until morning, when she'd had time to get used to what he was going to do to her.

The moment the lamp went out, Evie clutched the top sheet with fear. She could see Tyler's silhouette against the windowpane as he came out from behind the screen. She couldn't see in the darkness, but she knew he wasn't wearing anything. He hadn't been wearing anything the last time he had come to her bed.

"Tyler." There was a question and a warning in her voice as he approached the bed.

Tyler threw back the quilt but left Evie the sheet as he climbed in next to her. The bed sagged beneath his weight as he reached for her.

"Tyler, I don't want . . ." Evie bit back a gasp as his hand captured her waist, and she was suddenly confronted with the warmth of his bare chest. "I mean, if I'm already pregnant . . ."

"Hush." Tyler's mouth closed over hers, not softly, not hesitatingly, but wide-open and demanding.

Evie gasped and found his tongue between her teeth. A flickering of the pleasure she remembered from before kept her from pulling away, and the questing touch of strong fingers against the side of her breast made her moan in despair.

She remembered this part all too well. Her toes tingled. The tips of her breasts grew tight and painful waiting for him to find them. The sensation grew stronger and moved downward as his tongue plundered and did sweet things to her mouth. She didn't know how to respond, but Tyler didn't seem to care. He was decimating all her defenses very effectively without her help.

His hand slipped inside the gown he had somehow unfastened already. His muffled curse moved against her mouth as he encountered still another barrier. Tyler raised himself over her, and Evie stared up at his shadow in the darkness, wondering what expression was on his face.

"From now on, I don't want you wearing anything in bed. I can keep you warm, so you don't need this folderol. Help me get it off of you."

Evie surprised herself by lifting her hips so Tyler could pull the nightgown up, then lifting her arms so he could pull it over her head. He rewarded her with a kiss that sent more than her toes tingling, and she was reluctant to stop when he reached for the edge of her chemise. Obligingly, Tyler held her lips captivated as he rolled the thin cloth inexorably upward, until her breasts were bare to the damp night air.

The sound Evie made as his fingers plucked her nipple was more like a kitten's mew than a human noise. Pleased with his success, Tyler bent to touch his tongue to this responsive tissue, and she literally jumped in his arms. Within seconds, the chemise lay tangled somewhere among the sheets, and Tyler's kisses moved unhampered over silken skin.

Evie dug her fingers into Tyler's shoulders in a vague attempt to halt this assault on her senses, but even this grip bombarded her with strange sensations. He wore nothing, and her fingers dug into hot, smooth skin and taut muscle. Instead of pushing him away, her hands clung there, smoothing the rippling muscle as he bent over her, riding downward as he lifted his head to tease her lips with kisses. She didn't dare go farther than his waist, but even that held a strange fascination to her. He was narrow there, but she could feel the cords of muscle jerking at her touch. She liked knowing he was responding to her.

She didn't like it when she felt Tyler's hands pulling at the drawstrings of her pantalets. She tensed and this time, she did pull away. Tyler kissed her again, murmuring soothing phrases across her lips, but she was too terrified to respond. She knew what would happen when he had her undressed.

He loosened the strings but didn't immediately pull the fabric away. Instead, he bent his head to suckle at her breast until Evie was whimpering for more, while his hand stroked her abdomen and then moved lower.

She didn't want to feel this way. She didn't want to feel every nerve end drawn to the man hovering over her. But she was awash with heat and desperate for his kisses and her skin craved his touch as if it were a balm to all her fears. When Tyler's hand slid inside her pantalets, the craving went with it, centering where she didn't want it the most.

"I'm going to make love to you, Evie," Tyler whispered against her cheek as he nibbled his way to her ear. "I'm going to put myself inside you and make you my wife and show you how much pleasure there can be in this. Tell me you'll let me show you, Evie. I won't hurt you again."

She was even ready to accept the pain again. His words were an incitement as surely as the fingers now touching her where she had been afraid to touch herself. Evie bit back a cry as Tyler's fingers entered her, but his mouth was smothering hers, swallowing all the cries and whimpers, taking her response and giving it back to her in the magic of his fingers.

She was weeping for more by the time he rolled the fine linen over her hips. His kisses moved downward,

caressing her breasts, roaming lower, as his hands skillfully played along her thighs, pushing away the hampering material until nothing lay between them but the air
and their need. When Tyler touched her again, Evie
nearly rose from the bed, and he knew she was ready.

Evie shuddered as Tyler gently parted her legs and
bent them so she could receive him more easily. She
didn't want him to do this, but she didn't want him to
stop when he stroked her there. She felt hollow and aching and scared, and the pleasant sensations were rapidly
receding as Tyler moved between her legs and she felt
the hot iron-like rod brushing against her.

But Tyler was teasing her lips again, parting them with
his tongue, moving back and forth and in and out until
she was writhing with hunger. His hands circled both
breasts at once, caressing them, kneading, tantalizing the
tips until Evie was crying for more and raising her hips
to the rhythm he created.

He moved his hands to her buttocks then and entered
her. Tyler caught her cry with his mouth, held himself
still while she adjusted, and moved slowly when he felt
her shudder with the need that filled him. He couldn't
lunge forward as he wanted, as his body demanded. She
was too tight, too scared, too everything. He moved gently, felt the ripple of response, and breathed a sigh of
relief as he kissed her lips.

Evie couldn't believe he was doing this to her. She
couldn't believe she was letting him. The intimacy was
incredible, overwhelming, but she didn't even know this
man. She had a stranger's body inside hers, filling her
until she felt stretched at the seams, retreating until she
grabbed his shoulders and asked for more. She couldn't
bear it when he moved away. Her hips followed his, and
he began moving faster.

This was Tyler Monteigne, the gambler, the ladies'
man. He was using her as he had used countless other
women, and she was letting him. She was more than
letting him. She was wrapping her legs around him, raising herself to him, and begging and crying for more as
he slipped back and forth, plunged in and out until her
head spun with desire and her body was out of control

and there was nothing more to this world than their two bodies joined as one.

He gave a harsh cry and drove deep inside her, but even as his body rocked into hers, his hand slid between them and Evie felt the vibrations give way to uncontrollable quakes of pleasure beneath his expert touch. Tears rolled down her cheeks as the entrance to her womb clung to him, closing around him while Tyler buried himself inside her and exploded beneath her touch.

It hadn't hurt, and it had been more pleasurable than she had ever imagined. Why then, did she feel such terror when Tyler kissed her again and moved inside her?

"You're my wife now, Evie," he whispered against her ear. "You're going to be mother of my child."

Just the words enhanced her terror.

"When are you going to stop lying to me?"

His eyes seemed to shine golden in the darkness above her, and Evie had all she could do to keep from screaming as she felt that man part of him stir to life within her again.

He wasn't going to stop until she told him. She didn't know if she ever wanted him to stop.

Chapter 17

It was nearing dawn and they lay entangled in sweaty sheets, their bodies glistening as they entwined around each other. Evie couldn't move if she wanted to, and she didn't have enough energy left to know what she wanted. She liked the slick sheen of Tyler's hair-roughened leg against hers. She couldn't imagine her breast without Tyler's strong fingers wrapped around it. Idly, drifting in and out of sleep, she tried to imagine him lifting his hand away from her, and all she could envision was cold and loneliness.

Whatever they had just done was better than cold and loneliness. She was vaguely aware that she was sore. Tyler was large, she was inexperienced, and they had done "that" more times than she could count. Once they had just lain joined, too exhausted to do more, until their bodies had rebelled and rocked them together and exploded within minutes of their first movement. Another time they had woken from sound slumber and rolled into each other's arms, and instead of sliding back to sleep, had found themselves rolling across the bed again. Where they should have been oil and water, they were fire and kindling. Evie definitely didn't feel cold or lonely anymore.

Or not cold, anyway. With the coming of dawn, the loneliness began to form like ice around her heart. She couldn't remember the first time she had felt its sting. She supposed when she was very little she had just assumed that Nanny was her mother and never questioned her lack of father. It was only later that she questioned why Nanny was called Nanny and asked why she didn't have a father like the other girls had. Nanny had never lied. Nanny hadn't told the whole truth, but she'd never lied.

But Evie did. When she was fourteen, she had told her friends that her father was a railroad baron who spent all his time riding the rails, seeing that his trains ran properly. She had her mother dying of some romantic illness that made him incapable of ever loving again.

By the time she was eighteen, she had become a little more subtle. Her wealth was obvious, so she made Nanny into her maiden aunt and invented a story of her wealthy father's enemies wanting to harm him through her, so he had to keep her hidden. The romantic illness served just as well this time around.

But Nanny never lied, so all the neighbors knew Evie and Daniel were "adopted." That was a polite euphemism for saying they had no parents who would claim them and Nanny was being paid to do so. There weren't many reasons why parents didn't claim their children. Everyone could see why Daniel's parents hadn't wanted him. He was a cripple, lame for life, and when he was born, it was thought he would never walk upright. Evie had only been two years old when they'd brought Daniel to Nanny's house. She didn't remember his parents, but she remembered his infant screams. He had screamed night and day for months.

Although Evie had always kept the hidden dream that her parents would come to claim her someday, the realization that they were paying Nanny to keep her away had shattered that image. Lying there wrapped in Tyler's arms, Evie tried to imagine how to tell her husband that even her parents didn't want her. It was much easier to say they were dead.

But that wouldn't explain why she was here.

Rain clattered against the roof again. The gray light of dawn was erasing the darkness. Evie wondered if she had the courage to turn over and really look at her husband. She knew what he felt like. His hand on her breast was long-fingered, not callused, and stronger than she had ever imagined. The broad chest pressed against her back had a light mat of hair that tickled and made her want to touch him there. The man part of him made her curious, but she was uncertain as to whether she wished to explore that curiosity any further.

The hand on her breast began to move, the thumb scraping lightly up the side while her traitorous nipple hardened and surged against his palm. Evie could feel Tyler's warm length all down her back and wrapped around her legs. He was very definitely awake. Defiantly, she turned on her back to look at him.

The rain pounded overhead as she stared through the gray morning light to the man now hovering over her. In the shadows of dawn, she could discern the rough stubble of beard on his lean jaw, the tousled curl of golden hair as it fell over his face, and the faint lines drawn by years of pain along the sides of his mouth. He wasn't as shining handsome as he could be when he put on his happy face, but he was more real this way, more man than she was prepared to encounter.

"Did you know you have the most beautiful eyes I have ever seen in my life?" Tyler murmured, staring down at her as she stared up at him.

The compliment startled her. She had received enough flattery in her lifetime to start a book of poetry, but none quite like this. Tyler had already had what he wanted of her, and still he took the time to say something nice. That ought to count for something. She was ready to build a life out of any small thing he handed her. She grasped this bit of straw readily.

"Did you know you have the most silver tongue of any man I have ever known?" she replied wickedly, not yet ready to give him more than that. He had too much control in his hands. She would retain what she could.

Tyler grinned and applied his silver tongue where it would do the most good. When Evie finally gasped for air, he relented and returned to resting on one arm while he studied the wife he had so blindly taken the night before.

He cupped his hand around her breast as if to test its weight and flicked the rosy tip with his fingers, watching with growing hunger as it responded readily to his touch. Evie watched him warily through shadowed eyes, however, and he satisfied himself with kissing her there before releasing her to meet her gaze.

"If you're too sore, just tell me, Evie. A man and wife ought to be able to tell each other these things."

She found little relief in his words. How did she tell him she didn't know what she wanted? Yes, she was sore, but that didn't stop her from aching for more now that he'd aroused her again. Biting her tongue, she studied him as he had studied her. The bare arm resting above her was rounded at the top with an alarming amount of muscle. She had never really noticed a man's arms before. If she'd seen men with their shirts off, she didn't recall them to any extent. But she would remember this one. She could see the hair on Tyler's chest was little more than a light brown fuzz that arrowed down to his narrow waist, but the sheet rested there and she couldn't see any farther. She could feel, however. He was as aroused as she was.

Evie wasn't timid by nature. She reached out to scrape her fingers gently across Tyler's beard, liking the texture, and she smiled with this small pleasure. "It's sort of like being handed a box of chocolates and knowing you'll be sick if you eat them all but not knowing when to stop, isn't it?"

Tyler grinned and slid his arms around her and rolled over on his back, pulling Evie with him. Her hair cascaded in a waterfall around them, filtering the room's gray light through a curtain of silk. He pulled the heavy mass over one shoulder so he could see her more clearly. She was magnificently beautiful from the thick lashes of her sloe eyes to the upright tilt of full breasts and right on down to her toes, if he could see that far. He would in a minute. That one sheet wouldn't last long with what he had in mind.

"I've no taste for chocolates before breakfast. A sweet juicy orange is more what I had in mind. I've never got sick on oranges yet."

Evie gasped as Tyler lifted his head to suckle at her breast. She should have known what was coming, but it hadn't occurred to her that they could do "that" in this position. But he was making it very obvious that they could. One large hand was pressing at her hip, guiding her downward, and just the thought of what was waiting for her there made her ready.

A pounding on the door overrode the sweet murmuring of their lips as they met. Evie jumped at once at the noise, but Tyler wasn't so swift to allow the intrusion. Holding her still, he continued to ply his tongue and teeth in little nips along her throat.

"The whole damned river's coming out of its banks! We've got to get to the horses." The voice was peremptory and accompanied by staccato curses and continued pounding.

Tyler grimaced. "That's what happens when you treat them as equals. No courtesy at all. I expect better from you, woman."

Frightened by Ben's words, frustrated by the interruption, Evie remained frozen until she heard this crack. Tyler's humor belonged on the gallows. Pinching him in a soft place beneath his arm, she slid away, rolling up in the sheet as she did so.

"Expect to be disappointed then." She pulled the sheet defiantly over her breasts. She wasn't about to do what he had in mind with Ben standing outside the door, pounding it like a bass drum.

"I like a little sauce in the mornings." Tyler grinned, grabbed the sheet, and tugged as he swung his legs over the bed. "Ben, stop that infernal pounding before I come out there and throw you over the rail," he shouted at the door. "I'll be there shortly."

Evie scurried for cover as Tyler pulled the sheet around him, leaving her naked. He succeeded in getting a good glimpse of deliciously round hips and pert buttocks before she found the blanket and covered herself.

"There's no sense in getting dressed," he reminded her as he stepped behind the dressing screen to pull on his pants. "It won't take long to get the horses to high ground. Ben's just an old worry wart. I'll bring up some coffee and biscuits when I come back."

Evie wasn't paying him any mind as she wandered to the window with the blanket around her. She had every intention of going next door to see how Daniel fared. If

Tyler Monteigne expected an obedient wife who bowed to his every whim, he'd certainly taken on the wrong woman.

Her gasp as she looked out the window brought Tyler quickly to her side. He looked over her shoulder, cursed, and leaving his shirt unbuttoned, fell down in the chair and began tugging on his boots. "That river was only a trickle the other day. Where the hell did that come from?"

Stunned by the immensity of the rapidly spreading waters, Evie could only stare out as Tyler finished dressing. The nearly dry riverbed she had noticed when they arrived in town was now filled to overflowing. Water poured down the streets, lapping at the boardwalk, and seemed to rise even as she watched. Bales of cotton floated down the alley below. An empty crate bumped against a post by the sheriff's office. Men were loading up wagons with goods from the various businesses up and down the street, and the water was halfway up the wheels.

"Tyler, be careful out there. That current seems awful strong." Evie turned just as Tyler rose from the chair, fastening the rest of his shirt and shoving it into his pants. She didn't know why she should feel concerned about this man who had stolen her independence, but it seemed the natural thing to do.

Tyler noted her worried frown and felt an uneasy tug, but he disregarded it in the concerns of the moment. He pressed a kiss to her forehead and started for the door. "That coffee might be a little later than I promised. I'll see what I can do."

He walked out, leaving Evie wrapped in her blanket staring after him. When she realized what she was doing, she glanced down at herself and shivered with horror. She was standing here *naked*, with nothing but a blanket around her while she discussed floods and coffee with a man she barely knew.

And the memory of that man between her sheets and gazing down at her sent a hot flood of heat to her cheeks. She had never considered herself a wanton before, but it was all too obvious that Tyler Monteigne had made her into one. She was more than certain that ladies simply didn't do those kind of things.

Deliberately turning off the images in her head, Evie hurriedly washed in the cold water from last night and looked for the most stiffly correct gown that she possessed. Unfortunately she didn't possess many, and she'd been wearing them to school these last weeks. Not one of them seemed suitable for the day after her wedding.

She had to keep the proper gowns clean a little while longer, until she had enough money to have them laundered. It wasn't exactly with resignation that she donned the white Swiss muslin with sprigs of green on the ruffled overskirt and green ribbons at the heart-shaped neck. She liked pretty things, and the schoolteacher clothes had been a trifle depressing.

Evie didn't attempt an elaborate coiffure but merely twisted her hair in several loops, pinned it, and covered it with an old-fashoined net until she could do more. She had to see how Daniel fared.

He was lying propped against his pillows, throwing wads of paper against the windowpane when she entered. She glanced at the Pecos Martin book in his lap and saw the jagged tears of pages ripped from the seam. She wasn't going to question that particular piece of rebellion.

"The water's up to door fronts now. It's a good thing we're on the third floor." Evie lifted her skirt from the unswept floor and went to the window to check the flood's progress.

Daniel studied her turned back sullenly. "I suppose Monteigne is out there making a hero of himself."

Evie raised her eyebrows as she turned around. "He and Ben are moving the horses to high ground. What on earth is wrong with you this morning? If your leg is giving you pain, I'll fetch you some medicine."

"I don't want any damned laudanum." Daniel picked up a book from the bedside table. "Ben said he'd bring up breakfast when he got the horses out. You don't have to wait around on me."

"Daniel Mulloney, I do believe you're jealous!" Evie threw herself down in the overstuffed chair and watched the dust fly up. The discovery of Daniel's feelings had floored her, but she didn't intend to let him know that.

"I am not!" Red-eared, Daniel slammed his book down against the covers and glared at her. "I just don't see any reason why you had to go and get yourself married like that. And I don't believe for a minute that you're ..." He stumbled over the word and turned even redder.

"Pregnant? With child? *Enceinte?* I'm not sure I believe it, either." It would be easier to lie, but Evie didn't like lying about this, not to Daniel. He deserved better than that. But her words sounded cruel even to her ears. Heaven help her, what was she going to do with a child?

Daniel relaxed as the subject came out in the open. He looked at her with curiosity. "You said you didn't think you'd ever get married. I didn't think you even liked men. You flirt all the time, but you never get serious."

Evie examined her nails. "Well, things happen, I guess." She didn't want to say that she didn't have much choice. There was no sense in Daniel hating Tyler. They were going to have to learn to live together somehow, and Daniel needed a man in his life. She wouldn't have chosen Tyler had she been given a choice, but beggars couldn't be choosers. "At least Tyler is a little more fun than most." Remembering what they had done in bed, Evie didn't think "fun" was the correct word, but she let it slide.

Daniel didn't say anything, and Evie suspected his mind had followed the same path as hers. They were closer than brother and sister, but the topic of sex had never been discussed between them, and probably never would. That was one reason Daniel needed Tyler.

Daniel finally ended the silence with an awkward question. "Is he going to find you a house? I wouldn't mind living somewhere besides a hotel for a change. I'm starving right now."

"We haven't discussed it. I'm of the impression that Tyler doesn't have much more money than we do. I suspect we'd better keep on looking for our checks and waiting for that lawyer to turn up."

Evie rose and checked the window again. The water was lapping at the windows of several buildings already. She couldn't see Tyler from this angle. Daniel's room overlooked the livery and the tiny house attached to the rear, not the front entrance where Tyler would be. She hoped whoever lived in the house had moved everything into the stable lofts. It looked as if that back alley behind the hotel and past the house was a valley where all the water from the streets congregated. It rushed along like a river of its own.

She swirled around at a knock on the door, and gave a cry of relief as Ben sauntered in with a tray of coffee and some covered dishes that smelled mighty good. Tyler came in behind him, swiping his dripping hat from his head and leaving it on the floor, discarding his long coat and piling it on top of it.

Daniel sent Evie's new husband a suspicious glare, but the smell of food was more overpowering than jealousy. He struggled into a better position as Ben set the tray down beside the bed.

"Flapjacks, folks, and sorghum syrup. Don't eat too fast, it may be all you get the rest of the day. John's packing up his kitchen and moving for higher ground as we speak."

Evie turned a worried gaze to Tyler. "Should we be moving out, too? How long can the water stay this way?"

Tyler's gaze rested on her wholly inappropriate but beautifully feminine gown before rising to meet her eyes. He hadn't seen many women dress like that since before the war. Only the carpetbaggers' wives had that kind of money. She reminded him of a number of things he didn't want to be reminded of, but his smile was gentle as he answered.

"We won't let you starve. This is one of the safest places in town, and John is moving his supplies up here. It might not be the best fare, but there will be something to eat in those cans and barrels."

Evie nodded a trifle uneasily beneath the odd glow in Tyler's eyes. She didn't know what he was thinking when he looked at her like that. It wasn't the same look as when he wanted to bed her. She recognized that one well enough. This look came closer to the one he'd had in his eyes that day he'd first proposed marriage. It was almost a haunted look, and she didn't like it.

Evie ate a flapjack without tasting it, sipped at her coffee, and tried to pretend everything was normal. She and Tyler had not once discussed their plans for the future. She had no idea if she would have a house to live in, a place to raise a child, or where the money would come from. Until these last few months she'd never had to worry about such problems, and now they seemed immense and overpowering. She wanted to think Tyler would take care of them all, but she had this nagging feeling that he was as scared as she was. It didn't add to her sense of well-being.

Setting aside her coffee, Evie wandered back to the window. Water rushed like a river through the alley. A crate slammed against the side of the hotel, narrowly missing the top of a first-floor window. A rooster sat dripping and bedraggled on the livery roof. Her gaze drifted idly to the little house in back, and she screamed.

"Tyler! There are children out there. On the roof. They're going to drown!"

As she gathered up her skirts and ran for the door, Tyler jumped up and grabbed her by the arm, shoving her back to the chair.

"Don't leave this room. The place is filled with rats, both the four-legged and two-legged kind. Daniel, keep her here." He glared pointedly at the boy in the bed. "Ben and I will see what we can do."

Ben was already checking the window and whistling a dubious note, but like Tyler, he grabbed his hat and headed for the door.

Chapter 18

"What are they doing now, Evie?" Daniel leaned toward the window, as if he meant to join her there.

"They've got a ladder, and they're tying it between the roof and some room down on the second floor. They're all going to get themselves killed." Panicking as she saw Tyler's head peering out that second-story window, Evie headed for the door.

"Don't you dare, Evangeline Howell! You heard Tyler. He can't be worrying about you and those kids, too. You're the one who sent him down there. You can't stop them now."

Frustrated, Evie knotted her fingers into fists. "There has to be a better way. Men are such foolhardy idiots." She strode back to the window and glared down.

She had recognized the children by now, if just by their sizes. There was fourteen-year-old Carmen clinging to the toddler in her arms, and Manuel, the eleven-year-old, helping Jose, the youngest boy, hold on to the slippery tiled roof. They had been edging their way toward the livery when Tyler had yelled at them. Evie glanced at the big barn and the loft door. They could never have reached it unless they were skilled acrobats. With a baby in arms, there wasn't a chance.

She gave a gasp as Tyler tested the ladder by crawling out on it. The water pouring down the alley was already swirling past the first-floor windows. If he fell, he could be swept away in a minute. Evie clenched the windowsill and prayed.

The ladder held and Tyler continued across. The children sat stunned and uncomprehending until he was almost there. Then Manuel was excitedly sliding down the

roof to meet him, holding on to his six-year-old brother
and pushing him toward Tyler when he reached the edge.

Evie gave a cry of relief as the normally rebellious
José willingly crept up on the ladder with Tyler. Crawling
was the only means of progress, and they needed both
hands and knees. Tyler wrapped a rope around both
their waists before setting out over the water again.

"He's got one across. Ben's untying him and lifting
him in the window. The ladder's holding!" Evie reported
events to Daniel as they happened. She knew his frustration at having to stay in bed while others acted, but more
hands weren't needed. She had seen John from the res-
taurant down there, and Phil, the hotel owner. There
were more hands than could be used.

Manuel crawled across rapidly, but getting the toddler
across was a difficult task. Tyler had Carmen strap the
child firmly to his back, then waited for the girl to start
across before following. Evie held her breath as the ladder sagged beneath their combined weights. Tyler hesitated, making himself available if the girl should miss a
step, not daring to go too far out and risk them all. She
could see Ben jerking Manuel back through the window
before the lad could go back out and help. She wanted
to go to them, to reassure them, but she couldn't add to
Tyler's worries. She remained where she was.

She gave a scream of relief as Carmen crawled in the
window and Tyler followed. She hadn't realized how terrified she had been until she saw how her hands were
shaking. She knew what she had to do now, and she
threw Daniel a look of defiance. "I'm going to get those
children. I don't know what happened to their mother,
but they know me. I can't leave them down there alone."

Daniel bit his tongue as Evie rushed out. As usual,
there was little he could do to stop her.

The youngest was screaming, and Carmen was trying
to comfort her while Manuel and José yelled at each
other about somebody's cat when Evie rushed into the
room. The men were hauling in the ladder and one of
John's boys was stiil lugging supplies into the room, and
they didn't halt immediately at her appearance.

"Manuel, José, stop that nonsense immediately. We've

got to get you upstairs and find you some dry clothes.
Carmen, come along. I'm sure I have something you can
wear. You'll catch your deaths in those wet things."

The no-nonsense words that Nanny had used for
twenty years came out without effort as Evie set the
children to order. The men in the room turned to stare
at her then, as the boys hushed their fighting and even
the toddler seemed to quiet with her calm control of the
situation. Tyler took a step toward her, but Evie merely
shook her head.

"I'm taking them upstairs. We'll be fine. You go back
to whatever you need to do."

In the gloom of the unlighted chamber, her white muslin glowed like a candle as she shepherded the children
to the door, guiding her petticoats gracefully past cartons
and crates with the elegance of a lady. One of the
younger men whistled softly, and his father cuffed him
on the ear. A man didn't whistle at a lady.

Evie didn't notice her admirers. Men staring at her
were nothing new, but four bedraggled youngsters were.
José whooped as he left wet tracks up the carpeted stairs,
and he occasionally turned around to admire his foot-
prints as Manuel led him upward. The wide-eyed toddler
stared over Carmen's shoulder as Evie followed them up.

Evie threw open the door to Daniel's room and shuffled the two boys in. "Daniel, direct these two to the
proper trunks where they can find something dry. A shirt
or your long johns or something ought to do for now."

Daniel stared at Evie with incredulity, but she shut the
door before he could protest. Leading Carmen to the
next room, she opened the door. "You're almost as tall
as I am. We can deck you out nicely. I'm not certain
about the baby, though. What's her name?"

"Maria. Do you have towels? I will dry her off."

The room was a shambles from last night. Evie hoped
Carmen knew nothing about what happened behind
closed doors, because anyone with any knowledge at all
would know what had happened here. The bottom sheet
had parted from the mattress and was half off the bed.
The sheet Tyler had used was still lying on the floor in
a puddle beneath the dressing screen. She had at least

folded the blanket and laid it over the chair arm, but she hadn't put away last night's clothing. Parts of it could still be seen beneath the screen. And her nightgown and private clothes were scattered all across the floor where Tyler had thrown them. Why hadn't she noticed that before she left?

Because she had still been in a sodden haze from his lovemaking. Kicking the offending garments out of sight, Evie reached for the used towels beside the washstand. The hotel wasn't up to its usual standards today.

Carmen began stripping Maria and toweling her off while Evie searched for clothes. "Where is your mother?" Evie asked as she rummaged in a trunk. "She'll need to know where you are."

"She went to see a friend who was having a baby last night. She said she would be gone just a little while, but I suppose the river rose faster than she expected." The girl's voice was anxious, but she hid it well to keep from frightening the toddler.

"She must be frantic worrying about you. I guess there isn't anything we can do until the river goes down. Does it do this often around here?"

"No, señora. I have heard people speak of the flood of '55, but I was not born then. It rains sometimes like this in the spring, and the river gets high, but not like this."

"Here, this gown is too small for me. I don't know why I brought it. Go behind the screen and change. I'll look after Maria. We can wrap her in a blanket if nothing else."

Tyler didn't return until after dark. By that time Evie had raided the supplies for dried apples and pickles and cans of beans and the six of them had picnicked merrily throughout the day. Daniel had taught the boys how to play Hangman until even José had learned enough of his letters to hang Daniel on "cat." Maria fell asleep wrapped and pinned in one of Evie's linen chemises, and Carmen had raptly fallen in love with the trunk of books.

She wasn't the only one who was in danger of falling in love. Daniel kept sending Carmen surreptitious glances, but Evie had caught enough of them to guess their meaning. Once Carmen's hair dried, it was a luxurious black that she tied back with a ribbon from Evie's collection. Her face was an oval of creamy perfection, accented by the slash of black eyebrows and lashes too thick to be real. Although little more than a child, she was already developing the shape of a woman. It was easy to see what Daniel was seeing. And her love of books was no strike against her with a bookworm like Daniel.

Evie had intended to make pallets in Daniel's room for the boys and put the girls on the floor in her room when dark came. But by that time the pain in Daniel's face was evident, and Manuel and José were bickering and had to be constantly separated. Resignedly, she directed Manuel to move the overstuffed chair in Daniel's room to her room, then sent him back to make a pallet for himself with Daniel. Carmen and the two youngest she installed in her own bed.

Tyler wasn't going to like it, but she hadn't seen more than his hat all day as he came and went below. Apparently a boat had been found somewhere, and the rescue mission had spread to stranded families throughout town. The hotel was filling with people. He couldn't object too mightily to just these children.

After they settled down to sleep, Evie carefully folded her muslin gown and hung up her petticoats and donned her nightgown. She didn't fool herself by wearing chemise and pantalets beneath it. If Tyler was coming, he had enough to object to. She wouldn't give him more.

Taking a spare blanket from her trunks, she curled up in the overstuffed chair and rested her feet on the padded seat of her bedroom chair. Tyler would have to find a place on the floor if he returned. For all she knew, he'd gone over to the saloon to fortify himself. She couldn't object. He didn't have to marry her. He hadn't wanted to marry her any more than she had wanted to marry him. She wasn't certain what their relationship could be called, but it certainly wasn't husband and wife. She wouldn't pamper him by playing a role they both knew to be false.

*   *   *

Tyler had to walk across sleeping bodies in the hall by the time he returned to the hotel. He was drenched to the skin and had survived the day on little more than black coffee and the flapjacks he'd had that morning. There was only one thing on his mind at the moment, and that was getting out of these clothes and into bed with Evie.

He had his coat and hat off and was starting on his shirt by the time he reached her room. Ever since he had returned from that federal prison camp to learn he no longer had a home or family, he had turned his back on the life he had known and created a new one. There wasn't any place in that life for a wife and children, but there was always a place for a woman in his bed. As long as he thought of Evie like that, he would do just fine.

The room was dark and silent when he entered, but Tyler hadn't expected anything else. It was late. He dropped his coat and hat on the floor, and stripped off the soaked shirt. He could see the outline of the dressing screen near the window, and he started for that, knowing he would find the washstand and towels there. He stumbled over an unexpected object, and his hand caught on the back of a chair that hadn't been there this morning.

Eyes adjusting to the dark, he glanced down to a pair of blanket-wrapped legs. He followed the blanket upward to thick chestnut hair falling over a white-clad shoulder huddled on a pillow laying over another chair arm. He knew only one woman in this world with hair as thick as that. Evie.

Cursing silently, Tyler sat down and removed his boots, then tiptoed to the bed. He didn't think Evie was the type to give up the comfort of her bed just to get even with him for some imagined wrong. He looked down at three sleeping heads and ran his hand through his hair. He hadn't known she was the mothering type, either, but then, there was a hell of a lot he didn't know about Miss Evie Peyton.

He didn't like having those children in here. He didn't want anything to do with children. But he could see where she couldn't put them out for the night. Silently, Tyler went behind the screen and stripped off the rest of his clothes. He didn't even have a clean shirt in here. He hadn't planned on an extended stay in town. His beard itched, and he wanted a hot bath. Most of all, he wanted Evie in a warm bed. He didn't know how to correct any of that.

He couldn't wander around naked in front of children, but he sure as hell wasn't going to put those wet clothes back on, either. Remembering Evie's trunk of linens, Tyler pulled on his wet pants and crept back out to look for it. She'd left it open for him, and he helped himself. There was something to be said about a woman who came prepared.

Deciding if he couldn't have a warm bed he was going to make do with the willing woman, Tyler left his pants on the floor, tucked the sheet around his hips, and came to stand beside Evie's sleeping figure. She couldn't be that sound asleep in that position. Lifting her gently, he slid into the chair and settled her on his lap.

Evie woke instantly. Tyler smothered her gasp with his fingers. She wriggled around to stare at him and discovered immediately where she was sitting. He chuckled as she tried to scoot away. The chair wasn't big enough for either of them to go anywhere but where they were.

Tyler pulled her blanket up around her shoulders. "I'm cold and hungry, wife. What do you mean to do about it?"

Evie knew she was occasionally naive, but she wasn't dumb. The hunger he talked about had nothing to do with food. She had managed to prop her buttocks against his thigh, but even so, she could feel him stirring beneath her. There were layers of material between them, but Tyler's hands were already roaming beneath the blanket, pulling at her rumpled nightgown.

"Find you a hot chocolate?" she asked sweetly.

"Best idea I've heard all day. I'm ready for chocolate now."

Tyler's mouth closed over hers, and Evie drowned in the taste and heat of him. She could smell whiskey on his breath, but he was far from drunk. His fingers were sure and accomplished as they moved along her thigh, now bare of any encumbrance. Instead of sliding into the

warmth of her as she had expected, they stroked her
backside, applying pressures that had her writhing as
surely as if he had stroked her elsewhere. Evie wanted
to cry out, but Tyler's mouth had prior claims, and her
tongue entangled with his as his hands worked their
magic.

"The children!" she whispered frantically as she felt
his sheet go the way of her nightgown and skin brushed
tingling skin.

"Practice being quiet," he replied as he turned her so
her breasts brushed against his chest.

Her knees were on either side of his thighs, and Evie
could feel him rubbing against her. She couldn't believe
she was doing this, but as Tyler unfastened her gown
and bent his head to tug at her breast, she didn't stop
to think what she was doing. In Tyler's arms, everything
was sensation. There wasn't time for thought.

His hands lifted her breasts and pulled her upward
so he could suckle them at leisure. Then they drifted
downward, circling her waist, sliding over her hips until
he cupped her firmly, bringing her closer.

Evie gave a muffled cry as his hands opened her over
him. The word "Tyler!" escaped in a breathless rush before his lips closed tenderly over hers, and then he was
in her, and around her, and pushing her wildly to that
brilliant horizon he had shown her the night before.

She was ready, more than ready for him. Pulling her
mouth away from his, she bit his neck in an effort to be
quiet. Tyler groaned and buried himself deeper, pulling
her down hard and long until she bucked against him in
frustration. He let her go, letting her make the moves,
but responding with a wildness that his controlled perfor-
mances of the night before had kept in line.

Evie remembered the wildness from the first time, only
this time it wasn't pain that it brought but rapture. She
wanted to scream with the pleasure of it. She wanted to
scream with the sheer frustration of having to be quiet.
She wanted to bury herself inside of him, take him
deeper, find that place where they could each enter the
other's skins and become one. She knew it was there,
she could sense it, feel it coming closer, and she rocked

and rode him in desperate search for what she was being denied.

In the end, it was too much for both of them. The children stirring in the bed put an edge on the pleasure. Tyler caught Evie's lips and branded them with his kiss while his fingers found the place that would give her release. She convulsed around him, and he gave a smothered cry of relief as he pushed deeper and finally gave up his seed. She was still hot and pulsing and he wanted to do it again, but they would have to wait for another night. Gently, Tyler eased Evie's legs around so she could stretch them free once more.

She fell asleep on his shoulder almost at once. Tyler stayed awake awhile longer.

He had seen the initials on her pillowcases. EPH. He didn't even know what the Evie stood for. And Maryellen had nothing to do with the "H." She had been a virgin; he knew that. So she couldn't have been married before, could she? So who in hell was the "H"?

In the morning, he was going to have a long talk with his wife. After they got rid of the kids.

Chapter 19

"Thtop it, Hothay," a tiny voice whispered indignantly. A rustle of bedcovers and a giggle followed.

Evie stirred. The whispers continued. "Stop it, both of you" came from a properly horrified Carmen. Evie wiped her eyes.

And realized where she was. Tyler was practically snoring in her ear, and he was jaybird naked beneath the blanket. She was lying across his bare thighs, and her fingers were curled in the hairs on his chest. Opening her eyes cautiously, she got a glimpse of his two-day beard and decided she had finally hit rock bottom. She was lying in the arms of a naked gambler with children tussling in the bed across from them.

At least there wasn't any liquor on the premises. She may have behaved like a drunken wanton, but she hadn't been drunk. Evie wasn't certain that was anything to be proud of. She grimaced as she moved her sticky thighs and tried to pull her nightgown down around her and keep Tyler covered at the same time. It wasn't an easy maneuver, but she managed it.

He was stirring by the time she got her feet to the floor, but she made a hasty dash for the dressing screen. This was not at all as she had pictured married life from her chaste bed in Nanny's house.

As she stripped off her nightgown, Evie gazed in dismay at the stains of red on the fragile lawn and the dried stains on her thighs. She scrubbed in the fresh water she had brought up last night, but the evidence didn't disappear with washing. She was bleeding.

Hastily supplying herself with a cloth and dressing in yesterday's underclothes since she'd not had the forethought to put fresh ones behind the screen, Evie wrapped herself in her robe, pulled a brush through her hair, and exited to see if she could keep the children from waking Tyler entirely.

It was too late. Maria had escaped while Carmen was busy trying to keep José from ransacking open trunks. The toddler had happily climbed up on the mountain of blankets and sheets that was Tyler and perched herself with a finger-sucking grin in his lap. Tyler scowled back at her through bleary eyes and stubbled jaw, but Maria only added a second finger to the first and continued to peruse him with wide-eyed wonder.

Tyler growled as Evie hurried to relieve him of his unwanted burden. Jerking the blanket around him, he rose with uncertain dignity and took advantage of the dressing screen while Carmen politely kept her back turned. If the fourteen-year-old thought it odd to wake and find a man in her teacher's room, she was too polite to mention it.

Evie flung Tyler's still-damp pants and shirt over the screen to him. It wouldn't do any good to go next door to Daniel for dry ones. Tyler would bust the seams just trying to get them on. He should have thought of that while out playing hero the day before.

Maria's tiny gown was dry if spectacularly wrinkled, and Evie busied herself pulling that on the toddler as she listened to Tyler splashing clean water into the washbowl. Would he notice? What was he going to say? If she weren't so terrified, she would be hideously embarrassed. Would he think she lied? Of course he would.

José made a dash for the door, and Evie caught him by the collar just before he could escape. He wriggled and hollered, "I gotta go! I gotta go!" while she held him.

Tyler stepped out from behind the screen, menacing in his height and in his appearance, and the youngster silenced at once. The rough beard and wrinkled clothes made him appear more an outlaw than a handsome gambler, and when he reached for José, even Evie had second thoughts about letting him go. The look Tyler gave her was sufficient to release him.

"The privy is underwater," he rumbled as he deposited the boy behind the screen with the chamber pot. "Use that. That's what it's there for."

Having solved that minor problem, Tyler turned a stony look to Evie. So he knew. The color drained from Evie's face as he glared at her, and when he jerked his head in the direction of the door, she nodded faintly and followed him out.

The children's racket had apparently roused the guests sleeping in the hall, for the bodies he had stumbled over last night had disappeared elsewhere. They had the hall to themselves. Tyler watched as Evie pressed herself against the wall, trying to become part of the wallpaper.

"Have I done something to the child?" he demanded in a low voice that didn't sound as if he believed his own question. He rested his hand above her head, preventing her from escaping easily.

He was giving her an easy out. The lies came swiftly and surely to mind. She could tell him the doctor had warned her it would be a difficult pregnancy, but she hadn't wanted to worry him. She could tell him there was a history of miscarriage in her family. She had heard enough women's talk to make up a dozen different lies, each one better than the next, particularly since she didn't think Tyler knew all that much about pregnant women. The worst of it all was that she wasn't even sure what was the truth. Evie struggled with her conscience and fear.

"I don't know," she finally answered. That was as close to the truth as she could come.

Tyler scowled, but there was an element of worry in it this time. "Should I find the doctor?"

Evie shook her head, embarrassed at the idea. "There's no pain," she whispered.

Tyler removed his hand from the wall and stood in front of her, hands hooked in his front pockets as he stared down at her. "Could you have just been late?"

She was so embarrassed she thought she would burn right through the floor in another minute. She should have known that Tyler would know more about women's things than she did. A practiced womanizer would have to know. "It's possible," she admitted. "It's never happened before."

Tyler sighed and rolled his shoulders back, looking anywhere else but at the confounded woman in front of him. He wanted to blame her. He did blame her. She should have known better. But so should he have. And he had been the one to press the point. He was still so angry he could spit, and getting angrier by the minute. He clenched his hands against his pants.

"I'll go find some coffee. What do I get for those birds in there?" He threw a grudging jerk of his head in the direction of the bedroom door.

Evie closed her eyes and tried to breathe deeply. He'd had her almost fainting with fear. "Milk, if anyone has some. Fruit, if you can. There's nowhere to cook anything."

Tyler nodded curtly and stalked off. Evie peeled herself from the wall and stared after him. Her knees were still trembling. He was furious, she could tell by the set of his shoulders. He was furious, but he hadn't taken it out on her. She ought to count her blessings.

She hurried back into the room to find Carmen regarding her curiously, but she was in no humor for answering questions. She sent the children scurrying for clothes while she searched out something new to wear. She wanted something frivolous, something defiantly gay. Her choices were growing limited. She needed a laundry. There was little chance of Tyler helping them out now. She would be lucky if he didn't ride out of town by sundown.

Pulling out a sultry blue-gray silk with an almost immodest neckline, Evie grinned in triumph. It was then that José knocked over the water bowl and Maria fell down in it, screaming her lungs out. By the time Evie had grabbed up the little girl and comforted her, prevented Carmen from boxing her brother's ears, and restored order once more, she decided silk wasn't precisely the thing to wear today. She was beginning to have some idea why the women in town with children didn't wear anything but aprons and cotton.

She didn't own an apron, and her cottons were a far

cry from the gingham and stripes of the town matrons, but Evie pulled out one of her schoolteacher gowns and made do. It didn't require a bustle or a hoop, and the dove gray would stand up to attack by a two-year-old. She would at least look clean and unrumpled for a while. Glancing at the loose gold ring on her finger, she carefully set it in her jewelry box. She wouldn't want to lose that; Tyler might want it back.

She went to look in on Daniel and found him engrossed in a deadly game of checkers with Manuel. Neither of them paid her much notice, other than to complain that they were hungry. Evie glanced out the window, found that the water had almost retreated to mud-puddle level, and left them to the battle. It was time she found out what had happened to Mrs. Rodriguez.

Benjamin was carrying the tray upstairs as she started down. Evie had him set it down in Daniel's room and explained her problem. She wasn't about to ask where Tyler had gone. Maybe if they pretended this whole thing hadn't happened, it would go away.

Benjamin gave her a look that said he knew more than he was telling, but he agreed to go looking for Mrs. Rodriguez. After questioning Carmen, he set out, leaving the children to their noisy meal together.

Tyler didn't return. When the sun came out and set the spongy mud and puddles of the main street to steaming, Evie finally gave Manuel permission to check their home for clean clothes. He came back with tales of a snake in the rafters and mud over everything, and Evie's heart plunged a little lower. What was she going to do with these children?

She owed a gown and an explanation to Starr, but there wasn't a chance of going to her under the circumstances. Starr would certainly understand, but Evie could use the money the other woman had promised for the gowns. Eventually, somebody would come collecting for these rooms, and she didn't have the cash for both.

As the day wore on, Evie kept telling herself to be grateful that she wasn't pregnant. Watching Maria and José jumping on the bed and Manuel running up and down the staircase on mysterious errands, she was doubly grateful that she wasn't pregnant. She had always got along well with children, but children needed the firm hand and discipline that only a father could provide. Tyler was never going to be that father.

Jason Harding appeared late in the afternoon, hat in hand. He asked to speak to Evie alone, and when they were out of hearing of the children, he offered her a chair he appropriated from a nearby room.

"You'd better tell me straight out, Mr. Harding. After these last few days, my nerves aren't likely to take much hemming and hawing," she told him bluntly.

"There isn't anything to tell you straight out. We found the place where Mrs. Rodriguez went Friday night, but they say she left early in the evening." Jason's solemn face hovered near, his eyes a kind gray as he watched her carefully.

Evie twisted her fingers in her lap, thinking of the four rambunctious children bouncing around in the rooms overhead. Mrs. Rodriguez would not have left them alone all this time willingly. She knew what Jason was trying to say.

"How do people usually cross the river?" she asked quietly.

"It's usually so low, a horse can cross it."

"And Mrs. Rodriguez had a horse?"

Jason nodded slowly. "It was part of the deal when she sold the livery. Tom had to supply her with a horse whenever she needed it."

"And the horse isn't back, either, is it?" At Jason's shake of the head, Evie sighed. That was that, then. Mrs. Rodriguez had tried to cross the river to get back to her children. Somewhere, far down stream, they would find her body one of these days, if the coyotes and buzzards didn't get there first.

"Do they have any relatives in the area?"

Jason twisted his hat thoughtfully. "Rodriguez wasn't from around here. I don't know his family at all. Angelina grew up here. I don't remember the family name right off; I was just a boy when her folks died. She had a brother, I recollect. He went off to California to find gold. I don't know if she kept in touch. You might ask the kids."

Evie assimilated this progression of facts and stood up. "Thank you, Mr. Harding. Have you checked the school yet? Will it be in any condition for use tomorrow?"

"I'm sending some of my men over to clean it out. It may be a week or so before we ought to put school back in session. There's too many need the children at home right now."

Evie was afraid to ask what that would mean to her pay. The money she had earned at the school in St. Louis had been so insignificant to her that she had never questioned when it came or how. She didn't have the experience to negotiate her way through these channels now that it was her only income.

"All right. If you don't mind, I'll help the children clean out their house tomorrow. I can't keep them here for very long. What will happen to them if we can't find their uncle?"

"Don't worry about it yet, Mrs. Peyton. If nothing else, the two oldest can find work and the youngest can go to good families. Let's take it one step at a time."

Jason Harding had all the tact of a buffalo. Evie held her temper since he was her boss in a manner of speaking, but she gave him a look that made him take a step backward. The fact that she didn't come up to his chin and was half his breadth had no effect on the fury blazing in her eyes. "You'll separate those children over my dead body, Mr. Harding. They need each other now more than ever before. Try thinking what it would be like without your own brother."

Swinging on her heel and stalking off before she could say more, Evie was halfway up the stairs before she realized Harding had called her Mrs. Peyton. Tyler hadn't told him of their marriage.

She didn't know whether that was good or bad. She didn't know how he could disguise the fact since the preacher traveled through here regularly. Ben and Daniel might keep their mouths shut if ordered, but what would that prove? They were still married, legally and in the eyes of the church. Closing their eyes to the truth wouldn't solve anything.

But she had too many other things on her mind to worry about that one right now. Tyler Monteigne could wait for another day.

Tyler wasn't in any humor to wait for another day. He had spent the day shoveling mud out of John's café and hauling supplies so there would be food to eat that night. He had struggled with his fury and nearly floored Ben for suggesting they check on Evie and the children at lunch. The battle between his conscience and his anger had taken more strength than the donkey work of cleaning and hauling. By the end of the day, he was too exhausted to think.

But by the end of the day, his feet automatically turned back to the hotel. He wouldn't think "home." He didn't have a home, didn't want a home, didn't need a home. Coming to Texas had stirred him out of the rut he had fallen into in Natchez. He had always planned to travel. He had taken a few trips up and down the Mississippi, but he had seldom seen more than the card tables of the steamboat cabin. Now he meant to see the country. He'd settle things here and be moving on when he'd seen enough.

Evie would understand. He'd buy her a divorce in Houston. He'd heard it could be done. If no one knew they were married, then no one could complain of the scandal. She'd be as relieved as he, he was certain. It might take a bit of a bribe to make the Reverend Cleveland understand, but Tyler suspected it could be done. The preacher would be out riding circuit shortly anyway. When he came back, Tyler would be gone, a ninety-day wonder. A man of the cloth would be too sympathetic to say anything aloud.

Wiping his dirty face wearily, Tyler knocked at Evie's door. It wasn't home if you had to knock, he reasoned. He could hear them in there. Why didn't they answer? With a scowl, he threw open the door.

The first thing he noticed was the enormous bouquet Evie had created out of the flowers he had given her.

They made a spray of color on the dull wall over the bed where she had carefully placed them on a shelf out of reach of little hands.

The next thing he noticed was the youngest boy scampering back into place behind the baby and in front of the next oldest boy. The girl and Evie stood behind them. Once the wanderer was in place, they beamed and began to sing about "Wayfarin' Strangers."

If that was supposed to mean him, Tyler wasn't impressed. The scent of fresh bread made his gaze wander to a table beside the window. There hadn't been a table there this morning. A damask tablecloth covered what looked to be a plank braced up by four flat-topped trunks. Candles flickered in a silver candelabra. Bowls of fine china were set out, and he was more than certain that the kettle sitting on the dresser contained soup or stew. He was starved.

And they were still singing. For him. The table had been set for him, too, he realized. Panic began to rise in Tyler's throat. Childish voices rose in tremolo, and Tyler took a step backward. The baby grinned and broke rank, toddling in his direction. José reached for her, and the whole ensemble crumbled into chaos at his feet. Sweat broke out on his forehead as Tyler saw Evie coming forward, a frown of confusion marring her lovely face as she wiped her hands on the towel at her waist.

"I came to tell you I'm heading back for the ranch," Tyler announced loudly—too loudly—over the heads of the children. And before anyone could say otherwise, he backed out the door. "I'll see you next Saturday."

And he was gone.

Chapter 20

"He bolted like a wild stallion with the paddock gate left open," Evie complained the next day. She wasn't entirely certain her audience was sympathetic, but she needed an understanding ear.

Since Daniel had been there when she had discovered the children's musical talent and used it to keep them occupied instead of worrying about their mother, he didn't need to ask why Evie had greeted Tyler with a chorus of children. Ben looked at her as if she were crazed.

He scratched his black head and shook it with amazement. "You ain't got a clue, do you? That man's dead-set against having any ties at all, and you give him a room full of them all at once. I'll be lucky to find any trace of him at all after that. Sorry, Miss Evie, but you plumb picked the wrong man when you picked Tyler. He didn't used to be that way, but the war kicked it all out of him."

"I didn't pick the blasted man; he picked me." Indignantly, Evie kicked a chair leg. "He could fall off the face of the earth for all I care. I just wanted to know if he was demented or something."

"Or something might cover it," Ben agreed grimly.

"Fine, then. The children and I are going over to clean their house. Unless one of their relatives shows up soon, I'll be over there for a while. Carmen can't look after them all the time." Evie threw open the door and walked out without the usual rustle of silk. She was wearing the same dress she had worn the day before.

Ben raised his eyebrows at Daniel in unspoken question.

Daniel shrugged uncomfortably. "You never can tell with Evie. She lives in a world of her own most of the time. I wish I could get out of this bed. She needs someone with her."

"They ain't much interested in breaking mustangs when the branding is going on. I think I'll hang around awhile. Looks to me like the man at the livery could use a little help." Ben ignored the relief in the boy's eyes, put his hat on, and wandered out.

Following Ben's direction, Kyle Harding appeared at the little house behind the livery about midday. His eyes widened with amazement as he watched a boy with a fresh snakeskin wrapped about his middle climb up on a stack of crates and sweep the uncovered rafters with a long-handled broom. He continued to stare as a young girl used a shovel to heave the mud's debris out the open back door while carrying a dark-haired toddler on her hip. But mostly his gaze followed the beautiful schoolteacher he had last seen in satins and lace and who now wore a sadly bedraggled gray gown hitched up between her legs to expose her mud-covered stockings as she scoured an iron stove on her knees.

A younger boy came up from behind Kyle, barreling through the doorway practically between his knees and sliding across the wet floor with a whoop as he dropped a pitiful, yowling cat at the schoolteacher's feet. The woman Kyle knew as Mrs. Peyton looked at the poor creature and immediately began to towel it off with her makeshift apron.

It was only then that she noticed Kyle standing in the doorway. She gave him a surprised glance and continued toweling the complaining cat as she greeted him. "Good afternoon, Mr. Harding. Are you looking for someone?"

"You, as a matter of fact. I had to come in for supplies, and Jace told me to look in on you, said you had a handful after the flood. He thought maybe I ought to offer to bring you out to the ranch for a while, until things are cleaned up better here. The branding is keeping us all pretty busy, but there's more than enough room at the house."

Evie wanted to ask if Tyler were there and what he had to say about that, but she merely smiled and returned the indignant cat to its feet. "That's kind of you, Mr. Harding, and you can thank your brother for me, too, but someone needs to look after the children. I'm not much inclined to sitting around while everyone else is working."

"I can see that." He hesitated there in the doorway, seeing the amount of work yet to be done in just this one room. He ventured to say the back rooms were worse. His glance returned to the schoolteacher's smiling face, the wickedly dark eyes and tempting lips, and he knew Jace didn't need him at the branding as much as this woman needed him here. He began rolling up his sleeves. "Let me haul that table back where it belongs for you. It's too big for a woman to handle."

The overturned table thrown against the back wall by the flood was quickly restored to its proper position in front of the fireplace. Under Carmen's direction, Kyle was soon righting furniture in the other rooms and hauling soaked mattresses out to air. Evie watched him with laughter on her lips and continued directing the boys to search out unwanted animal life with brooms. Much of the mud on the floors went out the door with their efforts.

Ben wandered over in curiosity later that day and found himself chopping empty crates and broken boards for firewood. The wood dried quickly over a smoldering tinder fire. Before he could escape, he was coerced into nailing a bed back together while smells of cooking began to lace the air in the front room.

The sheriff stopped by as they were preparing to put dinner on the table, and Evie deliberately sent the two boys out of the house with a covered tray for Daniel. When they were gone, she offered Sheriff Powell a cup of coffee and made Carmen sit down in one of the kitchen chairs that still had four legs.

"What have you found, Mr. Powell?" Exhausted, Evie was in no humor for male equivocations. The truth might be painful, but it was better than knowing nothing and suspecting everything. She knew that from experience.

The sheriff glanced nervously at dark-eyed Carmen sitting in the chair, following his every word. An infant version of her sat in her lap, watching him solemnly, and his gaze returned to the schoolteacher. For an instant, he saw a certain similarity in their dark-lashed, exotically shaped eyes, but he shook his head and the image went away. Mrs. Petyon had the peach-and-cream complexion of a Southern lady. The children had the olive complexions of Mexicans. There could be no resemblance.

"We found the remains of a horse we think belongs to the livery. Tom thinks it's the one Mrs. Rodriguez took out that night. It doesn't look good. There were Indians camping in that area right before the flood. We're looking for them now, but we think they were reservation Indians and had no place being there. They won't be easy to find."

Carmen shivered and a tear glittered briefly in her eye, but when Maria patted her face with chubby hands, she straightened and began feeding the child small pieces of the tortilla growing cold on the table. Evie's heart nearly broke at the sight, and she wiped away a hasty tear of her own.

"Thank you, Sheriff. Carmen has an address for her uncle. We're going to send a telegram in the morning. I'm going to take the children back to the hotel again tonight, but I think once the house is returned to order, I'm going to have to move in with them. I'd appreciate it if you'd let me know of anyone who can help me move my trunks. I can't pay much . . ."

Kyle intruded. "I'll make certain there's someone back to help. What about your brother, ma'am? I understand he's laid up."

Evie glanced around the small house uncertainly. It had three rooms instead of the two they were living in at the hotel, but it wasn't her house. She made a helpless gesture. "We'll have to see. I need to talk to Daniel and the doctor. He's still in a lot of pain, and I don't want to hurt him by moving him too soon."

One by one the men departed, calling promises and reassurances, until Evie was left alone with Carmen and the baby. The boys evidently intended to entertain Daniel through supper. The two women exchanged glances.

"I can go to work, but what will happen to the children?" Carmen whispered as she helped Maria sip from a glass of milk.

If they didn't discuss her mother's death, they could discuss the facts of their current existence without grief. Grief would come later. Right now, they had to find some way to survive. Evie understood that, and she wove her fingers together and tried to think.

"The school term will be over in a few months. I want you all to finish it out. I have a little money for food, and if I can move Daniel out of the hotel, there should be enough for everyone. By the time school is out, your uncle may have come. We won't worry about looking for jobs until then. We'll just need someone to mind Maria while you attend class."

She would have to sell every evening gown in her collection to have enough money to pay for food for all of them, but it wasn't much of a sacrifice. She didn't need the gowns anymore. These children were more important. Evie knew what it felt like to be an orphan.

They were a silent troupe that night when they returned to the hotel. With the children in bed, Evie and Daniel discussed alternatives. Neither of them mentioned Tyler. He hadn't been the one to come to help. He hadn't even been the one to ask if they needed any. Evie went to bed that night in her chair without glancing at the flowers that were already beginning to fade, all except the paper roses.

By the end of the week her hands were raw from scrubbing, her knees were sore from spending so many hours on them, but the Rodriguez house was clean and liveable again. With additions from Evie's trunks and donations from some of the townspeople, there were beds and linens enough for everyone, and fancy china in the cupboards for eating. A surreptitious trip to the rooms over the saloon had procured a healthy purse for food and Starr's admonitions about men and their company.

Evie was carefully tying the purse of coins to her inside

pocket when Starr caught her arm and forced her to look up at her.

"What did you decide to do about that baby?" she demanded without any preface.

Too exhausted even to be embarrassed, Evie faced her without flinching. "There wasn't any. It was a mistake."

Starr looked relieved. "Well, then, you'd better do something so that mistake doesn't happen again. Tyler ain't the kind of man to stay away once he stakes his claim. You'd better let me teach you a few things before you wind up in the family way for certain."

The mention of Tyler's name sent Evie's stomach plummeting to her feet. She stared at the beautiful saloon girl, unable to get past her knowledge of Tyler to listen to what else was being said. "Why do you think Tyler's the one?" she asked in what she hoped wasn't a desperate whisper.

Starr grinned. "When a man as handsome as that one comes into town with money in his pocket and doesn't find his way to my bed, I know he's got something good going on the side. It doesn't take a genius to figure out who that can be. The two of you came here together, didn't you?"

Tyler hadn't been with Starr. Evie stared at her with wonder and relief and didn't bother to answer. She hoped no one else had put two and two together as quickly as Starr had, but then, Starr was the only one to know her predicament.

"I'd better be getting back to the children," Evie replied irrelevantly.

Starr shook her head and wouldn't let her go. "Not until I tell you about vinegar and sponges and what to do after. I don't even want to know how that man talked you into his bed, but if he hasn't got the sense to marry you, then you don't want to be carrying his baby."

Evie didn't think there was much chance of that. Tyler would stay far away from her now that he knew he was safe from fatherhood. But she wasn't averse to a little knowledge. She had always wondered how prostitutes managed to sin without retribution. The information might be useful sometime.

When Starr was done with her, Evie was quite certain that she never wanted to sleep with another man again if that was what she would have to go through. But she thanked Starr politely, offered to send her a pie as soon as they got in supplies, and hurried back to the little house she was slowly making into her home.

When she counted Starr's money later, Evie discovered it was more than they had originally agreed on, but for the sake of the children, she wasn't going to argue. Carmen had showed a distinct aptitude for doing laundry and had nearly washed all the children's clothes that Evie had thought were lost to the damage of the flood. That saved them the expense of buying clothing as well as laundering her own and Daniel's things. For that reason alone she was willing to allow Carmen freedom to buy whatever groceries she thought were needed. She wouldn't begrudge her a dime.

Daniel chose to move in with them. Evie wasn't certain if he thought he was protecting them with his presence or if he just wanted to be closer to Carmen, but she was grateful for his company and his common sense. Although he grumbled and complained and refused to listen when she told him he was trying to do too much too soon, he also kept the boys entertained in the evening and gave them something to do besides roaming the street looking for trouble.

They divided the two bedrooms up between the girls and the boys, with Daniel and Evie having their own cots in each room and the children sharing a bigger bed. It was almost like having a home again, and Evie practically forgot about their other problems. The lawyer's absence nagged at the back of her mind, but Tyler's absence was much more demanding.

With her nest nicely feathered and anticipating no other trouble, Evie staggered slightly and clasped her chest in surprise when José came running and screaming through the door one day at the end of the week. Ben had just gone back to the ranch, and Kyle Harding hadn't been back since he finished helping her with the moving. She was expecting him today or tomorrow, but it was too early for him now. Daniel was sound asleep in the

back room, and he was helpless anyway. Whatever José
was screaming about was going to have to be handled
without the help of any man. Evie lowered her hand and
tried to follow José's excited yells.

"He's hurting Manuel! Help him, please. Hurry!" José
darted back out the door again.

Carmen came racing in from the front bedroom where
she had been putting Maria down for a nap. Evie gestured for her to remain and grabbing up the closest thing
she had to a weapon—an iron skillet—she ran after José.

She didn't have far to run. In the street just outside
the livery a nearly bald-headed man with muscles twice
the size of any man Evie had ever seen grappled with a
boy dangling from his hands like so much straw. Manuel
was putting up a valiant fight, kicking and screaming and
swinging his feet, but with his arms caught in vises, he
couldn't cause much damage.

"Put that boy down at once, sir!" The skillet forgotten,
Evie stood outraged before the giant.

"He stole my money, and I want it back." The man
shoved both Manuel's arms into one massive grip and
reached for the boy's kicking, squirming leg.

"I did not! I did not. Let me go!" Manuel kicked backward, narrowly missing a vulnerable part of his captor's
anatomy. The man swore vigorously and shook him.

"José, go get the sheriff, pronto!" Evie demanded,
knowing the boy was there without looking for him. Remembering the skillet, she shook it in the man's face,
although her reach was decidedly extended to do so.
"Put him down this instant! If he stole money, the sheriff
will decide what to do with him. You have no right to
touch him."

"I didn't, Miz Peyton. Honest, I didn't." Manuel was
nearly weeping, although he was trying valiantly not to.

"Peyton? You Peyton's daughter? Where is that bastard? I've been trying to track him down for years." The
giant lowered Manuel slightly, as if he had forgotten the
boy while he confronted the furious, slender woman in
his path.

Stunned by the direction of the attack, Evie could
only stutter. She wanted to know more about a man

named Peyton, too, but she certainly didn't want to turn this beast's rage on her. Her creative abilities lagged behind her greater fear for Manuel. "I'm not telling you anything until you put that boy down, sir. I insist you release him at once. You ought to be ashamed of yourself, picking on a child."

As if remembering what he held in his hand, the man abruptly turned the boy up by his heels and began shaking him. Manuel screamed, and Evie rushed in with her skillet, slamming it as hard as she could against the giant's broad side. He roared and swung one fist backward to knock her away as another man would a fly.

The click of a six-gun could scarcely be heard over the commotion, but the man's voice following it was cold and clear and deadly.

"I'd suggest you put that boy down very gently, mister. And if you've hurt the lady, you'd better come around with your gun in your hand."

Caught off balance dodging the blow, Evie staggered and righted herself and swung to stare incredulously at the man standing on the other side of the giant, aiming a pistol at the man's back.

Tyler.

Chapter 21

Evie's words might have failed her, but her wits had not. She did what any sensible woman would have done when her husband put himself in danger of being shot down by a giant bully. She screamed.

She screamed when the man dropped Manuel. And she screamed as she swung her skillet with all her might and nearly took the man's gun hand off before he could reach for his holster. And she screamed when Tyler jumped on the man's back and caught his neck in a stranglehold as the giant tried to reach for Evie. That last scream was just for good measure. Evie was quite certain Tyler had the man well in hand as she swung her skillet at her attacker's kneecaps.

The man went down with a bellow of rage and pain. Tyler went with him, pinning his knee in the hollow of the man's back and jerking his head backward until his captive could no more than gurgle a protest.

"Don't kill him, Tyler," Evie told him calmly. "He says his money's been stolen. José has gone for the sheriff." She turned a thoughtful look on Manuel who had forgotten his own peril in the excitement, and was now bouncing up and down with glee and offering murderous threats.

He stopped bouncing when he caught Evie's look.

"Why did that man think you stole his money?" she asked with a deceptive calm.

"Evie, for Christ's sake, that can wait. Get this brute's gun and let me get him out of here." Tyler threw her an exasperated glance over his shoulder.

By this time a small crowd had gathered. Most of them were women who had been shopping in the general store, but one of the clerks came out and was busy snapping his suspenders while watching the proceedings, and Phil from the hotel had sauntered over to see the fun. Neither of them seemed much interested in helping until Evie bent over and removed the stranger's gun. Then they grabbed his arms and held them so Tyler could get up and dust himself off.

By the time the sheriff made his way through the crowd, Tyler was returning to his normal dapper self. He straightened his string tie, pulled his ruffled cuffs into place, checked the buttons on his expensive brocade waistcoat, and glared daggers at Evie.

Evie was more concerned with the boy whose collar she held as he tried to make a dash through the crowd. "Manuel, I want the truth now. If you didn't do it, I want to know why that man thought you did."

"Because I'm a greaser, that's why!" the boy spat out with anger and shame. "Anything goes wrong, and they always point the blame at me."

"A greaser?" Evie lifted a questioning gaze to Tyler, who shrugged, then to the sheriff who came in for the last of this conversation.

Powell offered the explanation she sought. "A Mex. They're considered lower than a snake's belly around these parts. You got to know the history, Mrs. Peyton. During the war, the Mexicans would lie and connive and shoot a man as soon as his back was turned. Some consider them worse than red devils."

Red devils. Indians. Evie sighed and gave Tyler another glance, but his mouth was pursed tight with disapproval, and she couldn't tell whether it was for this prejudice or for herself. She donned her sweetest smile and turned it on the sheriff.

"Why, I believe my father was of Spanish origin, Mr. Powell. I guess that means I'm a greaser, too. But I like to think of myself as a schoolteacher. Manuel"—the tone of her voice changed, and the boy straightened obediently—"you are an eleven-year-old boy with a talent for trouble, but if anyone calls you a greaser again, I give you my permission to hit him where it hurts. And then hit him one for me, too. Is that understood?"

Manuel stared at her as if she had lost her mind, but he nodded eagerly enough. The people around them were staring, too, but the schoolteacher stood there as cool as a sip of water, her chestnut hair piled in sophisticated curls and ringlets above a slender neck bearing no stain of Mexican origin, her expensive skirts spreading in a wide pool over a lady's hoops, and her smile as pleasant as a gentle summer day. They didn't know what to make of her.

Tyler did. She was a liar, pure and simple, but the lie had been extremely efficacious. She wasn't Mexican or Spanish any more than he was, but the sheriff was questioning the boy with considerable more gentleness than he would have otherwise.

"I was in the livery," Manuel explained defensively. "It used to be my pa's, and Tom lets me work there sometimes. But I didn't take nothing."

The sheriff turned to the giant still held captive by Phil and the clerk. Rage burned in the man's eyes, but it wasn't directed at Manuel or even his two captors right now. It was directed at Tyler and Evie.

"Where were you carrying the money and when did you last see it?" the sheriff asked his prisoner.

"It was in my saddlebag, and I last saw it when I put it there. Those bags were in the livery with my horse when I went over to the saloon. That's the only time they were out of my sight. I just want the money back. I ain't gonna press charges 'gainst no whippersnapper."

"Manuel, turn your pockets out." It was a silly gesture, but it was the only way Evie could convince the sheriff Manuel wasn't responsible. The boy was reed slim and wearing clothes two sizes too small for him. Anyone with half an eye could see he couldn't be carrying wads of money.

The boy did as told and the crowd murmured their approval. There was nothing in his pockets but a small penknife and a marble.

The sheriff turned to Evie and Tyler. "You want to press any charges?"

Evie could feel Tyler stiffening with anger as he remembered how the bully had swung at her, but she hadn't been hurt, and she caught his arm and spoke first. "I think we're even. There's no sense pressing charges. Maybe someone ought to help him search the livery and see if his money fell out somewhere."

Once the giant was released, he didn't give them a second glance. He walked immediately to the stables, and several of the townspeople followed out of curiosity. If there was money in the straw, everyone would like to find it. Evie watched him go almost with regret. He knew something about a man named Peyton. It was an unusual name. She had always wondered why her parents had given it to her instead of something normal like Maryellen. Maybe they were trying to tell her something.

Tyler caught her look and growled, catching her arm and leading her away. "Don't you even think it. Spanish! Christ, Evie, you're going to tell one tale too many one of these days, and people are going to quit believing anything you say."

"Watch your language, Tyler. I won't have the children learning blasphemy." Evie watched as Manuel and José scampered ahead. The little brats knew that livery inside and out. She had no doubt that they were heading for some secret passage or hiding place right now. If she found they had been stealing from people's saddlebags, she was going to have a rough time ahead. She hoped their uncle received the cable Carmen had sent days ago.

"To hell with blasphemy! Ben tells me you've moved in with those brats. I know that's not what you came here for. Are you planning to settle here? Or are you just waiting for that lawyer to get back? I heard Jace tell Kyle that Hale's wired them that he'll be back shortly."

Evie caught her skirt and stared up at Tyler with suppressed excitement. The lawyer! She would know something soon now. Her eyes danced with delight, but she replied coyly, "Why, I daresay that depends on you, my husband. Whither thou goest, so should I, shouldn't I?"

Tyler caught his breath before he could say something he shouldn't. He had just seen her fighting like a raging schoolboy in the streets, but she was looking up at him through the lashes of a demure young lady. She wasn't

what she seemed, but neither was he, so he guessed they
were even.

"Let's not fool each other. You don't want this marriage any more than I do. I'll admit, it could be mighty
convenient to tell marriage-minded females that I'm already taken, and I have no objections to sharing your
bed. You're damned good in bed and it's almost worth
taking the chance, but I don't want to do that to you.
You were meant to have a home and children and all
that folderol, and I'm not the man for that."

They had stopped in the alley between the livery and
the hotel, where the sun couldn't reach. Evie stared up
at Tyler with a growing sense of frustration. He had done
"that" to her, even admitted that he enjoyed it, and still
he couldn't see that they could work it out together. He
knew more than she about these things; maybe he was
right. But when she looked in his eyes, she didn't believe
him. The golden flecks disappeared into deep pools of
pain, and the lines were back around his mouth again.
Tyler's looks made all the women swoon, and his elegant
clothes bespoke the gambler the world saw, but she had
seen the man without his clothes and looks. He was just
a man, like any other. And right now, he was her man.
She had always thought Jane Eyre a bit of a prig for
walking out on Mr. Rochester.

She smiled at that. "I'm sure you're right, Tyler. Won't
you come in and have some supper with us? Daniel
would like to see you again. He's rather depressed because he can't get out and about. It would do him good
to see you."

Put like that, Tyler couldn't refuse. He had told her
he wasn't a family man, and she hadn't argued or cried
or tried tearful persuasion. She had simply agreed with
him and invited him to dinner for her brother's sake.
Tyler supposed she was as devious as the next woman,
but he liked the way she went about it. The pregnancy
trick had been despicable, but he was the one who had
contributed to that. Whatever other wiles Evie wielded,
she wielded with creativity and grace, and an innocence
that he couldn't refuse. He followed her down the alley.

He had forgotten about the children. The minute Tyler

walked through the door, he knew his mistake. It had been easy enough to forget who the boy in the street was when he had seen Evie attacked, but he couldn't forget the rest of the menagerie easily. The ankle-biter toddled forward with grinning gabbles as soon as he entered. She had some fascination with his trousers; her little fingers crushed them as she clung to his leg.

"She just wants to be picked up, Tyler. I daresay it gives her a whole new perspective on the world from your height." Evie set the skillet back on the shelf and added another plate to the table that Carmen was setting. She frowned at Daniel now sitting in the corner. He wasn't supposed to be up and around yet. "We'll be eating shortly. Let me get you something to drink while we call Manuel and José." She poured Tyler a cup of coffee and disappeared out the back door on some errand.

Tyler wanted to run. He wanted to disengage his pant leg and bolt out the door and never look back. But he'd had a week to think about his last hasty departure, and it looked mighty like he'd turned tail that time. He wouldn't be thought a coward because of a few rambunctious juveniles. They weren't anything to him. Someone was bound to come and claim them sooner or later. Then he'd have Evie to himself again, figuratively speaking. Tyler threw a glance at the boy reading a book in the corner.

"Well, Daniel, you've changed locations. Does that mean you're going to live?" Tyler bent and picked up the termite on his leg, unable to move without moving her.

Daniel looked up with casual interest as Tyler lifted Maria into his arms and stared at her as if she were a bug from outer space.

"I'll make it," he answered with his best effort at manliness. "Maria might not, though, when Evie discovers she's been ransacking through her paints. Carmen only just got her cleaned up."

Tyler eyed the toddler's fresh-scrubbed face with suspicion. Maria giggled and patted his cheeks with both hands. Tyler blew his cheeks into big puffs and shook his head and made an impolite noise. Maria erupted in gales of laughter.

Tyler gave up and sat down with the toddler in his lap. "I suppose this one is Maria. Evie surely wouldn't do anything to her. She's just a baby."

Coming in from the back porch with some fresh kindling, Evie asked, "What won't Evie do to whom?"

Maria reached for the mug that Tyler was lifting with studied nonchalance. The hot coffee threatened to tilt on her head, and he hastily returned the mug to the table. "I suspect there isn't anything Evie won't do to anyone, given a chance, but it's none of your business. We're just all getting along real friendly like here."

Evie threw Tyler a suspicious glance. "So I see. You better scoot your cup away from the table edge. She'll have it in your lap."

The brat curled up in his lap and spread her arms around him until Tyler was forced to hug her back. Then crowing with delight, she scrambled up and planted a sloppy kiss on his cheek, slid down his leg, and toddled merrily off in another direction. She didn't play fair. Tyler reached for his coffee and wished it were something stronger. He could have had that once, but he didn't want it any longer. And it wasn't the coffee he was thinking about.

Daniel chuckled and went back to his book with a final gambit. "Ask Evie how her painting is coming along."

"Painting? What have you two been up to while my back was turned?" She threw a suspicious glance to Tyler, who was finally getting a drink of his coffee.

He shrugged and figured in for a dime, in for a dollar, and asked, "What have you been painting lately?"

Evie threw an irate glare at her brother. "Daniel! What have you been telling Tyler? And how do you know what I've been doing? You're supposed to be lying in bed and resting that leg."

Daniel shrugged and ignored her tirade, leaving Tyler to handle it. Tyler threw him a look that said Daniel would pay for this later, but he maintained his calm in the face of the storm.

"I just asked a simple question. You don't need to fly

off the handle. Maybe I should ask what you mean to see that lawyer about when he returns." That made Daniel's ears perk up, Tyler noted with satisfaction. Let the boy work that one out for himself.

"Let's just take one topic at a time. When did you ever see my painting? Have you been sneaking around here while my back is turned?" Evie shook a piece of silverware at him as she finished setting the rest of the table.

Tyler grinned. The light in here wasn't the greatest, but he could see the flame of irate color on her cheeks. He could see that getting under Evie's skin could be an interesting pastime, particularly since she was so good at getting under his. Besides, it was safer than thinking what else he would like to be doing with her.

"I rummage through ladies' things all the time. It always pays to know a little more about a lady than she knows about me. Are you going to tell me about the painting, or am I going to have to find out on my own?"

"I paint." She said that emphatically, slapping down a spoon she had just polished until the silver should have worn off. "Why don't you go wash before Manuel and José get here?"

Tyler rose obediently, but he couldn't resist temptation. He stopped behind Evie and catching her waist, kissed the nape of her neck. He could feel her stiffen, but he didn't dare do more under Daniel's nose. With a chuckle, he tugged one of her curls. "Yes, ma'am, I'm going, ma'am. Do I get to see your painting after we eat?"

"No one will ever see my painting again," she answered with a dramatic sniff and a glare that pinpointed Daniel specifically.

Daniel looked over his glasses in the direction of Evie's bedroom. "Guess again, sister." He nodded toward the doorway.

Maria stood there, both chubby hands wrapped around a piece of wood as tall as she was. She dragged it farther into the room, grinning hugely. "Mine," she pronounced adamantly.

Tyler whooped and grabbed the board, lifting it into

the air before Evie could beat him to it. It wasn't a board but a wood frame for a canvas, and he was nearly thrown off balance by the lightness of it as he tried to keep it over his head and catch the subject in the light.

"Tyler Monteigne, if you don't give that back to me right now, I'll never speak to you again!"

"Promise?" Tyler whistled as he recognized the dark-eyed urchin in the front corner of the canvas. The figure in the background was barely sketched in, but he had the ominous feeling that he might be the subject. There was something vaguely familiar about the figure's stance with hands in pocket and shoulders thrown back. The child in the picture was apparently offering him something, but the object wasn't finished yet. The whole subject made him uneasy.

Manuel and José burst in at that moment, followed by Carmen. Evie scowled at Tyler as he continued to peruse her work, but she was forced to ignore him as she shepherded the boys into washing and cleaning up before they came to the table.

Without comment, Tyler handed the piece to Daniel. Then he bent and picked Maria up and put her on the high stool evidently meant for her. The boys' excited chatter filled the sudden silence between the adults as they settled at the table.

Tyler watched as Evie bustled around making certain everyone had what they needed, including Daniel, who had to eat in his corner. She was not only a beautiful liar and a woman who could handle four children and a rebellious adolescent at once, but she had talent that he had never suspected.

What else was he going to find out about Evie Peyton before she put the noose around him and lynched him good?

Chapter 22

"That was a delightful dinner, Mrs. Peyton, but I've got a game waiting for me over at the Red Eye." Tyler moved his chair back from the table and eyed Evie warily as she passed the dishes to Carmen, who was washing them. He didn't know how she would take to being addressed by her maiden name instead of the one he had given her. As far as he could tell, she hadn't told anyone of their marriage, and she wasn't wearing his ring. He didn't know what to make of that, either.

The look Evie gave him was fulminating, but not particularly clear as to which particular subject she objected to.

"Why, go and play and have a good time, Mr. Monteigne. Perhaps we'll see you again before you move on."

She didn't even need to lace her words with scorn. They were quite effective all by themselves. Tyler stood up and reached for his hat. She knew he made his living by gambling. She didn't have to make it sound like he was just out for a good time. And that crack about moving on deserved some kind of retribution, but not in front of the kids. He needed to come back and have a good long talk with Miss Evie Peyton, but now wasn't the time. He had new reasons for wanting to add to the stack of cash he was accumulating in that bank back in Natchez, and time was wasting while he stood here arguing with this woman he wasn't certain he could call wife.

"I need to talk with you when you get a chance. Alone." Tyler added the emphasis when Evie just gave him one of those tantalizing smiles.

"I'm sure you do, sir, but as you can see, that's not

likely to happen any time soon. But we'll be happy to have you for dinner if you happen by." Evie removed the damask tablecloth and took it to the back door to shake it out, deliberately turning her back on the man wanting to shake her in the same way she was treating the cloth.

Tyler sent her a dark look, said his farewell to Daniel, gave Carmen a charming smile that almost had her melting to the floor, and left.

Several hours, a few hundred dollars, and a few drinks later, Tyler gazed with satisfaction at his winning hand until he caught sight of one of the saloon girls sweeping down the stairs in a pink gown that he had reason to remember very well. His hand halted over his stack of coins. Instead of raising the ante, he laid his cards out and collected his winnings while following that pink dress through the crowded saloon with his eyes. He felt fury simmering somewhere inside him, a fury that he had long ago buried and thought under control until a certain infuriating female had appeared in his life.

He wasn't going to let her do this to him. He was in control of his life now. He was comfortable, with nothing to lose. He had no reason to fight, no reason to get angry, and all the world at his feet. He ought to just sit back down and continue with his game, but he was on his feet and following that pink gown without giving his actions a second thought.

From out of the corner of her eye, Starr watched Tyler rise and noted his direction. For a saloon this far west, the Red Eye had a certain elegance, and Tyler Monteigne's formal frock coat and tie suited it well. The cowboys lined along the polished mahogany bar with its brass railings were the ones who looked out of place. One of these days, if she had her way, there would only be men in suit coats and hats lined up in here. But the saloon wasn't hers yet, and she couldn't treat it as if it were.

Still, she had an interest in the girls under her command, and giving the cowboy at her side a light buss to the cheek, Starr whispered a few promises and set out after Tyler.

She literally cut him off at the pass, accepting the drink

he was offering to Rose and sending the other girl back to a table waiting for a little attention.

Tyler sipped his own drink and eyed the garish blonde who had intercepted his questions. Starr had a good head on her shoulders, and some other more unique assets. He let his gaze drift down to admire them as she expected, then returned to watching her face.

"I don't like men, Monteigne," Starr informed him with a smile that said otherwise. "They're a passel of lying, cheating bastards with only their own self-interest in mind."

Tyler admired the performance. She was almost as good as Evie, but Evie lied with a cheerful insouciance that made you want to believe her. He just wanted to smack Starr. He waited politely.

Starr gave his cool demeanor a look of annoyance. "You're a smug bastard. I don't know what that schoolteacher sees in you. She certainly deserves better, but I guess she's not likely to find anyone else out here, unless it's those Harding men. They're a bit tough for a young girl like that."

Tyler felt his earlier irritation growing with leaps and bounds. "I'll thank you to keep Mrs. Peyton out of this."

"Mrs. Peyton, is it? Is that what you call her when you've got her in bed? Get out of here, Tyler Monteigne, and go do the right thing by that poor widow woman so she won't have to be selling her gowns to eat." With that pronouncement, Starr slapped her glass down on the bar and walked away from him.

The effect was the same as if she had thrown the whiskey in his face. Tyler stood, stunned, watching her retreating back as Starr found a new customer and left him standing there. He glanced hastily around to see if anyone else had heard, but the bar was too rowdy and no one was paying him any mind. Feeling sick to his stomach, he paid his tab and headed for the door.

The air outside didn't serve to cool his head any. After the rain, the weather had returned to its normal sun and heat, and there wasn't a sign that it had ever been anything else. Even the nighttime held the hint of the summer to come, and Tyler gulped the muggy air without relief.

It didn't make any sense, but he turned his feet in the direction of the livery and the little house behind it. Evie was surrounded by children, and he couldn't talk to her. She was probably asleep. There wasn't anything he could say to her. He had thought her wealthy. She and the boy were always tricked out in expensive clothes and carried a fortune in whatnots with them. But he felt like the biggest jerk alive and kept walking.

She was selling her gowns to whores. He was going to wring her neck for that. He was her husband, damn it. She should have come to him first. She had no business even talking to women like that. The memory of that night when he had found her coming down the stairs of the saloon still rankled. Evie was too innocent to have to deal with the likes of that.

The house was dark when he arrived. Tyler knew they were all asleep. He stopped in the shadows of the hotel and tried to decide what to do. He knew what he ought to do: he ought to get the hell back to the hotel and sleep it off. But that wasn't what he wanted to do.

While he was standing there contemplating which dark window might conceal Evie behind it, Tyler caught a furtive movement at the side of the house. He thought his eyes tricked him at first, but then the shadow moved again, and its bulk was discernible. Even half-drunk as he was, he could figure out what a shadow of that size represented.

He reached for the six-gun he carried continually in these hostile environs. He hadn't wanted to wear weapons ever again, but it hadn't taken him long to discover why these Texans always wore enough guns to start a war. If it wasn't Indians or rattlesnakes or raging steers, it was gallows bait like this one that tested a man's endurance. Tyler clicked the hammer back and started forward, only to hesitate at the sight of a second shadow approaching from the rear.

He didn't have to stretch his imagination to figure out who that slender silhouette was. It was going to be a repeat of this afternoon if he didn't get that skillet away from her. He really wasn't in the mood for tangling with a man that size again if he could avoid it.

"Evie, get your rear end back in that house before I paddle it. You, sir, better move away from those windows before she brings that skillet down over your bald pate and I have to shoot you for getting between us." Tyler stepped nonchalantly from the shadows of the hotel into the alley, brandishing his gun clearly.

The giant growled and swung around to stop the skillet he remembered altogether too well. He wasn't quick enough. It swung down and smashed the hand he reached with, and he howled.

Evie stepped in and easily removed his gun before stepping back out of his grasp again. She threw Tyler a look of unconcern as he approached. "I want to talk to the man, Tyler. Just hold that gun on him awhile longer."

"You've got a gun, now. Why don't you hold it on him?" Tyler asked derisively, irritation overcoming his usual even temper. She had a way of doing that to him that wasn't healthy for either of them.

Evie shot him a look that didn't bode well for later, but turned her attention back to her captor. "What's your name, sir?"

The giant gauged the distance between himself and the fool woman with the gun, kept a wary eye on the man who had jumped him earlier this day, and answered cautiously, "Logan."

"And what is your interest in a man named Peyton?"

That made the bullheaded man look up. "He owes me money."

Evie concealed a shiver of apprehension. She was dressed only in a nightgown and a robe that was little more than gauze, and her feet were bare. She blamed the coolness for her shiver, but the air wasn't cool. She tried to hold the gun steady. "Who is he?"

The man glared at her. "You're the one with his name. Where is he?"

Tyler watched Evie's lips clench in a formidable frown and knew they weren't going to get anywhere soon at this pace. He had seen Evie in a rage before. He returned the pistol hammer to its seat and let the click bring Logan's attention back to him. "Just tell the lady everything you know about Peyton and why you're looking for him."

Logan looked as if he were ready to bite someone's head off, but faced with two guns he had little choice other than to reply. "I haven't seen the man in over twenty years. He borrowed all I had and took off for California, promising to come back in a year, a wealthy man. Ain't seen him since. I trusted that scum, thought he was a gentleman. I've learned better since then. Now I don't loan nobody nothing, and I keep what's mine. That money is mine, and I want it."

"Was he from around here?" Evie asked eagerly.

Logan glared at her. "You ought to know." As she lifted the gun menacingly, he scowled. "Yes, he was from around here. I worked out at the Double H, and his folks owned a piece of land back east of here. His mother was a 'breed, and folks don't cotton much to them 'round here."

There was no reason in the world that she could associate this man named Peyton with herself, but Evie couldn't help the excitement running down her spine. She prodded him further. "How old was he when you knew him? What did he do for a living?"

Tyler gave her an odd look but remained silent.

"How in hell should I know how old he was? Twenties, I reckon. He was old enough to get drunk at the saloon and start fights. He used to draw pictures of people in the bar and they'd pay him for them, but he drank and someone always said something about his mother, and then the fun would start. All I want is my money back, lady. If you don't know where he is, I'll be on my way."

"Have you checked to see if his parents are still alive? Did he have any other relatives?"

Logan was growing seriously annoyed. "I ain't exactly a fool. I tried to get my money back out of them the first time I came through here. The second time, they were dead. He had a kid sister, but she married and went away. You living here and having the last name and all, I figure you got to be his. Just tell me where to find him, and I'll be on my way."

"The lady's name is *Mrs*. Peyton. She's a widow, and she's just moved here. If her husband knew anything about the man you want, he took it with him to his grave." Tyler was tired of this game. He wanted to get Evie away from this giant before somebody did something rash. Or before Logan really started paying attention to the woman standing there in next to nothing instead of to the gun in her hand.

Logan scowled. "It's only been twenty years, and the man didn't have a son. Unless you married a baby, we ain't talking about the same people. Let's just call it quits."

Evie politely lowered her gun. "Did you find the money you lost earlier, Mr. Logan?"

Tyler clicked the hammer back again as the man's fists clenched. Logan threw him a furious look, but he kept his hands to himself. "I mean to find out who took it. I keep what's mine."

Tyler could see what Evie was going to do even before she did it. With a sign of exasperation, he grabbed her hand and gently removed the gun from it. "Get in the house, now. Then I'll give him back his gun."

Evie sent him a petulant look, thought better of replying in kind, lifted her robe and gown, and gingerly traced her way to the rear of the house and out of sight. The two men watched her go.

"Just leave her alone and you'll do fine. Half the men in this town are ready to kill for her, and the other half haven't met her yet. You really don't want to get into that." Tyler kept his gun primed, but handed Logan his.

Logan took the weapon, gave Tyler a long look, and shoved it back in his holster. "If I find she's been lying . . ."

"It wouldn't be anything new. But take my word for it, she's from back East and doesn't know a thing about your man."

Accepting that, Logan shrugged and made his way back down the alley to the lights of town. Tyler watched him go, then turned back to the house and the lying, conniving brat hiding inside.

Except she wasn't inside. She was tiptoeing around the

far end of the building and up on the front porch. Tyler nearly winged her before he realized what he was aiming at. Disgruntled, he released the trigger and shoved his gun back where it belonged.

"Damn it, Evie, you're going to get yourself killed creeping around like that. I told you to get back inside."

"I can't talk to you inside. Daniel or Carmen or someone would hear." Evie sat down on the front step and wrapped her feet under her for warmth. The white robe spread in a halo around her.

Hell, that was what he'd wanted anyway, along with a few other things he didn't dare mention. Crossing his arms over his chest, Tyler slumped against the porch post and regarded her warily. "So, talk."

Evie threw him an irritated look. "You don't have to treat me like a criminal. You know why I had to call myself a widow."

"But you're not. Your name is Peyton. I assume that means your father's name is Peyton, too. And you came back here looking for someone. It wasn't any sister, was it?"

"It could be. I don't know." Evie looked away. Tyler in frock coat and cravat was too handsome to endure for long. She wanted to be in his arms, and it wasn't his shirt that she wanted to feel beneath her hands. "I don't even know that my father's name is Peyton. I don't know who my father is."

Tyler slid down the post to sit beside her and contemplate that thought for a while. It could be another lie. He had grown up knowing his father and his grandfather and his grandfather's father. He could recite his family history back to the first Monteigne who came to New Orleans back in the late 1700's. But his family wasn't so insulated that he didn't know about orphans and bastards and the rest of the world's refuse. He just couldn't place Evie among their numbers. She breathed wealth as naturally as air.

"All right, let's say for the moment that you don't know who your father is. What about your mother? Couldn't she tell you? And what about other relatives?

And this Nanny you keep talking about? Are you telling me no one knows who your father is?"

Evie slanted him a look that could have meant anything. "Surprised? Who did you think you married, Louisa May Alcott?"

"You're not half as good a storyteller." Tyler leaned back against the post and contemplated the woman before him. She was a liar, but she was the most wholly desirable liar he'd ever met in his life. And she was his wife. It set a whole war of conflicting feelings rampaging through his middle. He didn't want to acknowledge any one of them. "And I doubt that writing books makes Miss Alcott as rich as you."

Evie shrugged. "Nanny was the one with money. We haven't seen any since she died."

"That doesn't make any sense," Tyler pointed out. "Would you care to tell me the whole story?"

"No, I wouldn't." Evie crossed her arms and glared at him. "Would you care to tell me what you intend to do with me? I'm your wife, but no one seems to know it. That's just fine with me, but you can't keep hanging around here like this without someone calling me other names."

There was that. Tyler wiped his palms against the knees of his trousers. "I can get you that divorce if you've got your cap set for some other man. But if you haven't, what's the hurry? I'm not planning on marrying anyone else. I owe you some support, I guess. I'll not have you selling your gowns to whores anymore."

"So that's what brought you down here." Evie pulled the robe more firmly around her and tried not to shiver at the cold way he was discussing their marriage. It wasn't just the marriage. Those few words muttered over their heads meant nothing to her. But what they had done in bed afterward had meant everything in the world to her. She'd had dreams that what they had done had meant something. She had never been closer to any person in her life, and she had thought it would stay that way. But Tyler was acting as if it had never happened. She had a hard time keeping the tears from her eyes.

"That's not an answer. As long as you're my wife, I'll

take care of you. Now tell me if you want me to go back to Houston and get that divorce."

Gathering her robe in her hands, Evie stood up and glared at the man hastily getting to his feet. When they were face-to-face again, she leaned over and practically spit in his face. "Take your damned divorce, Tyler, and shove it where it hurts."

As she walked in the house and threw the bolt behind her, Tyler reflected that he had finally taught her how to swear.

Chapter 23

"Where the hell do you think you're going all geared up like that?" Standing on the boardwalk in front of the sheriff's office, Jace stuck his thumbs in his gun belt and eyed his younger brother skeptically as Kyle swung off his horse.

Wearing his best white linen shirt, a cravat, and a fawn-colored corduroy coat that had all too evidently been dragged from the back of his wardrobe, Kyle wiped the dust off his polished boots with his handkerchief and stuffed the now-dirty cotton back into his pocket. He merely grinned at his brother and joined him on the boardwalk.

"Pheewy!" Jace held his nose. "You've got on more stinkwater than a polecat. If you're not careful, you're going to resemble our resident dandy here." He nodded at Tyler who was leaning against the wall, carving an unoffending stick into a point. Tyler looked up at the reference, gave Kyle's Sunday clothes a disinterested look, and returned to his whittling.

Kyle grinned even wider. "He's just a boy. I'll show him how a man courts a lady."

Tyler closed his knife and put it in his back pocket. He pushed his broad-brimmed hat back on his head, revealing more of his golden curls, and gave Kyle another once-over. "I'd loan you my waistcoat, but I'd be afraid you'd stretch it over that paunch of yours. Why don't we have a game of cards and discuss fashion later?"

Kyle was admittedly a larger man than Tyler, but there wasn't an ounce of fat on him, and he took Tyler's insult for what it was worth. He gave the gambler's French-cuffs and embroidered waistcoat a look of scorn. "I've got some time. I'll win enough for a bottle of fancy wine and some candy for the lady, then I'll be on my way."

Fatal last words.

While Tyler skillfully played one hand into another well into the afternoon, Evie excitedly tried on one walking dress after another, debating the merits of the formal gray merino over the more elegant ecru foulard.

"Philly and Delphia have no reason to lie, Daniel," she called through the bedroom door. "You know your boss gets all the news first. Mr. Hale is back, and I'm going to see him."

"Evie, I don't want you going over there until I can come with you." On the other side of the door, Daniel restlessly reached for his walking stick. He wasn't using his leg yet, but he was getting better at hopping around on one foot with the stick for support.

"Oh, pooh! He's just a lawyer. What can he do but look at me as if I'm deranged? It wouldn't be the first time." Evie decided on the foulard and rummaged in her jewelry box for a gold locket to add a bit of brightness. She was grateful Carmen had taken Maria with her to the store. There was never time for the little niceties like accessories when the children were around.

"I don't think you ought to tell him who you are. I think I ought to go over there as a friend of the family and make inquiries. There could be a lot of money at stake here. You don't want to rush things." Daniel pulled himself up and hopped toward the door.

Evie swung it open and pointed back to the chair. "Sit, Daniel. The doctor said exercise the leg, but he didn't mean for you to walk on it."

"If you go without me, I'm going to send Manuel looking for Tyler. I know he's still in town." Daniel met Evie's gaze defiantly.

Evie knew it would take time and effort to locate Manuel, and she could be there and back before Daniel's threat could have effect, but she didn't want Daniel going even as far as the livery with that leg. She pointed at the chair again. "Sit. You can't go ruining your future by damaging that leg. And that's what you'll do if you come with me. And I'm not about to let know-it-all Tyler have any part of this. It's none of his business."

Daniel sat, but the rebelliousness hadn't left his face. "He's your husband, Evie. The two of you can pretend all you want, but the fact of the matter is, you're married. And even if you're right and there isn't any baby, the marriage isn't going away by ignoring it. So as your husband, Tyler should be the one to go with you to see Hale."

The only mirror in the house was the small one she had brought with her. Evie propped it on the mantel and examined her hair in it. Everything seemed in order. She turned back to her room to find the matching hat. It had a veil of sorts that would cover her hair and keep it in place. Keeping a decent coiffure in this heat and dust was a trial.

"Well, I'm not about to go into a saloon looking for Tyler, so you can forget it, Daniel," she called from the bedroom. Finding the hat, she turned to examine its placement in the mirror. "I won't tell Hale who I am. How's that?"

That was more than he could expect, Daniel decided. "What will you tell him, then?"

"I don't know. Whatever comes to mind." Airily, Evie adjusted her hat, inspected her skirt to be certain all the flounces and petticoats were in their proper place, and swept out.

It was Saturday and there was no reason to expect that the lawyer was going to be in his office, but Evie went anyway. She couldn't wait one minute longer than necessary to find out how much the man knew. She had waited a lifetime already. There really could be very little danger in just asking a few questions.

She climbed the stairs to the lawyer's office in full view of the town. There wasn't any reason why the local schoolteacher couldn't go to see a lawyer. They were both perfectly respectable people. Garbed in full regalia, her bustle swinging her train in proper elegance, Evie felt prepared for anything.

Below her, Manuel whistled softly in appreciation before darting off to inform the man who had paid to notify him as soon as she put in an appearance.

Evie knocked politely, then walked in at the call from someone inside. The room was cast in the half-light of pulled shades, but she could tell it was a lawyer's office. The stale air reeked of ancient cigars. There was a horse-hair sofa in one corner that she knew would exude dust if she sat down. An oil lamp with a green shade to force its light downward sat on one corner of the old mahogany veneer desk. The veneer was coming loose in places, and the leather of the two chairs in front of it was cracked and mottled.

But Evie's interest was more in the man behind the desk. He wore unrimmed glasses as he studied a stack of papers that had apparently accumulated in his absence. His blond, thinning hair seemed barely able to cover his skull. But when he looked up, his smile was genial, and then appreciative, and Evie felt right at home.

He wasn't much taller than herself when he stood up. Accustomed as she had become to tall men like Tyler and the Hardings with their wide shoulders, she was slightly taken aback at Mr. Hale, who seemed almost slender and effeminate. But she remembered men like that from St. Louis—very successful men—she reminded herself, and she relaxed.

"Mr. Hale?" she inquired.

"Jonathan Hale, at your service, ma'am. How may I help you?" He gestured toward one of the leather chairs.

Evie chose the chair without arms and spread her skirts carefully as she chose her words. "It's a rather delicate matter, sir. I don't know how to put it." She smiled a little, just enough to get him slightly flustered. It was purely ridiculous the way men would fall for a woman's smile, but she had very few weapons in her arsenal, and she had learned to use them skillfully. "I'm Mrs. Maryellen Peyton, the new schoolteacher here in Mineral Springs."

Hale had reason to remember the name "Peyton" very well, and his interest immediately intensified. As he studied the woman before him, he grew even more excited. The hair, the eyes, the clothes, all fit the description. The name was baffling, and her appearance here was a matter of some concern. Unaffected by her skillful smile, he listened carefully as she continued to speak at his nod.

"I've just come from Natchez, but I have corresponded for a long time with a friend of my childhood in St. Louis. When she heard I was coming here, she was most anxious that I make a few inquiries, and she gave me your name." Evie hesitated a moment to see how this elaborate network of lies was being absorbed. The lawyer nodded thoughtfully, waiting for her to continue. He wasn't being very helpful.

Slightly miffed, Evie elaborated a little further. "She's an orphan, but she has reason to believe her parents are from this area." Evie silently cursed her choice of assumed name. There would be questions about that "Peyton" if she wasn't careful. She summoned all her powers of creativity to the problem. "As a matter of fact, she was quite excited when I married Alexander Peyton, my late husband, because she thought Peyton might be part of her family name." There, that should do it. She had Tyler to thank for that little absurdity.

Hale formed his fingers into a little tent and studied her intently. "Are you asking me to find your friend's family, Mrs. Peyton?"

Evie took a deep breath, but the little man didn't seem to appreciate the sight. She exhaled slowly to give herself time to place this as delicately as possible. "She found your name on some papers, Mr. Hale. She thinks you might already know about her family. Her name is Evangeline Peyton Howell."

Evie waited in triumph while the lawyer took off his glasses and polished them. He knew the name all right. She could see it in the way his hand shook. The test of his honesty would come with his next words.

Hale replaced his glasses on his nose. "The Howells were a prominent family in this town, Mrs. Peyton. They paid well to keep their secrets. They're all dead now, of course, sad to say, but I can't ethically give secrets to a stranger. Perhaps you should have Miss Howell write to me."

Swamped with disappointment, Evie folded her hands

in her lap. She wanted to know now. She had half a mind to tell him who she was just to shake him out of his complacency, but she had promised Daniel to be cautious. She didn't want to be cautious. She saw no reason to be cautious. This man had what she wanted, and she wanted it with every hair and particle of her body.

But she stood up and smiled sweetly. "I'll do that, Mr. Hale. I do appreciate your time. Evie will be quite delighted to hear you know of her family. You don't have any idea what that will mean to her."

Hale rose and saw her to the door and watched as she swept down the stairs in a flurry of silk petticoats and a cloud of cinnamon-rose scent. It was all he could do to keep his heart beating as she walked out of sight. When he closed the door, he gave a sigh of relief and felt what could only be a shiver of anticipation. It had been a long time since he'd had a feeling of anticipation. He'd given up hope long ago when he was just a boy and his father had informed him that he was going to be a lawyer and not a cowboy.

He no longer had a child's dream of roping cattle and riding a horse in the hot sun all day, but the life of a cattle baron could be a very lucrative one. The Hardings lived simply, it was true, but as their lawyer, he knew how much wealth had accumulated out there. And he knew to a dime how much more would accumulate now that the war was over and profits were skyrocketing. And that bundle of living joy who had just walked out of here owned half of all that.

The knowledge was sweet in his mouth. He wanted to savor it for a long time, a very long time. But he was going to have to make plans.

He almost laughed as he stared at the pile of work on his desk. He had come back here a failure. He had searched St. Louis high and low for the elusive Miss Evangeline Howell, but she had disappeared with all her worldly belongings and hadn't been seen since the funeral of her guardian. Who would have believed that the little heiress would have turned up here, right under his nose?

And under the nose of her stepbrothers. Hale wondered what the Hardings would do if they knew their beautiful new schoolteacher was the owner of half their spread. He didn't think he would let them know right away. If things worked out well, he wouldn't let them know until his wedding day, his wedding to Miss Evangeline Peyton Howell, formerly known as Maryellen Peyton.

Tyler was waiting for her around the corner. Evie stopped in her tracks and regarded him suspiciously. After last Friday night, she wasn't at all certain that she wanted to speak to the cad. She certainly hadn't thought he'd want to speak to her.

"You're tricked out mighty fine this afternoon, Miss Peyton." He removed his hat and offered her his arm. When she didn't take it, he caught her gloved hand and pulled it through the crook of his elbow.

She didn't want to be this close to Tyler Monteigne. She could smell his shaving soap. And she smelled the smoke of the saloon he'd probably been in since this morning. She remembered the strength of the arm she was holding, and she tried to draw away.

It was a futile battle. His hand covered hers, and she couldn't struggle with him in full view of everyone. Digging her fingers in and hoping they hurt, she turned her saccharine smile on him. "And it's a pleasure to see you, too, Mr. Monteigne. To what do I owe this honor?"

"I just thought you might be interested in telling me why you went to see the town lawyer as soon as he got back. Another man might think it suspicious after our discussion last week, but I'm a better man than that. I figure you're bound to be looking for your long lost sister."

"Maybe I was looking for a way to sue you for everything you have, Tyler Monteigne. After all, a man who does what you did ought to be forced to a little responsibility."

Tyler kept smiling as charmingly as she was doing. He stopped in the window of the millinery shop and pretended to show her a hat there. "I had the clerk at the general store set up an account for you, and I've told Daniel about it so you can't pretend it isn't there." He had never tried to talk through clenched teeth before. It wasn't easy, but it was better than shaking her until her teeth rattled. "I told you I was willing to support you."

"Why, that's generous of you, I'm sure." Evie disengaged her hand now that he'd loosened his grip. "Perhaps I won't be needing a lawyer after all." She picked up her skirt and hurried in the direction of the livery, but Tyler was too swift for her. He caught her arm before she could escape.

"I think I'll walk you back home. You never know when a lady will be accosted by strangers in this town."

His grip was hard as it steered her in the proper direction. Too furious to speak, Evie let the angry tap-tap of her shoes on the boardwalk speak for her.

Kyle Harding was just coming out of the house as they turned down the alley. He saw them approach and pulled off his hat to hurry toward them.

"Monteigne, it's mighty thoughtful of you to find the lady for me. Mrs. Peyton." He grinned and saluted her with a gallant bow. His eyes danced as he looked up to note Tyler's scowl and the lady's blinding smile. "I've come a-courtin', Mrs. Peyton, just as I promised. Do I pass inspection?"

Kyle held out his arms so she could fully admire his formal attire. The cravat was now askew and his linen slightly crumpled, but he was a well-built man with a masculine assurance that didn't require fancy clothes. Tyler didn't require the refinement, either, but she wasn't speaking to him right now. Evie smiled her appreciation.

"You are quite the most handsome man I've seen today, sir. Have you spoken with Daniel?" She ignored the grip tightening around her arm.

"I have, and he gives me his permission to take you over to John's to eat and then to dance out at the church afterward. I think he regrets he can't go along as chaperon, but I very much suspect one or more of your little charges will have their noses pressed against the windows to keep an eye on you, so I'll behave."

Evie could just imagine Manuel or José peeking in

windows and hiding under chairs at Daniel's instigation, not to mention Tyler's. She threw her escort a look of indignation and discreetly removed her arm from his hold. This time, he was the one who couldn't struggle.

Kyle grinned easily, not having missed a moment of his opponent's discomfiture. After losing the better part of his cash to the gambler this afternoon, he wasn't extending him any sympathy. "Well, Monteigne, you know what they say about being lucky in cards and unlucky in love . . ." He held out his arm for Evie.

She took it and walked off without looking back.

And from the second-floor lawyer's office, Hale watched the woman he intended to marry emerge from the alley with Kyle Harding on her arm. First the fancy stranger, now Harding. He was going to have to work fast if he meant to capture Miss Evangeline Howell.

Knowing full well how his looks compared to her other two suitors, Hale applied his active mind to other methods of persuasion. They might look prettier, but he was smarter. He was certain to come up with something, sooner or later.

Chapter 24

"I didn't think to ask before, but I'm not trespassing on another man's claim, am I, Mrs. Peyton?" Sitting across the table from her at the café, Kyle Harding didn't look particularly worried, but they were both aware of the other couple who had just seated themselves not far away. They couldn't help but be. Tyler had stopped by to make introductions. Without a qualm, he had introduced Evie as a friend of his family, made a smiling jest about schoolteachers letting down their hair, and led his newfound friend off to another table.

Evie listened to a soft trill of laughter as the other woman responded to some remark of Tyler's. She managed a generous smile at Kyle. Her face was going to crack before long if they didn't get out of here. She'd been smiling ever since Tyler had introduced the banker's spinster daughter. The woman had a horse face and abominable taste in clothes, but she had all the other assets a man looked for in a woman: a fine body and the ability to give him all the attention he could want.

Evie managed to look genuinely surprised at Kyle's words. "You mean Mr. Monteigne? Don't be silly. He's an old friend of the family, just as he said."

Kyle threw a circumspect look to the other table. Tyler hadn't bothered to rig himself out in anything fancy, but his usual duds were sufficient to turn a lady's head. Claudine was practically panting over that golden head and charming smile as Tyler spun some tale for her amusement. Neither seemed to be in the least interested in their table. But the coincidence of their arrival was suspicious.

"An old family friend who just happened to follow

you all the way out here so he could punch out any man who dared look at you twice?" Kyle wasn't particularly afraid of Tyler, but he had an aversion to stealing another man's claim. Jace had been put through that once before, and he wasn't going to do it to another man. There might not be a lot of law out here, but the spirit of fair play ruled. A man didn't take what belonged to another.

Evie patted Kyle's hand gently. "Mr. Monteigne is a gambling man, not a family man. I'm not young and foolish enough to fall for a man who won't be around long enough to be remembered. I'm the marrying kind, Mr. Harding. I enjoy good conversation and music and dancing as well as the next person, but when all is said and done, I aim to have a home and family."

Kyle turned his attention entirely to the lovely young woman across from him. He was nearing thirty years of age and ready to settle down. Women weren't plentiful out here, and he'd not seen any to hold his interest before this, but Mrs. Maryellen Peyton had all that a man could possibly want. Perhaps she was a little more outspoken than he had imagined a wife should be, but she had been married before and wasn't any half-grown innocent. She'd add a spark of life to the old ranch house. He held out his hand for her to take.

"You couldn't find a man more settled than I am, Mrs. Peyton. Let's try that dancing part for a while."

As the handsome couple rose and walked out, Tyler smiled deep into Claudine's eyes and asked what a beautiful woman like her was doing in a town like this. Inside, he was counting how many minutes it would take before he could gracefully leave.

"I can't find Manuel anywhere." Carmen stood by the open front door, staring out into the night, a worried frown crossing her usually serene brow.

"He's probably following Evie. He and José were whispering together over supper." Daniel glanced covertly at the beautiful girl in the doorway and went back to bending his injured leg up and down as the doctor had told him. It hurt like hell, and his muscles felt like they were on fire, but he was determined to walk again, and walk straight.

Carmen turned and looked at him curiously. "Why do you call her Evie? I thought her name was Maryellen."

Daniel blushed, but in the dim light the color wasn't noticeable. "Evie is her other name. She prefers Maryellen," he answered with a touch of curtness.

Before Carmen could respond to his rudeness, Manuel came barreling down the alley, swinging up on the front porch, nearly colliding with his sister as he slid into the house. "They're over at the church hall, dancing. Do you think she'll marry Mr. Harding?"

Daniel gave him a furious look, then reached for his glasses to hide his expression. "I doubt it. She just likes to dance."

"But Mr. Harding is *rich*. He has horses. Maybe he would let us ride them if they got married." Manuel grabbed the crust end of a loaf of bread from the stove and sat cross-legged in front of the empty fireplace, munching, building dreams of his own.

Evie could already be rich, but she hadn't come back here after seeing the lawyer, so Daniel didn't know. He shrugged. "She's more likely to tan your hide if she knew you were spying on her."

Manuel dug a coin out of his pocket and flourished it. "Mr. Monteigne gave me this to follow after them, but he's there with her now, and I didn't see why there should be two of us."

"Besides, you were hungry." Daniel gave the disappearing bread a knowing look while hiding a chuckle. Evie would be up in the rafters if she knew Tyler had been paying Manuel to spy on her. His hopes soared. Evie needed someone like Tyler to look after her, and after all, they were married. It was time they started acting like married people.

"Did you find Mr. Logan's money?" Carmen asked anxiously, closing the front door and peering into the bedrooms to be certain the two youngest children were asleep.

Manuel looked uneasy. "There wasn't any sign of it. You reckon he made up that story?"

Daniel looked between the two of them and continued bending his leg. Both sets of dark eyes were worried as they exchanged glances. He wanted to take away the worry, but he was stuck here like a useless lump of lead. There was something odd about the way Manuel had been behaving lately. "Was there anyone else near the livery while he was gone?"

The question made Manuel even more nervous. The boy fidgeted, finished his bread, and hopped up, heading for the door again. "I better go see if the dance is over yet. Do you think Mr. Monteigne will pay me more if I catch Mrs. Peyton smooching with Mr. Harding?"

"Manuel!" Carmen caught her brother's shirt and jerked him away from the door. "Answer Mr. Mulloney."

Mr. Mulloney. Daniel wanted to crawl in a hole and hide at the same time he swelled with pride. She thought of him as a "mister." Evie's decision to call herself "Mrs." had at least given him back his name, but their deceptions made him feel lower than a snake. He watched Manuel with concealed curiosity.

The boy shrugged and looked at the floor. "I'm not supposed to say."

Daniel felt a knot form in his stomach. "Manuel, if you know someone stole that money, you're an accomplice if you hide that information from the sheriff."

Manuel looked defiant. "I didn't see anybody do anything. And you can't tell me what to do. You're not my father."

He ran out the door before anyone could stop him, leaving Daniel and Carmen to look at each other through worried eyes. There was something wrong, but who could they tell and what could they say?

"I'll talk to Evie. Maybe she'll know what to do." Even as he said it, Daniel knew it was a lie. Evie was too caught up in a dozen different things to think anything of Manuel's minor rebellion. It could mean nothing. It was just something in the pit of his stomach that felt wrong, and maybe something in Carmen's expression.

"Jailbreak! There's been a jailbreak!" The voice shouted from somewhere at the front of the church hall,

and the music skidded and crashed to a reluctant halt as
word reached the musicians.

The dancers stopped where they were, and Evie found
herself on the arm of one of the Double H cowboys. The
man had brown-stained front teeth and a distinctive odor
of tobacco. He spat a wad as the call for a posse came
through loud and clear. Without taking another look at
the woman he had been do-si-do-ing around the floor,
he stalked off to join the rush of other men going out.

Another arm caught her waist and began leading her
to the edge of the crowd. Evie recognized Tyler's embrace without having to look at him. He was different
from any man in here. He didn't lift her or shove her,
but steered her firmly and with gentleness out of the
crush of people. She didn't spare time to be angry for
his presumption. She was worried about the children.

"I need to get back to the house, Tyler. What if those
men make a break for the livery?"

Tyler's thoughts were plunging along those lines, too,
but it was Evie's safety that concerned him. He just
wanted to keep her from running into the night and
smack into the arms of those desperadoes. Looking at
the fear in her fair face now, he knew the trouble was
multiplied.

Kyle Harding plowed through the crowd to come up
beside them. He noted the placement of Tyler's arm but
disregarded it in the importance of other events. "I'm
going to have to go join the sheriff. Are you staying
here, Monteigne?"

"I brought the bastards in once; somebody else can
have the pleasure now. Those kids are back at the house
alone. Somebody needs to go check on them."

It was obvious that Kyle was struggling to remember
what kids and why anyone should care, and Tyler felt a
surge of impatience. "You go on, I'll take care of it."
He turned to Evie. "Let me take you over to Miss Horton. You can stay with her while I look in on the kids.
I'll be back shortly."

Relieved of any further responsibility, Kyle made a
bow and said his farewell to Evie, then hurried after the

others. Evie clutched Tyler's arm before he could make his escape, also.

"I'm going with you."

"You're not going out there until it's safe. Be sensible, Evie." Tyler steered her in the direction of Claudine Horton. Even from here he could see the other woman's fury, but he wasn't much inclined toward soothing ruffled feathers at the moment. He needed to get outside.

Evie jerked her arm away, caught up her skirt, and started for the door on her own. When Tyler tried to catch up with her, she started to run. She didn't care if everyone stared. She'd left those children alone with only Daniel to watch over them. The horror of what could happen to them in the hands of those outlaws kept her moving forward. It would be all her fault.

Tyler gave up trying to halt her. He wasn't about to be charged with assault, and that was more than likely what it would take to bring Evie down now that she was in full flight. He simply caught her upper arm, slowed her down slightly, and hoped for a graceful exit.

Outside, men were running for horses, checking ammunition, and unfastening rifles as they swarmed through the town's main thoroughfare. Shouts and yells could be heard up and down the street, but the search party hadn't reached a stage of organization yet. Torches flared here and there, and Tyler grabbed one from someone's hand as they ran by.

He released Evie's arm and unhooked his holster flap as they hurried down the street. The alley would be black. He needed more hands and more guns. He gave a whistle of relief as a dark shadow stepped out of the hotel doorway.

"Where the hell have you been?" Tyler shoved the torch into Ben's hand.

"Around. I'll tell you later. One of the kids just ran down the alley. I ain't seen anyone else." Ben glanced down at Evie's pale face. "You'd better get inside the lobby, Miss Evie. Tyler's gonna need both his hands."

She gave the rifle in Ben's hands a nervous look. "I can hold the torch."

"Then you stand right here and hold it, 'cause we don't

need it yet. You just stand here and holler if you see anything." Ben passed the torch to her, primed his rifle, and started down the alley.

Tyler followed without a backward look. Evie wondered how she had been hoodwinked into this position. It seemed much safer to her if the alley were lighted as they walked down it, but then, it also seemed wisest if someone guarded their backs. She hesitated, and before she could make any decision, she could see Tyler running up to her front porch and Ben disappearing down the side to the back.

No one followed. No one interfered with their progress. She could see the shadow of Tyler pressed against the front wall as he looked through the lighted window. When he threw open the door, she breathed a sigh of relief and started down the alley after them. The posse was already beginning to form, and she wasn't going to be left standing here alone on the street.

She had forgotten about the side door of the hotel. As she hurried down the alley, the door opened and a dark figure stepped out. Evie gave a scream of surprise, but it wasn't a loud scream, not more than a squeak after the man's gloved hand closed over her mouth. The torch fell to the ground and went out.

Chapter 25

Daniel and Carmen looked up in surprise as both the front and back doors burst open simultaneously. They were huddled together on the pallet that served as Daniel's couch in the front room, their heads bent over some book they had been reading. They jumped apart with guilty looks as Ben and Tyler rushed into the room.

Tyler wiped the back of his forehead with his sleeve and regarded the two with amusement. "Lord, when I didn't see anyone in here, I thought we were all in trouble. First thing tomorrow, I'm going to see you get some proper furniture. That way I'll at least be able to see what you're up to from the window."

Daniel grimaced and regarded the pulled guns with interest. "Were you planning on shooting us if we were up to no good?"

Ben laughed and shouldered his rifle while Tyler tucked away his gun. "No, but your sister might. We'd better go round her up."

Tyler started for the door. "Are all the others in their beds?"

Carmen nodded. "Manuel just came in and went straight to bed. The others are asleep."

A cry echoed down the alley, a slight cry, but carried by the night air it magnified in Tyler's imagination. He started, and hand on his gun, threw open the door. The torch at the end of the alley was gone.

His curse sent Ben running after him. Daniel grabbed for his walking stick and struggled to his feet with Carmen's assistance. Behind them, Manuel crept into the front room, still fully dressed.

Evie wasn't there. Tyler knew she wasn't there. He

cursed every word he knew and some he hadn't known he knew as he stumbled over the torch in the alley. He grabbed it and held it like a cudgel as he glanced around.

The darkness was against him, but the light scrap of material that was Evie's hat stood out even in the pitch-black of night. He and Ben both saw it at the same time, and Ben grabbed for the door above it. Silently, he swung it open and slipped in, gesturing at Tyler to go around.

If Evie was inside that door, Tyler wanted to be there, and he cursed Ben for taking the part of older brother as usual. The damned man had never known how to be a servant. Still cursing furiously, Tyler ran to the front of the hotel and entered through the lobby.

Phil was at the front desk counting the night's receipts. He glanced up with disinterest at Tyler's entrance, then jumped when Tyler slammed the torch across the desk.

"Who's come through here in the last five minutes?"

Phil stared at the dapper-dressed gentleman as if he were crazed. The fury in Tyler's oddly colored eyes could easily be insanity. Nervously, he shrugged. "Just Hale going up to talk to a client. Tom from the livery was here a bit ago. There's a drummer out of Houston came in drunk as a skunk." Realization suddenly dawned. "If you're looking for those jailbreakers, they didn't come through here. The posse's already tracking them."

The side door apparently went up the back steps. Phil couldn't see it from the lobby. Tyler glanced toward the wide staircase leading to the upper rooms. All evidence of the flood had been carefully polished away but boards that had been too warped to repair had recently been replaced. The new treads were a different color. There was an outline of mud on one of the lighter treads. Mud, in a town as dry as dust. He started for the stairs.

A crash and a thud echoed from overhead, and Tyler took the stairs two at a time, with Phil following close behind.

Ben was already there, ramming the door with his shoulder. Tyler could hear Evie's irate screams as she ranted at someone, but she didn't sound hurt. He almost grinned as the words "you demented son of a female dog" floated from the room. And then the door suddenly opened before Ben could hit it, and he fell through, sprawling at Evie's feet.

Choking on laughter, Tyler stepped over his friend's long form, blocking Evie from the sight of the curious crowd beginning to form in the hallway. With a few curt words, he ordered Phil to close the door and go find what remained of the law in this town.

Tyler held Evie firmly in his hands as he looked her over. She was slightly disheveled, her usually orderly curls falling lopsidedly over her face, and one of her flounces was badly torn, but fire and not fear burned in her eyes. He pulled her close and planted a kiss possessively on her lips. He deserved that much reward for this wildly pounding heartbeat she had caused.

Evie allowed it for a few minutes. Tyler could feel her collapsing into his embrace, turning to him for reassurance, welcoming his kiss with parted lips and arms that clung to his shoulders. He held her tighter, concentrating on the taste of her and not what had led him here. He didn't want to think about the fear racing in his heart. She wasn't his to lose, and that's the way he wanted it.

But as if sensing Tyler's inner thoughts, Evie shoved away from him a moment later.

"Unhand me and go after that cad! I want him strung up by the neck. So help me, if he ever lays another hand on me . . ."

Tyler placed his hand over her mouth and glanced at Ben who was checking out the window.

"Went out this way, all right. There's a bit of a roof down there, over the back door. He just jumped down and slid to the ground, I reckon. Must have had a horse waiting. I don't see nothin'."

Someone was pounding on the door. Tyler waited until he was certain Evie's tirade had silenced, then released her mouth. She glared at him but held her tongue.

"Good girl. Did you get a look at who did it?"

Evie wanted to smack Tyler's face for that patronizing tone, but she was too glad of his arm around her waist to do anything that would release it. She didn't want him to ever let her go. Gathering her resources, she glanced

down at her lovely gown and tried to patch the flounce
at her neckline back where it belonged.

"No, he had a sack over his head. I don't think I've
ever seen him before." Her voice shook, and she hated
that. The pounding on the door increased.

"Better let them in." Tyler put his gun back in the
holster and gently pushed Evie into a chair while Ben
went to let in whoever Phil had fetched in the name of
the law.

The scrawny youngster didn't look any older than
Evie, but he wore a badge and a gun and a certain familiarity to the rest of the Powells. He frowned menacingly,
as if that was expected of him, but his eyes lit with sudden admiration as his gaze fell on Evie.

"Miz Peyton, ma'am! Are you all right?"

"Of course she's not all right. She's been abducted and
dragged up here like a sack of corn, and she's half scared
out of her mind. Why don't you just stand there and
listen instead of asking stupid questions?" Tyler was getting damned tired of seeing that look in men's eyes when
they saw Evie. But he blamed his irritation on the
scrawny lawman and not the fear of these last few
minutes.

Evie sent him an admonishing look. Holding her
flounce, she turned back to the boy. "I don't suppose
you have a pin on you? I must look a complete disaster."

Tyler thought he would strangle her. The boy was patting his pockets as if he were in the habit of carrying
straight pins, and his eyes were wider than saucers as
they noted the place where the gown was torn. To Evie's
credit, she wasn't wearing one of her low-cut evening
gowns—she'd probably sold all those—but the respectable walking gown still had a less than modest neckline
that would reveal more than was necessary should she
remove her hand. Tyler shrugged off his coat and threw
it around her shoulders.

"Tell us what happened, E—" He corrected himself
and finished, "Mrs. Peyton."

Evie pulled the coat around her, let her gaze flicker
over the men pushing through the bedroom door, and
waited.

Tyler sighed, gestured at Ben, and between the two of them, they shoved the sightseers back out into the hall and slammed the door.

"The children are waiting, Mrs. Peyton, if you could hurry?" Tyler prompted politely.

That did the trick. Evie was on her feet and heading for the door. "Some donkey grabbed me in the alley, covered my mouth with his nasty hand, stuck a rag in it, and dragged me up here. I couldn't see his face. He had it covered with a sack, and there weren't any lights. He smelled like horse manure." She stopped to pull Tyler's coat over her arms and around her torn bodice, then turned to look at the men waiting for the rest of the tale.

"He told me if I behaved, everything would be all right. I didn't recognize his voice. I'd say he was a head taller than me, maybe not much bigger than Tyler. He wore gloves and boots. When he got me up here, he had to set me down to get that rope." She nodded at the rope no one had noticed lying on the bed. "I knocked over the lantern, kicked the chair, took out the gag"— she nodded at the handkerchief lying on the floor—"and then you were pounding at the door. He ran for the window and was gone before I could stop him."

Evie reached for the door, then remembering the crowd behind it, turned back to the room. "Tyler?"

Tyler looked at the scrawny boy who was standing, still dazed, in the center of the room. "Go back to the office and write all that down. I'll come back and tell you more if she remembers it."

With that, he caught Evie's arm, gestured at Ben, and holding her protectively to the side nearest the wall, he eased her out the door while Ben pushed the sightseers out of the way.

Evie went without a word. Tyler in shirtsleeves and waistcoat was still an impressive sight to see. Only one person questioned his right to lead her away. Jonathan Hale stepped out of the crowd to confront them.

"Mrs. Peyton, I came running as soon as I heard the screams, but apparently your friend here was quicker." He sent Tyler a look of mixed irritation and suspicion before turning back to Evie. "Are you sure you're all right? I could arrange for your security. It is difficult to trust anyone in times like these. I hope you realize you can rely on me."

Evie looked down at the lawyer's hand grasping hers and wondered dully what in heaven's name he was talking about.

Tyler merely disengaged her hand and half carried her past the irate lawyer without a word.

Gratefully, Evie followed Tyler down the back stairs that she had just been dragged up, not protesting his strong arm at her back. She could hear Ben clattering behind them, but her thoughts were drifting forward to the children and Daniel.

She tried not to think of the man holding her. As they popped through the back door into the alley, she asked the question uppermost in her mind. "Do you think he was one of the thieves who escaped?"

It was the same thought Tyler had been chasing around in his head. She wasn't going to like his conclusion. "Maybe we better get back to the house before we talk."

Evie accepted that. She was suddenly very tired. Her arm ached where it had been yanked behind her. Since she had left St. Louis, she had been subjected to more overt hostility than she had ever suffered in her life. If this was what real life was like, she wanted her Nanny back. She would take her adventures from between the covers of a book from now on.

Before they reached the house, Tyler was nearly carrying her. Ben grabbed the door to let them in. Evie looked up to see Daniel and Carmen safe and waiting with terrified expressions, and she started for the bedroom to check on Maria.

With an empathy he couldn't explain, Tyler caught Evie's arm, gently removed his coat from her shoulders, threw it on a chair, swung her into his arms, and carried her into the bedroom. Maria was already sound asleep in the big bed. Tyler laid Evie beside her, brushing a kiss across her forehead.

"I'd take your clothes off, but I'd shock the children.

Get some rest. I'll be right outside until morning, so you don't have to worry about a thing."

He was saying words Evie wanted to hear. She closed her eyes and nodded. Tyler would take care of everything. He would make certain Manuel and José were in their beds, keep away the goblins, and explain everything to Daniel. She could just lie here and pretend she was back home in St. Louis.

Except she wasn't in St. Louis. As she lay there, inert, Evie could hear the low rumble of Tyler's voice in the next room. She wanted that voice whispering in her ear again. She wanted his arms back around her waist. She wanted his body in the bed next to her, holding her, keeping her warm, making her feel good again.

Just the thought brought a flush from her head to her toes. She wanted Tyler naked next to her. Would he know she thought things like that? The idea didn't bear considering. Her imagination had gone completely out of hand to think such things.

In the next room, Tyler heard the soft sounds of Evie rising from the bed, her shoes falling to the floor, her bare feet pattering across the old wood as she took off her gown. He kept his explanations to Daniel and Carmen brief. He didn't think he could concentrate for long on what he was saying while he listened to Evie undressing. They were a sensible pair; they didn't question him long.

Tyler watched them go off to their respective rooms and breathed a sigh of relief. Daniel caught the one they called Manuel hiding around the corner and dragged him off by the back of his shirt. Tyler hid a weary grin, threw his hat on the table, and waited for Ben to speak.

"I'm goin' to mosey 'round the hotel awhile. Mind if I borrow your room?"

"Someone might as well get my money's worth out of it." Tyler handed him the key.

Ben looked him up and down carefully. Tyler was in his shirtsleeves, his usually immaculate hair disheveled, and his patented grin sagging slightly. He shook his head. "You a mess, boy. That woman got you by the back hairs. You better get on out or start accepting it."

Tyler scowled and removed his tie. "I'll be back at the ranch on Monday. Just you mind your own business."

Ben gave a sour chuckle and walked out shaking his head. Tyler growled and contemplated going after him, but he had promised Evie he would stay. Sitting down on the pallet and pulling off his boots, he wondered what in hell he'd got himself into this time.

He was almost positive that Evie's abductor wasn't one of the escaped thieves. They wouldn't have hung around or bothered dragging a woman to a hotel room.

Someone was after Evie.

Back at the hotel, Hale listened sympathetically as Phil ranted about the room's destruction and the fact that since it hadn't been rented to anyone, he had no one to pay the damages. Suggesting that Phil start changing his locks, the lawyer took his departure on that piece of free advice.

Returning his hat to his head as he reached the street, Hale turned his feet in the direction of the dreary rooms he called home. He showed no surprise as Tom slipped out of the livery to join him.

"Some hero you make," the larger man sneered as he fell in step. "You were right there and still couldn't get to her in time."

"Some criminal you make," Hale replied mockingly. "Your man let her go. Where do you find the stupid bastards?"

"You get what you pay for," Tom replied with unconcern. "That was a damned stupid idea anyway. Women don't look twice at heroes. They like their men strong and mean to keep them in line. Take her out in the woods and put it to her, and she'll be so grateful you won't even have to ask. When you get her back to town, she'll be thoroughly compromised and begging you to marry her."

Hale gave this crudity a look of disgust. "You want to see me shot, don't you? With the likes of that gunfighter hanging around, I'd have a bullet through my middle before I opened my mouth."

Tom pulled thoughtfully at his long cigar. "Sheriff

don't cotton to gunfighters. And he's riled a few of my friends. He shot the brother of one of them. Why don't I see what I can do about eliminating your competition?"

Ignoring his roughneck client, Hale took the steps to his room two at a time.

Below him, the red glow of a cigar lingered thoughtfully for a few minutes more, before disappearing in the direction of the saloon.

The next morning, Evie wasn't quite prepared to accept Tyler's conclusions when he gave them, but her own conscience worked against her. As she readied the children for church, she tried to think what she could have said to whom to give herself away, but the lawyer seemed the only logical suspect, and second consideration didn't even make that thought logical. It was definitely not the namby-pamby Mr. Hale who had dragged her up those stairs. And he thought she was just a friend of Evangeline Howell's.

Logan was a little more logical suspect. He'd already been caught once sneaking around the house. Perhaps he hadn't believed her story. She should never have used her middle name. She was beginning to think that it was the cause of all her trouble.

Tyler had gone back to the hotel to change his clothes after she got up, but he was back in time to escort them to church. Evie supposed she ought to be worrying about her reputation after last night and with Tyler walking at her side as if he belonged there, but her mind was on more important things.

Letting the children get farther ahead, she tugged on Tyler's arm and whispered, "Have you told anyone about where I come from or anything?"

Tyler lifted a golden brow and looked down on her. "What is there to tell? I know about as much as anyone around here."

"You know my name is Evie," she pointed out.

"I know you call yourself Evie upon occasion," he agreed, "but I haven't mentioned the fact to anyone. Why?"

She embarked on a different tactic. "Have you heard anyone mention a family named Howell?"

The children were already in the church. Tyler wanted to stop and haul her back and put her through an inquisition, but he could only smile and nod at the people standing around the church door as they entered.

Through his smiles, he whispered back, "I remember Jace saying his mother's maiden name was Howell."

Evie's face went pale. "Oh, hell."

A sudden silence fell around them, and she looked up to discover they were standing in the church doorway, and every face in the place was turned toward her.

The acoustics in here were very good.

Chapter 26

"I wonder if that was the sermon the reverend meant to preach this morning," Tyler mused aloud as the church crowd departed in different directions around them and he casually steered Evie through it.

"I think I like Maryellen's version of it much better." Kyle laughed, and came up on Evie's other side.

Tyler raised a disapproving eyebrow at the familiarity of using first names, but Evie was going red, and he held his tongue. "Harding, you're intruding. Go away."

Kyle kept his pace. "I've been commissioned to ask Mrs. Peyton if she would join us out at the ranch for Sunday dinner. At least I haven't driven her to swearing at me yet."

Evie's fingers clenched Tyler's arm tighter. Surprised but more pleased than he cared to admit at her unspoken plea, Tyler dismissed Kyle's request. "You'll have to plan further in advance than that. She's already accepted my invitation."

Kyle looked to Evie for confirmation. She offered a small smile. "The excitement last night was rather wearing on my nerves, Mr. Harding. And I have lesson plans to put together for tomorrow. Maybe another time?"

"Next Sunday?"

Evie's fingers were digging deeper, but Tyler let her field this one on her own.

"It might be better if you were to dine with us, Mr. Harding. I have the children to consider, and Daniel would be disappointed to be left behind. His leg still gives him a great deal of pain."

Kyle was obviously disappointed, but he succumbed to

her plea. "Of course, I should have thought of that. Just let me know, and I'll be there."

He walked away, and Evie relaxed and released Tyler's arm. Completely out of the blue, she asked, "Tell me, Mr. Monteigne, when was the last time you attended church?"

Tyler could find no clue to the reason for this question in her placid expression, and he watched the children skipping ahead as he debated his answer. If this were some kind of test, he was about to fail it. "Sometime before the war, I reckon."

Evie nodded. "That's what I thought. And why did you choose to attend today?"

"Because I'm not going to let you out of my sight until I get a few explanations."

That was a lie. She was very good at recognizing lies. Avoiding looking at the handsome man beside her, Evie watched Manuel and José run off with several of their friends. She was about to reprimand them for not changing their good clothes, but she needed to talk to Tyler more. She let them go as she subjected him to the questioning needed to shore up her confidence in the only man in town she might trust. He had gone to church for her sake. Could she trust him with the truth?

"I see," she murmured complacently, then thrust from a different direction. "I understand some men like a challenge. If I hand you all the pieces to the puzzle and you put them together, will you lose interest and go away?"

Astounded at this course of their conversation, Tyler didn't reply immediately. When he did, it wasn't an answer. "Do you want me to?"

"That isn't the question at hand. I need someone I can trust. Daniel has a broken leg and can't help me. You and Ben are the only ones I know, but you've been here long enough to be getting itchy feet. If you're ready to roam, I'd just as soon you move on now, before I come to rely on you."

Tyler squinted up at the sun, as if the answer were to be provided there. When no bluebird wrote it across the sky, he returned his gaze to the lady walking at his side. Wherever they went, she turned heads, but she didn't seem conscious of it. She was intent on this conversation and waited for an answer.

There was no getting around the question she hadn't asked. They were almost at the house, and Carmen would already be starting Sunday dinner. Catching Evie's shoulders and holding her to one side, Tyler leaned in the open front door. "Daniel, I'm going to take your sister for a walk. Tell Carmen she doesn't have to do a thing but relax until we get back."

He didn't linger to translate Daniel's reply. Releasing Evie, Tyler started down the path leading away from town, out into the countryside. He jammed his hands in his pockets as she hurried to catch up with him.

"I don't want the responsibility of marriage, Evie. And I sure as hell haven't planned on taking care of a house full of kids. I've not had to plan beyond tomorrow since before the war. That's the way I like it. But I pay my debts, and I know what I owe you. I'm not going to leave you to fend for yourself. Now you can take that any way you want to take it, but I'm not going anywhere until I know you're safe."

Evie straightened her shoulders and marched alongside of him. Her best white organdy skirt trailed in the dirt of the path they were following. The sun overhead was beating unmercifully against her hair, and she feared she would turn pink shortly. A wide spreading oak threw a welcoming patch of shade over the prairie grass ahead, and Evie anticipated its coolness as she pondered Tyler's words.

She had to give him credit for honesty. And he had been amazingly decent about the proprieties since discovering she wasn't carrying his child. Another man might have taken advantage of the situation and then wandered off, leaving her pregnant and alone. Perhaps Tyler didn't desire her any more, but she had learned a few things about a man's needs and wants in these last years, things that couldn't be found in the books she read. She didn't think lack of desire was keeping Tyler Monteigne out of her bed.

"All right. I believe you." Evie stopped in the shade of the oak and turned to face him. He was wearing his hat, and she couldn't discern his eyes, but she sensed they were focused on her with an intensity that would burn could she but see it. "I'll tell you what little I know, if you will stay long enough to help me. Then we can go our separate ways. Agreed?"

Tyler relaxed. That sounded simple enough. He nodded, and a slight breeze wafted the scent of cinnamon and roses around him. Perhaps it wouldn't be quite that simple. He was going to have a devil of a time looking at her for any length of time without stripping off her clothes and making mad, passionate love to her. Hell, he was growing hard just looking at her. Maybe he could devise a scheme for helping and staying a thousand miles away.

"It sounds all right, for now. You want to start with telling me why you asked about a family named Howell?"

"Because that's my name, Evangeline Peyton Howell."

The first blow, and already he was crumpling. Tyler stared down into that innocent face with those exotic eyes and swore vividly. When he was done, he managed an unpleasant smile. "That isn't the name you put on our marriage papers. We might not even be married."

"I didn't know the legalities." Evie turned away and stared out over the prairie. "Shall I stop there, then?"

"No. Keep on going."

"I'm an orphan. Or I assume I'm an orphan. My parents may very well be alive, but they don't claim me. They just pay—paid—my guardian a healthy sum to keep me, until Nanny died. A check hasn't come since then. All I know of them is my name and that the checks come from the Bank of Mineral Springs, Texas, and they are sent by the legal firm of Hale and Son. That's it." She swung around to see how he was taking this.

Tyler removed his hat and let the breeze ruffle his hair as he studied her. He thought there might be a suggestion of a tear in her dark eyes, but she held her chin with a proud defiance he had to admire. For all he knew, she could be half Spanish, just like she'd said. But he didn't think so.

He rubbed his knuckles against the velvet softness of

her cheek. "All right, Miss Howell, now that we have that established, what did you find out at the firm of Hale and Son yesterday?"

Evie's lips trembled slightly, but she held strong at this sign that Tyler didn't mean to turn tail and run. "Nothing. I went in as Maryellen Peyton, and he wouldn't tell me anything. He said to have Evangeline Howell write to him. He also said the Howell family had once been prominent citizens and they were all dead."

"Which could very well mean that there are large sums of money sitting around in that bank over which he has complete control. Nasty situation. Do you have proof that you are who you say you are?"

"I have a baptismal certificate with my name on it, the letters from the attorneys to Nanny, and a letter I assume is from my mother turning over my guardianship to Nanny. The letter uses my name. If there's more, I haven't found it."

Tyler thought about this for a minute. "Well, no one has jumped out of the woodwork and declared you look just like any Howell or whatever. It seems to me you've done a good job hiding your identity. None of that explains why you were abducted last night. I can't see why anyone would want to harm an innocent schoolteacher. Somebody, somewhere, must know something, and the lawyer seems the most likely prospect."

Evie nodded. "That's what I thought, but then I thought about that man, Logan. Do you think the 'Peyton' could be a family name, too? He might not have believed our story. And the lawyer might not have believed it, either. It may be this Peyton person that they're after. But what were you telling me about the Hardings' mother's name?"

"That's all I know. I asked where the Double H brand came from, and they explained it stood for Harding and Howell, that their mother's maiden name had been Howell. She and their father died in a tragic accident some months ago."

"They're not wearing mourning," Evie pointed out.

"People don't hold much with those things out here, particularly men. Life isn't easy, and people come to expect death. Look at that crew of yours. Are they going around moping and moaning like they're expected to do back East? They haven't got time. They've got to survive."

"I suppose." Evie had heard the children's sobs late at night, but there was nothing she or Daniel could do that they weren't already doing. They couldn't bring Mrs. Rodriguez back from the dead. She supposed grown men like Kyle and Jason would deal with the death of their parents in a more grown-up fashion than sobbing in their beds at night. "I guess we need to find out more about the Howells. What do you suggest?"

"I suggest that Evangeline Howell write from St. Louis and tell Mr. Hale that Nanny is dead and ask for instructions. We can crumple the letter up some and walk on it and put it in the mail and it will look like it's been through every mailbag between here and there. I assume you've made some arrangement to have your mail sent down here."

"Yes, but it could take months for Hale's reply to go to St. Louis and back. There's got to be a faster way. I had hoped to get Daniel hired on as a clerk, but with his leg . . ." Evie made a gesture of frustration.

Tyler didn't have any intention of sitting around idle waiting for a letter to appear, but he wasn't going to tell Evie that. There was no telling how much dust she had already stirred up by going to that lawyer yesterday. He was keeping her clear of any other proceedings.

"Give me time to make a few more inquiries, Evie. We can't do much until we have some facts. You just get busy writing that letter. I'll let you know when I've found out anything." Tyler steered her back in the direction of town. With a definite task ahead of him, he felt a little more comfortable. This business of vague worries about Evie and the children made him itchy. He preferred direct action, and now she had given him enough information to act.

Evie smiled and let him steer her away, but she wasn't about to sit back and do nothing while waiting for Tyler to do all the work. She had a few plans of her own.

*   *   *

"There's mail, Daniel," Evie whispered excitedly, with a trace of worry as she came in after school the next day. Two slim envelopes waved in her hand as she stepped from the bright sunlight of outdoors into the dimness of the front room.

Both envelopes had an Ohio return address, and Evie handed them unopened to Daniel. They both knew what that return address meant. The fact that they were addressed to the "executor of Delilah Witherspoon's" estate told a whole story.

"We shouldn't have these, Evie." Daniel stared at the envelopes hungrily, without opening them. "There must be a lawyer out there somewhere taking care of Nanny's unfinished business."

"Of course there is." Impatiently, Evie threw her books and papers down on the table. Carmen had gone to pick up Maria at a neighbor's, but she would be returning any minute. "We just didn't wait around for him to hem and haw and decide what to do with us. Maybe that's where my check has gone. That would mean that Mr. Hale already knows Nanny is dead, if this other lawyer has sent out notices."

Another lawyer with the power of their future hanging over their heads. Daniel sighed. Maybe he ought to study law. It might be the only way to ever untangle this cursed mess.

But he'd much rather be a newspaper man. With determination, he ripped open the first letter and scanned it.

"It's the check for my upkeep." Daniel glanced at Evie. "Do we dare cash it now? If there's a lawyer out there, he might accuse us of stealing."

"How can you steal your own money? Cash it, and let them come find us." Evie crossed her arms defiantly. There was no doubt pots of money sitting around in banks and lawyer's offices all over the country that they were entitled to. She didn't see any reason why they should have to starve and do without while lawyers debated the disposition of all that wealth. "Open the other one."

The other envelope contained a lengthy sheet of vellum that Daniel scanned quickly, then went back and read more thoroughly. His hands were shaking as he handed it over to Evie when he was done.

"They want to know how I am progressing, if it is possible for me to attend a university. They are willing to continue providing funds to the estate and for this executor to act as my guardian until I am of age. There isn't any note to me or any mention of condolences. It's a business letter."

"And you're unfinished business, just like Nanny's estate." Evie read the letter with disgust. "If I were you, I'd write to this lawyer and tell him you're ready to accept their offer. Get an education. Get everything out of them that you can. Then when you come of age, go back there and walk in on them and say 'hello, folks, here I am, ready to take over the family business.' I'd like to see their faces."

Daniel managed a painful smile. "It would be even more amusing were I whole again." He folded the letter up and put it in his pocket. "But I'm not going anywhere until we find out about your family. Take the draft and put it in the bank. José is practically barefoot, and they can all use new clothes."

Evie glanced at him speculatively. "And you will need transport out of here. This may be all we get. We can't spend much of it."

Daniel looked annoyed as he returned to his reading. "Don't be a goose, Evie. I'll write the lawyer and tell him to forward the money here. We'll be fine. Go deposit the money."

He was hurting, and there wasn't a thing she could do. Quietly, Evie folded the bank draft and put it in her skirt pocket. She had felt the pain of never knowing who her parents were, but it was as nothing compared to knowing she was not wanted. She knew exactly what Daniel was feeling right now.

Returning to the sunshine outdoors, Evie hurried down the alley toward the bank. Tyler had warned her not to go out alone after dark, but she felt no insecurity in traversing the streets during day. This was a small town, and she was always in sight and sound of someone.

The other night had been a fluke with the jailbreak causing so much commotion that her abductor might have got away with it had it not been for Ben and Tyler's quick reactions.

She almost bumped into Mr. Hale as she came around the corner. She caught herself just in time, pulling her skirt out of the dust as he raised his hat and made a gentlemanly bow.

"Mrs. Peyton!" He gave her a look of warm concern. "I am happy to see you doing so well after Saturday night's little contretemps. I tried to be of some assistance, but the sheriff's son kept everyone shut out. I cannot understand such a thing happening in Mineral Springs."

"Mr. Monteigne believes it was one of the escaped outlaws. I'm certain nothing of the kind will ever happen again." Evie began strolling toward the bank. She wanted to get as much information from this man as she could, but the bank draft was burning in her pocket.

Mr. Hale offered her his arm, and she accepted it, giving him a delighted smile that he promptly returned.

"I understand Mr. Monteigne is a friend of your family's. Will he be staying here for any length of time?"

She was supposed to be the one asking questions. Evie made a vague gesture. "He has business with the Hardings, I believe. Tell me, Mr. Hale, if I go to the cemetery, will I find graves for the Howells? I have already written Evangeline about what you said, but the mail takes so long, I thought I'd find out what I could on my own. My letters are likely to reach her before there is time for her to write you and you to respond."

"I can see no harm in your visiting their graves. I would be delighted to escort you. Do you have time now?"

Mr. Hale was a very polite man. Evie smiled at him approvingly. She wished he wasn't so darn ethical about keeping family secrets, but she couldn't complain if the family lawyer was an honest man.

"I have to stop in the bank. I don't wish to delay you."

"There's no delay. We're already here." He opened the door for her and escorted her inside.

She didn't want him watching her as she tried to deposit Daniel's check. It was going to be a tricky business as it was. Evie bit her lip in frustration and glanced around the tiny building. There was one teller's booth behind bars and a desk in the far corner of the room behind the teller. She could see the safe built into the wall behind the teller. It wouldn't take much to rob this place.

Sighing, she patted Mr. Hale's hand. "If you'll just wait here for me, I'll be right back."

The teller was only a few steps away, but if she talked low, perhaps he wouldn't hear. She removed the check and stepped forward to transact her business.

Several minutes, several smiles, and several blushes and reassurances from the male teller later, Evie returned triumphantly to Mr. Hale. Daniel now had his very own bank account.

"Your brother is lucky to have a sister like you." Hale opened the door. "Your maiden name is Mulloney, then?"

So he had heard. Evie held her chin up. "Yes. We're originally from Ohio, but we've lived in the South for some considerable time now. The war was devastating to us all." Distraction worked best at times like this.

"I'm certain. Was your husband from around here, by any chance, Mrs. Peyton? There are still remnants of a Peyton family in these parts, but I don't remember any of the name Alexander."

Evie tried not to tighten her grip on the lawyer's arm as they entered the churchyard. "Alexander grew up in Natchez, sir, but it is possible there are cousins."

"It's quite a coincidence your coming to Mineral Springs to teach, and then taking on the Rodriguez children, if so, Mrs. Peyton." Hale stopped before two small, nondescript gravestones and pointed at them with his cane. "There lies the Rodriguez children's maternal grandparents."

Evie could just barely make out the inscription: James and Rosita Peyton.

Chapter 27

Evie smiled, made several noncommittal remarks about her husband's wandering cousins, and allowed Mr. Hale to lead her toward the grander monuments in the Howell family plot. She refused to reveal how shaken she was already as she listened politely to his explanations. He pointed out the patriarch of the family, Cyrus Howell, his wife beside him, a son who had died at an early age, and various and assorted relatives. But none of the graves were new. Tyler had said the Hardings' mother had only recently died.

Evie placed her gloved hand on the lawyer's frock-coated arm and turned away. "I'm afraid my friend is going to be terribly disappointed. She is only my age. It seems most of those people were much too old to be her parents. But I do thank you for your time, sir."

Hale hesitated, then led her farther down the same path. "All the Howells aren't buried in the family plot, of course. Wives are usually buried with their husbands. Louise, for instance, was Cyrus's daughter. She's buried in the Harding family plot. I believe you are acquainted with the Hardings? It was a tragic accident."

They came to stop before a newly erected monument, and Evie held her breath as she swiftly scanned the writing. She scarcely paid attention to the name of Randall Harding. Her whole being focused on the name below it: Louise Evangeline Harding, born 1829, died 1870.

Evie quivered. She reached out a hand to touch the stone, but didn't dare in Hale's presence. Tears filled her eyes. She wanted to fall to her knees and weep, to pour out all the grief and pain and frustration of twenty years into the grass just barely started over the dirt mounds.

Her mother. She knew it. Evie could feel it to the very bottom of her soul. It was as if Louise were standing over her now, holding out a hand in sorrow. She had died so young. If only Evie had come a few months sooner. She would have known her, spoken to her, maybe come to love and understand her. Just a few short months, and now eternity separated them. It was more than Evie's heart could bear.

She turned away sharply and started down the path before her tears could betray her. She pulled out a handkerchief and neatly dabbed at her eyes, forcing herself to behave as Maryellen Peyton, disinterested observer. She should be handed an acting award. Her very foundations had been shaken, and she was walking with this man as if she didn't have a care in the world.

"How sad for the Hardings. Their mother must have been terribly young. It is always tragic when someone dies young." Evie was doing mental acrobatics. Applying her mind to a problem always helped to alleviate emotion. She had no reason to cry over a mother who had abandoned her, even if that mother could barely have been twenty years old when she had her. Her age. Evie could very well remember the terrible fear of being pregnant with no man's name for her child. She didn't want to feel sympathy for the dead woman, but it would come later, when she didn't have to think.

"Actually, she was just their stepmother. I'm right between Jace and Kyle in age, and I can remember when she married their father. She probably wasn't much more than ten years older than Jace, but she made us boys jump when she came around. She was a mighty fine woman. She's the one who put up the money for the school. The government has finally got around to saying we ought to have public schools, but the money just isn't there. Without her, the children around here would be growing up ignorant."

Evie liked hearing these things. Her mother was a good woman, a well-respected woman, and a good mother. It gave her some small sense of pride. She supposed if she thought about it she could be furiously bitter that such a good woman would desert her only daughter, but Evie was certain there were mitigating circumstances. She couldn't have done what her mother had done, but was abandoning a child so much worse than killing an unborn one? That's what she had meant to do.

Lost in the torment of her thoughts, Evie almost didn't hear Mr. Hale's words. She halted a minute as if to adjust the buttons on her gloves, then looked up at him through her lashes. "I'm so sorry, Mr. Hale, I believe I missed what you were saying."

He tucked his cane beneath his arm and took her arm to guide her over a tree root as they left the cemetery. "Perhaps it would be better if I did not repeat it. I have no business talking so freely to you like this, but I can see you are a woman of compassion, and that you have Miss Howell's best interests in mind. I do not know how to phrase this without going beyond my authority to do so."

"You mentioned the Hardings. I fail to see how they could be of any interest to my friend."

Hale answered evasively and in low tones as they traversed the main street. "Mr. Harding had a younger brother. Really, Mrs. Peyton, I cannot say more. As long as your friend does not come to Mineral Springs, there is no need to worry. The Hardings are very attractive young men. It would just be . . . shall we say, indelicate, if she should develop any relationship with Kyle or Jace."

It didn't take too long to work out that hint. If Kyle's uncle were Evie's father, the Hardings would be her first cousins. So much for her mother being a good woman. Evie's lips tightened.

"I'm certain that won't be a problem. Evangeline is happily affianced to a very wealthy gentleman back in St. Louis. You can understand why a woman on the brink of marriage might be concerned about her heritage." Since Mr. Hale was being so considerately open to her, Evie boldly pushed forward. "As a matter of fact, I have given thought to what we discussed the other day. I have already written Evangeline, you understand, but wouldn't it be better if you were to write her immediately and tell her what you know? Her wedding is a few short months from now, and it would be so much better if her concerns were answered quickly."

Hale hesitated, giving the young woman on his arm a quick look. She had to be the woman he had sought in St. Louis. But she spoke so easily of this "friend" of hers and her impending marriage, that it made him doubt his conclusions. If she spoke about herself, could she be contemplating marriage? He had heard no such rumor in St. Louis.

"As a matter of fact," Hale said carefully, "I have been trying to get in touch with Miss Howell. You'll understand that I am not in a position to divulge the details. I have left my card with both her guardian and her legal adviser in St. Louis, but I have not heard from either of them."

Evie was jubilant, but she didn't dare reveal anything yet. If she could only tell him who she was ... it would save a great deal of time and worry. But the abduction the other night made her hesitate and give Tyler's and Daniel's warnings more consideration than she would have otherwise. She was almost positive she knew who her mother was, and Hale had insinuated at her father's name. Those were pieces of information she could savor for a long time. She could wait for the rest of the details a little while longer.

"Her guardian has only recently died. I'm sure there is just a certain amount of confusion involved. She will be in touch, particularly if she gets my letter. I thank you so much for your kindness, Mr. Hale." They had come to the alley by the hotel, and Evie held out her hand in farewell. For some reason, she was reluctant to let Mr. Hale see where she was staying, although he certainly seemed to know everything about her.

"May I be so bold as to ask for your company one evening over dinner, Mrs. Peyton? It is not often that we have an attractive young woman in this town, and I will admit to being most interested in you."

She hadn't thought she'd made much of an impression at all on this dry stick of a man. Evie hid her surprise at his request. "I would be honored, Mr. Hale, but as I have told Mr. Harding, it is rather difficult for me. My brother suffered an accident recently and is confined to bed, and the Rodriguez children look to me for their welfare while we search for their uncle. Perhaps another time."

He bowed over her hand. "I will find some way to see you again. However, I am unhappy to inform you that I have heard the children's uncle was killed in California some years ago. You may do better to let the town see to their placement in homes."

Evie frowned at this piece of news, and absently dismissed the lawyer before going her own way. Why would Mr. Hale have heard of the death of someone in California, if the man's own niece and nephews hadn't heard of it? But Mr. Hale had been so extremely helpful in other ways, she couldn't just put the information aside.

She needed time to assess all the facts and innuendos she had accumulated this day, but as she walked in the door, the sight of Tyler spread-eagled on the floor decimated all else.

Maria and José sat on each of his arms and Manuel held his legs. When Evie entered, Tyler looked up and began scattering children across the floor. They giggled and laughed and came back for more, climbing into his lap and pulling on his arms and wrapping small arms around his neck to try to pull him down again. Evie gaped, amazed.

"It's the only way I could keep them all in one place," Tyler explained, embarrassed, as he rose from the floor with Maria still clinging to his neck and José hanging on to his knee.

"Where are Carmen and Daniel?" instantly on the alert, Evie looked to the pallet where Daniel usually lay. Finding it empty, she started for the back bedroom door.

"I'm fine, Evie," Daniel called from his bed. "They're just making a fuss about nothing. I need food more than I need a doctor."

Tyler pulled the leech off his neck and dropped her into Evie's arms. "He was trying to stand and the pestilence here knocked him over." He tickled Maria on the belly, sending her off into a fit of giggles. Obviously, she felt no remorse. "Carmen's gone to find the doctor."

"Oh, Daniel, no!" Carrying Maria into the bedroom with her, Evie tried to determine the extent of the damage by the paleness of Daniel's face. He was in pain, she could see that. But the leg still seemed to be lying straight.

"It's fine. I know it's fine. I just bruised myself a little. I'm going to walk again. I'm going to ask the doc if I can take some of these bandages off. It will be easier to exercise if I'm not all wrapped up." Daniel shifted his weight against the pillow and leaned over to look at his offending leg. He'd been wearing the same set of trousers for three weeks now rather than slit all his clothes up the side to accommodate the bandages. He was getting mighty tired of the whole routine.

Tyler came in behind Evie, holding José like a sack of grain beneath one arm. The six-year-old kicked and squirmed, but Tyler acted as if he weren't there. "Daniel's made of tough stuff. He'll survive if you'll get a little food in him. I managed to keep an eye on this nest of rattlesnakes, but I'm not getting near that stove of yours."

José squealed at being called a rattlesnake and started throwing punches, but Tyler upended him by the ankles and threatened to bounce him off the floor. José laughed with delight.

Evie watched this play dubiously. Tyler was wearing buckskins and boots, but his shirt was the white linen of a gentleman and not a cowboy. Still, he wasn't wearing the ruffles and waistcoat of the gambler, and she had never seen him in anything else before. And it wasn't just the clothes that were different. Could this be the same Tyler who had backed out and practically run when he'd returned to the hotel to find the children singing?

"What are you doing here?" she asked suspiciously as she accepted Daniel's reassurances and returned to the front room to try to fix dinner.

"I've been asking myself that for the past hour. The question is, where have you been for all that time?" Tyler had dropped José, and the two boys were now wrestling on the floor at his feet. Maria was quietly sitting at the sewing basket by the fireplace, pulling out threads and needles one by one and scattering them across the hearth.

Tyler appeared to be completely untouched by the confusion. He stood beside Evie, hands on hips, waiting for an explanation she didn't feel prepared to give. She slapped a bowl at his middle so he had to grab it, then poured in some cornmeal.

"If you're going to be underfoot while I'm fixing dinner, you're going to have to help. Add milk until it gets thick."

Tyler stared at the bowl as if it were a pig that had sprouted wings. Evie ignored his expression and turned back to the stove to add onions to the beans that had been soaking all day.

Refusing to be intimidated by a termagant in an apron and a room full of children, Tyler set the bowl on the dry sink and began adding buttermilk from the pitcher Evie had set out. "What do I do with it now?"

"Mush it around so everything's moist, throw in a little sugar, some of that bacon grease in the can over there, and anything else that seems good." Evie wiped the onion juice off her hands onto the apron she had donned when she came in and reached for some of the dried chili peppers hanging from the shelf.

"Aren't you supposed to measure these things?" Tyler looked at the sugar and grease with bafflement. The mixture in the bowl was more than moist, and he had a suspicion he'd added too much milk.

"Do you win at poker by counting cards or watching people's faces?"

"I've spent years watching people's faces. I've never looked at a bowl of cornmeal before." In disgust, Tyler threw a lump of grease in and a spoonful of sugar. The mixture was beginning to look a mite peculiar. "Counting cards works better when you start out."

Throwing in the chopped peppers, Evie removed the bowl from his hands. "Then go entertain the children or keep Daniel company."

"All I wanted to know is where you've been." Tyler stepped back out of her way, but not so far that she couldn't hear him.

"And all I wanted to know is why you're here. Stalemate. Now scat. I've got to keep my eye on this stove."

She was in a flurry of motion, and Tyler stood back to admire the choreography. She was in one of her schoolteacher gowns today: no bustle, no flounce, no crinoline. The simple-figured cotton swirled around her as she moved from stove to table to sink to cabinet. She sent Manuel out to bring in vegetables from the root cellar and José to fetch a pail of water. He couldn't remember reading any novels where the heroine was a homemaker, but he bet there was one, and Evie had read it.

Tyler remembered the kitchen back home with black slaves singing and moving about and his mother occasionally testing a dish and instructing the younger girls how to properly mix a cake. He remembered the scents of baking bread, frying chicken, and peach cobbler bubbling on the windowsill. He remembered feeling at home and content in this small world that was all he knew.

And he remembered how it had exploded all around him. Turning his back on the scene, Tyler started for the door, only to halt when it flew open with the entry of Carmen and the doctor on her heels. With a sigh, he caught Carmen as she tripped on one of the spools of thread rolling across the floor. Setting her straight, he grabbed Maria before she could go after the doctor and set about picking up the contents of the sewing basket as Carmen led the way to Daniel. He'd be damned if he ever had children of his own. They ought to be avoided like measles.

But Maria was patting his cheek and kissing his ear, and Tyler wandered over to catch the screaming argument between Carmen and Daniel so Evie wouldn't have to drop what she was doing to investigate. Even if Carmen's words were half in Spanish, it wasn't very difficult to translate. Tyler dumped Maria into her sister's arms, turned Carmen around, and shoved her back through the bedroom door. Sometimes, men had to stick together.

Daniel gave him a grin of relief and finally submitted to the examination. "She's afraid I'm going to die, too," he explained shyly. "I guess 'cause she's lost her mother and father in this past year."

Tyler nodded his understanding. Daniel had a good head on his shoulders. He seemed to take the vagaries of the world with a calm that Tyler had worked for years to develop. There were times when he still wanted to rip things apart at the injustice of fate, but he wasn't going to let this solemn adolescent know that. He watched carefully as the doctor unwrapped the bandage.

"How's it knitting, Doc?" Tyler asked casually. He didn't want to care what happened to the boy, but he did. If Daniel never walked again, Evie would never forgive herself, and Tyler would have one more black mark to chalk up against a God who hated his creations.

"Satisfactorily, it seems to me." The doctor had Daniel move the leg around in different directions, checking the development of the disabled muscles. "I wouldn't want any pressure on it just yet, but with a crutch to keep the weight off, he might get around a little. The idea is to keep that leg moving just as if you were walking on it. The bone has to knit before you can use the leg, but you've got to get those muscles working for you." These last remarks were addressed to Daniel, who nodded eagerly in understanding.

"How much can I be up? Can I go down to the newspaper office for a while each day?"

The doctor frowned. "That's a bit of a risk. You could stumble or fall or be knocked down again."

The disappointment in Daniel's face was so apparent that Tyler couldn't hold his tongue. "What if someone were to walk with him, just in case something happened? Is there any reason he couldn't walk that far?"

The doctor shrugged, closed his bag, and got up from the bed. "None that I know of. It would be a good stretch for him."

Daniel didn't dare look excited until after the doctor had left, and then only a note in his voice gave him away. "Who can I get to walk with me? Evie's teaching every day."

"I reckon Ben or I or somebody or another can show

up most mornings. It's no hardship to walk those few blocks."

Evie was at the door, wiping her hands on a towel as Tyler said this. Her eyes widened, but she left the questions to Daniel.

"I don't want to put anyone out any," he replied cautiously.

"That's all right, looks like we're going to be around anyway." Tyler turned and held Evie's gaze with his own. "They caught one of the thieves last night. It seems someone from outside helped them to get free."

The same someone who wanted a distraction for Evie's abduction is what his eyes said.

Chapter 28

"You're imagining things, Tyler." Evie tucked her hands under her elbows and walked away from him. The sun hadn't gone down yet, but it was throwing long shadows across the grass as she headed out of town.

"Damn it, Evie, this isn't a dime novel where nothing ever happens to the heroine. Will you come down out of those clouds of yours and listen to me?"

Frustration pounded at his brain and clenched his hands into fists. Not in all the years since the war had he been bombarded with so many frustrations at once. He didn't want the responsibility of worrying about a house full of kids and a crippled adolescent. He sure as hell didn't want to play nursemaid to a beautiful dreamer who couldn't tell the difference between fantasy and reality. The worst of it all was that he couldn't keep his mind off that dreamer's swaying skirts and tiny waist and kissable lips. He needed a woman, and he needed her now.

"I'm not a complete incompetent, you know," Evie replied thoughtfully, as if he were offering an intellectual debate rather than a screaming argument. "I like colors. I wish I could paint that sunset." She gestured toward the horizon. "I suppose I read a lot, but that's because Daniel and I are so close. He could never go out and play with the other children, so we read together."

Aware that Tyler was keeping his distance, Evie stopped and waited until he was beside her. "And I like to write stories in my head. I don't think that's a crime. It's mostly because I want a story to go with the pictures I like to paint."

"And maybe sometimes you like to act them out,"

Tyler finished bluntly. "I'm not Pecos Martin, Evie. I'm not going to come riding to the rescue when the bad guys arrive. I think you'd better leave this town and let a proper lawyer find out the answers to your questions."

"You want me to leave the children? And leave the school without a teacher again? And disappoint Daniel? Do you think he could find a job at any other newspaper office? Not a chance in a million, Mr. Monteigne. You may think I'm a dreamer, but I know what responsibility means. I'm staying here. I'm not running away."

Perhaps there wasn't accusation in her voice, but Tyler heard it anyway. He steeled himself against the guilt and kept his hands in his pockets. "Fine. Stay here and play Joan of Arc. But don't expect me to come to the rescue when they start lighting fires under you."

Evie continued to cup her elbows as she turned to face Tyler. The setting sun cast brilliant highlights off his hair but left his face in shadow. She desperately wanted him to hold her. Without his fancy gambler's clothes she could see the strength in his wide shoulders and muscled arms, and she needed to borrow a little of that security, just for a little while. She thought she would pay him back with interest someday, but he wasn't likely to appreciate the form of payment. Tyler would never admit to needing what she had to give.

"I never imagined myself as a martyr. I like it here, Tyler. I want to stay. Help me to do that."

Tyler kept his curses to himself as he gazed down into her pensive face. He didn't want to consider this aspect of his wife. Evie was meant to be a wild and beautiful butterfly. He liked watching her. He liked hearing about her wilder flights. He admired her beauty and cleverness. He didn't want her tied down with all the baggage the world would pile on her shoulders. But if he left her to do things on her own, that was what would happen. Evie needed a man to take the burden from her. And he didn't want anyone but himself to be that man.

That was a damned foolish thought, and he didn't intend to think it again. He needed a woman and this one appealed to him and that was all there was to it. Without a qualm, Tyler pulled his hands from his pockets and caught Evie by the waist, pulling her to him.

She came without protest, fitting into his arms as if she belonged there. As he bent his head to her, she slid her hands around his neck, and he swelled with pride that she came to him so trustingly. He had never tamed a butterfly before. He held her gently and plied her lips with kisses.

Evie closed her eyes and let her hopes soar as Tyler's arms closed around her. She took his kisses and gave them back twice over. His hands were warm and strong where they held her waist, and when he pulled her closer, tightening his arms around her, her breasts brushed against his shirt and she felt it to her toes. He wanted her; she knew he did. It was a glorious, dizzying feeling, and she reveled in it.

It couldn't last. A carriage rolled by on the dirt path behind them. Tyler set Evie back down and glanced after it. News of the gambler kissing the schoolmarm would be all over town by morning if that was one of the town's biddies. The driver, however, was definitely male, and he breathed slightly easier. It looked to be the lawyer, but the carriage was well on its way now, and he couldn't tell for certain.

He looked back to Evie. Her lips were puffy from his kisses, and her dark eyes were watching him questioningly. She was his wife, for heaven's sake. There wasn't any reason for feeling guilty for kissing his wife.

But remembering the wrong name on the marriage papers and the promises they had made, Tyler dropped his hold on her waist. "That was a mistake. I'm sorry." He turned and started walking back toward town.

Evie stayed where she was. He could ride off into the darned sunset and kiss his horse for all she cared. She wasn't going to follow him. He knew where to find her when he missed her.

The following Saturday, Tyler watched as Hale came down the steps and headed for the café as he always did at noon. As long as he was hanging around town, he might as well put himself to good use. His gut feeling was that the sooner they found out about Evie's parents, the better off they all would be. He wasn't certain where the relationship between the thieves and Evie's abductors and her unknown past might be, but he had a suspicion a few clues were locked away in that lawyer's office.

Nodding at Ben lingering in the shadows beneath the gallery, Tyler casually strolled down the alley behind the building in which the office was situated. He had examined the territory earlier. The building had a back entrance as most of them did. And that entrance led to interior stairs. He didn't have to use the outside ones where all could see.

He was inside Hale's office within minutes. The man didn't believe in locked doors. Admittedly, few buildings around here even had locks, but the secrets held in this office should have required a minimum of caution. Hale either had nothing to hide or he had hidden it well.

Tyler started with the huge oak filing cabinet. Most of the files inside were coated with dust and yellowed with age. Cryptic notes made it impossible to determine the file's contents without examining them. Tyler cursed and looked for some pattern. There didn't seem to be any that he could discern. Old wills for one family were intermixed with mortgage deeds for another family. Scribbled notations fell out of files without any clue as to whom they applied. Hale didn't need a key to open his secrets; he needed an interpreter.

Giving up in disgust on that source, Tyler turned to the mahogany desk. He'd seen one like it over in Georgia during the war. That one had been over a hundred years old and shipped from England. Chances were good that this one had come across the Sabine with some Hale ancestor with more respect for his past than Jonathan. The veneer had cracked and broken in several places.

Tyler found the secret drawer that all these old desks had, but there was nothing in it but fifty-year-old dust, some old coins, and a ledger with meaningless entries from years ago. He could almost swear that Jonathan Hale didn't know the drawer was there. It probably hadn't been opened since his father died.

Evie's lawyer might be honest, but he was a nitwit.

Scowling, Tyler scanned the papers littering the top of the desk. There were a few legal briefs, some deeds in the making, an assortment of ancient books, and the usual tools of the trade. He didn't want to disturb anything that might be noticed, but curiosity had him lifting the large blotter in the desk's center. He could remember his father shoving papers he referred to often under there.

A thin file of papers lay casually beneath the heavy blotting pad. Holding his breath, Tyler eased it out, attempting to leave the rest of the contents of the desk undisturbed.

The first paper inside was a yellowing copy of the last will and testament of one Cyrus Howell. Not taking the time to read it yet, Tyler flipped to the next document. A trust agreement entered into by Elizabeth Howell Harding. Tyler glanced over it swiftly, finding the name Evangeline Peyton Howell almost immediately. He wanted to grab the file and run, but Hale was certain to miss it.

The last document in the file was the will of Randall Harding. Tyler frowned. Hale's filing system left a lot to be desired. Maybe Evie had the right idea. Daniel could clean this place up with one hand behind his back. Unfortunately, those stairs outside presented a certain obstacle to a man with only one good leg.

A sharp whistle from the porch below caused another curse. With regret, Tyler shoved the file back where he found it, checked to make certain he hadn't left anything out of place, then slipped to the door. He heard footsteps coming up the back stairs.

Cursing inwardly, Tyler cast a quick look around. There was no place to hide in here. His gaze fell on a door down the hall. It had no transom or window, so he suspected it was little more than a closet, but that suited him just fine. Hale's visitors weren't likely to visit a closet.

The door was unlocked; the room was unlighted and windowless. Tyler caught a glimpse of towering stacks of old law books and crates of papers, then eased the door closed and waited in silence. Ben had been out front waiting for Hale to come back. The lawyer usually took an hour for lunch. Tyler didn't think it had been an hour yet, and the footsteps had come from the rear of the building. If Ben had seen Hale's visitors, he would have whistled sooner. That must mean Hale was coming down the street to meet the men now pounding noisily down the hall.

"Look, I just want to check on something, all right?"

Tyler didn't recognize the voice, but it was loud and clear enough to carry through the wall and the crates of junk. He stood motionless, afraid any wrong move would start an avalanche. The next voice mumbled, and he strained to hear, but all he caught was the first man's reply.

"Look, I don't trust lawyers any more than you do. That's why I'm here. I saw him put those papers in a drawer, and I want to take a look at them."

The other voice was closer now, just outside the door. "I don't like it. I don't like messing with no kids; I told you that before. I can take this Pecos fellow out without touching the damned kids."

The first voice hissed angrily. "Shut up. We're not doing anything unless I know we're going to get paid. Because of those damned kids, I'm going to have to pull up and start operations somewhere else. I want something out of this. Go keep an eye out the window."

Tyler felt something in his chest constricting. There were probably dozens of kids in town, but there were only a few who might be mentioned in connection with "this Pecos fellow." Damn, and double damn. He wanted to throw open the door and grab these two and send them flying down the stairs. He wanted their necks broken. His hands clenched into fists as he strained to keep control. He knew what happened when he lost control. He couldn't afford to lose control. He didn't even have a gun on him this time.

Tyler felt like every blood vessel in him would burst as he waited for these two to ransack the lawyer's office and leave. He could hear drawers opening and closing, but no further conversation. Then there was a shout from the one watching the window, and two pairs of boots hastily retreated down the back steps. Hale was coming.

He had to get out of here now. He didn't know what they were looking for or what they were talking about. He just knew he had to find out who they were and get the kids somewhere safe. To hell with the damned lawyer.

Tyler left the closet fast on the heels of the two intruders. He cast a look out the window overlooking the alley, but he couldn't see anyone down there. He prayed Ben had got a look at them, but he had a sinking feeling that they·had stayed to the back. Heart pounding faster than was good for all concerned, nerves on edge, Tyler clattered down the back stairs.

The street behind the building was empty. How could they have disappeared so fast? Not daring to attract attention by running, Tyler strode swiftly down the alley to where Ben waited.

Ben heard him coming and whistling, left the porch, and met him in the alley. His expression didn't change as he caught sight of Tyler's grim look. "Hale went on to the livery. Did you find anything?"

"Did you see anyone coming out of here?" Tyler demanded, walking swiftly toward the main street.

Ben raised his eyebrows but replied in an even voice. "Not a soul. What's going on?"

"Have you seen any of the Rodriguez kids?"

Tyler's tension was beginning to make Ben uneasy. He glanced at his friend and picked up his pace. "Not lately. Why?"

"I'm going to check the house. You check the livery. Be careful. If you find them, just get them over to the sheriff's office. I'll figure out what to do with them from there."

They were already to the hotel. There wasn't time for further questioning. Nodding his head in acceptance, Ben took off in his long-legged stride while Tyler tried not to run the distance to the little house behind the stables.

Evie looked up in startlement as Tyler came bursting through the door without any warning. Although his expression revealed nothing, there was something in the way he moved that terrified her. She dropped the pot she was holding and hurried toward him.

"Where are the kids?"

Evie didn't stop to question why he wanted to know. The urgency in his voice was apparent. "Daniel's at the newspaper. Carmen and Maria are at the general store. Manuel and José could be anywhere."

"Get Carmen and Maria over to the sheriff's office. I

don't think they'll bother Daniel, but get him anyway. Tell the sheriff I'll be over as soon as I find the boys. Do you have any idea where they might be?"

Evie took off the apron she'd found in the kitchen. Her hands were shaking. "The livery, most likely. Tyler, you're terrifying me. Can you tell me what this is about?"

"If I knew, I'd tell you. Just do what I say, as quickly as you can. I'll tell you what I know after I find the boys."

He was gone as quickly as he had come. Evie stared after him with a fear that threatened to suffocate her. Picking up a fire iron from beside the fireplace and hiding it in her skirts, she hurried down the alley in Tyler's path. If anyone else meant to jump out at her, she intended to take a piece of their shins first.

She saw Tyler slipping into the livery from the back, so she hurried toward the newspaper office. The printing presses were going, creating a racket that made it nearly impossible to hear, but Averill was apparently used to the cacophony. He nodded at her request and although he gave her a questioning look, he didn't hold her. Evie ran out the door and on down the street to the general store.

She took a deep breath of relief when she found Carmen admiring a red ribbon and dawdling over the counter with Philly and Delphia. The twins gave Evie big smiles, but she merely nodded at them, took Maria into her own arms, and hastened Carmen out the door.

Evie tried not to panic. At least, she tried not to let the children know she was panicking. They could see Daniel making his awkward way toward the sheriff's office at the other end of the street, and they hurried to catch up with him. He gave Evie a searching look, but she shook her head.

"Go on without me," he ordered. "You can go faster than I can."

Evie gave him a stricken look. They had always done everything together. Daniel was her partner in crime. She couldn't leave him behind. But the stoic look on his face warned that his pride would be damaged more if she insisted on hovering over him. Daniel was growing up.

With one last desperate look, she hurried the girls toward the end of town.

Tyler wasn't there. The sheriff looked up in surprise when they entered, so he didn't know what this was about either. Evie wished she had her gloves and hat on instead of a fire iron and a child in her hands. She always felt better when she was dressed properly. Handing Maria back to Carmen, she looked blankly at the fire iron, then glanced back to the sheriff who seemed to be waiting expectantly.

"Tyler's looking for the boys. I think they're in danger. I've got to go find them." She hadn't expected to say that, but as the words came out, Evie knew that was what she had to do.

She turned in a swirl of skirts and started for the door, but Daniel blocked her way. He stood in the doorway leaning on his crutch, and she couldn't get by without knocking him over.

"I've got to find Manuel and José." She waited for him to move.

Daniel looked pointedly at the fire iron. "Not if Tyler told you to come here, too, you're not. Sit down and wait for him to explain."

"He's not here!" Evie cried. "I've got to go find them. I don't know what's going on, but I can find them. I'll be fine. Just let me by."

The sheriff rose and came forward. "Now Mrs. Peyton, I'm sure Tyler will be here in a minute. You just sit down and relax and everything will be just dandy."

A shot echoed in the street outside.

Daniel swung around and nearly toppled as Evie shoved to get next to him. Carmen bit back a scream and clutched Maria. Cursing, the sheriff physically removed Evie from his doorway and stepped out to the boardwalk.

Standing in the center of the street were two of the gang that had escaped earlier. And in their hands were Manuel, José, and two smoking guns. Tyler was nowhere to be seen.

Chapter 29

Murderous rage pumped through Tyler's veins as he gazed down from the hotel roof to the scene in the street below. He'd grabbed his rifle on the way up, and his hands clenched it with years of familiarity. He knew what the weapon felt like in his hands, how it sounded when it went off, the destruction it would wreak when it did. He knew it all too well. The years since he had last held a rifle in ambush like this telescoped to nothing, and he was a terrified, furious boy again. Sweat popped out on his palms as he lifted the weapon into position.

José and Manuel struggled futilely in the arms of their captors. That fact alone made Tyler see red. Grown men terrorizing helpless innocents had that effect. His finger itched on the trigger as he lined up his shot carefully.

They wanted him. He could hear their shouts. Tyler wished for a real Pecos Martin right now. But he knew damned well that for some insane reason, these bastards thought he was Pecos Martin, and they wanted him dead. Every word carried clearly up to him. He could go down there and maybe they'd drop the boys. Maybe.

He hadn't ever wanted to get involved again. He didn't want to do this now. He knew what would happen. Something in him was screaming in terror as he took aim. But it had to be done, just like last time.

Without a shadow of a doubt of his ability to wreak destruction, Tyler squeezed the trigger. A shrill scream echoed up from the street. Taking the time to adjust his aim for the chaos suddenly erupting, he pulled the trigger a second time.

The boys were breaking free and running. He could see Ben grabbing them and jerking them back under cover. The sheriff was headed this way, Evie close on his heels. Tyler pulled the trigger again. The bastards weren't dead yet.

Fury flew through his veins. They weren't going to get away with this. Tyler watched as one man got up and limped for his horse. His finger closed over the trigger. It felt good again. He could feel the power whipping through him. Should he take the bastard's ear off? Go for the heart? How about a long, excruciating death with a shot to the belly? Savagely, he pulled the trigger and watched the man stagger and fall.

Only the vision of Evie running down the street, her gaze scanning the rooftops stopped him from finding the second man in his sights. She avoided looking at the men lying in the street. She couldn't even look at what he had done. The blood and the anguish hurtled up at him through her eyes and ears. Not until then did Tyler lower the rifle.

The shooting had stopped. Keeping her cries and screams inside, Evie ran up on the porch and grabbed the boys from Ben, wrapping her arms around both of them at once and hugging as hard as she could. She couldn't close out the sound of shots ringing in her ears. She couldn't stop hearing the boys' anguished cries for help. She wouldn't look at the carnage behind her.

Tyler had done that. She knew it deep down in her soul without even looking at Ben. She didn't know if there could have been a better way of doing it. She didn't know anything except the boys were alive and in her arms.

Tears were rolling down her face, and Manuel had wriggled free of her embrace by the time Carmen and Daniel made it down the street. Jonathan Hale hurried down from his office to help Evie stand up and to steady her. He murmured reassuring words and tried to steer her in the direction of the hotel lobby. She scarcely even knew he was there.

She waited for Tyler, but he didn't come. Horror and fear wove a suffocating web around her heart. The sheriff was busy rounding up the injured man and giving orders for taking care of the dead one. Daniel and Carmen had the boys firmly in hand. A crowd had started filling the street. But still Tyler didn't come.

She glanced at Ben. His dark face was expressionless, but he gave a curt nod toward the hotel door. Then he stepped forward to usher the children out of the crowd and toward the alley.

That was all the signal Evie needed. Shaking herself free from Hale's sympathetic embrace, she picked up her skirt and headed for the hotel lobby under her own sails, leaving the lawyer behind. By the time he followed her in, she was halfway up the stairs. He called after her, but she ignored him.

She knew where Tyler's room was. She had seen him standing in the window, watching over the house late at night. There had been times she had been tempted to go to him, but she knew the physical realities of romance now, and she had resisted. She wanted more than he had to offer.

But she didn't give a fig for reality right now. She didn't know where Tyler was, but he needed her. She could feel the need welling up inside her. His cries echoed in her ears with their silence. He should be down there now, giving explanations to the sheriff, reassuring the boys, holding her. But he wasn't. He was hiding somewhere in this hotel, avoiding what he had done. That wasn't the Tyler she knew. Something was wrong.

She knocked on his door and got a muffled curse in reply. He was in there. Setting her jaw, Evie threw open the door.

Tyler was sitting on the bed, calmly cleaning his rifle. When he looked at her, his eyes were perfectly blank. That terrified her more than anything else he could have done. Tyler's eyes always danced with mischief and laughter or darkened with fury and anguish. They never stared blankly.

Heart plummeting to her stomach, Evie closed the door behind her and moved into the room.

"You'd better leave, Mrs. Peyton." Tyler snapped the rifle shut and began to wipe down the outside with a rag.

"Why? Will you shoot me if I don't?"

That brought a thread of fury to his eyes. His gaze hardened as it drifted over Evie's schoolmarmish gown. She had quit wearing her fancy silks and laces in preference for the practicality of cotton, but the high-necked gown did nothing to disguise her distracting figure. Tyler's knowing gaze reminded her of things she didn't want to remember.

"If you mean to stay, I can think of better things to do with you than shoot." He set the rifle aside and stood up.

Evie supposed she was supposed to feel threatened. She didn't. Perhaps she was mad, after all. She stepped closer to meet him.

She was almost within reach. Tyler's fingers tightened into fists. "Don't, Evie. Get out of here while you can."

"I won't." She was close enough to smell the sweat on him. On other men, it might be unpleasant, but not on Tyler. She inhaled the masculine musk with the scent of his shaving soap, and she wanted to peel his shirt off and get closer. Her fingers itched to touch his skin. She clenched them as he was clenching his.

"We have an agreement, Evie. Don't make me break it." Tyler's muscles tensed with the effort to keep from reaching for her. His arms ached with rigidity as he held them at his side. The scent of cinnamon and roses engulfed him, and he almost broke down and cried.

She didn't even have to think about her response. A lifetime of reading novels made it instantaneous. When the one you loved was hurting, you reached out for him. She had never been given that opportunity in her life. She grabbed it now.

Evie slid her arms around his waist and hugged Tyler until he clutched her close and she could lean her head against his chest and hear his heart beat. She heard his muffled groan, sensed his rejection, but still she clung. She wasn't going to let him go until she was inside his skin.

Tyler held her as if she were a lifeline. His arms wrapped around her shoulders and waist and pressed her slender body into his until there wasn't an inch of space between them anywhere. Along with the cinnamon and roses of her bathing soap, he could smell the vanilla on her hands from her baking and the heated woman scent of her as their bodies ignited. He held himself stiff and straight as he stared at the wall, but he couldn't let her go.

"Evie, you've got to get out of here. I don't want you to see that side of me again. I don't want you hurt."

"I wasn't hurt last time, Tyler. You didn't hurt me. Tell me what's wrong. Talk to me, Tyler." Evie dug her fingers into his shirt and had shocking visions of tearing it open with her teeth. She wanted him to bare his soul, but she would start by baring his body.

"What do you want me to say that you haven't just seen? I'm a killer, Evie. I kill people. I'm very good at it, if you didn't notice. I've been practicing since I was a boy. Ben says some people have a talent for writing or painting or riding horses. I've got a talent for hitting targets. I could shoot better than my brothers before I was ten. I used to amuse myself by shooting peaches off of trees and letting Ben catch them. And then I grew up and went to war and learned to shoot people."

Evie did find a button with her teeth then. She jerked it open and found the salt of his skin beneath her lips. Tyler shuddered as she kissed him there, but he didn't release his rigid stance.

"I thought you said you spent most of the war in prison." If her kisses wouldn't do it, her words would have to. She began to nibble at the base of his throat.

He ought to fling her from him, but the warmth replacing the ice in his veins felt too good. He'd used this form of solace before, knew how well it worked, and he wanted it. He wanted Evie. But he couldn't have her. He steeled himself and hoped she would understand.

"I did, after taking out a squad of Union soldiers who'd captured my brother. I was holed up in the rocks where they couldn't reach me, and I just picked them off, one by one. I must have killed a dozen of them; they couldn't avoid me. I finally ran out of ammunition. And they still had my brother. He died in prison. So I accomplished nothing. I met the brother of one of the men I'd killed later. He wasn't any different from Michael. We

could have been friends if he'd worn a different uniform.
Do you understand any of this, Evie?"

"No. I don't want to. You did what you had to do to
save your brother. Why are you blaming yourself?"

Her cunning teeth had nipped another button and now
his shirt was spread wide. Tyler felt her lips nibbling at
his nipple, and a livid streak of desire shot through him.
He was only a man. He could resist only so much. His
fingers found the hooks at the back of her dress.

"I killed a dozen good men, Evie. Killed them. Shot
them in cold blood. I aimed and fired and reloaded and
kept on killing until I ran out of ammunition. It was like
there was someone else inside me, some savage beast
lusting for blood. I couldn't stop. Even when I knew it
was useless, I cried and aimed and fired again. I was
seventeen years old, Evie, and I wanted to be dead."

Tyler could feel her shivering in his arms; he didn't
know whether from passion or fear. The back of her
gown gaped open, but all he could touch was her corset.
He wished for a knife to cut the damned strings. Instead,
he started pulling the pins from her hair.

"You wanted to save your brother." Her imagination
was too vivid not to picture the scene. She didn't want
to see it. She closed her eyes and concentrated on the
movements of Tyler's hands. She could feel her hair slipping, tendril by tendril, down her back.

"I had to save him. He was the oldest. He was the
only one who could save the plantation. I couldn't do it.
Nobody had ever taught me how. I was the baby. If
Michael died, everything was lost. But I couldn't stop
him from dying any more than I could stop from losing
the plantation. A dozen men died for nothing. I put my
gun away and swore never to be put in that position
again. And now look what you're doing to me."

She was pulling his shirt from his pants and running
her hands up his back, but she knew that wasn't what
he meant. She thought she knew what he meant, but she
didn't want to think about it. Defiantly, Evie released
him and jerked her arms from her bodice, pulling the
gown down to her waist. Her hands began working at
the ties holding it over her petticoats.

Her corset pushed her breasts up until they strained at the edge of her chemise. Tyler stared down into the valley between and felt what remained of his control slipping away. His fingers reached of their own accord for her corset strings.

The contraption sprang open as he released the ribbons. He took an edge in each hand and ripped it wide, flinging the lace and bones across the room. Evie stared at him wide-eyed, but he had warned her.

The tapes at her waist parted easily, and the hoops and petticoat fell with the gown to her feet. She ought to be shaking in her shoes by now, but she merely stepped over the puddle of material and reached for his shirt.

Tyler stared in astonishment as Evie grabbed his shirt front and ripped until the remaining buttons flew across the room. When she attempted the same trick on his trouser front, he gave a curt laugh and caught her waist, throwing her toward the bed.

Half on and half off the bed, she kicked as he fell down on top of her, but she wasn't trying hard enough. Tyler settled himself between her legs to keep from being maimed, then caught her flailing hands above her head as he reached for her chemise.

Evie gasped as the thin material fell in two, exposing her nakedness. She had known what she was doing when she started, but the hard bulge pressing between her legs now sent shivers of as much fear as anticipation through her. It wasn't the laughing, charming Tyler leaning over her now. The darkness in his eyes was terrifying. This was the Tyler who had taken her that first time. She didn't know what to expect from this Tyler.

He still had his trousers and boots on as he leaned over her, but his tattered shirt had been discarded to the floor. Up close, the golden-brown breadth of his chest held her fascinated, but he wasn't allowing her to touch. She wriggled in frustration as he bent to draw one breast into his mouth.

There wasn't any reasoning after that. Evie cried out her ecstasy at the touch of Tyler's tongue, and he moved to cover her mouth with his kisses. His tongue plundered and invaded, and she pushed herself upward to better take him. His hand loosened its grip on hers, and she tangled her fingers in his hair, grabbing it by the roots and holding him in place until both their mouths were bruised and hurting.

His hands closed over her breasts, molding them, driving her wild until he turned his mouth to suckling at them. Alternately weeping and moaning, Evie dug her fingers into Tyler's ribs and tried to force him away or force him closer. She finally found his buttons and began tearing at them recklessly.

Her frantic fingers decimated what remained of Tyler's control. Ripping at the heavy cloth of his trousers, he pulled them open until he felt the freedom of release. To his shock, she grabbed him, but not for long. His hand had already untied the opening in her pantalets, and he spread her legs wide to position her. All other thoughts fled as he felt her lift her hips to welcome him and tasted her moistness with his fingertips. There was only one place he wanted to be, and he was almost there.

Evie cried out as Tyler entered her, but he was too far gone to hold back now. Cupping her bottom, he drew her roughly against him until he was situated as deeply as he could go. Then he pulled back and repeated the motion until she was writhing and screaming beneath him, just the way he wanted her to be.

And then she was exploding around him, her muscles tensing and holding him captive and milking him until he could hold back no longer. With a curse and a sigh of relief, Tyler buried himself and his demons deep within her.

Chapter 30

"I'm sorry, Evie," Tyler whispered quietly, spreading her hair across the mattress with his fingers before kissing her cheek and reluctantly getting up. He surveyed the destruction of the room and ran his hand through his own hair in a gesture of confusion and dismay.

Becoming aware of her wanton position, Evie gingerly sat up and pulled the bedcover up to wrap around her. Still shaken by the riot of emotions Tyler had set loose within her, she could only watch as he visibly pulled himself together.

"Sorry for what?" she managed to murmur. She felt odd, as if everything she had thought she was had disappeared, replaced by some stranger.

Tyler's expression was wry as he turned back to face her. She looked deliciously rumpled with her chestnut curls tumbling down over partially bared breasts and her lovely face wearing a dazed look that made him want to tumble her again, this time with a whole lot more tenderness. He resisted pulling her out of the bed and taking her in his arms.

He gestured with his hand instead. "Stop a minute and listen."

Totally attuned to Tyler, Evie had ignored their surroundings. At his words, she took the time to realize where they were and what they had done. It was the middle of the day and half the town had seen her coming up here. She could hear voices down the hall. She heard footsteps in the room above this one. She heard someone coughing. Slowly, a flush rose to her cheeks.

Seeing that hint of color, Tyler shoved his hands in his

pockets and walked to the window. "We weren't exactly quiet," he mentioned, as if she needed to be reminded.

"I'm sorry," Evie whispered. She flushed even deeper as a vague memory of how loud she had been came to her.

Tyler swung around, and a bit of his usual grin clung to his lips. "Don't be. I like knowing I'm appreciated. And with you, I know it's no act. You don't know how good that makes a man feel."

Evie buried her cheeks in the bedcover, but she smiled back. Tyler couldn't resist any longer. It was obvious he had spent what self-control he possessed. Why fight it any longer? He sat down beside her and pulled her into his arms. None of this was her fault. She was a sprite from another world given into his protection. he had failed at that as he had failed at almost everything else, but right at the moment he didn't feel sorry.

"We'll have to tell them we're married, Evie. They'll whisper and wonder and gossip, but you'll be able to stay here and keep your teaching position as long as they think we're respectably married."

Evie nodded against his shoulder, but a lump came to fill her throat. "What about you? You didn't want to be married. And I didn't do anything to prevent babies like Starr told me to. I didn't mean to tie you down, Tyler. Honest, I didn't."

Tyler looked down at her in amazement. "Starr told you about those things? She ought to be taken out and shot. I'm going to have to have a word or two with that woman." He stroked Evie's lovely hair and tried to imagine having babies with her. The thought was too tempting by far. He sighed and held her close. "Chances are that one time won't make a baby. We need to talk about making a marriage first."

A pounding on the door jerked them away from that frightening thought. Tyler scowled and called, "Go away."

"Open up, Monteigne. I want to talk to you, and I want to talk to you now." The sheriff's voice carried enough authority to make the badge he wore a formality.

"Your timing is not auspicious, Powell. I'll be out shortly."

"Now. And if you've got Mrs. Peyton in there, I want to see her out here, too. You can't get away with molesting innocent women in this town, Monteigne."

Tyler cursed, rose from the bed to grab his shirt, and discovering it's lack of buttons, threw it on the floor again. "I hope your job is an elected one, Powell. I'm going to have you run out of town for invasion of privacy. What my wife and I do behind closed doors is none of your affair."

Ignoring Evie's corset and torn chemise, Tyler threw her gown to her while he rummaged in drawers for a clean shirt. The stunned silence from the other side of the door gave them a few moments' reprieve.

Evie wriggled into her gown, but Tyler hadn't been gentle with the fastenings, and without her corset, it didn't fit properly. She felt scandalously bare with nothing beneath it and the back gaping open. She hurriedly pulled up her petticoats while Tyler put on his shirt.

She thought she recognized Hale's furious whispers on the other side of the door. She remembered leaving him in the hotel lobby. He would have been the one to send for the sheriff. Sighing, she accepted Tyler's offer of a coat to go over her gown. It might be ninety degrees in the sun, but she couldn't go out the door with her dress open.

"Are you coming out of there, Monteigne, or am I coming in?" The sheriff had evidently recovered his self-possession, not to mention a load of anger.

Still tucking in his shirt, Tyler flung open the door. He blocked any sight of the interior with his body as he faced his audience. Hale stood white-faced and furious just behind Powell. Everyone else had evidently chosen to stand out of range of a potentially dangerous killer.

"What has he done with Mrs. Peyton? The man is a menace, Sheriff. You'd better lock him up until we find out what's going on. I don't believe for a minute that they're married. I've talked to Mrs. Peyton myself. She's a young, innocent widow, and this man is obviously trying to take advantage of her."

Tyler lifted a cynical brow at the lawyer's tirade, then turned affably to the sheriff. "My wife has that effect on men." He shrugged in dismissal of Hale. "I'll be happy to tell you what I know about this afternoon's incident, Sheriff, but it doesn't require an audience. And Mrs. Monteigne would like to return to the children, if you don't mind."

Hale puffed up like a banty rooster. "I insist on speaking with Mrs. Peyton. She's by way of being my client, and as her attorney, I must insist on seeing her."

Having found enough pins to shove her hair into a caricature of a chignon, Evie came up behind Tyler and moved the door enough to peek around him. She smiled at their audience, fluttered her lashes, and grasped Tyler's arm. "Gentlemen, you are embarrassing me enormously. Could you please wait until another time to interrogate Tyler? I have to get back to the children."

Tyler stifled a chuckle as the two men visibly blanched and stepped backward. Men might stand up to a man's weapons, but they fell before a woman's without a qualm. It was absolutely amazing what the power of a woman could do.

"I'll see you safely back to the house, Mrs. Pey—" the sheriff hesitated as Tyler shifted position—"Mrs. Monteigne. Then, if you don't mind, I'd like to borrow your husband for a while. I've got one man dead and another seriously injured, and I've got to have some kind of report."

"I understand that, sir, and you deserve some explanations. It's a pity we don't have many." Evie tugged Tyler's arm and reluctantly, he stepped into the hall to follow the sheriff toward the back steps.

He halted when Hale made it apparent he meant to follow. "As you can see, Mr. Hale, my wife doesn't need your assistance. We'll let you know if we need your services."

Hale glanced furiously from one participant in this tableau to another. "If she's married to you, the lady came to me under false pretenses. I think I deserve some explanation."

"When we're ready to give one, we might consider it.

Until then, I'm asking you to leave, Hale. This is none of your affair." Tyler pulled Evie possessively to his side, out of reach of the man who all too obviously had meant to court her.

Evie glanced around Tyler's broad shoulders to smile her regret at the lawyer. "I'm so sorry if I've misled you, sir. It's a long story. Maybe we'll have time to talk later."

Tyler rolled his eyes heavenward, then dragged Evie toward the stairs. How in hell had he got himself hitched to a temptress who would inevitably attract every man within a fifty-mile radius? It was fitting punishment for his wandering ways, he supposed, but he didn't know how he was going to keep from killing every one of them.

Not wishing to follow where that thought led, Tyler started down the stairs. He'd get her back to where she would be surrounded by kids. He'd noticed she never looked at a man when the kids were around. That was the safest place for her to be.

When they arrived at the little house behind the livery, José threw himself into Evie's arms, Daniel gave an audible sigh of relief, and Ben discreetly removed himself from the scene with the entrance of the sheriff. Evie took a rocking chair and pulled José into her lap, hugging him close, and he surprisingly allowed it.

Maria wandered to Tyler and pulled on his pants leg. He scowled down at her, but she smiled almost as convincingly as Evie. "Tywer, up," she commanded.

Tyler glanced helplessly to Evie.

"She just wants to be picked up and held, like anybody would after a day like this."

Tyler scowled blacker as he read the significance of Evie's words in the flashing look of her dark eyes. But he leaned over and picked up the little imp. Maria crowed with delight and snuggled against his shoulder as if she belonged there.

The sheriff coughed nervously, and Manuel eyed him with a degree of speculation, keeping a safe distance from the hand of authority. Carmen caught his shoulder before he could back off any farther.

"I don't mean to impose on your family, Monteigne." The sheriff didn't notice the sudden look of interest passing between several members of that "family." "But I've got a report to write. The city board will have my job if I don't explain this shooting to their satisfaction."

Tyler bounced Maria in his arms. "There isn't much I can tell you. I overheard some men talking about drawing out Pecos Martin and using the kids for shields. They found Manuel and José before I could. You need to talk to the boys about that part of it. I saw them carry the kids out to the street, so I slipped up to the hotel. It's the best lookout in town. You know the rest."

Powell didn't look appeased. "I told you I didn't want any gunfighting in this town, Monteigne, or Martin, or whoever you are. I want to know who those men are and why they were looking for you and if I can expect any more of this kind of riffraff around here. I'll have to ask you to leave, if so. I've never seen shooting like that in my life, and I'm not willing to see it happen again. You near killed those men from a distance and at an angle that most men would never try. You could have killed those kids just as easily."

"No, he wouldn't. He saved us." Manuel placed his fists belligerently at his waist and glared at the sheriff.

Tyler grinned and ruffled the boy's hair. Manuel dodged the show of affection, but he didn't move far from Tyler's side.

"I'd like to know who they were, too, but you'll have to ask the brats here or the one the doc is tending to. The one I killed was one of your escapees. Maybe he resented being caught. But I'd like to know who told them I was Pecos Martin." Tyler turned an accusing look to the sheriff.

"Half the town heard the boy there tell Phil that Pecos Martin was coming to town and that Ben was your friend. Word spreads. And if you're not Martin, how did you learn to shoot like that?"

"The war, Sheriff, same as you and a lot of other people. I'm just better at it than some." Tyler glanced to Manuel. "Have you ever seen those men before?"

Manuel shrugged. "There's always strangers at the livery. I don't notice them none."

Tyler frowned. The boy was as tense and nervous as

a high-strung yearling, but he wasn't going to force the boy. Not yet. He turned back to the sheriff. "You'd better talk to your patient, Powell. And let me know what you find out. My wife has a hankering to stay in this town, but if the law can't keep her and the children safe, we'll have to be thinking about moving on."

The word "wife" caused the children to grow wide-eyed, but they remained properly silent while the adults conversed.

Powell turned his gaze to the woman in the rocking chair with the child in her arms. Evie returned his look with an innocent smile. She was just a schoolteacher he tried to tell himself. Just a female with no knowledge of a man's world. Monteigne was the man with the answers. But even as he returned a wary gaze to the gambler, Powell felt like he was missing something.

"You haven't explained why you've allowed your wife to pose as a widow yet."

Tyler deposited Maria in Carmen's arms and moved toward the door. "And I don't intend to, not yet. It has no bearing on the matter at hand. If you have any other questions, Sheriff, feel free to come by." Gently, but firmly, he edged Powell to the door.

When the sheriff was gone, the room erupted in an explosion of questions. Tyler held up his hand and waited for silence, then pointed at Manuel for the first question.

"If you and Miz Peyton are married and all, does that mean you're going to stay here? Will you be working at the Double H? Can we go see the horses?"

Tyler heard Evie's faint chuckle behind him. He'd done this to himself. The last time he'd lost control like that, he'd wound up in prison for three years. That should have been enough lesson for any man. But no, now he'd shackled himself for a lifetime, and not just to a wife. He didn't think there was a chance in hell that Evie would give up these kids, even for him.

"The horses at the Double H aren't anything to see. They're half-broke mustangs. And I wasn't exactly working out there, so I'm not promising anything."

Tyler could see the disappointment already spreading across the boys' faces. He wasn't meant to be a family man. He wasn't any good at it. He wasn't good at much at all but playing cards, shooting guns, and winning women. Helplessly, he turned to Evie.

She set José back down on the floor. "Go get wood for the stove. We need to get dinner started. And don't you dare go sneaking back to that livery. I don't want you anywhere near that place ever again." She stood up and shook out her skirt and answered the children's unspoken questions. "We don't any of us know what we'll do until we hear from your uncle. California is a long, long way away. So you might as well be patient."

"He didn't answer my telegram," Carmen pointed out reasonably.

"Maybe he didn't get it. Things like that get lost all the time. We'll send another one tomorrow." Evie tried not to think about Hale's declaration that the uncle was dead. If he were dead, shouldn't somebody have wired back with that information? She would believe the best until informed otherwise.

She saw Tyler standing helplessly by the door, and her stomach did strange little flip-flops as she watched him there. Her husband. It seemed impossible to conceive. She knew he was incredibly attractive, but that wasn't what she saw now when she looked at him. She saw a man as lost as she was, a man with spectacular strengths and a vast store of knowledge but lacking roots and an incentive to grow them. Or was she just seeing what every other woman of his acquaintance was seeing—a man who needed to be tied down?

She went up to him and touched one of the arms folded defiantly against his chest. "Will you be staying?" She touched the tip of her tongue to her dry lips as she sought the right words. "I'd like you to stay, but you don't have to if you don't want."

Tyler watched that enticingly pink tongue slip over kissable lips and felt his insides slipping. She still wore his coat over the gown he'd literally ripped from her back. He'd treated her like an animal, ruined her chances for a good husband, showed her what he was, and still she didn't retreat from him. Evangeline Peyton Howell was a very odd woman.

And he didn't want to lose her.

He didn't accept that fact gracefully. He didn't want a house or a passel of kids. He didn't want ties of any sort. Marriage meant all those things and more. But marriage meant Evie was all his.

Tyler shrugged. "I'll be back for dinner. Save a place for me."

He walked out, leaving Evie staring after him, wondering.

Chapter 31

"You fool! You incompetent, bumble-headed, pea-brained fool! Why did you have to go dragging those kids into this? Didn't I tell you I didn't want anybody hurt? I just wanted that gambler out of here."

The man sitting in the shadows of Hale's office glanced disinterestedly at his dirty boots. "You didn't specify how you wanted him out of here, and the boys were getting a little nervous about those kids poking around all the time. They thought they'd take care of two birds with one stone."

"They thought? That's the trouble with the lot of you—you don't think! That's what you have me for. Unless you want to go to jail for a real long time, you'd better start paying attention. You're going to have to sell that livery and set up elsewhere. That will take care of the damned kids."

The man in the corner gave the lawyer's irate face a considering look. "I haven't got the money to start over again, and it looks to me like you'll not be getting it anytime soon. It appears the widow is already taken."

Hale's face turned even redder with fury. "She's lying to protect him. I don't know what he has on her, and I haven't got time to find out. I've got the Hardings out of the running with that story about first cousins, but the gambler has to go before she starts telling people who she really is."

"You'd think the whole damned town would have figured that out by now, the way she's moved in with those Rodriguez kids."

"The whole damned town thinks Elizabeth Howell was a saint. And it's been twenty years. People don't remember old stories that long. Hell, even I was too young to pay attention back then."

"I wasn't. Logan wasn't. He's been hanging around, you noticed? He's dumb, but even he smells something fishy."

"He just plain out and out smells." Hale wrinkled up his nose in distaste. "It's not going to be easy, but nothing worth having is. Just take the gambler out of the picture for me. I'll do the rest."

The man in the corner shrugged and gradually unfolded himself from the chair. "You keep those kids out of my hair, then. They know too damned much already."

Hale nodded absently. His mind was already elsewhere.

"Come with me back to the hotel. Ben can stay here and look out for the kids." Tyler pulled Evie into the shadows by the door as the children readied themselves for bed.

Evie looked up at him uncertainly. "I'm not certain this is the right thing to do, Tyler. I'm not even certain we're really married."

"We're married if we say we are. I'll get you a ring that fits in the morning. The old biddies will be looking for one."

"Tomorrow is Sunday," she whispered back. "You can't buy a ring on Sunday. We'll have to get up and go to church. Can you imagine what people are going to think when we walk in there after spending the night at the hotel?"

"They're going to think I'm finally doing my duty by my wife. Damn it, Evie, there isn't any other woman in this damned town for me. Now that it's respectable, I want you in my bed." Frustration laced Tyler's words as he gazed down at Evie's troubled expression. He took her hands in his and rubbed them gently.

"But you don't want to be married and you don't want babies and you don't want to settle down. That's not a marriage, Tyler." Evie pulled her hands from his. Temptation was close enough without adding to it. The possibility of spending the night in Tyler's bed caused rivers of anticipation to flood through her. She remembered their wedding night very clearly. She wanted that closeness again. But Tyler had had that closeness with other women, and he'd not settled down because of it.

"We exchanged vows, Evie. You're my wife. I'm willing to face up to that. I know it's not fair to you. I'll make a rotten husband and a worse father, but what's done is done. If we get a divorce now, you'll have to make it public. They'll run you out of town then. They won't let a divorced woman teach their kids. And every man in town will look at you as easy pickings. I won't let that happen, Evie."

He was right, of course. She had tried not to face it when he'd made their marriage public. She wasn't at all certain why he had made their marriage public. Surely they could have lied their way out of that little episode. People would gossip, but she could lead an exemplary life and the gossip would go away. But now he was standing here saying he wanted her to be his wife. How much of that could she believe?

"There will be babies," she answered sadly, crossing her arms beneath her breasts to protect herself from the hurt. "We can't give them a proper home. You can't even promise to be a proper father. I never wanted that."

Tyler fought the despair washing over him. With any other woman he could have given her a peck on the cheek and walked out. But not with Evie. Evie had gnawed a hole into his middle and burrowed there, and he couldn't get her out. He didn't want to get her out. He was growing comfortable carrying her around inside of him. He was tired of going from female to female, avoiding their claws and traps and stratagems. He wanted just this one woman, if he had to turn into a savage to keep her. He had done that today, and she had brought him out of it. Maybe that was all he needed, one woman who could tame the beast.

"We'll use Starr's suggestions and not make babies," he whispered desperately. "I've got some cash saved up. Maybe I can buy a herd and lease some land. Maybe I can learn to settle down here. Just come back with me, Evie. I want you in my bed tonight."

She didn't know what swayed her. She wanted babies, so it certainly wasn't that. Perhaps it was knowing that he wanted her enough to actually think about settling down. Or perhaps it was just the fact that the womanizing gambler had finally offered to make the final commitment. *He* was actually pleading with *her* to be his wife. It was an occasion of sorts.

Tyler certainly hadn't mentioned anything about love. He wanted a woman in his bed, and she was that woman. She wasn't exactly flattered. But there was a certain ring of truth to his arguments. He wanted her, and she wanted him. They were married. Why shouldn't they go to bed together?

Feeling a panic much like the one of their wedding night, Evie met Tyler's anxious gaze. He really did want her. That could be enough. It was more than she'd ever had before.

Throwing an anxious glance to Daniel who was politely keeping his head buried in a book, Evie nodded. "All right, but we have to come back here in the morning to get the children ready for church."

He would have sung the "Hallelujah" chorus if she'd asked it of him. He didn't want to go back to that empty hotel room without her tonight. There were too many fiends in the dark, too many ghosts from the past. Evie's presence would chase them all away.

Tyler reached for her shawl and pulled it around her as he spoke to Daniel. "I'm taking Evie with me tonight. You and Carmen behave yourselves. I'm sending Ben over to keep an eye on things. We'll be back in the morning in time for church."

Daniel peered over the top of his glasses, but he didn't raise his head. Evie's on-again, off-again marriage contained several embarrassing elements that he wasn't prepared to acknowledge. He just held his tongue and watched her go.

Outside, Evie felt deliciously free, as if she were indulging in an illicit affair as Tyler led her determinedly toward the hotel across the alley. It was rather like a Gothic tale where the heroine sneaks into the forbidden tower at night. She had always wondered about the "fate

worse than death" that the heroines feared in those novels. Now she knew what it was. She'd much rather be in
Tyler's bed than dead, of course, but just the thought of
what she was deliberately about to do led to dangerous
anticipations. She felt Tyler's long legs moving next to
hers and remembered what they had felt like earlier
today, and she thought she might explode with desire.
She tried not to think too closely about Tyler's legs.

By the time they reached the top of the stairs, they
were practically running. As Tyler had expected, Ben
was waiting for him when he threw open the door to his
room. But Ben had only to take one look at the two of
them before reaching for his coat.

"Stay over at the house and keep an eye on the kids.
We'll be back in the morning." Tyler repeated the words
he had said to Daniel, but morning was too far off for
him to even think about. He had Christmas wrapped up
and in his arms right now. He wasn't about to consider
the day after.

Ben nodded his head, gave Evie's flushed cheeks a
wicked look, and departed without a word. They heard
him clambering down the stairs as they closed the door.

Suddenly inexplicably shy, Evie couldn't look Tyler in
the eye as he reached to take her shawl. She looked
down at the gown she had changed into and realized
Tyler was looking there, too. She had worn one of her
more daring dinner dresses, and without the shawl, she
suddenly felt very exposed.

"This time, I want to see all of you, Evie." Tyler
tipped her chin up with his finger until she met his eyes.
"Are you having second thoughts?"

Evie shook her head soundlessly. She could easily
drown in the tenderness of Tyler's eyes right now. Maybe
he did love her, just a little. That wasn't just lust reflected
there; she was sure of it. She raised her fingers to the tie
he had donned before coming to dinner.

"I'm your wife. I want to be a good one." She undid
the tie and reached for his collar button.

Her reply wasn't what Tyler wanted to hear. He didn't
know what he wanted to hear; he just knew a vague
disappointment. But she wasn't arguing, that should be

enough. If she was just playing another one of her roles, that shouldn't trouble him. He would take her any way he could get her.

They undressed each other slowly, exchanging tentative kisses at first, then growing more greedy as need overcame propriety. Evie felt the rush of cool night air as Tyler lifted her out of the puddle of her petticoats and gown, but it was as nothing to what she felt when he removed the rest of her undergarments.

She stood there in nothing, with even her stockings and garters lying at her feet, while Tyler looked his fill. The single lamp threw shadows over the walls and turned her skin to flickering waves of alabaster and ivory, tinged with pink and accented with brown. Tyler reached out to touch her breast, and she sucked in her breath, but she didn't retreat.

"There isn't an angle or plane on you. You're all curves," he murmured wonderingly, exploring the circle of fullness of her breast before dipping lower, to the inward curve of her waist.

He still wore his trousers. Evie didn't think that quite fair, but she was willing to be patient. She wanted to be able to paint Tyler just like he was now. She wasn't certain she could do justice to the way the light glinted off the golden-brown hairs on his chest, or if she could manage the ridge of muscles beneath, but she wanted to try. It would be much safer to paint just the upper half of him. She didn't think she dared even think about the lower half.

As if he had followed the path of her thoughts, Tyler pulled off his belt. "I'm ready anytime you are."

Evie cast a quick look downward, then back up again. He was smiling at her embarrassment, but his fingers continued to work at his trouser buttons. She backed toward the bed. "Tyler." She licked her lips nervously. Every nerve in her body was tingling with the need to have him touching her again, but they had a lot of unfinished business. "I don't have ..." She hesitated, not knowing how to say what she needed. "Starr said I'd need ..."

Tyler backed her toward the bed. "I don't keep vinegar and sponges in my room, Evie. We'll find those another day. I'll take care of myself this time." He pulled something out of his trouser pocket before he stripped the trousers off.

Evie wasn't paying any attention to what was in his hand. She had never really seen Tyler in an aroused state before, and her eyes widened into saucers. She knew it was possible. He had shown her it was possible. But she never would have believed it otherwise. He seemed to grow bigger as she watched.

Tyler caught her by the waist and lifted her to the bed. "Have you ever read *Tom Jones,* Evie?" When she shook her head, he lay down beside her and leaned over her. "I'll have to find a copy for you. There's a scene in there where the hero . . ." And he leaned over and whispered in her ear.

"That's in a book?" she asked incredulously, but the question was strictly rhetorical. Tyler was already showing her what he wanted. She felt the faint rasp of his whiskers against her flesh as he took her breast into his mouth, and she lifted herself completely into his embrace.

"Perhaps I'll find a copy of *Fanny Hill* for you, too," he murmured against her lush fullness as Evie came readily into his arms. "I can remember they tried a variety of interesting places besides a bed. What do you think, Evie? Shall we try a couch next? How about on a ship?"

She didn't know whether it was Tyler's words or the sound of his voice that acted on her like an aphrodisiac. She was on fire all over. The brush of his hair-roughened legs between her thighs made her quiver with excitement. The touch of his hand as he flattened it over the mound there drew her attention downward. She knew he was watching her, but she couldn't look away as he covered himself with something and began to probe gently where his fingers played.

And then the feeling began to swell and rise up in her, and Evie jerked her head back to meet Tyler's gaze as he entered her. She saw the look of possession in his eyes, the determination, and her heart nearly leapt from her chest. But then he lifted her hips and slid deeper, and she was beyond awareness of anything at all but the thundering earthquakes exploding through her middle.

Tyler took his time. He had been too quick earlier, too savage, and he wanted to savor the sweetness now. He plundered her mouth, paid homage to her breasts, and moved relentlessly slowly until he felt her breathing quicken again. Then he rocked against her until she cried out and raised her legs of her own accord, taking him deeper, until he could go no more. He set the rhythm then, finding it in his own desperate need, wanting the release and the comfort and the ecstasy only she could offer.

Tyler took Evie's cries into his mouth and drowned them with his own. As his body exploded into hers, it wasn't enough. He knew it wasn't enough. But it was better than anything he had ever known before. He kissed away a tear rolling down her cheek, and let the perspiration between their bodies oil the friction of their skin as he covered her with his weight. He didn't want to move off of her. He didn't want to leave her. But he had to.

Evie moaned a little as he moved away and discarded the sack that had protected her from his seed, but she didn't seem aware of what he was doing. Tyler pulled her into his arms and brushed her hair down over her breast.

"Do you think we can borrow the couch in the lobby next time?" he whispered in her ear.

Evie giggled but didn't reply. She snuggled closer, laying her leg across his.

"Evie, I'm not Ivanhoe," he murmured, more to himself than to her.

"Who did Fanny Hill have?" she asked sleepily.

"A lover who left her to make her own way in the world for the better part of her wicked life." Tyler stared up at the ceiling. The lamp was flickering low and would soon be out. He didn't feel called upon to rise and blow it out.

"Well, when it comes to that, I suppose that's what we all have to do." With dreamy philosophy, Evie curled up against his shoulder and went to sleep.

Tyler lay there a little while longer, his stomach tightening into knots of fear. He had a wife now, and he didn't know what he was going to do with her. He didn't even know if he could protect her. He had made a dismal failure of protecting his loved ones earlier. How much had he improved in years of playing at gambling tables?

Not very much, he feared.

Chapter 32

Tyler watched the sun slowly crossing the windowsill to burnish a strand of auburn in Evie's otherwise dark tresses. Looking down on her face innocent with sleep, he felt seventeen again: nervous, terrified, and proud. He'd thought he'd grown up a little since then, but only on the outside, apparently. Inside, he was still that boy with a frightening job ahead of him.

He leaned over and kissed the corner of her eye. Her lashes fluttered, brushing against his nose, and he kissed her again, this time near the corner of her mouth. She turned and caught his lips with her own before he could get away.

It would have been nice to dally here awhile longer, but he'd made promises and he would try to keep them. He was hard and eager for her when his hand tenderly caressed her breast, but the hour was already late. Reluctantly releasing her, Tyler reached for the cover and pulled it around his waist as he climbed from the bed.

Evie lay sprawled wantonly across the sheets. She was even more beautiful in the sunlight, like some exotic cat stretching in feline pleasure. There was no shyness in her now as she wiped at those dangerous sloe eyes and considered him openly. Ruby lips smiled as she flexed her legs and turned on her side.

So much for taming the beast. Tyler felt a bolt of overpowering need strike through him, and in seconds, he was kneeling over her on the bed, and the lateness of the hour grew later.

"I feel like I ought to have a scarlet letter *A* branded on my forehead," Evie giggled as she held Tyler's arm and hurried after the children on the way to church.

"*F* would be more appropriate," Tyler muttered. He could think of a damned number of other things he would rather be doing than rushing around getting a passel of children ready for church and then spending hours listening to a preacher rant and rail. Most of those things had to do with getting the woman next to him naked again.

"*F?*" Her eyes widened as his meaning came clear. "For fornicate?"

"Fornicate?" Tyler choked back a grin at this ingenuous translation of his intended vulgarity. "Fornicate, of course," he agreed. "Or frigging." His lips curled upward as he searched for a few more equally adequate substitutes for the subject he had in mind.

Evie laughed. She had been as cheerful as a chirping bird all morning. Married life suited her. Tyler allowed himself a degree of satisfaction for that, but he didn't let her see it. She would only chirp and twitter some more.

He loved hearing her chirp and twitter, if he would admit it, but he wouldn't. He didn't want to love anyone or anything. Love was a painful business that he was better off avoiding. Good sex was an entirely different proposition. That's what he and Evie had—good sex.

Caught up in his selfish thoughts, Tyler didn't even see Kyle coming until Evie gasped, and by then it was too late. The blow shot through his jaw with the power of two hundred pounds of muscle, sending him sprawling in the dust right before the church and half the townspeople.

"That's for being a low-down, good-for-nothing snake in the grass. Now get up and let me give you another for being a rotten, no-account sidewinder."

Tyler didn't listen to Evie's indignant cries. Leaning back on his elbows, he remained where he was, gazing up at the larger man with his square jaw set in murderous rage.

"I accept your congratulations, Harding, but I'd prefer to leave the rest until after church." Odd, but the beast didn't stir at this direct assault to himself. It didn't take any effort at all to lie here grinning back at the man who had it all—except Evie!

"Dadblast you, Monteigne, get up and take it like a man. You've got no business nosing around a little filly like Miss Maryellen. You ain't even got a roof over your head. I'm going to kill you just as soon as you stand up."

Tyler lay back down and placed his hands behind his head. "Well, in that case, I guess I'll just do my worshiping right here. Maryellen," he said the false name with a wry twist, "tell the preacher to speak up loud and clear this morning."

Evie couldn't keep a bubble of laughter from forming on her lips. The children had stopped to stare, and people were coming out of the church to watch the performance. Tyler looked quite ridiculous in his best Sunday frock coat and crisp ruffled linen lying in the street, but he seemed perfectly content to continue perusing the sky. Kyle, however, appeared on the verge of a volcanic explosion.

Doing her best to keep a relatively straight face, Evie patted Kyle's rumpled coat sleeve. "Do try to understand, Mr. Harding. Tyler's been a friend of the family ever so long, and I've come to rely on his help and advice. Daniel looks up to him as if he were an older brother, and the children adore him. He's really a very nice man, Mr. Harding. And he literally swept me off my feet. I had no idea he returned my feelings like that. I do love him, Mr. Harding, and I wish you wouldn't hurt him too much."

Tyler liked the sound of that, even if it were a pack of Evie's usual lies. He propped himself up on his elbows again and grinned hugely at Kyle's discomfort. "Yeah, Mr. Harding, don't hurt me too much, or I'll not be any use at all to my wife."

Kyle almost erupted again, and Evie gave Tyler a swift kick with her little shoe. Giving a surprised "oomph," he caught his bruised rib, sat up, and glared at Evie. "Kick a man while he's down, will you? You'll pay for that later, woman."

Kyle bristled and clenched his fists again, but Evie just smiled sweetly and held out her hand to her dusty husband. "We're going to be late for church. I want to hear you singing this time instead of grumbling in my ear."

Laughter tittered through the crowd as the handsome gambler eyed his wife warily and stood up without the aid of her helping hand. Ignoring Evie's triumphant expression, Tyler dusted himself off and met Kyle's furious gaze.

"Don't know that I can say the best man won, but it's not as if I forced her." Tyler groaned inwardly at the sound of his own words. He was becoming as much a liar as Evie.

Before he could correct himself, Evie took his arm and smiled pleasantly at her erstwhile suitor. "Why don't you come to dinner after church, Mr. Harding? We'd be happy to have you. I'd hate to think I'd come between two friends."

Kyle growled, "He ain't no friend of mine," but he walked by Evie's side as they headed toward the church.

Not until Jace joined them did Tyler realize the big man was in the crowd. Thanking the heavens above that the brawl had been settled amicably before Jace could join in, Tyler expressed his gratitude by consenting to join in the hymn singing. He wasn't certain it was good for his soul, but it could very well be good for preventing aching ribs.

It had been a long time since he had raised his voice in song and he was a bit rusty, but the notes came back to him with a little practice. So engrossed did he become in remembering the harmony that he didn't notice Evie's curious glances, nor the startled looks on the faces of the children around them. He just felt better for having conquered one more ghost from his past.

It wasn't until they were leaving church and well-wishers came up offering both congratulations on their marriage and comments on Tyler's singing that he realized what he had done. Jace pounded him on the back and grinning, dragged Kyle away after making polite excuses about dinner. After swallowing one more compliment than he could handle, Tyler caught Evie's arm and hauled her from the crowd.

Evie had the pensive look on her face that Tyler had cause to remember too well, and he attempted to forestall her next leap of imagination. "Don't even say it, Evie," he warned.

She gave him a thoughtful look from behind long lashes. "Did all your family sing as well as you?"

He should have known he couldn't stop her. Tugging uncomfortably at his tie, he answered evasively, "My father wasn't much good at it."

"But the rest of you did: your mother, and your older brothers."

"Yeah." Tyler refused to say more. He wasn't going to stir any more old memories than was necessary. His family had lived too far up the river to attend church regularly, but they had often spent Sunday morning around the piano, singing hymns to his mother's accompaniment. And at Christmastime, they were often called upon by the neighbors to do the carols that became second nature to them. His mother sang at weddings, and singing was a form of entertainment at any number of other social occasions. Just thinking about those times brought painful tears to his eyes. That had all been before the war, of course.

Evie respected Tyler's silence. It didn't take her good imagination to know what was going through his mind right now. Children were just naturally jubilant and loved to sing. The Rodriguez children had eagerly learned that tune she had taught them. It was a wonder Tyler hadn't taken to his heels and never turned back when they'd met him at the door with that song. The painful memories that must have brought back made even her heart flinch.

Unaware of the thoughts of their elders, the children came rushing up around them, chattering like magpies. Even Daniel was grinning and talking excitedly about some plan of his for the afternoon. Evie wound her fingers around Tyler's hand and squeezed, and he pulled her arm behind her back and rewarded her with a kiss on her forehead.

The children took the affectionate gesture in stride and continued chattering as they walked down the alley. Not until they got close to the house and saw the stranger standing on the porch did they go silent, one by one.

Tyler pressed Evie slightly behind him, but the stranger didn't look particularly dangerous. He looked as if he had been traveling for a long time. His long canvas dust coat was wrinkled and dirty and thrown over a satchel that looked as beaten and weary as its owner. The man himself wasn't particularly tall, but he sported a pointed goatee that had the children staring. Threads of gray laced the beard and his otherwise dark hair. But it was the eyes that Tyler noticed.

They were Evie's eyes.

And the children's eyes.

With a growing lump of panic in his middle, Tyler looked around him again to be certain he wasn't mistaken. He had never really noticed the resemblance before. The children were unmistakably of Spanish origin, with the olive coloring, black hair, and slight stature of their Mexican father. Evie's complexion was as fair as an English rose, her hair shimmered with strands of auburn, and while she wasn't particularly tall, he would never call her short. There was absolutely no resemblance at all, except in the eyes.

Those mysterious, slightly slanted, long-lashed sloe eyes of hers had always fascinated him. Perhaps knowing Evie made it easier to accept the same eyes on the children without a second glance. But seeing those eyes on this stranger who pulled the two sets of characteristics together caught his attention with a vengeance.

Gesturing for Evie and the children to wait, Tyler advanced upon the stranger alone. "Is there something we could help you with?" His voice was neutral, but his gaze quickly scanned the newcomer for guns or other weapons. He could see none. There did seem to be a paintbrush sticking out of his coat pocket, however. Tyler's breath caught in his throat.

The man looked over the crowd of heads ranging from Maria's small one to Daniel and Evie's taller ones, and an expression of puzzlement crossed his brow. "I was told this was the Rodriguez place. Does Angelina Rodriguez live here?"

That question wasn't as easy to answer as it should have been. The man had to be a relation, a close relation

to the children and therefore a close relation to their
mother. He didn't want to blurt out that Angelina Rodri-
guez had been washed away in a flood some weeks back.
But he wasn't at all certain how to explain why he and
Evie and Daniel were now living in this little house.
Tyler opted for the evasive answer.

"I'm Tyler Monteigne. May I ask your name?"

The older man grimaced and brushed the dirt off his
hand before extending it. "My manners are lacking, as
usual. I apologize, Mr. Monteigne. I'm James Peyton,
Angelina's brother."

Tyler heard Evie's gasp behind him, and obviously, so
did Mr. Peyton. Not daring to turn around and see the
questions in her eyes, Tyler shook the man's hand.
"Well, Mr. Peyton, in that case, we're mighty glad to see
you, but I'm afraid we have unhappy news for you. Why
don't we all go inside first?"

In his words and the gracious gestures he used to escort the other man into the house, Tyler revealed his
plantation upbringing. Heart pounding, Evie watched the
two men go in, but she didn't think she could move a
foot. The children followed her example, standing in the
dust, watching her with curiosity and waiting for instructions. Daniel was the one to limp up on his crutch and
tug at her elbow.

"Come on, Evie. That has to be Carmen's uncle."

Evie's gaze swung to Daniel's familiar face for reassurance. "His name is Peyton." She had known that. She
had seen the gravestones in the cemetery and sent the
second telegram. She had hoped, but she had hoped for
twenty years. Hope was about as real as Don Quixote
and Sancho Panza.

Daniel's excitement danced in his eyes. "He could be
the clue you're looking for. Come on, Evie. We've got
to go in."

The boys were already deserting her. Curiosity won
out over the security of Evie's company. They were at
the door and listening to the conversation within. Carmen and Maria waited patiently for Evie's decision.

Evie nodded. "He must be your uncle," she agreed,
speaking to Carmen and ignoring Daniel and all their

hopes. "He has traveled a great distance. Bring him some of that beer your mother kept in the cellar. Have Manuel run over to the butcher's for another chicken."

Carmen accepted the orders with grave dark eyes that belied her years. She disappeared with Maria into the interior, leaving Evie to follow at an unsteady pace.

By the time she entered the cool darkness of the house, Evie had found her shield again. She shook out her skirt and touched a hand to her hair, then donned a sympathetic smile as she practiced the feminine walk she had been taught in school in St. Louis. Even through the grief written across his face, the gentleman near the hearth watched her approach with appreciation.

"Mr. Peyton, my sincere condolences. I trust Tyler has explained everything to you, but if you have any questions, please feel free to ask away." She took the mug of beer that Carmen carried in and handed it to their guest. "Please, don't stand on formality. Have a seat. We'll have dinner ready shortly. You have to stay and join us. You'll want to hear all about the children."

The stranger set the mug on the table and searched Evie's face inquisitively. "I have dozens of questions, thank you, but I don't want to be in your way. I can remember being a young boy and starving impatiently for Sunday dinner. Please go on and work without worrying about me."

Evie felt tighter than a bow string as she accepted the excuse to leave the two men while she and Carmen went to work at the kitchen stove. Most everything had been put on to simmer before they went to church. It was just a matter of frying chicken, putting in the biscuits, and finishing up the last-minute things that couldn't be done ahead of time. It gave her time to breathe and steady her nerves.

Although the stranger and Tyler sat not that far away, both men spoke in low tones, and with the clanging of pots and the chatter of nervous children, their conversation was not easily discerned. Evie tried to pretend she was just preparing a meal for a friend of Tyler's. The coincidence of his name meant absolutely nothing.

She heard José ask the stranger if he was going to stay

and be their new daddy, but she couldn't hear the man's reply. That gave her one more subject to fear. He would take the children away. What would she do without the children?

She would have to stay with Tyler in his hotel room. They would have to take a room for Daniel, but he couldn't manage the stairs yet. She couldn't cook their meals. She would feel like a kept woman, sitting on the bed and waiting for her man to come home from the saloon. And she wouldn't have the children.

She tried to keep the tears from her eyes. Perhaps Mr. Peyton was a wealthy man and could take care of them much better than she could. The streets of California were said to be paved with gold, and he had just come from there. He would take the children back with him, and they would go to good schools and dress in fine clothes. They would be just fine. She didn't need to worry about them.

Carmen set the table while Evie put the new chicken Manuel brought into the skillet. She ordered the boys to go wash their hands, and the men went outside to clean up, too. There was a great deal of noise and jockeying for position around the washbowl. Evie could hear Tyler ordering José to get the dirt out of his ears before potatoes grew in them, and she smiled. Tyler might be terrified at the thought of children, but he was good with them.

Freshly scrubbed, they trooped in and took their places around the table. Evie started setting the food out in bowls while Carmen got Maria arranged on her high stool with a towel around her neck. She could pretend this was a family gathering. It was a family gathering. She just wasn't part of the family.

When everything was served, Evie took her place beside Tyler and said grace. Hands reached and grabbed after that. Nervously, Evie ordered them to mind their manners, and instantly aware of the stranger in their midst who might disapprove and go away again, the children went stiff and silent, passing the bowls as they had been taught.

Evie thought she might break like brittle glass. She

forgot to take a piece of chicken as it went around, and she only rolled the peas around on her plate. She kept watching the stranger furtively as he ascertained each child's name and made an awkward comment or two to get them talking. They responded with wariness, making Evie's tension shoot up another notch.

She had been cooler-headed in a saloon filled with gamblers and when she had been abducted than she was in this perfectly normal setting with a man who might know her father. Or be her father. Evie closed her eyes and shut out that thought. She was a Howell. Just because her middle name was Peyton she shouldn't get her hopes up. Her mother may have been a Peyton. There was nothing to prove her speculations right or wrong.

But she wanted to know. All her soul screamed to know. She couldn't eat for wanting. And at the same time, she was afraid to find out.

When José dumped his glass of milk and it flooded across the table to Mr. Peyton's lap, Evie calmly cleaned up the chaos, soothed José's terror, offered the use of the bedroom so Mr. Peyton could change into dry trousers, and when all was calm again, walked out the front door and didn't look back.

Chapter 33

Sending an apologetic look to the man who had watched Evie's exit with perplexity, Tyler stood up, made his excuses, and went after her.

She was wandering aimlessly down the street, looking bewildered and sad. When Tyler caught up with her, Evie donned a bright smile and gestured to a bolt of cloth in the mercantile window.

"That would look nice on Maria and Carmen. Do you think they would wear matching dresses?"

Tyler grasped her shoulders and forced her to face him. "I'm not Peyton or Hale or any of those other men you've fooled with that face, Evie. I know what's worrying you, but worrying about it isn't going to make it go away. Now let's get back to the house before the kids' uncle thinks you're crazed and unfit to take care of them."

Evie searched Tyler's face. He had known enough pain of his own to recognize hers; she read that in his eyes. The determined set of his jaw reassured her somehow. Tyler turned a smiling, easygoing face to the world, but he wore the same kind of mask she did. Only what was behind his mask had been shattered long ago, while she was still relatively whole. She thought maybe she was beginning to understand him just a little bit. He needed something to replace what had been lost, but he was afraid of it, afraid of suffering the pain again.

Her smile faltered slightly, but she offered a brave face. "Kiss me, Tyler."

They were standing there in the eyes of the whole world, but Tyler didn't hesitate. Gently, he cupped her face with both hands and touched his lips to hers until they both warmed and moved closer together. Nothing could tell him that they had something special more than that small movement, that natural gravitation between them. It was a little frightening, but Tyler dropped his hands to Evie's waist and pulled her into his embrace for a brief moment before releasing her.

"Hold your chin up and let's beard the devil. What would Jane Eyre do if she were you?"

Evie didn't want to pretend that Mr. Peyton was Mr. Rochester, but she knew what Jane Eyre would do. Picking up the skirt, she sailed back down the street to confront the man directly.

Carmen was cleaning up the table and Daniel was embarrassedly entertaining their guest when Tyler and Evie came back through the door. The boys were fidgeting, not wanting to miss anything, but reluctant to hang around the house on a Sunday afternoon. Evie sent them to change clothes and go play, put Maria in for a nap, and helped Carmen finish cleaning up. Carmen was old enough to know what was going to happen.

When the children were out of the way, Evie set cups of coffee around the table, invited Daniel and Carmen to join them, and sat down beside Tyler to face the man who could take the children away.

"We sent several telegrams, Mr. Peyton, but never received a reply. We had just about given up hope." Evie had learned to take the initiative a long time ago. It was the best way she knew to get what she wanted.

"I didn't receive any telegrams. I was probably already gone." Peyton's face clouded in memory of the letter that had sent him on this journey. "Angelina had written to me some months ago. It took me a little while to wind up my affairs, and finding transportation in this direction from California wasn't easy. I've gone through two horses in the process. I had no idea what I was going to find when I arrived here."

He looked up at Tyler and Evie. "The children have been blessed in finding someone as thoughtful as you to look after them. Had I come here and found my sister gone and her children scattered to the winds, I would have been desolate. Thank you for keeping them together."

"It's been our pleasure," Evie answered. "They are beautiful children, and I really don't know what I would have done without them."

"But you and your husband will be wishing to set up a home of your own," he said with understanding, sipping his coffee. "It is difficult for newlyweds to be suddenly endowed with four children."

Evie panicked, but Tyler placed his hand across hers and held it to the table, steadying her.

"My wife has always wanted a family, sir. She has none of her own, so she is being honest when she says it has been a pleasure. We can't help but be worried over the children's future. I know this has come as a surprise to you, and you'll need time to make plans. We'll be happy to stay until you say otherwise."

Peyton looked a trifle relieved. He reached in his pocket and pulled out a handkerchief, and his paintbrush rattled to the floor. He looked at it with bemusement, then leaned over and tucked it into his pocket again. Absentmindedly, he tucked the handkerchief back in without using it, either.

"I'll admit to a certain amount of consternation on my part. I'm a bachelor with no children to my name. Angelina was all the family I had left. I'll make provisions for them one way or another. There isn't as much money as there used to be, but I suspect it's cheaper living here than San Francisco, and I've got a little land near here. We'll make it work." He smiled at Carmen, and she gave him one of those grave little looks of hers.

Evie clenched her fingers in disappointment at the mention of his lack of progeny, but he hadn't said he was taking the children away yet. She tried to keep her voice even. "I'll be happy to look after them in any capacity. Carmen is very good, but she is too young to shoulder all the responsibility of her younger brothers and sister."

Peyton leaned back in his chair and tapped his fingertips on the table as he watched the anxious faces around him. He cast a speculative glance at the boy with spectacles in his pocket and a crutch leaning against his chair, then to the young girl who sat interestingly close to him. But his gaze most often came back to the woman with the thick chestnut tresses of a woman he had known too long ago.

"You're quite right, of course. If it is no inconvenience to you, I'll ask you to go on as you are. I'll take a room at the hotel while I take a look around, reorient myself as it were. Tell me, Mrs. Monteigne," he couldn't help asking, "are you from around here?"

Tyler crushed Evie's fingers against the table to keep her from answering. "My wife was born in St. Louis. She never knew her parents, but it seems they come from these parts. That's not something we speak openly about, if you understand me."

Peyton looked momentarily thoughtful, then drifted off on a memory of his own. "I used to hate this town. My mother was half Mexican, half Indian, and people around here despise what they call 'breeds.' It's a hard enough life out here without having your neighbors hate you. But I can remember one little girl who wasn't from around here. She went to school in St. Louis, and she didn't have the same kind of prejudices. She made me see that the rest of the world was different and that I could go out and find my own place in it. She probably saved my life, 'cause I was an ornery cuss back then. Mrs. Monteigne reminds me a little bit of her."

Tyler's fingers squeezed warningly around hers, but Evie was tired of waiting and being cautious. Jerking her hand free, she said, "Elizabeth Howell. Her name was Elizabeth Howell, wasn't it?"

Peyton jerked back to the present with a start and a sudden guilty look that he quickly erased. "Maybe so. Well now, I suppose I'd best go back to the hotel and see if there's room for me. It was a mighty fine dinner, Mrs. Monteigne. I'm obliged to you."

Evie rose with him. "My name is Evangeline Peyton Howell, sir. That's the name on my baptismal certificate. Would those names mean anything to you?"

"Evie!" Tyler stood up and grabbed her shoulders, but he knew better than anyone that there was no holding her back once she got rolling. She was throwing months of caution into the lap of a stranger, but he couldn't help but be curious at the stranger's reaction.

Peyton stared at Evie for a long time, then shook his head. "Elizabeth Howell married Randall Harding while I was in California looking for a gold mine. That's the last I heard of the lady. Perhaps you ought to talk to her." He pushed his chair under the table and gave the door an uneasy look as if he wished to walk out and keep on walking.

"Elizabeth Harding is dead, sir," Tyler said gently, pinching Evie on the arm to keep her quiet.

The man looked shocked, and the hand around the chair tightened until the knuckles whitened. He stared at the young couple on the other side of the table, then shook his head in a gesture of despair. In a moment's time, he seemed to wither into an old man. "I see." Without another word of explanation, he picked up his bag and walked out.

Tyler pulled Evie around and held her. She buried her face in his shoulder and wrapped her arms around his waist, but she didn't cry. She had cried those tears long ago. There weren't any more to shed.

"He's had a lot of nasty shocks, Evie. Let him go." Tyler rubbed her back gently.

Daniel couldn't hold his tongue any longer. "If they weren't married, Evie, he couldn't say anything that would jeopardize her reputation. He loved her. Anybody can see that."

That was true. James Peyton had known Elizabeth Howell a lot longer than he had known one Evangeline Howell Monteigne. His loyalty would lie with the woman he had loved. Evie straightened her shoulders and offered Daniel a small smile.

"My uncle is a very famous painter. Did you know that?" And with those enigmatic words, Carmen picked up the coffee cups and went to the sink.

"Excuse me, Mrs. Peyton, may I have a word with you privately?" Jonathan Hale lifted his hat and fell into step with Evie as she hurried from the schoolhouse to home.

"Why, go right ahead, Mr. Hale. I doubt that anyone will hear us as we walk. And the name is Monteigne now." Still annoyed with this little man for having called the sheriff the day she had gone to Tyler's room, Evie hurried along the boardwalk, her stiff pongee skirt sweeping over several layers of petticoats. She had needed lots of fortification when she had dressed this morning.

"Excuse me, Mrs. Monteigne, but that is precisely what I wished to talk with you about. It doesn't seem at all politic to be discussing your marriage on a public street."

"It doesn't seem at all politic to be discussing it at all, Mr. Hale," she rebuked him. She wasn't certain why she was feeling so irritated at the man. He had given her loads of invaluable information, and she really shouldn't provoke him. She was quite certain he had much more information if she could only pry it from him. The letter she had sent supposedly from St. Louis might have reached him by now, but there hadn't been time for a reply to go to her St. Louis address and return here.

"You are quite right, of course, but I can't help taking an interest in your behalf. As a good friend of Miss Howell's, you are my best connection with the lady. And I can't help feeling protective of any innocent woman."

Evie sent him a doubting gaze. "How very thoughtful of you, sir, but I am in something of a hurry. We will be at the house shortly, and there will be no privacy there at all."

"Very well. I understand that you and Mr. Monteigne were married by Mr. Cleveland?"

She didn't know how he'd come across that piece of knowledge, but she supposed the record had to be on file somewhere. "You understand correctly, Mr. Hale."

He sighed heavily. "I was afraid of that. I don't know how to put this delicately, my dear lady, but Cleveland is not really a minister. I have checked his credentials before. He has a large following on his circuit, but the man is a complete impostor. He will do anything for a dollar."

Evie felt a quiver of fear, but there had always been

a question about the legality of their marriage. She kept walking. "How unfortunate. Well, then we shall just ask Mr. Brown to repeat the ceremony for us. We have been attending the Presbyterian church anyway."

Hale coughed and hurried to keep up with her. "Pray, think a moment before you do so, my dear. There will be those who will be scandalized that you and Mr. Monteigne have been living in sin all this time. It is quite common knowledge in these parts that Cleveland isn't the man to go to for a marriage. They will think the worst."

Rather than being shocked or fearful, Evie was getting angry. She sent Hale a baleful look. "People always do think the worst, don't you agree, Mr. Hale? They haven't a great deal better to do, I suppose."

"Quite often they have very good reasons, Mrs. Peyton. I know it must be difficult to be an unprotected widow in this world, and you are probably very grateful for the care of Mr. Monteigne, but you need an older and wiser head to guide you. Mr. Monteigne may be very handsome and charming, but there is much you don't know about him. Men have ways of knowing more about other men than the ladies do. I would advise you to think twice before making your marriage legal."

That was certainly a shocking statement. Evie looked at him incredulously. "You are asking me to live in sin?"

Hale choked on her honesty, turned red about the ears, and hastened to say, "Of course not. It is well-known that Mr. Monteigne has his rooms at the hotel and that you live with the children. I'm certain you can arrange something."

Arranging something had been precisely their difficulty, but not in the way that Hale meant it. Sneaking out at night to stay with Tyler and then coming back in the morning to look after the children had a certain lack of propriety to it that rankled. Tyler hadn't pressed her last night, but she hadn't liked sleeping alone, either.

Before she could respond appropriately, a familiar figure walked out of the hotel as they passed. Nervously, Evie halted to greet Mr. Peyton, but she wasn't too nervous not to note the shock on Hale's face when she made the introductions.

"Peyton?" he inquired cautiously. "There haven't been Peytons hereabouts for years, aside from this dear lady." He nodded at Evie.

"My sister's been here," Peyton responded wryly, giving the lawyer a quick once-over. "Don't suppose you're related to that pompous ass, Andrew Hale, are you?"

"My father, sir." Hale nervously fiddled with the brim of his bowler. "He was a bit of a stickler, but we shouldn't speak ill of the dead."

"Not as long as they're dead, I reckon." Satisfied on that account, Peyton offered his arm to Evie. "I was just going around to see to the children now that school is out. Will you accept my company?"

Politely, Evie turned to Hale. "Was there anything else you wished to discuss? Have you heard from my friend, perhaps?"

"Yes, yes, I've heard from her. It's just as you said. She's going to be married and would like to know more about her parents. I will be in touch with her guardian, of course." He sent Evie a suspicious look, but refrained from voicing his doubts about the letter's authenticity.

She didn't want him writing to her darned guardian, but Evie hid her displeasure, smiled, and took Peyton's arm. "Well, thank you very much for our informative discussion, sir. Good day."

As they strode rapidly down the alley, Peyton glanced at her curiously. "Hale made you mad, did he? Elizabeth often threatened to kick his father. All lawyers aren't alike of course, but there seem to be a damned lot of pompous asses among them."

Evie smiled at that. "Well, I suppose donkeys have to live, too."

"Donkeys?" His startled look received no answer as Evie hurried up on the porch and into the house.

"José went out in his good clothes," Carmen reported as soon as they entered.

"Well, then, we'll make him wash them when he comes back in." Evie lifted her hat and went into her room to set it on the dresser. "Give Mr. Peyton something cool to drink," she called as she checked her hair in the mirror.

"They'll have to start calling me Uncle Jim, I reckon." Peyton watched her carefully as Evie sailed out of the bedroom tying an apron around her waist.

Carmen had already rescued Maria from the neighbor's, and Evie swept the child into her arms and gave her a hug, then presented her to their guest. "This is your Uncle Jim, Maria. Say hello."

She stuck her thumb in her mouth and said "hewwo" around it.

"It's an honor and pleasure, Miss Maria. Will you let me hold you?" Peyton offered his arms.

Maria looked uncertain for a moment, then finding something of interest, she eagerly went into his arms and pulled at his beard.

"Umph. I guess I asked for that." Peyton wrapped his long fingers around the child's smaller ones and gently untangled his goatee. He propped Maria where he could see her face more clearly. "You have eyes and hair like your mama's and grandmama's." He informed her with a smile.

Then he turned to Evie who was watching this display protectively. "And you have eyes and hair just like your mama's and grandmama's, too."

Chapter 34

Evie couldn't believe he'd said what he had. She'd never had a family to be compared to. She stared at him with a glazed look on her face, waiting for the punch line. When Peyton didn't say more, she didn't know where to look. She wiped her hands nervously on her apron, then turned to see what Carmen was doing.

The younger girl was listening unabashedly. Shaking her head to herself, Evie gestured at the rocking chair. "Won't you have a seat, Mr. Peyton? I have to start dinner. Tyler and Daniel will be home soon."

Peyton gave her a look of exasperation and still carrying Maria, walked in the direction of Evie's bedroom. "Your husband mentioned your interest in painting, Mrs. Monteigne. Are you working on anything now?"

Evie swung a frantic look to Carmen at the stove, then back to the stranger disappearing into their bedroom. She had spent too many years hoping. She couldn't believe her prayers would be answered so easily. She needed time to think, time to formulate questions, but her mind was a blur of madly spinning wishes and hopes and cries, and she could only follow the man who might hold her secrets.

He was studying the canvas propped on the easel by the window. Maria was swinging her chubby fist at the picture and saying "Tywer" over and over, to make sure the stranger got the point.

"It's a very good likeness of Tyler, my dear," Peyton informed the child calmly. "Your Miss Maryellen is a very talented young lady." At Evie's appearance, he swung around questioningly. "Why on earth do you call yourself that awful name? You did say your mother named you Evangeline, didn't you?"

"She also named me Peyton and Howell, but those names don't belong to me any more than any other. Maryellen had a nice, sweet sound to it, like someone who had a loving family around them." Now that she had come to accept that this man knew some of the answers, Evie calmed down. She would remember Jane Eyre and behave sensibly. She pulled out one of the paper roses Tyler had given her and twirled it between her fingers.

"Evangeline was your mother's middle name, and it was her mother's name before her. It's a good old-fashioned family name. Elizabeth must have wanted you to have your family if in name only. I still can't believe she did that." He shook his head and put down the child who had begun to wriggle to get loose.

"Can't believe she did what?" Evie stood there helplessly, watching this stranger who was examining her canvas with a professional eye and telling her the things she had always wanted to hear.

"There's no proof, I suppose." Sadly, he looked up from the painting to examine Evie in the same way he had examined the canvas. "But I don't know where else you would have come across such a name. Or those looks. And this." He gestured at the half-finished painting of Tyler and Maria.

"Perhaps, if you would explain?" She wasn't following all this. No one else had ever commented on her looks. And she didn't know if he meant the painting itself or Tyler. She knew what she hoped he meant, but Texas had taught her a thing or two about reality. She wasn't going to daydream the most important story of her life.

"I don't suppose you would have any wine, would you?" Peyton turned to stare out the window at the narrow, dirty alley.

"I can send for some. The mercantile might have a bottle."

"It's no matter. I just thought we both could use a drop of something strong." He looked over his shoulder. "You ought to take a seat. I'm not sure I should be saying anything at all, but you have more suspicions than I have answers, and we need to sort through them."

Evie obediently dropped to the edge of one of the beds. "What did you mean about my eyes and hair?"

"You have eyes like mine, like the children's, like my mother's—your grandmother's. Rosita Peyton was a very lovely woman, but you look nothing like her except for the eyes. My father used to call them Spanish eyes. I never met Angelina's husband, but I suppose he had dark eyes, too, and the same coloring as my mother. That's why the children look Mexican, I guess. My sister Angelina was a lot like our mother, too. I was the different one; I looked more like my father. He was an Irish-American with a big laugh and a talent for trouble. He wasn't tall, but his hair was auburn and he never could stay out in the sun much. Neither can I. Do you find you have the same problem?" He turned to look at her.

Evie nodded. "I turn red quickly, but I try to wear a hat and carry a parasol. There's not much call for me to be out in the sun."

He nodded and turned back to the window. "I hated farming. My father claimed his father felt the same way and that he died a terrible death in a barroom after he lost his farm while frittering his time painting silly pictures."

Silence fell, and not knowing what else to say to get him speaking again, Evie said, "Carmen tells me you are a famous artist."

Peyton's smile twisted. "I once sold a portrait for two thousand dollars. Money was plentiful back then. I made a lot of it. I don't know if that makes me famous. Anyway, fame—like money—is fleeting. My eyesight is going bad, and my hand is developing a tremble. I can't do as well as you have done there anymore." He jerked his head toward the easel. "I can teach you a few techniques, I suppose, but it looks like you've had some professional training."

"An artist from Paris came to stay in St. Louis one year. Nanny insisted that I study with him. He said my work was too feminine, not strong enough. I asked if he thought a woman ought to paint like a man, and we had a terrible fight, but I tried to learn everything he knew."

Peyton chuckled and finally turned around, leaning back against the windowsill and crossing his arms over his chest. "You sound just like your mother. She once told her father that she wasn't a man, she didn't want to be a man, and if he wanted her to think like a man, then he'd better find her a man's head. Until then, she was a going to do things like a woman, which was a hundred times better than any man could do."

Evie managed a smile. Her mother had said something like that. Those words were music to her ears. Her mother existed somewhere besides in her imagination. This man knew her mother. She looked up at him expectantly, waiting for more. "My mother and I must think alike, then."

His smile disappeared. "Let us hope not. Tell me about this Nanny of yours. How did you know your parents came from here if you grew up in St. Louis?"

Evie explained about the arrangement with the lawyer that she had learned about after Nanny's death. Peyton began to shake his head slowly in dismay halfway through her tale.

"Elizabeth had too much of her father in her. She thought money would take care of the problems of the world. Maybe it does. Who am I to say? But if she had just written to me, told me, I could have come and found you. Maybe that's why she didn't. She wanted you to grow up a lady, and not an itinerant artist's daughter without a penny to her name."

Tears stung Evie's eyes as she gazed at this bearded stranger who seemed to be saying he was her father. It was too frightening to take in all at once. What did he want from her? Did he think she ought to run into his arms and accept his story and forgive him for a lifetime of neglect? Or was he more interested in her mother's money? Why did she have to let him know so much about herself? How long would it take before the news would be all over town? And then everyone would know what she was. An unwanted bastard.

She stared down at her hands. "Why didn't you marry her?" she asked through a voice choked with tears.

"I wanted to. But as I said, I didn't have a penny to

my name. Elizabeth said she didn't care, that she loved me, that she always wanted to be with me. But when I decided to make our wealth in California, she heeded her father and not her heart. She said she'd wait for me." He had taken to staring at the far wall, but now his head turned in her direction again. "When were you born?"

"September 10, 1850," Evie answered without hesitation.

A glimmer of warmth lightened his eyes. "A farewell gift. I left for California at the end of January, the year after the great rush for gold in '49. I'd heard the tales about gold and didn't think I'd make much of a miner, but I thought I might find another way or two to make a penny. I'd thought Elizabeth would be coming with me, so I wasn't very careful. You're a married woman, am I embarrassing you?"

Evie shook her head. "Tyler was ... Well, I know what you mean."

"Jumped the gun, did he?" Peyton chuckled. "Well, then, you know what me and your mother felt like." He rubbed the back of his neck. "The night she told me she couldn't go with me, I felt like I'd been poleaxed. I didn't think to inquire about intimate details, although I suppose it would have been too soon for her to know anyway. I just packed and left in a rage."

"Did you ever write to her? Let her know where you were?" Evie wasn't certain if knowing why she was a bastard would assuage the hurt any, but all these years of curiosity demanded answers.

"Hell, I wrote to her all the time. I wrote to her every night and mailed the letter whenever I got a chance. It takes months for mail to be delivered, so it was a while before I realized I wasn't getting any answers. Then I started to write once a week. When I still didn't hear from her, it dwindled to twice a month. By the end of the year I was making a little money, and I offered to come get her. I sent one of those letters every day in case they got waylaid. Finally, I lowered my pride and wrote Angelina. She was just a kid, but she wrote Elizabeth had left town and hadn't come home."

"She went to St. Louis to have me," Evie answered

quietly. "I didn't know she stayed that long. I don't think
I could give up a baby I'd come to know and love."

"Elizabeth was a strong woman. She knew her own
mind. She hated Mineral Springs. She fought constantly
with her father. She couldn't let anyone know she'd carried the child of a half-breed penniless farmer, and out
of wedlock at that. So she did what was best for you.
She gave you the life she had known before she came
here." Peyton gave Evie's expensive dress a knowing
look. "You didn't lack for anything, did you?"

"Only love." Evie turned at the sound of the front
door opening. Tyler didn't explain what he did all day,
but he came home at this time every night. She supposed
he was gambling at the saloon, but the big games were
at night. He couldn't be making much.

Tyler filled the doorway, his eyes taking in the scene
without expression. As usual, he was dressed like a gentleman, wearing the frock coat and tie and low-crowned
Stetson that set him apart from the rough ranchers and
farmers and merchants of town. He took the Stetson off
and spun it toward the bed with a proprietary air.

"Peyton." He nodded laconically.

"My daughter and I were just getting acquainted."
There was a note of defiance in Peyton's reply.

Tyler's gaze instantly swept to Evie's strained face. She
looked to be on the verge of tears, and he crossed the
room in two strides. Pulling her up from the bed, he
brushed a kiss across her cheek, and she came into his
arms as willingly as a lamb. He held her protectively in
his embrace, and something dangerous inside of him
clicked into place. He turned back to Peyton.

"I wondered if you were man enough to admit it."
Tyler felt the shock rippling through the woman at his
side, but Evie would come around quicker if he made
her mad. He gave her a glinting look of satisfaction when
she tried to pull free. "Sorry, darling, but the resemblance is pretty clear even without the name. I'm surprised you haven't got around to carrying paintbrushes
in your pockets."

"Tyler Monteigne, I'm going to smack you if you don't let
me go right now. You've no call to be rude to my father."

Tyler reached around her and slipped his hand into the deep pocket of her gown. He pulled it out again with his fist clenched triumphantly around an assortment of oddities. Pulling a charcoal pencil from the litter, he held it out to the man watching them with uncertainty.

"Are all artists absentminded dreamers, or did she inherit that trait like the talent?"

Evie elbowed Tyler and grabbed the pencil still wrapped in his palm before he could drop it. "I am not absentminded. There are perfectly good reasons for everything in there. Now give me back my things, Tyler, or I'll start going through your pockets."

Tyler dumped the jumble into her hands, then held his palms free of his clothes. "Search away, woman, see what you can find."

Evie's gaze drifted dubiously to the area where his trouser pockets were located. She knew better than to put her hands anywhere beneath his belt. If they had been alone . . .

But they were never alone. With a wry grimace of acceptance, she reached for his inside coat pocket and pulled out the derringer she knew he kept there. "Does it have real bullets?" she asked with wide-eyed innocence as she pointed it at him.

Gingerly, Tyler disarmed her, and putting the gun back where it belonged, he turned an apologetic look to Peyton. "She really isn't as dumb as she pretends to be."

Since the "she" in question was now alive and kicking instead of pale-faced and teary-eyed, Peyton nodded in masculine appreciation of Tyler's tactics. "I wouldn't expect her to be. Her mother was an intelligent woman. I'm the one missing in the brains department."

Tyler grinned as he caught Evie's arms to keep her from any further assaults. "Well, I've been told the same thing, but I'm smart enough to know a good thing when I see one."

"I am not a *thing*, Tyler Monteigne," Evie hissed, struggling to be free of his grasp.

"Who says I'm talking about you?" Tyler released her wrists and held up his hands again. Seeing the bouquet of paper roses filling the vase on the dresser, he grabbed

one and added it to the one in her hand. They weren't
the real thing, but they were all he had to offer. "Truce,
OK? Am I going to get to hear the whole story or do I
make up my own?"

Years of details tumbled out over the next few hours
as Daniel came in and dinner was served and everyone
had their own stories to tell. Although James Peyton had
left Texas long before the children were born, they had
memories of their mother reading his letters, of the gifts
she bought for them when he sent her money, and excited voices carried the meal long after dark.

When Evie and Carmen finally took the youngest off to
bed, Peyton glanced around the main room with puzzlement. Daniel sat on the straw pallet by the fireplace reading
a book. The boys had gone off to the back bedroom, and
Maria was being bedded down in the front bedroom. He
shook his head and gave Tyler a considering look.

"They don't leave you much privacy, do they?"

Having discarded coat, tie, and waistcoat in the evening heat, Tyler sat at the table in shirtsleeves, sipping
his coffee. He shrugged lightly at the question. "There's
a few problems we haven't conquered yet."

Peyton's eyes narrowed suspiciously. "What do you do
for a living? Seems to me if you're in a position to marry,
you ought to be in a position to offer a wife a house of
her own."

Tyler merely set his cup down and offered his most
charming grin. "I prefer challenges, sir. Any man can
find himself a sweet little wife and settle her in a cozy
cottage and bring home enough coins to keep her happy.
But that's not enough for me."

Daniel spoke up from his corner, glancing over the top
of his glasses. "He means he's a gambler who'd rather
take his chances on a crazy woman for wife. Evie isn't
precisely the settling-down sort."

Tyler leaned back in his chair and gave Daniel a puzzled look. "They don't come much more settled down
than Evie. Who else would land in town and immediately
cover herself up with children?"

"A woman with more energy than sense," Peyton replied with a chuckle. "The boy's right. Evie's got a restless soul. It doesn't take a father to see that."

Disgruntled to be told something he hadn't discerned for himself, Tyler went back to sipping his coffee. He fully intended to wait out the lot of them. He'd let Evie go to her own bed last night because he'd known she was rattled by the day's events, but he had no intention of being so generous tonight. She could mother the whole damned town all day if she liked, but at night, she was his.

When Evie finally came out of the bedroom, Tyler watched her closely. She was so beautiful that she made his heart ache, along with other parts of his anatomy, he acknowledged wryly. But it wasn't just her beauty that held his interest. Perhaps it was her restless soul as her father called it. But it certainly didn't seem restless tonight. She looked a trifle subdued in the light of the lantern she was adjusting.

Tyler couldn't stand the waiting any longer. He stood up and announced to the room at large, "I think we need to turn in early tonight. Evie, is there anything you want to take with you?"

She shot him an uncertain look, then looked at the lantern as she set it down. "Mr. Hale says Cleveland isn't legally a minister."

Tyler felt the knife going through his middle even before her words registered. It was in the tone of her voice, the way she turned away from him. He was in trouble now, but he'd found his way out of worse spots. He gathered his shattered wits and applied them to the problem.

"Hale is a troublemaker, but if it will make you happy, we'll do it again at the church."

Evie gave him a sideways look as she played with the crocheted doily on the table. "You'd better think about it first, Tyler, while you still have a chance."

He felt like he'd just been hit by a timber and abandoned. He stiffened and reached for his coat. "If that's the way you feel about it, then maybe you're right."

He walked out, leaving everyone else in the room staring at Evie. She stood there frozen, the crushed doily in her hand. Then donning a familiar smile, she made her excuses and returned to the bedroom, shutting the door firmly behind her.

Chapter 35

"Are they still at it?" Evie whispered anxiously as she walked Daniel home from the newspaper office. He really didn't need assistance any longer. It was almost six weeks since the leg had been broken, and he maneuvered fairly well on crutches, but she wanted this time to talk to him.

"Last I heard," Daniel replied noncommittally. Since Tyler had walked out over two weeks ago, Evie hadn't been particularly communicative. She had gone about her schoolteaching as if she didn't have a care in the world while the town gossiped around her. Knowing Evie, he reckoned a crisis was imminent, but he was staying out of it this time. This one wasn't any of his business.

"Nobody can play poker for three days straight." Evie tightened her lips into a worried line. "It's not natural. There isn't enough money in this whole blamed town to be worth sitting through that."

"That's one opinion." Daniel shrugged. He gave Evie a sideways look. "Averill told me he hears that you and Tyler aren't legally married, and that you're planning to sue him for misrepresentation or something like that. Where do you think he got that news?"

"Not from me." Evie's lips tightened even further. "If that's what Tyler is telling everybody, I have a bug to put in his ear."

"Don't you dare, Evie," Daniel warned as they came close to the alley. "You'll stay out of that saloon, or they'll likely take your job and the kids away. The scandal is enormous enough as it is."

"Tyler Monteigne can rot in that saloon, if he wants.

He can play poker until his eyes drop out and his hands fall off. But I'll be doggoned if I'll let him go around telling false tales about me."

"Lies, Evie. The word is lies. And you've told your fair share of them at one time or another. They're just coming home to roost, like I warned you they would."

Evie picked up her skirt and started down the alley. "You're the one who said we needed to be careful. You're the one who agreed I might be in danger if I used my own name. Now don't go preaching honesty at me now, Daniel. And I haven't told a single lie in ..." She contemplated the last time she'd let her imagination stretch the truth a little. "Well, I don't think it's been since I told Mr. Hale about my friend in St. Louis. There hasn't been a need to lie about anything."

"That's because the truth has become more fantastic than your imagination. Now that you know who your parents are, why don't you just go over to Hale and ask about the money? You know there has to be some. Those lawyers in St. Louis may be keeping it for themselves."

"That's what Mr. Peyton says. My father," she amended. Evie halted before the porch and looked at Daniel with bewilderment clouding her eyes. "But I just have this feeling that telling everyone who I am will come as an unpleasant shock to too many people. How will the Hardings feel when they learn the stepmother they idolize had a child out of wedlock? The children don't mind knowing I'm related to them, but what if there are other Howells out there I don't know about? How will they feel knowing Elizabeth wasn't a saint? For all that matters, the whole town thinks of her that way. And it's only my father's word against everyone else's that she wasn't. Who do you think they will believe?"

Daniel ran his hand through his hair in a gesture reminiscent of Tyler's, and Evie looked away. Tyler's absence was like a festering abscess in her center, but she couldn't let anyone know that. She waited for Daniel's reply without looking at him.

"Danged if I know, Evie, but you can't put it off forever. Your father says the house on that land of his isn't habitable, and it looks like he hasn't got much to put it back together with. If you could just get your hands on your mother's money, you could fix things up and insure that the children had a decent roof over their heads and clothes on their back."

"This roof is secure enough, and my father is helping out with groceries and clothes. We don't need any more than that." Evie started up the porch before Daniel could bring up the subject of Tyler's support again. Tyler didn't owe her any support. She wouldn't touch the account at the general store. It would be much better for everyone concerned if he would just win his darned card game and leave town. Maybe if she let him know that their foolish encounters hadn't borne fruit, he would go.

As they entered, Manuel came dashing in through the back door with a huge grin plastered across his face. "Tyler's winning! Old Tom just put up his half of the saloon, and they're down there arguing over its worth. I've got to go back and see if Tyler took the bet."

Evie grabbed Manuel's collar before he could rush out. "You have no business being in a saloon. Where's José?"

Manuel glanced up at her in astonishment. Evie always smiled and never laid a hand to him. He didn't even try to struggle out of her grasp. "He's with Uncle Jim back at the saloon. I just came to tell you what's happening."

Evie sighed and let his collar go. "I am beginning to think your Uncle Jim and Tyler Monteigne are two of a kind. Go fetch José back here. It's almost time for supper."

Daniel sent Evie a swift look as she disappeared into the bedroom to take off her hat. How could she be so quick to recognize the characters of other people and never understand her own? She had been as restless as two tomcats in a box these last weeks. She had left Carmen to do most of the cooking while she finished that damned painting. Her classes at school had gone on more field trips in this past week than they had in an entire year. And unless she was painting, she never sat still. Her latest project involved replastering the old adobe walls with tinted materials. Admittedly, the sunny yellow was less dreary than the peeling mud of before, but she stayed awake all hours working on it. Even Evie's energy couldn't last that long.

When official word arrived with James Peyton later that day that Tyler had indeed won half of the saloon, Evie showed no interest in the news. She finished setting food on the table and took her place, insisting on grace before she allowed anyone to eat. While the others chattered excitedly about the news, Evie silently chewed her food.

She didn't want to hear about Tyler. He had taken the opportunity for freedom that she had handed him with an alacrity that was embarrassing. She didn't know why she had been foolish enough to think a man like that needed her in any way but one. And now he had a whole saloon full of women at his command to take care of that particular need. And Starr wouldn't forget to prevent babies.

Damning Tyler to the hell he deserved, Evie rose from the table and returned to her painting. The light stayed strong for a few hours yet at this time of year. She was almost finished, and she wanted it done so she could shove it out of her life. It wasn't turning out as well as she had expected, but she disliked leaving a project unfinished. And the portrait of Maria seemed to be fairly decent. When she was done, she could put the whole thing behind her and look for something new to do.

The sunlight prevented Tyler from seeing in the front window of the little house behind the livery, but he knew she was standing there, working on that damned painting as she had every night these last weeks. Manuel had told him what she was doing when he'd asked about the light that came on in there every night. She was going to ruin her eyes just like her father had if she didn't give it up pretty soon.

Tyler turned away. It wasn't any of his business any longer. Hale had served him with some papers that had enjoined him from being in Evie's company and told him that the marriage was legally null and void, but he hadn't seen Evie's writing on the papers anywhere, and he'd thrown them out. He'd thought he could walk away now that Evie had found what she wanted, but he didn't seem able to make the move. He still felt married, and he wanted to know for certain that Evie didn't feel that way any longer.

He had seen her eating dinner with Hale twice, and even Kyle Harding had been over, sniffing around again. Rumors were rampant, but Tyler hadn't given credence to any of them. Not until he heard the words from Evie would he begin to believe.

So he supposed he ought to talk to Evie, but he couldn't bring himself to do it just yet. He needed to dig her out of his flesh first. She was the glue holding him together. He had to see if he could still walk away without her. Winning that card game was the first step in the right direction.

Tyler started throwing his clothes in the valise he had brought here with him. He owned half of a saloon. The jubilant triumph of that knowledge warred with the other Tyler, the one who didn't want any ties. He could lose the damned saloon as easily as he had gained it. He couldn't look at it as his. But the pride of ownership kept creeping up on him.

He could show Evie and the whole town that he could be somebody. The saloon was just a start. He had enough in the bank to buy a herd of cattle if he chose. And the sum he had won at this last card game would give him enough to live on for quite a while. He didn't even need to gamble if he didn't want to. He could become a rancher, or run for sheriff against Powell, or anything else he applied his mind to.

But his mind was on Evie.

Not acknowledging that thought, Tyler slammed the valise shut and started out the door. Ben met him on the stairs.

Ben threw the valise a shrewd look, then narrowed his eyes as he looked back to Tyler. "Going somewhere?"

"I'm a landowner now. I've got to look after my property." Tyler pushed by him and continued down the stairs.

Ben followed. "Thought for a minute there you might

be thinking of leaving town. You have a tendency to do
that when things start tying you down."

"I'll go when I'm damned good and ready to go.
There's still some unfinished business here."

"That's good to hear. I thought you might be inter-
ested in a few things I found out over at the livery."
Ben waited until Tyler turned around to stare at him.
"Somewhere private, my friend."

Tyler nodded, and they clattered out of the hotel
together.

"Mr. Harding, this is a surprise. Won't you please
come in?" Evie tried to hide her astonishment at the
sight of Jason Harding standing at the front door. His
expression was grim, and she had a sinking feeling that
his call wasn't purely social, but she put on her best lady
face and smiled.

Inside, Jason gave the man named Peyton sitting in
the corner with Maria in his lap an even more furious
look before turning to his hostess. "Is there somewhere
we can talk private?"

Evie looked around desperately for some support. She
wished Tyler were here, but she had to face the fact that
he might never be here again. Catching sight of Daniel's
questioning look, she remembered his words of earlier,
and taking a deep breath, she faced Jason Harding directly. "There isn't anything we can say that my family
can't hear."

"Your family?" Jason gave the assorted collection of
children and adults an incredulous look. "Tyler said you
had a tendency to stretch the truth, but that's stretching
it a little too far. Let me take you down to the café for
a cup of coffee."

He was just a man, after all. Evie could forgive him
for his stupidity. She smiled and taking his arm, led him
toward a chair. "My father, James Peyton." She gestured
to the man in the rocker who nodded his head in greeting
but didn't offer his hand. "I believe you know Daniel.
He's more of an adopted brother than a blood brother,
but we were raised together, so it's the same thing to us."

If Jason weren't so tall, she'd shove him into a seat,

but she did the next best thing. She sat down in the chair beside the one she offered to him. He was forced to follow suit. She gestured to the children. "And of course you know my cousins. Their mother was my aunt."

Jason sat in stunned silence, trying to take in the enormity of the misconception that he had arrived here under. Glancing to the older man and catching his cynical look, he almost flushed. He gripped his hat brim like some greenhorn adolescent and tried to summon apologies for words he'd thought but hadn't said.

Evie smiled brilliantly. "To what do we owe the pleasure of your company, Mr. Harding?"

"I . . . uh." He stammered and turned red under that brilliant gaze. Evie was even more beautiful up close than he had ever noticed. It was no wonder Kyle was head over heels. Gulping and remembering the reason he had come here, Jason forced the words out. "I came here tonight as a representative of the school board, but it's Kyle I'm concerned about. He's been on a rip-roaring drunk these last two days, and you're to blame, Mrs. Peyton, or Monteigne, or whoever you are."

Evie turned to Carmen. "I think you better bring Mr. Harding some of that beer, Carmen. And if José and Manuel show up, send them into the bedroom." She returned her attention to Jason. "As far as I am aware, I am still Mrs. Monteigne. I tried to explain to Kyle, and I'd thought he'd understood. Is there anything I can do?"

Jason threw Peyton a curious look. "You can tell him this man is your father, for one thing."

Evie looked surprised, but Peyton gave their visitor a disgusted look. "He thinks you've found a new suitor more to your liking," he explained.

Evie's eyes widened as she turned back to Jason. "Why, Mr. Harding, that's an evil mind you have! Even Tyler could see the resemblance. Shame on you."

Carmen set the beer on the table, and in the background Daniel snickered behind the pages of his book. Carmen threw him an enigmatic glance and took the other half of his pallet.

Jason had the grace to look embarrassed. "Well, it seemed mighty odd that Tyler moved out when this man moved in. And there's all these rumors flying around about you and Tyler not being married when everybody knows ..." He shut up under the curious gaze of the pair on the pallet. At least Maria seemed to have fallen asleep in the other man's arms. He turned his attention in that direction. "You look mighty familiar to me, Peyton." His forehead wrinkled in a slight frown as he turned back to Evie. "And I thought your married name was Peyton, not your maiden name."

Before Evie could reply, Peyton answered for her. "Daniel thought it safer if she traveled as a widow since she didn't have any servants to accompany her. Although I grew up here, my daughter has never been in Texas. She wasn't certain what to expect."

Jason began to relax in understanding. "And she came here to meet you. Are you a traveling man, sir?"

"I've been in California," Peyton acknowledged stiffly.

They were making up lies for her. Evie listened in amazement, but she wasn't about to correct them. Her concern was for Kyle and for her job. "Now will you tell me if there is anything I can do for Kyle, Mr. Harding? I've tried to be just as plain as can be with him, but people have such wicked tongues. He really shouldn't listen to them."

Jason's expression went grim again. "You can't deny that your husband has taken rooms at the saloon. It doesn't set a good example for the children. Kyle accepted the fact that you married another man, but it's a bit difficult to accept that you don't live with your husband. He's thinking he should have done something to keep you from making the wrong decision, and he's blaming himself."

Evie would have preferred to scream and throw a tantrum and tell everyone to mind their own business, but she managed a small smile and straightened her gown and folded her hands in her lap. "It's a little difficult for all of us to live in this small house, Mr. Harding. And admittedly, Tyler and I have had a little tiff, but that shouldn't be anyone's concern but ours. My father is seeing to the repair of his old home while Tyler is making a place for us here. Everything will be straightened out with time. You just tell Kyle I'd be appreciative of his support. Your brother is the sweetest man I've ever met, but you can see for yourself that we would never suit. Why, I'd up and die of loneliness out there on that ranch all by myself."

She thought she'd almost smoothed everything over when the front door crashed open and a giant, bald-headed man stood there.

Before she could even catch enough breath to scream, Logan pulled his gun and aimed it at the man with the child sleeping in his lap.

"Peyton, I'm going to kill you."

She did scream then, as chairs crashed to the ground and the men in the room scrambled to their feet.

Chapter 36

"Logan, you old bastard! Angelina told me you were dead." James Peyton calmly handed a now wailing Maria into Evie's hands as Jason put his hand on his gun and moved threateningly to block Evie and the children from the intruder.

"Don't give me that bullshit, Peyton. I want my money." Logan left the door open behind him as he held his gun high, but his gaze drifted nervously to the screaming child and the woman and girl in long skirts trying to calm her.

"And you'll get it, but there's no sense in making the womenfolk hysterical. Let's go over to the Red Eye and catch up on old times." Peyton threw a glance to the tall young man watching carefully with his hand on his gun. "Harding, you want to join us? Your stepmama was a friend of ours. We'd like to hear a word or two about her."

That statement was more likely to make Evie hysterical than the giant with the revolver, but she bit her tongue and watched the men warily holster their weapons. She'd like to take the skillet to all their heads at the moment, but Nanny had taught her to be a lady. Quieting Maria in her arms, she merely smiled as Jason gave her an apologetic farewell. The other two men were already out on the porch, arguing loudly.

"If you see Tyler, tell him everything's just fine," she said maliciously as Jason started for the door. He turned and gave her a curt nod, then strode out.

Daniel had scrambled to his feet with the aid of his crutch when Logan made his entrance. Now he looked longingly at the door through which the men had left.

Once again, he'd been left behind with the women and
children.

Seeing that look, Evie spoke up. "Do you think you
can find José and Manuel? I'm going to start hog-tying
those two rascals if they don't start coming home by
dark."

With relief, Daniel accepted this assignment. "My leg
needs the exercise anyway," he responded gruffly, refusing to look at Carmen as he swung out the door.

Evie threw the girl a harried look. "I think the Shakers
have the right idea. Men and women ought to be kept
separated, if just for their own sanity."

Carmen smiled shyly. "But then where would babies
come from?"

As Carmen took Maria to put her to bed, Evie contemplated her comment with despair. Babies were the
least of the trouble men could wreak. She hoped Carmen
never had to know a breaking heart.

From his seat at the card table, Tyler watched the
three men at the bar with curiosity. He'd never seen
a more unlikely combination than James Peyton, Jason
Harding, and Logan. Drawing on his cheroot, he threw
down a card and continued the game, but he kept one
eye on the trio at the bar. They spelled trouble if anything did.

Starr approached them, and Logan gave her a hug.
Apparently the lout was happy about something for a
change. Tyler blew a smoke ring and pulled in the pot
he'd just won. He didn't have to gamble anymore, but
he didn't know what else to do with his time. Except
watch for trouble.

His gaze slid to the corner where Tom was drinking
away his misery. He didn't feel the least bit sorry for
robbing the man of his half of the saloon. After going
over the books, Tyler could tell he'd been robbing Starr
for years of her share of the profits. Now he'd like to
see the sales agreement that had bought the livery from
the Rodriguez family. He was willing to wager that had
been another form of robbery. Tom wasn't an honest

sort of man, and his voice was naggingly similar to one he'd heard on a rather inauspicious occasion.

Suspicion wasn't enough to hang a man. Tyler shuffled and began dealing the deck, but his attention wandered back to the three men who had entered just a while ago. Apparently James Peyton was the man Logan had been hunting for and Logan was celebrating having the debt paid. Tyler wasn't certain where Peyton got his cash, but that wasn't any of his business. Only he couldn't help wondering how Harding had got in on it. Peyton was usually with Evie at this time of night.

That made him restless. Every damned man in town had a right to go call on Evie but him, and he was her husband. Sort of. He was going to have to do something about that situation sooner or later. With Peyton over here right now, maybe now was the time. She'd be alone except for the kids.

Except for the kids. Tyler snorted at that understatement. How in hell did Evie think she was going to keep a rein on those two wildcats, Manuel and José? They needed a man's firm hand, and the only man around was standing here at the bar. There was always Daniel, of course, but the boy had enough on his shoulders without being saddled with a couple of brats who could run circles around him any day. In a few years Daniel might be useful, but right now there were other things he needed to be doing besides riding roundup on children.

At the sight of the object of his commiserations appearing in the doorway, Tyler folded his cards and called it a night. If even Daniel was out of the house, someone had to see to Evie.

Daniel looked relieved as Tyler stood up and strode toward him. It was a weekday, and the bar wasn't crowded. The three men who had been joking and laughing together grew silent as Tyler strode by, but he didn't acknowledge their presence. He was more concerned about the expression on Daniel's face.

"Tyler . . ." Daniel glanced over the other man's shoulder to the bar where everyone seemed to be staring at him. He backed out into the street at the nod of Tyler's head. The door closed, and darkness enveloped them.

The light streaming from the saloon's lone window was on the opposite side of the door from where they stood. Daniel hurried to speak to the silent man crushing his cheroot beneath his boot. "José and Manuel have disappeared again. And I can't find Ben, either. Do you think they're together?"

"If they are, Ben has them bound and gagged. Evie's too lax with those brats. They ought to be home and in bed this time of night." Tyler started walking toward the livery, adjusting his stride to Daniel's halting one.

"She would if she could find them. They went out after supper and haven't come back."

"They've been told to stay out of that livery." Tyler wished he hadn't crushed his cheroot. He needed something in his hand right now besides a gun. Instinct was itching at him. Ben had always said he'd had a nose for trouble, and Tyler could smell trouble brewing now. The boys were probably just up to mischief somewhere, but that wasn't what his nose was telling him, not after what Ben had said earlier.

"That was the first place I searched. They aren't there." Daniel gave up on the extra crutch and propelled himself along with one as Tyler's speed increased.

"Did you see Ben?"

"No, I told you I didn't."

"He's there." Instead of taking the wide front doors used for carriages and wagons, Tyler hurried down the alley toward the side door, avoiding the corral and the other entrance on the far side.

Pulling his gun, Tyler stood in the dark doorway and whistled. An answering whistle echoed from the interior and a moment later a shadow slipped from the stable. Ben materialized in the dim light thrown from the hotel windows into the alley.

"Somethin' wrong?"

Tyler shoved his gun back in the holster. "The brats are missing. Have you seen them?"

Ben shook his head. "But I went out for a bite to eat earlier. They could have slipped in then."

Tyler cursed. "All right, you'll have to go down and look for them." He turned to Daniel. "Can you whistle?"

At Daniel's nod, he ordered, "Then you stand here and whistle if anyone comes. Then clear out of here. Make like you're just wandering home. Don't try to run. If anyone questions you, just bluff. You've been around Evie long enough to know how to do that."

Daniel nodded without argument. "Where are you going to be?"

"I'm going to see Evie." His tone was grim, but his step was quick as Tyler continued on down the alley.

The front room was well lit, but even if it hadn't been, Tyler knew she would be up. She wouldn't get any rest until she had those boys back under the roof. He cursed the little brats again, but his brow was creased with worry as he stepped up on the porch. He should have done more to protect them besides order them out of the livery. Those men who had held the boys hostage could easily have others working with them. If Ben was right about what he'd found in the livery, they almost certainly had someone working with them.

Before Tyler could reach for the door, a large form rose from the shadows at the side of the house. The light from the front window glinted against the polished steel of a gun.

"Monteigne? Hale told me you'd try this. You've got orders to stay away from the lady." Sheriff Powell stepped up on the porch and gestured with his gun to indicate that Tyler back away from the door.

Tyler held his hands up so the man could see he wasn't going for his own gun. "The lady is my wife, and her cousins are missing. I'm just checking to see if they've got home yet."

"Let their uncle look for them. I've got someone back at the office you ought to see. He was swearing out a warrant for your arrest when I saw him last."

Tyler glanced longingly to the brightly lit front window, wishing for just a sight of Evie. He missed the warmth of that little room. It had been nice for a change to smell bread baking, listen to childish laughter, and have a woman who required only his presence, no matter what his mood. He could be churlish instead of charming, and Evie would tease him out of it. He could sit there and just talk with Daniel, and she wouldn't be leaning over his shoulder, demanding his attention. Evie was the least demanding woman he'd ever known, and that included his sainted mother. But then, that's what happened when a woman didn't need him. She could lock him out without a qualm. He'd finally found a woman who didn't require commitments, and look where it got him.

Tyler glanced at the sheriff's gun and shrugged. "Whatever you say, Powell. But if anything happens to those kids, it's on your head."

They walked back down the alley. Daniel had disappeared from sight. Tyler was relieved that the boy didn't see him with the sheriff holding him at gunpoint, but he had to wonder where he'd disappeared to so fast. That livery had to have more hiding places than the badlands.

When they reached the sheriff's office and opened the door, Tyler wished he'd been a little more forceful in resisting Powell's arrest.

Silas Dorset looked up from the papers he was signing, and his smile was genial as Tyler and the sheriff walked in. "That's one of them, Sheriff. Now find the woman and the nigger, and you've got the thieves."

Tyler's hand reached for his gun, but Powell jerked it away before he could free it.

"Mr. Hale, this is unexpected. It's late." Evie glanced uncertainly around the lawyer to see if her father or Harding accompanied him, but there was no one else on the porch.

"I realize, and I apologize, but this is important. I tried to speak with your father first, only . . . He and his friends are a trifle under the influence. Mr. Monteigne has just been placed under arrest, and I understand there will soon be a warrant for you. We've got to get you out of here before that can happen."

Shocked, Evie swung the door open and gestured for Hale to enter. He shook his head and remained where he was. "There isn't time. I've got my carriage out back. I'll take you out to the Harding ranch where you'll be safe until I can straighten this out. Does the name Dorset mean anything to you?"

Evie shook her head in puzzlement. The name rang a bell—Dorset! The man who had stolen Tyler's plantation. The man who had tried to cheat at cards. Her eyes widened. "That's ridiculous. The man's little better than a cheat and a thief. I can't believe he came all the way out here to make such false accusations."

"Well, he has, and it will take some time to disprove them. Unless you wish to suffer the unpleasantness of sitting behind bars while I straighten this out, you'd best come with me." Hale held out his hand.

Evie refused it. "I can't. Manuel and José are missing. I can't go anywhere until I know where they are. Daniel's out looking for them now. I'm certain they will be back shortly." She felt Carmen coming up silently behind her. This was a terrible way to bring up children. They should be protected from these kind of sordid goings on.

"I'm certain matters will be in good hands with their sister and your brother in charge. Go pack a few things in a bag. There isn't any time to spare." Hale finally entered the house, his nervous energy adding to the urgency of the situation.

Evie wanted to resist, but Carmen had already gone for a valise, and Mr. Hale looked as if he were ready to suffer apoplexy. She would almost rather go to jail than accompany him, but she supposed it would be much more pleasant to hide at the Hardings' ranch. She would be of more use to Tyler if she were free and could come to his defense.

"Is Mr. Harding going with us? He left with my father. I really need to see them before I run off like this."

"Miss Howell, there is no time to wait. Carmen will tell them where you've gone when they come back. If you'll just hurry, I can explain everything."

Howell. He called her Howell. She caught his eye, and the knowledge was there. He knew, and he was going to tell her everything. Excitement rippled through Evie's veins. No more charades. No more pretending she was what she wasn't. He was going to explain about her mother and the trust and then she would have the funds to help Tyler fight Dorset and to give the children a good home, and everything would be all right again. It would be almost like having Nanny with her again.

Giving Hale a quick look, Evie hurried to the bedroom to gather a change of clothing and her nightgown.

She was back in minutes, wrapping a mantle around her shoulders and adjusting her hat. "Are you certain the Hardings won't mind? They're friends of the sheriff. Won't they object to hiding a fugitive?"

"They're family, Miss Howell. The Hardings stick by family. Now lets hurry."

"Daniel still isn't back. I'm afraid something has happened to the boys. Let us take a quick look first. I can't leave without telling them why." Evie hurried toward the door.

Hale grabbed the valise that Carmen was carrying and hurried after her. He caught Evie's arm as she started down the alley toward town. "You can't go that way, Miss Howell. Someone will see you."

"Well, they'll have to see me. I need to see Daniel." She kept going despite Hale's hampering grip. Spying a movement in the shadows, she shook off his hand and almost ran down the alley.

"Daniel!" She knew his movements anywhere. The shadow stepped forward, and she could see the jerk of his crutch.

"Evie, what's going on? I just saw the sheriff with Tyler. Is something wrong?" Daniel gave Hale a quick look, but his attention was focused on Evie. He didn't fail to notice her hat and mantle.

"Dorset is in town. He's swearing out warrants for Tyler's arrest and mine. Mr. Hale is taking me out to the Harding ranch where they can't find me. Have you found the boys?"

"Ben's helping me look. Don't you worry. We'll take care of them. Is there anything we can do?"

"Just tell the boys something unexciting. Tell them I've gone to see an old friend or something. Mr. Harding can tell the school board that I've been called away. Tomorrow was the last day of the term anyway. The children were expecting a party. Maybe you could see that they got one."

"Miss Howell, we must hurry. The sheriff could be back any minute." Hale tugged on her arm.

Daniel stared at this use of Evie's name, but before he could comment, Evie hurried off in the company of the lawyer. Maybe it was going to be all right, then. If Hale knew who Evie was, then he knew she had the funds to make everything right.

Daniel turned back toward the livery at a whistle from inside. He'd thought he was supposed to be the one to whistle. What was he supposed to do now?

Chapter 37

With a gun at his back, Tyler could do little more than offer his enemy a sardonic grin. "Well, well, Dorset, did you miss me so much you had to come find me?"

Dorset's handsome face was a little more lined than when he had seen him last, and the glitter in his eyes wasn't amusement. Tyler thought the other man looked like he'd been rode hard and put up wet. As a gambling man, he knew when his opponent had reached the point of desperation. He'd say Dorset had reached it and gone past.

"I don't know what you do with card cheats and thieves in this town, Sheriff, but I want the book thrown at him." Dorset signed the remaining paper on the desk with a flourish. "He's probably still carrying that watch he stole from me in his pocket. Pretty little thing, it is, with a picture of my mama in a fancy pink gown inside. I'd like it back, Sheriff."

Powell pulled the watch from Tyler's vest pocket and snapped it open. The picture was just as the man had said. He prodded Tyler with a gun. "And I bet you told your poor wife this was your mother, didn't you? Damn, but you almost had me believing you. Get in there." He shoved him toward the cell.

"It *is* my mother, Powell." Tyler didn't budge. He ought to be sweating with desperation about now, unleashing the beast that crawled in his guts, but he was suddenly cooler and calmer than he'd ever been in his life. He wouldn't let Evie be branded a thief or the wife of one. He wouldn't bring shame to the small family under his protection. He was damned well going to do something right for once in his life. He turned and calmly snatched the gun from the sheriff's hand. Powell tended to be a little slow on the uptake.

Emptying the bullets from the gun, Tyler gave it back to the furious man behind the badge. "Telegraph the sheriff in Natchez. Make inquiries about both of us. See which one of us has the longer record. Dorset there is one of those Yankee carpetbaggers who came down to nab every ripe plum on the market. He swiped my family's plantation and everything in it, including that watch. There's plenty back in Natchez who will tell you the story."

Dorset stood up and rested his fists against the desk. "I bought that plantation fair and square. You're the cheat who stole the money I needed to run it." He turned to the sheriff. "You ever tried to plant cotton or run a plantation without cash, Sheriff? Those damned niggers don't work for nothin' no more. I want Monteigne and his shill locked up until they're old and gray. And I want my money back."

Powell gave both men a look of disgust, but he reserved his worst epithets for the stranger. "I'm from Texas, mister. If I'd known what you were when you walked in here, I would have bounced you out again before I listened to your sorry tale. I've seen enough of your kind to last me a lifetime and then some."

The sheriff gave Tyler a shrewd look as he reloaded his gun. "Tom over at the saloon's been complainin' about you, too. Maybe we ought to settle this the Texas way. I'll send those telegrams right enough, but I think we all ought to mosey over to the Red Eye. A good game of cards ought to answer the question without having to call in any judge."

Dorset fumed, but Tyler accepted the decision with a curt nod. He just hoped Daniel and Ben had found the boys and got them home to Evie so she wouldn't be worrying. There was no reason she ought to hear about any of this until it was all over.

Daniel and Ben had their hands tied and weren't going to be telling Evie anything any time soon.

Ben looked disgusted as he struggled with the rope

wrapped around his wrists and ankles and tied in between. The bastards had done a thorough job for a
change. There wasn't a chance in hell of getting out of
this one.

"There might be a knife or something farther down
the tunnel." Daniel rolled into a sitting position and tried
to see beyond the circle of light from the lantern beside them.

"Well, you'd better look quick. They had so much fun
making a birthday present out of me, they're bound to
come back to finish the job on you." Ben threw the two
silent boys at the edge of the light a quick look. Bound
as tightly as he, they looked terrified, but they hadn't
said a word since he and Daniel had been thrown down
to join them.

"I'm a cripple, remember? They won't be worried
about me." Daniel's reply was bitter as he scooted carefully toward the darkness. "A cripple, a nigger, and two
babes. I'm sure they're just as worried as can be."

"I'm not a babe." José was the only one to protest
this assessment of their predicament.

"And Daniel's not a cripple. And just because Ben's
a different color doesn't mean he's not a man. That's
what Evie says. We're better than they are. We'll get out
of here." Manuel spoke for the first time. His eyes were
wider than saucers in the darkness, but his small face
was set with determination. He turned his back on José
and using his fingers began struggling with his brother's
ropes.

Ben chuckled. "You boys got spunk but not a whole
lot of sense. Why didn't you tell the sheriff about what
was going on in here?"

Manuel shrugged and kept working at José's ropes.
"He don't listen to us. We're greasers. That's like being
a nigger, isn't it?"

"I think you need to listen to Miss Evie a little closer."
Muttering beneath his breath and working at his bonds,
Ben tried to keep an eye on Daniel as he used the freedom of his legs to inch farther into the tunnel beneath
the stable. They were in a hell of a fix, but he wasn't
about to contaminate the boys with that knowledge.

"We were going to catch the thieves ourselves." Manuel said as if Ben hadn't interrupted. "Tom stole the livery from us. That's what Mama said. And he's stealing from people like Logan. And I bet anything, he's the one who's running the gang stealing from the stagecoach."

Considering the looks of the thugs that had caught them and put them down here, Ben wasn't willing to take that wager. He'd seen them coming and going from this hiding place. He'd reported it to Tyler. Tyler would know where they were. He just had to hope that Tyler would notice they were missing before the criminals decided to rid themselves of any witnesses.

"There's crates back here," Daniel called. "I don't know what's in these others, but there's sticks of dynamite in this open one."

"Well, I'm not about to blast ourselves out of these ropes. A crate of knives would be more useful."

Daniel disappeared into the darkness of the interior. Someone in the stable overhead slammed a boot against the trap door in the floor and yelled at them to shut up or they'd shut them up. Ben grimaced but quit talking. He didn't want to do anything that would bring anyone down here just yet.

He was afraid the boy was hurting his leg by moving around like that, But Daniel was the only one with freedom to move. The young ones were tied together, and he was bent backward so he couldn't even sit up. Ben wondered what kind of minds thought up positions like this.

Daniel slid back excitedly, a grin beaming from ear to ear. As he entered the lamplight, he turned around, revealing a sharp piece of metal caught between his bound hands. "Let's get busy. I got an idea on how to get out of here if we can get these ropes off."

Ben didn't know how anyone could get two kids and a cripple past the passel of ruffians above, but he wasn't one to sit around and mope, either. He took the sharp edge and began to saw at Daniel's ropes.

Tyler carefully folded his cards and laid them face down on the table, waiting for Dorset to shuffle through his own hand and make the wager. On his right, Tom was nervously sorting through his draw. Tom was half drunk and jittery as a skunk at midnight, and the nagging sense of ill-ease Tyler had had all night multiplied. He'd thought Dorset had been behind this feeling, but something nagged at the back of his mind when he didn't need the distraction. He needed to settle the sheriff's idea of fair play and get back to Evie.

As the other men laid their bets, Tyler glanced up at the crowd around him. Peyton, Harding, and Logan were still here, watching the game with drunken interest. There hadn't been any sign of Daniel or Ben. Maybe they were back at the house. Maybe they weren't. The only two things keeping him here instead of running to see how Evie fared was the gun in the sheriff's hand and Tom sitting at the table with him. If anything was happening at the livery, Tom wouldn't be here.

Tyler threw in a gold coin against Dorset's voucher and Tom's greenback. This wasn't a game he could win. Dorset had only one thing that he wanted, and Tom had nothing. If he won, he won nothing but the sheriff's suspicion. If he lost, he might be free, but he would still have nothing. He didn't like the terms of this game.

He finally caught Jace's eye, and the big man wandered over, a little the worse for drink but more sober than the other two.

"Go see if Evie and the kids are all right. The boys were missing earlier, and she was worried about them."

Jason watched the fancy gambler at the card table, his fingers expertly sorting his cards beneath the frill of his shirtsleeves, his eyes never leaving the other players as he spoke. He gave a snort of contempt. "What do you care?"

The only sign of anger in Tyler's expression was a slight tightening of his jaw. "Just do what I ask, or have Peyton do it. If anything happens to me, he's the one who has to look after them."

Jason gave the sheriff standing close behind Tyler a second look, and enlightenment came gradually. He didn't know what was happening here, but this wasn't just an ordinary card game. Through the haze of liquor, he sensed the tension. He turned wordlessly and went back to the men at the bar.

Out of the corner of his eye, Tyler saw Peyton slip out. Jason remained by the bar, but his expression had gone from pleasantly complacent to wary. He would be a good man to have on his side. Tyler just hoped that was where Harding meant to be when the aces fell.

The vouchers in front of Tyler began to grow. Without his cronies to help him cheat, Dorset was at a disadvantage. Tyler was all too aware that he was the only man at the table without a gun. Only the sheriff's presence was holding off the confrontation that was inevitable. Tyler knew better than to play with desperate men. On his own, he would have walked away long since. With the sheriff at his back, he kept playing.

Peyton returned and whispered to his companions. Tyler wished he could hear what they were saying but the worried expression that appeared on Harding's face told him enough. Something was wrong back at the house. He almost missed the card that Tom played.

To hell with what the sheriff thought. He had to bring this game to an end. Spreading out his hand containing three deuces, Tyler snatched Dorset's voucher from the pot and deliberately began adding up the sum owed to him.

"Three thousand dollars, Dorset. That's more than I owed in back taxes when you stole my plantation. What are you planning on putting up as collateral?" Tyler tucked the vouchers into his coat pocket.

"The night's not over, Monteigne. You're cheating. I damned well know you are. Nobody's that lucky. We're staying right here until the sheriff catches you at it."

"I'm not lucky, I'm good." Tyler swept up the greenbacks on the table and counted them. "Tom, you're about cleaned out. You sure you want to keep this up? Have you got any more saloons you want to get rid of? How about the livery? My wife's cousins are mighty fond of that stable. Maybe you want to lose that, too?"

"Shut up, fancy boy, and play. We're sitting right here until you start losing or someone puts a hole through your head." Tom grabbed the deck and began shuffling.

The livery owner's hands were shaking as he dealt the cards. That wasn't a good sign. Tyler turned and lifted an inquisitive eyebrow at the sheriff. "Do I have to cheat to end this game?"

"The man's right, nobody's that lucky." Powell yelled at the bartender, "Bring us a fresh deck, Fred." He took a seat at the table. "I'll deal." He swept the old cards off the table and broke open the new pack.

Frustrated and fuming, Tyler sat back and accepted the new set of cards thrown his way. Peyton eased in behind him. Tyler didn't want to be accused of cheating, but he had to know what was happening. Feigning nonchalance, he leaned back in his chair to hear what Peyton had to say.

"Evie's gone with that duded-up lawyer out to Harding's place. The boys are still missing," Peyton whispered as if he were talking to the man beside him.

Evie with Hale. Fear boiled up inside Tyler. Hale had Evie's money. He knew it in his bones. He knew this was what it was all about. Hale and Evie's money, and now he had Evie. He had to get out of here.

The cards Powell gave him were worthless. He could discard the entire hand and not lose by it. Not giving any sign that he'd heard a word Peyton said, Tyler shoved a stack of greenbacks into the center of the table. "No more vouchers, Dorset. Put up the Ridge or you're out."

"You can't do this." Dorset looked to the sheriff for confirmation.

The sheriff was glancing over his own hand. "I've got a family at home, boy. I'm ready to get out of here. Put up the cash or the collateral." He glanced up at Tom. "That goes for you, too."

The sheriff obviously had a good hand. Another time, Tyler would have been amused. As it was, he didn't care what happened. Hang the Ridge. Hang Dorset and the sheriff and the livery. He wanted out of here.

Without discarding, Tyler matched the bets and called their hands. Glaring at him, Dorset threw in the heavy packet of papers in his coat pocket. With the livery deed already in the pot, Tom folded and sat back to wait the outcome.

The sheriff reluctantly parted with a stack of coins and paper and added it to the collection. He wasn't much of a gambling man, Tyler recognized. Whatever cards Powell held, he wouldn't play deep. Tyler threw out another stack of coins and raised the ante once again.

Roaring, Dorset came to his feet and went for his gun. "You're bluffing, you bastard! You can't win every time. Show the damned cards."

Hands grabbed him from behind, removing the gun while Dorset struggled with fury. Tyler merely sat back, tipped his hat back on his head, and waited.

"That's the way the game's played, Dorset. You can't control the cards like you can a military government. Either meet the wager or fold."

"I'm going to kill you!" Dorset shouted, trying to shrug off his apprehenders.

The sheriff threw in his coins. "Meet the wager or fold, Dorset."

Dorset howled. "He's cheating! Can't you see he's cheating? I'll not let him have everything, damn you!"

The sheriff looked at his own cards and shrugged. "I never saw a cheat allow me cards like these. And if you're accusing me of cheating, I'll have you locked up until your veins bleed dust."

Tyler smiled slightly and added the rest of his winnings to the pot. "I'll see your hand, Sheriff. Or do you want to accuse me, too?"

Powell stared at the young gambler contemplatively. The pot in the center of the table was mighty rich, too rich for his tastes. The amount he needed to match Tyler's call was all he had in his pocket. He knew full well he'd dealt the hand honestly. He couldn't imagine any man being so lucky as to have a hand to beat the cards he held without even making a draw. But no man could bluff with a smug smile on his face like that. Tyler Monteigne just had God's gift of luck.

Swearing, the sheriff threw in his hand, too. The crowd around them roared as Tyler began to sweep up his winnings. Tom swallowed another jigger of whiskey and slid under the table. Dorset had to be forcibly restrained as he tried to grab back the deed to the plantation.

"Can I go now, Sheriff?" Tyler asked pleasantly, throwing his cards facedown on the table and rising.

The sheriff reached over and turned the cards up. A deuce, a four, a seven, and two face cards of different suits. Nothing. Cursing, he glared up at the young gambler. "You are good, aren't you?"

"Damned good, Sheriff. And I'm keeping a lady waiting. If you'll excuse me?"

Tucking the deed to the Ridge into his coat pocket, Tyler strolled toward the door, aware that half a dozen men were following him out.

"Daniel, if you're not careful with that, you're going to blow us all to kingdom come," Ben warned as the boy grasped the stick of dynamite in his fist and pounded on the trapdoor with his other hand.

"Just keep the lantern ready. Wielding these crutches has given me a damned good throwing arm. If they don't scram, I can throw this thing right into the street. All we've got to do is duck and be ready to run."

As their yells brought the trapdoor open, Ben held up the lantern and Daniel pointed his dynamite at their captors.

"He'd been right. They didn't believe a cripple and a nigger. With a sigh of regret, Daniel lit the fuse, flung it upward and out as far as he could, and covered his head while Ben leapt to cover the boys.

The men above them screamed and ran as the dynamite exploded behind bales of hay. Fire flickered instantly.

"Now you've done it," Ben murmured prosaically, reaching for the youngest and throwing him upward to safety.

As they scrambled out of the tunnel, they hit the floor running.

Coming out of the saloon, Tyler watched in amazement as the livery he had just won shook with a solid boom. Silhouetted against the first flickers of fire, dark figures dashed from the interior like rats from a sinking ship. Before he could recognize the small shapes of the boys or the awkward gait of Daniel, a rumbling began in the earth beneath them.

A hissing followed the rumbling, and smoke began to leak from cracks growing in the street. Tyler recognized Ben, recognized the way the tall man threw himself beneath the overhang of the porch, carrying two small boys with him. With a swift intake of breath, Tyler ran to grab the dark shape struggling to run with a crutch, and jerked him into the protection of the overhang just as the explosion hit.

Fire leapt briefly from the stable door, then sucked inward with a great whoosh from the force of the explosion. The street slowly and effortlessly collapsed straight down the middle.

Uncovering his head, Daniel peered out from beneath Tyler to the cave-in slowly crumbling the clay between the livery and the bank.

"Damn, but I should have known that's where it went!"

Tyler gave the boy an incredulous look, stood up, and shaking his head at the wonders of nature, began running to the little house standing untouched behind the partially demolished livery.

Chapter 38

A coyote howled in the distance, and though the night was warm, Evie shivered and wrapped her mantle closer around her.

"How soon until we get there?" Nervous, she turned to the man driving the horse at an unseemly pace.

"The Harding ranch covers thousands of acres. And they're surrounded by thousands more of government land. I've been telling them they need to be buying that land, but they laugh. There's so much land out here, nobody needs to buy it. But the day is going to come when they're going to regret it."

That wasn't what she had asked. Evie stared out over the flat prairie. An occasional shrub tree silhouetted against the night sky was the only landmark she could distinguish. She hadn't seen any sign of human habitation for what seemed like miles.

"I don't see how Dorset can have us arrested all the way out here." This was more musing aloud than an attempt to strike up a discussion. Hale hadn't spent much time listening to any of her earlier comments.

"You fell into bad company with Tyler Monteigne. I warned you of that earlier. I'll explain it to the judge, and everything will be all right."

He kept telling her that, as if saying the words was a magic incantation that would indeed make everything all right. Evie had some confidence in the power of words, but action usually worked better. She didn't like being separated from friends and family. She wanted to go home.

"I think we ought to go back, Mr. Hale. I don't feel right leaving Tyler to face the judge alone. And I'm worried about the boys. I just don't like running away. I doesn't solve anything. I've made a mistake. Won't you turn around and take me home?"

A muffled explosion in the distance made the earth rumble and the horse edgy. Evie threw a worried look outside the carriage but could see nothing untoward.

Hale bit his lip and concentrated on the horse rather than Evie.

She could jump. The carriage had a roof and sides, but it was open in front and had only a low-slung door. But they were moving so fast she feared she would break her leg. And they were so far out in the middle of nowhere, that she wasn't sure she could find her way back. Besides, there was nowhere to hide. And no reason to hide that she knew of, yet.

"Mr. Hale." His silence put a measure of panic in her voice. "We have to go back. Something dreadful is happening. I know it."

A log and frame cabin loomed on the horizon. With the horse under control again, Hale increased the pace. "Miss Howell, I've always had your best interests in mind. We'll be there shortly. Just be patient."

"Why do you keep addressing me as Miss Howell?" Nervously, Evie twisted at her fingers. She wished she had found her gloves before leaving.

Hale gave her an impatient glance. "Because your marriage to Monteigne is not legal. I told you that."

"Everyone else calls me Mrs. Peyton." Now that she was actually getting a response out of him, Evie pushed for more.

"Everyone else doesn't know who you are, but I do. I don't know why you insist on this charade, but there's no further point in it. It doesn't matter who your father is, but your mother was Elizabeth Howell Harding. That's a matter of some importance in this town."

"She's dead, but my father's not. That's a matter of some importance to me. I want to go home."

The carriage hit a deep rut in the road and creaked ominously. Hale slowed the horse just outside the cabin.

"I'd better check the wheel. I wouldn't want to be stranded out here without shelter."

Evie glanced at the house nervously. There weren't any lights. She was certain it was abandoned.

Hale climbed down and inspected the wheels, making clicking noises with his tongue as he did so. She didn't like the sound of that. She liked it even less when he came around to her side and held out his hand to help her down.

"The axle is almost gone. We'd better stop here where there's shelter. It's perfectly safe, I assure you. No one will find you here."

Evie kept her hands crossed in her lap and stayed where she was. "I'm not going in that house with you, Mr. Hale. It isn't proper. I'll sit right here, if you please."

That didn't seem to annoy him. He merely began unfastening his horse from the carriage. "You're quite correct. It isn't proper. I'll see to it that the situation is remedied when they find us. You must believe me, Miss Howell, I truly have your best interest in mind."

He was beginning to sound like a parrot. Seriously annoyed as well as increasingly frightened, Evie glared down at him. "I beg your pardon, Mr. Hale, but I don't feel the least bit safe. There could be rattlesnakes and wild Indians out here. Surely we can't be much farther from the Harding place. Perhaps we could walk the distance?"

"I assure you, we cannot. It would no doubt be dawn before we reached the ranch by walking, and your reputation would be ruined."

"I don't give a darn about my reputation, Mr. Hale, it's my life I'm worried about. What do I know about surviving out here?" Irritated, Evie climbed down from the carriage herself. For good measure, she checked the axle, but she couldn't tell a thing in the dark.

"There will be a lantern and water and food in there, Miss Howell. We only need wait until someone discovers us." He held out his hand to lead her into the house.

There wasn't much else she could do. If she knew how to ride, she'd steal the horse. The cabin seemed less frightening than that alternative. Ignoring his outstretched hand, Evie lifted her skirt from the dust and started toward the house.

It was far superior to the shack that Tyler had taken

her to. When Hale located the lantern and lit it, she could see that it had several rooms and real pieces of furniture. The dust had been disturbed, as if someone had been there lately. The furniture was of heavy Spanish origin, and Evie ran her finger wonderingly over the old ebony table. She had seen nothing like it out here in Texas. Actually, she had seen nothing like it anywhere. The French influence in St. Louis had been stronger than the Spanish.

The massive bed in the first room was of the same heavy quality. The mattress on it didn't look as if it fit, and she couldn't help but look at it warily. A mattress left abandoned for any length of time would become the home for rodents, but this one seemed relatively intact.

"As you can see, the accommodations are a trifle crude, but comfortable. You will be perfectly safe here, Miss Howell." Hale held the lantern up so she could examine the evidence of his words.

She didn't like it. She didn't like it at all. The place looked abandoned; the layers of dust were proof of that. But why was the mattress intact? She turned to examine the shelves in the main room that would have served as parlor and kitchen. As Hale had said, there were assorted boxes and bags and cans there, a veritable larder. Why?

"I won't stay, Mr. Hale. I will take my chances with the prairie." Even as she said it, she knew she couldn't. Another coyote was howling somewhere outside, and she was well aware of the snakes and other creatures inhabiting this vast land. She had read enough of Daniel's Westerns to know all the dangers.

"That would be extremely foolish. You are a wealthy young woman, and it would be a sin to throw yourself away on unreasonable fears. You must learn to rely on me. I will take care of you." So saying, Hale set the lantern on the table and took a flame to the tinder in the fireplace. "I'm sure we won't need the heat, but sometimes a nice fire provides company."

Evie didn't like the way he said that. She didn't like anything at all about this situation. Giving the lawyer's back a contemplative look as he bent over the fire, she swung on her heel and headed for the bedroom.

A moment later, the bedroom door slammed and a bar snapped closed behind it.

Hale looked up, but his expression was one of smug satisfaction, not disappointment.

Tyler tied his horse behind the lawyer's office and ran up the back stairs. Knowing the kids were safe was a relief, but he didn't trust that damned lawyer one bit. As before, Hale's door was unlocked. He didn't need a light to know where to look. Picking up the blotter, he grabbed the file, bending it and shoving it into his coat pocket. Then he gathered up the clutter on the top of the desk and took it to the window to see if any of it pertained to Evie.

He could barely discern the handwriting in the dim light. The scribbles looked meaningless, but he shoved them in his pocket anyway. Judging by his previous explorations, Hale kept all his current notes on hand. If he were innocent, he'd have every right to scream bloody murder at this ransacking, but Tyler didn't think Hale was that innocent. Hale would have to keep his mouth shut if any of the documents were incriminating.

He knew the one man who had been up here the day of the shooting was still at the doctor's office. The other man Tyler suspected of being here was over at the saloon drowning his sorrows. Those were the only two men he could identify in association with the lawyer. He would have to begin with them.

Dawn was breaking as Tyler spurred his horse out of town. A long night of questioning had given him the information he sought, but he didn't like the sound of it. He hadn't felt this terrified in years. He'd never wanted to feel like this again. But his heart was pounding in a frantic rhythm to accompany the fears racing through his blood, and he pushed his horse at an unmerciful pace.

It was different this time, he told himself. He was a man now and not a scared little boy. There wasn't a war on. He just had to battle a greedy lawyer. But that wasn't the real problem, and Tyler knew it.

The real problem was Evie. The farther he rode, the

more that fact ground into his soul. He didn't want to lose Evie. These last two weeks had been like being back in that Yankee prison camp again, a mindless blur of nothingness with no hope on the other side. Tyler thought he'd killed all emotion in that camp, but it certainly wasn't reasoning logic pumping through him now. It was terror and longing for Evie.

He refused to be reduced to a lump of quivering pudding for a woman. It wasn't worth it. She had as much as told him that she didn't need him any more. She had sent him away. She had not once come looking for him since he'd left. She'd had those damned papers served on him. And now she was out riding the countryside with that damned lawyer. She wasn't worth the effort.

But despite these common sense assurances, Tyler spurred his horse faster. Pictures of Evie flashed through his mind: Evie smiling and laughing with a room full of crude men as she calmly cheated the cheater; Evie standing on a riverboat with sunlight sparkling off her hair; Evie behind a line of children singing a greeting, a light of welcome in her eyes; Evie, naked and rosy and wrapped in his arms in the middle of the day. The last image defeated him. She had come to him that day. She had given herself to him without reservation, without expectation of anything but to comfort his grief and guilt. He would be a long time finding another woman like that.

And so as he galloped his horse across the miles, Tyler allowed the knowledge of Evie to slowly sink into his bones and become part of him. Wherever he went, whatever he did next, Evie would be with him. It was a terrifying thought, but he was man enough to handle it now.

Unfolding himself from the uncomfortable chair in the front room as sunlight crept through the windows, Hale stretched his aching back and looked out on a rosy dawn. He had just spent his first night with a woman. It wasn't as he had hoped it would be, but he had learned to be practical a long time ago. He could have bought a night of Starr's time anytime he wanted, but he liked to keep his money for better uses. Perhaps he hadn't actually slept in the same bed as Evangeline Howell, but the effect would be the same for all intents and purposes. In a few hours, he would have the right to sleep with her every night of his life. He would appreciate some gratitude from her for saving her not only from that degenerate gambler but from the stain this night would leave on her reputation—however, he never got his hopes up, particularly where women were concerned. Perhaps Tom was right, and he should have forced her, but he just wasn't that kind of man.

He had expected Tom and his boys to be here by now with the preacher. Glancing nervously at the horizon where no sign of rescue approached, Hale crept to the bedroom door. He hadn't heard a sound from there all night: no crying or bewailing her fate, just silence. He knocked tentatively.

"Miss Howell, are you all right?"

"Is Tyler here yet?" she called in dulcet tones.

The thought made Hale cringe. "He's in jail, Miss Howell. I have it under good authority that a warrant is going to be signed against him for murder. Gunslingers like Pecos Martin always have a trail of warrants after them."

Her laughter chimed clearly through the heavy oak door. "Tell me when Tyler gets here, Mr. Hale."

She didn't even have to add a warning. He heard it in her laughter, in the assurance of her words. This wasn't at all what he had planned. She was supposed to be weeping and near hysterics and agreeable to anything. They certainly didn't make women like they used to. His mother had been the last truly good woman he'd known.

Perhaps he needed to change his tactics. Tom should have been here by now. Something must have gone wrong. He was going to have to take matters into his own hands, as usual.

Hale wasn't very good at the shotgun tactics that Tom would have used. He didn't think he could force the preacher to marry them, and it certainly didn't look like the lady was going to cooperate without some incentive. Somehow, he was going to have to provide that incentive.

"Now that it's light out, will you feel safe while I go to fetch help? My horse doesn't have a saddle, so it may take me awhile."

"Take all the time you like, Mr. Hale," she practically sang. "Leave me some fresh water, will you? I'd like to freshen up some while you're gone."

That made Hale feel a little better. Maybe she was beginning to understand her predicament. She was an unmarried woman, a schoolteacher, and she had spent the night unchaperoned with a man. Harding would have to fire her. And the good moral ladies of town would demand that he do the right thing by her, or she would be consigned to the level of women like Starr.

"Miss Howell," he called tentatively. "I'll bring the preacher back. Everything's going to be all right."

"You do that, Mr. Hale. You just go and take care of everything."

Somehow, that didn't sound as reassuring as he would have liked. Frowning, he straightened his tie and went to fetch the water as directed.

Hearing the horse ride away some time later, Evie peeked out and finding the front room empty, began to explore.

Tyler had second and third thoughts about Evie and her place in his life when he reached the cabin he'd been told about and smelled smoke coming from the chimney and saw the abandoned carriage out front. Light flickered in the front window, and he had the picture of a cozy little love nest with Evie cuddled up in the arms of her fancy lawyer. Tyler's fingers itched on the handle of his gun as he circled the house.

The place was built like a fortress. There was only one entrance and high, narrow slits for windows. He wished for some of the explosives Ben and Daniel had set off. He'd blow some ventilation into the place.

Pulling his gun, Tyler tested the door. Warped by decades of exposure to the elements, the old oak protested loudly under the slightest of pressures. Tyler cursed to himself and stepped back into the shadows. He preferred surprise for his entrance.

No one came running to investigate the noise. Were they so engrossed in what they were doing that they couldn't be bothered? Livid, Tyler returned to the side

of the house and the largest of the windows. They were
designed primarily as air vents and contained no glass.
Digging his boots into the deteriorating clay filler to find
a foothold on the timbers beneath, Tyler pulled himself
up until he could see in. He could see only the outline
of a bed and a glimmer of light from the room beyond.

If he was walking in on some unsuspecting family, he
was asking to get his head blown off. But the image
of Evie in Hale's arms kept him from rational thought.
Carefully, Tyler pulled himself through the opening. The
scratch and thump of crumbling patches of clay falling
to the ground gave the only warning of his approach.

He lowered himself cautiously to the wooden floor inside and kept to the shadows along the wall while he
listened for any evidence that he had been heard. From
the other room came the sounds of soft humming.

Humming. If it was Evie in there, she didn't sound in
the least frightened. After what she had put him through,
Tyler meant to correct that. But he didn't mean to terrify
some innocent stranger. Keeping his gun raised, he crept
across the darkened bedroom to the doorway.

The sight in the other room nearly paralyzed him.

Hair piled in a tumble of chestnut curls on top of her
head, Evie stood naked in a small tub of water, soaping
herself with a cloth while firelight danced a pattern of
shadows and light across her glistening skin.

Tyler felt all his fears fall into a lump in his stomach
while the rest of him began to tingle with a desire that
would soon become a raging inferno if he didn't act
quickly. He didn't know what in hell she thought she
was doing out here, but he sure enough was going to
find out. Holstering his pistol, he stepped into the parlor.

"Mind if I join you?"

Evie swirled around, her hair coming loose and tumbling to her shoulders as she attempted to cover herself
with her hands. Blinded by the firelight, her eyes took a
moment to recover before they could see into the shadows. But Evie didn't really need to see to know who
stood there, arms crossed over his chest as he leaned
against the door frame.

"Tyler!" She grabbed for the towel on the chair and

wrapping it around her, stepped from the tub. Forgetting that he was supposed to be in jail, she asked eagerly, "Have you come to take me home?"

Tyler could feel the effect of her beauty shattering the lump in his middle. Or perhaps it was the eager light in her eyes that made his insides come alive again. He'd known many beautiful women. None of them had made him feel like this. He wanted to wrap her in his arms, kiss her until she melted, and carry her off into the sunset.

But she didn't necessarily want the same things as he did. Sighing, Tyler refrained from reaching out for her. "Not necessarily. Looks to me like you've got a right cozy little place here." He gave a glance to the far corners of the room, noted another doorway, and casually strode over to inspect this possible hiding place.

Finding only another empty bedroom, one without the advantage of a mattress, Tyler turned to face Evie again. She was hastily tugging on her chemise without having toweled herself completely dry. The thin cotton was clinging to the moisture on her skin, leaving her nearly as naked as if she had not worn it at all. Silhouetted in the fire's light, her lovely figure made a tempting shadow beneath the garment, and Tyler caught his breath as his gaze found the outline of her legs and their juncture.

His fingers went instinctively to the fastening of his gun belt. Principles flew out the window when confronted with the temptation of Evie in nearly nothing in the absolute privacy of this hideaway. Fear didn't enter those lovely dark eyes of hers as he lowered the belt to the nearest chair.

"Do you have any idea how long it's been since we've been alone together?" Tyler started across the floor toward her.

Evie clutched the open neck of her chemise and stared as Tyler approached. She wasn't prepared for this. Nothing could prepare her for the burning hunger she found in his eyes. Her skin was aflame even before he could reach for her. She felt consumed, reduced to cinders, and incapable of independent motion beneath that stare. A sudden breeze might blow her ashes across the floor, but nothing else would move her from this spot.

But as his hand went out to cup her elbow, he ignited a flame that restored her and caught her up in its raging glory. Evie's arms slid around Tyler's neck and her body arched against his, and he was no longer reaching for her elbow but sweeping her into an embrace that threatened to consume them both.

Their mouths met and meshed and clung and devoured until they discovered that their starvation could not be satisfied with just this one contact. Evie shivered as Tyler lifted her from her feet and carried her into the darkened bedroom, but she refused to release him as he lay her against the bare mattress. She clung to his shoulders and pulled him down until he was sprawled over her, his heavy weight pushing her back into the feather down.

"My God, Evie, I don't want to rape you. Give me time . . ."

But her warm hands were already inside his shirt, stroking, touching, making him feel like a warrior god as he jerked his shirt and coat free and started on his trouser buttons. If he didn't release them, they would almost certainly pop open of their own accord.

She was so soft and enticing beneath him. Tyler felt rough and grimy and completely undeserving of the scented silk and warmth of her, but her eager hands were pulling at his clothing, and he had no intention of stopping.

He cursed at the tangled confinement of his trousers and his drawers and finally forced himself to sit up and remove his boots and clothing before returning to her. In his absence, Evie had flung off her chemise, and Tyler reveled in his unobstructed access to her breasts. He felt her arch off the bed as he took one nipple in his mouth, and it took all his self-control not to come into her then. He wanted it so bad that he ached.

"Tyler, please, now," she whispered in his ear as her hands rode down his back, their motion giving meaning to her words.

He had wanted to take time, to love her slowly, to show her how he felt, but they were both raging out of control. The brush of those soft thighs he had just seen silhouetted in the firelight flamed along his hips as Tyler dipped his tongue one more time into the recesses of her mouth. His hand caressed her breast, and when she gasped and arched into him, he couldn't stop.

Evie gave a wild cry of triumph as Tyler plunged into her, filling her, stretching her, forcing her to follow him in his mad ride as he withdrew only to surge into her again. She didn't think about what she was doing. She only knew she was in Tyler's arms again, that he had come for her, and that she would never let him go. The violent joining of their bodies was testimony to that. Nothing could ever put them asunder again.

Evie cried out her ecstasy as Tyler delved deeper and deeper and carried her with him into regions hitherto unexplored. She was lost now, running through a mindless landscape with only Tyler for guide. And as her body slammed into an unseen mountain, she shattered in his arms, and knew the joy of his echoing shout as he joined her.

Still throbbing, they lay together afterward, their skins soaked with sweat as they gulped for air. Evie had never felt more alive in her life, and she stretched her thighs to wrap around him.

"Lord, Evie." Tyler felt himself stirring again, as if dying and coming back to life once wasn't enough. "We're going to kill each other if we keep this up."

"If this is the way to heaven, then I'll gladly go," she whispered in his ear.

"I don't know if it's heaven or hell where we're headed, but we're getting there fast." Tyler finally summoned the needed energy to roll over to keep from crushing her, but he pulled her with him, keeping her trapped in a tangle of legs and arms so he could feel her along the length of him.

"I love you," she murmured against his skin.

Tyler pretended not to hear, but his arm tightened around her as he stared up at the ceiling. "We've got some problems, Evie," he reminded her.

"You came for me." Evie stretched out along his length, enjoying the rasp of his hair-roughened legs against the smoothness of her own, loving the strength of them as they locked around her.

"I have half a mind to paddle your behind for run-

ning." Tyler ran his hand down her back to cup that soft
part of her anatomy. He could feel the heat build in his
loins as he stroked her there. Holding a naked Evie
wasn't conducive to logical thought.

"I didn't think I would be much help to you if I was
behind bars, too," she reminded him. "And I thought
the Hardings might help. I wasn't running away, I was
running to."

"The Harding ranch is west, not east. You'd better
start learning directions, sweetheart. Hale wasn't taking
you to the Double H. He was taking you here."

That brought Evie out of her moonstruck lethargy. She
pushed up on her elbow and stared down at him. The
sight of Tyler's amber eyes and wicked lips at such close
range startled her, and she had a sudden impulse to bend
over and kiss him, but she knew where that would lead.
She valiantly resisted.

"Why would he do that? The carriage axle broke. He'd
just gone back to get help. He'll be back shortly." At
that thought, Evie swung toward the edge of the bed.

Tyler's arm caught her waist and pulled her back.
Without any of the restraint that Evie had shown, he
closed his mouth over her breast and suckled until she
cried out and melted into his arms again. Then he raised
his head and kissed her mouth. When she was firmly
back in place, he leaned over her.

"I have a suspicion he won't be, but I think it would be
beneficial to his health if he realized that you're truly my
wife. What better way to show him?" he asked tauntingly.

"Tyler!" At this indication of his intention, Evie began
to wriggle beneath him. "If the preacher wasn't really
a preacher, I'm not your wife. Besides, that would be
embarrassing. Let's get out of here now."

Tyler pinned her shoulders to the pillow and held her
still. "You are my wife, and what better place could we
go but your father's house? We've not had this much
privacy since we married. And he assured me we could
have the use of the place for as long as we liked."

"My father's house? This house belongs to my father?" Evie stared up at the shadows of Tyler's face,
trying not to feel the length of him sprawled across her,

holding her down. But she burned in the place where they had been joined earlier.

"I'm certain your Mr. Hale had a reason for choosing this as his headquarters. Why don't we ask him when he returns? In the meantime, what better place could we be? I'm in no hurry to go anywhere. My only concern is that Ben and Daniel and your cousins may blow the whole damned town up while we're gone."

He was distracting her deliberately. Evie knew she shouldn't be here, doing this with him. They weren't really married, and they weren't doing anything to prevent babies. And she didn't really care. That shocked her, but she wasn't going to fight it. It felt right to be lying in bed with Tyler practically on top of her. She wanted to see the taut planes of his muscles as the sun rose in the window behind them. She wanted to see his eyes dancing with laughter or darkening with desire. She wrapped one leg around his to keep him from moving.

"I thought I heard something last night. Ben and Daniel made that explosion?" She shouldn't encourage him, but she would.

"That's what it looked like to me, but I didn't stay around long enough to inquire." Tyler brushed a kiss along the side of her mouth when he felt her tense. "Don't worry, they're all in one piece. The town isn't, though. It's got a gully right down the middle."

"Tyler, what are we going to do?"

Reluctantly, Tyler shifted to a less-tempting position. He knew what he wanted to do, but he'd already created enough problems by doing that once already. He was going to have to proceed at a more logical pace.

He leaned back on his elbows and stared at the dying embers of the fire in the next room. "Why did you have those papers served on me?"

"What papers?" Sitting up, Evie wished for a blanket or a sheet, but the morning air was warm and Tyler had seen all of her that was there to see already. She shoved a handful of curls over her shoulder.

That gesture was almost Tyler's undoing. If Evie had eyes at all, she had to see what she was doing to him. There wasn't any way he could hide his body's reaction to her. But she was staring pensively at the fire in the other room and ignoring him. Gritting his teeth, Tyler swung his legs over the opposite side of the bed and searched for his pants.

"The papers ordering me to keep away from you. What did you think I was going to do? Rape you in front of the children?"

Evie gave his back a puzzled glance. "Of course not. I don't know what you're talking about."

Locating his trousers and forgetting his drawers, Tyler began to pull them on. He hadn't really thought Evie would serve those papers on him. She might smile him into oblivion, but she would never use the courts to keep him away. It was comforting to know that if Evie ever did decide to tell him to get lost, it would be with lavish smiles and a flurry of lies.

"Hale gave me papers signed by a judge ordering me to keep away from you. I figured if you really wanted to see me, you knew where to find me, but you didn't come. Am I to take it that you don't need me around anymore?"

Evie continued to sit in the middle of the bed, naked, staring at his back. "Tyler Monteigne, have you been drinking?"

Tyler ignored the insane surge of hope rushing through him as he finally turned around to look at her. "Answer the question, Evie. You know who your parents are. If I give you the rest of the information in Hale's possession, do you want me to leave so you can be the town belle or whatever it is you want to be?"

She wanted to throw something at him. She wondered what Jane Eyre or Elizabeth Bennet might do in this situation, but those ladies would never find themselves in such a fix. She really was going to have to get her hands on a copy of *Fanny Hill*.

With a sigh of exasperation and as much dignity as she could muster under the circumstances, Evie raised herself up on her knees and swung her right hand and struck Taylor as soundly as she could manage across his handsome jaw.

Chapter 39

Tyler staggered backward and held his hand to his cheek. "What in hell was that for?"

"For coming in here and taking me like this if you didn't mean to make me your wife." Growing more furious by the minute, Evie swung her legs over the opposite side of the bed and started for the parlor and the fireplace where her clothes were.

"You *are* my wife!" Wearing nothing but his trousers, Tyler stalked after her. "You're the one who claims we're not married. Our agreement was for me to get lost when you didn't want me around anymore. I thought from the sounds of it that you've decided you've got what you want, and that I don't fit in those plans."

Evie turned around and swung for the other side of his face, but Tyler grabbed her hand before she could connect. She jerked her wrist free and picked up her gown, but discovering she had no chemise, she started back toward the bedroom.

Not daring to touch her anywhere else, Tyler grabbed her hair as she passed by. Caught up short, she turned and glared at him.

"Start talking, Evie, or I'll scalp you." Feeling a little more relaxed with the situation, Tyler grinned at the fury on Evie's gorgeous little face. If his assumptions were so wide of the mark that he drew this much wrath, maybe he was better off than he knew.

"You are a despicable, rotten cad, Tyler Monteigne." Evie grabbed her hair and tried to twist it from his grasp. When he wouldn't let go, she tried to trod on his toe, but he moved too quickly.

"Let's try this another way." Wrapping his arm around

her naked waist, Tyler swung her from the floor and carried her back to the bed again. He sat down on the edge and held her in his lap, although she squirmed furiously in his hold. "This isn't the way I would plan it if I had time to do otherwise, but would you do me the honor of being my wife, Miss Evie?"

That brought her to a halt. She turned widened eyes up to Tyler's golden face, but there were no signs of laughter there now. "You don't want a wife," she murmured, repeating his litany of vows carefully. "You don't want a family. You don't want commitment or responsibility."

"Nope," he answered cheerfully. "No sane man does. And I'll avoid them all to my dying day. But I want you, and if you come connected to all those things, well then, I guess I'll just have to take what comes with the package." Tyler caught her chin between his fingers and forced her to look at him. Her bones were so delicate, he almost felt like a brute, but there was wonder shining back at him from her face and not pain. He dared to go on.

"I'm not Ivanhoe. I'm not even Don Quixote or whatever other mixed-up hero you have in your head. But you're my sunshine. You're the stars that twinkle in the night sky. You're the puppy under my Christmas tree when I was four years old. You're everything I've ever wanted, Evie. And I don't want to be without you ever again. I'll understand if you don't feel the same way. I'm not much in the way of husband material. But I don't want you to think that you're anything less than my wife. I would never treat you that way."

Tears trickled down Evie's cheeks as she heard the longing in his voice and understood what he was trying to say. Sliding her arms around his back, she pressed fervent kisses into his bare shoulder. "I don't want to be like Bessie or Miss Priss or any of your other women. I don't want to tie you down, Tyler. I want you to be happy. I don't want to do anything that's going to make you leave."

Tyler clutched her close and laughter rumbled through his chest as he held her there. "We're quite a pair, aren't we? You keep sending me away to make me happy, and I keep coming back to keep you happy. Do you think we'll ever get it right?"

"Maybe with practice?" Evie peeked inquisitively upward to be certain he was truly smiling and not despairing over her inadequacy.

"Lots of practice," he agreed, tilting her head so he could kiss her squarely on the lips. Then tasting the sweetness, he pressed for more, until they were both gasping for air.

Leaning her head back against his muscled shoulder, Evie brought her hand up to her chest to control her breathing. Discovering her nakedness, she gasped and looked desperately around for a sheet.

Tyler laughed and cupped her breast in one hand. "Don't go playing modest now, Mrs. Monteigne. This is the way I intend to see you every night for the rest of our lives."

A soft flush seeped into Evie's cheeks. She had no clothes on, and she was sitting in the lap of a man wearing only his trousers. She should be grateful he wore that much, she supposed, as her gaze daringly took in the wide expanse of Tyler's chest and her fingers played in the light mat of hair there. She knew he was looking at her, and her nipples puckered in response to his gaze. She wanted to turn and rub them against his chest, but she supposed there were other things that needed to be done before she started that again. She was very aware that Tyler was quite ready to continue their lovemaking.

"We'll have to make certain we have a legal marriage," she warned him, hoping the depressing practicalities would return him to their plight.

"As far as I've been able to find out, we are legally married, but with Hale being the only lawyer in town and him being the one to say we're not, I guess we can play it safe and have it done in the church. That should satisfy all concerned."

Evie nodded. "Why do you think Mr. Hale is trying to keep us separated?"

Remembering the papers in his coat pocket, Tyler set Evie back on her feet and went in search of them. "I'm willing to wager the answer to your question is in this file."

Reluctantly, Evie pulled on her chemise and followed him out. She had wanted the answer to the mystery, but not right now. Right now she wanted to be in that bed celebrating her marriage with Tyler. But if Hale or the sheriff or someone showed up, Tyler would likely be back in jail, and there wouldn't be any more celebrating. If the answers to some of their problems were in those papers, they needed to know.

Tyler lit the lantern while Evie struggled with her corset. Laying the file on the table, he turned to see what was keeping her. He frowned at the sight, but he supposed she was right. He wasn't likely to get much done while she ran around tempting him with her nakedness. He reached over and tied off the corset strings for her.

With her breasts pushed up by the corset and the chemise beneath untied and revealing the valley between, she hadn't accomplished much in the way of removing temptation. And when she sat down in a chair and began drawing on garters and stockings, Tyler nearly crumpled the table he'd grabbed for support.

"Evie."

She looked up expectantly.

Tyler's gaze was fixed on the curve of her calf, and his voice was slightly strangled as he spoke. "It might be best if you dressed in the other room. I haven't quite got the hang of this husband business yet, and what I'm thinking right now hasn't got anything to do with responsibility."

Her smile was absolutely and utterly devastating. Tyler continued to clutch the massive ebony table as she stood up and eyed him seductively through those blasted dark-lashed eyes of hers. When he thought he was going to have to pick her up and carry her back to the bed again, she swished her little derriere and glided gracefully out of the room. Tyler heaved a sigh of relief. Life with Evie would never be dull.

When she returned, properly clad in a high-necked gown with dozens of tiny jet buttons, Tyler was poring over the papers spread across the table. He looked up and took in her appearance with a mixture of disappointment and relief. He preferred the naked imp, but the lady was much safer.

"Would you mind telling me what you were doing tak-

ing a bath in this forsaken place if you were just waiting
for Hale to return?" The question had finally worked
its way to his consciousness and worried at him while
she dressed.

Sitting hunched over the table with the morning light
setting off sparks of gold in his hair, Tyler was the picture
of the studious husband Evie had once imagined, only
better-looking. With a proprietary wiggle, she appropriated his lap and looked over the papers he was
reading.

"Mr. Hale kept talking about the nice fire and the
food and the bed and how everything was just fine, and
I had the nasty impression that I was going to be here
for a while." "She picked up the packet of papers labeled
"Trust Agreement." I had a really long, wretched night,
and I figured I'd feel a whole lot better if I met the
new day with a nice bath. It gives the world a whole
new perspective."

"I'll say it does," Tyler muttered, snatching the paper
from her hands. If she hadn't been standing there naked
when he came in, this whole thing could have had a
completely different ending. But he'd rather make love
than fight any day. He kissed the side of her neck,
wrapped his arm around her waist to hold her in place,
and began reading again.

When he was done, he sat there silently for a minute.
Evie took the papers away and turned back to a page
she hadn't quite finished. The dying fire crackled and a
spark shot up the chimney while they digested what they
had just read.

"When will you be twenty-one?" Tyler finally asked.

"September," Evie replied absently, rereading the beginning paragraphs. Even through the legal verbiage, she
could read her mother's despair. The trust agreement
had been written when Evie was three years old, upon
the death of her Grandfather Howell, after her mother
was already married to Randall Harding. Had her grandfather died just a little sooner, had her mother waited
just a little longer, she would have had the money to
come and get her daughter. The checks to Nanny before
that had come out of her grandfather's pocket and only

with the promise that Elizabeth would marry Randall.
Her mother had been coerced into giving her up, and
trapped after that.

Evie wiped at the moisture in her eyes and finally listened to Tyler's muttering.

"You'll be a damned wealthy woman in a few months.
You could go back to St. Louis and have your choice of
husbands. You'd better start reconsidering right fast."
Tyler caught her waist in his hands and tried to set her
back on the floor.

Evie sat right back down again. Tyler had pulled on
his shirt, but he hadn't fastened it. She ran her hand over
the silky fur exposed there. Tyler glared. She smiled.

"What do you think about babies?" she asked
innocently.

"They happen," he growled.

"So they do." Without further explanation, Evie turned
and picked up the next piece of paper on the table.

Tyler wrapped his arms around her waist and squeezed
until she looked over her shoulder at him. "Are you
trying to tell me something?"

She looked surprised. "Of course not. You already
know where babies come from, don't you?"

He had this giant abyss opening deep in his middle
and an insane desire to laugh with sheer joy, but all he
could do was stare at Evie's full ripe lips. His mind
sheared back from the edge and focused on reality. Evie
wasn't very good with reality. One of them had to be.

"Have we made a baby?" he asked cautiously.

She gave him an absent smile, patted his chest again,
and turned back to her reading. "After this morning, I
wouldn't doubt it. What do you think this means about
his wife inheriting one-half of everything he owns?" She
pointed at the phrase in Randall Harding's will.

Tyler briefly contemplated strangling her. The crashing
realization he had been harboring secret hopes that she
might be carrying his child struck him like a backlash
from a muzzle-loader. He stared at the slender woman
in his lap, circled her waist with his fingers, and wondered
how it would feel when she began ripening with his child.
His loins instantly responded to the notion.

Groaning at his one-track mind in Evie's presence, Tyler grabbed the will from her hand and read the damning phrase. More familiar with the legal niceties than the Harding brothers, his mind instantly grasped the implications.

"Didn't Harding die first? Your mother lingered some weeks after his death, didn't she?"

Evie nodded, and her gaze met Tyler's. She gulped when she saw the black intensity forming behind those usually laughing eyes. She didn't like his stare one little bit.

"I think, my wealthy wife, that you just may own one-half of the Double H."

Evie stared back. Tyler's tone was cold. She didn't like the sound of this at all. "What would I do with a ranch?" she asked, quite reasonably. "The money would be nice. I could buy new clothes for the children and maybe make the house bigger." A sudden thought staggered her, "That is, if you're planning on staying here."

Anxiety lined her brow, and Tyler gave up the battle. She was sitting on a mountain of gold and worrying about whether they were going to be able to stay in that miserable little shack behind the livery. He nuzzled her neck and resolved to work out the monetary details later. Evie was bright enough to translate the volumes of legal-ese, but she hadn't quite grasped the concept of what it would mean to them. Everyone else in the world would think he was after her money. Evie worried if he would stay in this wretched little town. Tyler shook his head in dismay at the impossibility of it all.

"It's your money. You can do what you want with it. My concern is Hale's plan for all this. If he knows who you are, why hasn't he told you about your inheritance? Isn't that what an honest lawyer would do?"

Distracted by this new question, Evie considered what she knew of the lawyer. "He's always been honest with me, except for not telling me he knew who I was, not until last night, anyway. I wonder how he knew?"

Tyler caught her hands and pressed them together, re-directing her wandering thoughts. "It doesn't matter how he knew. What matters is why he didn't do something about it. You've been living on beans with that teacher's salary of yours. Why wasn't he giving you the money the trust supplies?"

"He was, until Nanny died. I thought maybe the money was going to Nanny's lawyers, and I didn't want to let them know where I was, so I didn't write to them. But if he knew all along who I was, then he could have just given me the money. It doesn't make sense."

"Has Hale been courting you, Evie?"

She shrugged. "He says nice things and wants to take me to dinner all the time. He keeps telling me he's going to take care of everything for me. I suppose that would be pleasant if I was inclined to lean on others, but I'd rather take care of myself."

Tyler grinned and settled her more comfortably in his lap. "Then why did you go looking for Pecos Martin?"

Evie frowned at him. "That was different. That was for Daniel. Now quit looking so smug. Do you think Hale meant to marry me? Was that why he tried to get rid of you? I read something like that in a book once. The villain kept shooting at the hero and missing. It was terribly silly."

If Hale had been the one responsible for sending those two thugs out into the street with the children as hostage to draw him out, Tyler didn't find his actions very silly. But there were other forces at work here above and beyond Hale. Tyler wanted to rub his forehead and clear away the cobwebs, but Evie was right. It had been a long night.

What he wanted most was to pick Evie up and retire to that wonderful featherbed. But now that he had taken up the burden of responsibility, he wasn't going to set it down again. Tucking the papers inside his shirt, Tyler reached for Evie. "It's time to go find our villain, sweetheart. Are you going with me?"

As if he had to ask. Smiling eagerly, Evie swung around and started for the door.

Chapter 40

"You're either going to have to teach me to ride or find a saddle for two," Evie complained from her position behind Tyler. She shifted her arms around him as she tried to find a comfortable seat.

"The thought of you on a horse by yourself gives me the shivers, Mrs. Monteigne. I'll think about the saddle first."

She pinched him through his shirt, and Tyler laughed. It felt good to laugh again. He felt as if an immense burden had been lifted from his shoulders. He couldn't remember the last time he'd slept, but the knowledge that Evie was behind him sent energy singing through his veins. He could conquer mountains the way he felt this morning.

But it wasn't a mountain kicking up dust down the trail in front of them. If it was Tom and his gang of thieves, they were in a mountain of trouble instead, but Tyler tried not to let Evie sense this. Tom ought to be in the sheriff's custody by now. And after their hiding place was blown to pieces, the thieves ought to be halfway to Kansas. That line of dust represented trouble of a different sort, he suspected.

It didn't take long for recognizable shapes to ride out of the dust. Tyler brought his horse to a halt, checked that his gun was within reach, and wrapped his big hand around the small one at his waist. "Here they come, Evie. This is your last chance to get rid of me."

He felt her teeth nip into his shoulder and smiled. She had her claws into him deep, and he ought to be shaking her free. For her own good, he ought to push her out of his life. But he was a selfish bastard and wasn't going to give her up without a fight. After five long years of ambling peaceably through life, he was ready for a fight.

The sheriff led the pack. Right behind him rode Jason and Kyle Harding. Tyler frowned at the strangers behind them, the ones riding next to the lawyer, Hale. They looked surly and half-drunk. He could guess whose side they were on. His gaze drifted to the stragglers in the pack: Peyton and the real preacher from the church, quite a combination.

"There he is! Arrest that man, Sheriff. I told you to keep him away from the lady. My word, if he's molested her in any way ..." Hale signaled for his cronies to move in.

Tyler's gun was already in his hands as the strangers pulled out of the pack and began to circle him. He rested it calmly against his saddle horn as he met the sheriff's gaze. "I thought we'd come to an understanding last night, Powell. What is it you want now?"

Powell lifted his big shoulders uneasily against his tight shirt. "Hale says you're a danger to Mrs. Peyton. Claims he brought her out here for her protection until the two of them can get married." He threw a look to the woman peering out with interest from beneath Tyler's arm. She didn't look any too frightened.

Tyler shifted his position so Evie could see around him. The glitter of his eyes was decidedly dangerous as he looked down at her. "Is that right, Mrs. Peyton? Am I keeping you from your nuptials?"

She dug her thumb into the sensitive spot beneath his arm and made him twitch. "Actually, Mr. Monteigne," she answered sweetly, "these gentlemen are interfering with my plans. But since they so kindly brought the preacher along, perhaps that situation can be rectified. Reverend, my husband and I want to confirm our vows. Can you do that for us?"

Hale screamed in fury, and while confusion reigned, his surly companions moved in for the kill. The one closest to Tyler raised his gun, but the noise shattering the morning air wasn't from his weapon. That went flying out of his hand before he could pull the trigger. Screaming with pain, he grabbed his wrist and glared at Tyler.

Tyler was already opening fire on the other two thieves and didn't notice the glare. Their gun belts went skittering into the dust as their horses reared and screamed. Fighting to keep their seats, they had no time and little thought for retrieving their weapons.

Returning his smoking gun to its original position on his saddle horn, Tyler turned an unpleasant smile back to the lawyer. "You were saying, Mr. Hale?"

While the Hardings closed in on the would-be assailants, keeping them from retrieving their guns, Hale turned his rage to the sheriff.

"You can't let him do this! He's keeping an innocent young girl from her home and family. All he wants is Miss Howell's money!"

The name Howell instantly swung the attention of both Hardings to the couple on the horse. "Howell?" they echoed each other.

Evie smiled at them a trifle shyly. "Evangeline Peyton Howell. I was afraid of being murdered in my sleep if I gave my full name."

"Evangeline ..." Jason choked on the name and turned a glare to Hale. "Howell?" The word was more demand than question.

Hale swallowed nervously. "I only just found out. She's been leading me a merry chase."

"And that's why you brought the good reverend out here? To end the chase?" Jason was wound up good now. He inched his horse closer to the quivering lawyer. "You were going to use us to make her marry you? Just when were you going to tell us who she was? After the wedding? When you owned half our ranch?"

Kyle came up behind the terrified lawyer and grabbed his collar, lifting him bodily from the saddle. He silenced Hale's screech of terror with a shake. "What'll we do with him, big brother?"

"Put him down, Kyle," Tyler called wearily. "We'll need him to straighten out the god-awful mess he's created. Evie and I don't want your damned ranch. We just want to get back to the kids."

Peyton spurred his horse up next to Powell's. "My daughter is in need of a husband, Sheriff. I'd suggest we get the lot of them back to town and see that she gets one before the day is out. *Comprendé?*"

Having spent a long sleepless night himself, the sheriff was only too willing to turn his horse back to town. He only glanced to Miss Peyton-Howell or whatever her name was for assurance.

"Are the children all right?" she inquired brightly.

"If you call blowing up half the damned town all right, sure." He swung his horse around and started home.

Tyler watched with a frown as the thieves made a hasty departure in the opposite direction. They were going to have to go back and round up those three one of these days, but it didn't have to be now. Squeezing the arms wrapped around his waist, he set off after the shouting, squabbling men in front of them.

"I'd be a damned sight better husband for her than you are, Monteigne," Kyle grumbled as he straightened his tie with the use of the mirror over the bar.

"Yeah, and then you'd own three-quarters of the ranch and would probably try to drive me out." Jason spread his long legs across the barroom floor and examined his boot toes. "At least Monteigne won't stay put long enough to cause me any trouble."

"I don't want your damned ranch," Tyler repeated wearily, for the thousandth time this day. "Right now I've got half a saloon, half a damned livery, and half a wife. I don't need half a ranch, too."

The Hardings ignored him. "It would be good to have a woman around the house again," Kyle said thoughtfully. "The place is beginning to look like a derelict barn."

"And we still need a schoolteacher. Monteigne will most likely cart her out of here before the dust settles." Jason bent to polish a speck of dirt on his boots.

Sighing, Tyler slammed a deck of cards on the bar. "All right. High card wins Evie. And the kids. And her father. And Daniel. And hell, why not half the saloon and Starr and the damned livery? I'll just shuck the whole damned place off my heels if I lose."

Kyle stared at him in horror. "The kids? You mean

the kids come with her? They blew up half a damned town, Monteigne! Nobody's going to touch those kids."

"Actually, Daniel did that," a voice answered laconically.

The men at the bar turned their attention to the black man and the boy studying their cards unobtrusively at a table by the wall. The boy with the crutch leaning on his chair reddened.

"Daniel blew that hole down the middle of the street?" Tyler stopped worrying at the frills of his cuff and stared at the boy.

Ben shrugged and discarded a card. "He threw the dynamite. Would have sailed right out into the street and just made a little bang if the bastards hadn't tried to block the door with hay. Then José knocked over the lantern, and one thing led to another ..." He shrugged again and went back to his game.

Evie chose that moment to sail into the saloon and catch Ben's words. Smiling, she wrapped her arms around Daniel's neck and hugged. "The boys told me everything. He's a hero. He saved them all. And saved the bank, too. The sheriff said Tom and his gang were planning to tunnel into the bank and steal all our money. They would have done it, too, if Daniel hadn't stopped them."

Tyler cleared his throat rather loudly. "I don't suppose I get any credit for keeping Tom tied up at the saloon while Daniel worked his dastardly deeds?"

Magnanimous in her approval, Evie released Daniel—much to his obvious relief—and sailed into Tyler's arms. Wrapping her arms around his neck, she pulled his head down and kissed him soundly. Then she stepped back, crossed her arms, and glared at him. "Why aren't you over at the church? The preacher is waiting."

"Because your stepbrothers here can't decide who gets to be your husband." Tyler threw the Hardings a disgruntled look and straightened the cravat Evie had loosened.

Wide sloe eyes turned an incredulous look in the Hardings' direction.

Kyle stepped back and held out his palms. "Don't look

at me. I was just interested in keeping the peace. What
would I do with a passel of kids?"

Tyler caught Evie's waist and steered her toward the
door. "Besides, she lies and cheats at cards. Better leave
her to me."

Evie balked. "I do not cheat at cards, Tyler Monteigne! I don't even know how to play."

Tyler looked down at her calmly. "Yes, you do, too,
Evangeline Monteigne. You stood right there and smiled
every time Dorset had a bad hand and frowned every
time he had a good one. That's cheating."

Evie scowled. "Ben called them kings and queens, but
they all looked like knaves to me. They weren't wearing
any clothes, Tyler! I didn't like it when those cards
showed up."

Tyler stared down at her with dawning understanding,
fighting to keep the laughter from boiling up inside of
him. Cautiously, he turned to Daniel who was watching
this display with an amazing lack of expression.

The boy shrugged at the inquiry in Tyler's eyes.
"Nanny wouldn't let us play cards. She said they were
the devil's playthings."

"She didn't know they were high cards?" Tyler still
couldn't believe he was hearing this right. This whole
damned adventure had set out on the assumption that
Evie was something she was not. Why did he have such
a hard time believing that?

"She doesn't even know what a high card means.
But we know what card cheats are. We read about
them in ..."

"... In a Pecos Martin book." Tyler finished the sentence with him, throwing up his arms in defeat. "I give
up. I'm marrying into a family of lunatics." He punched
Daniel's shoulder. "The preacher's waiting. You're
standing up with me, remember?"

Sheepishly, the boy grasped his crutch and pulled himself up. "I wasn't sure you meant it. I mean, Ben ought
to be the one ..."

Tyler looked at the black man rising from the other
chair and watching him a trifle grimly. "Ben's the one
who ought to be giving me away." Tyler pulled a sheaf

of papers from his coat pocket and shoved them into Ben's. "But he's going back to Natchez."

Catching Evie's arm, Tyler began dragging her from the saloon. They only made it as far as the boardwalk outside before Ben caught up with them.

He caught Tyler by the elbow and jerked him backward, shoving the papers in his hand. "What in hell am I supposed to do with the damned place if you ain't goin' back?"

Tyler pulled his arm from the other man's grip. "Burn it to the ground for all I care. Sharecrop it. Put all your industrious relatives to work. It doesn't make up for your sister or pay what I owe you, but it's a start." He started to walk away.

Ben grabbed him by the shoulder and spun him around. "That was your daddy's place. You can't do this."

Tyler met Ben's dark gaze with aplomb. "It was your daddy's place, too."

Evie and Daniel stood quietly out of the way, their gazes flying back and forth between the two men, one black and lanky and possessed of a singularly unhandsome face, the other golden and compact and blessed with all God could give a man. Yet there was a resemblance there, if only in the proud way they held themselves and the independence of their thinking.

Ben scowled. "Mine, maybe. My mama wasn't a discriminating woman and your father was a philandering man. But he wasn't Cissie's father. You know that, don't you? And what happened to Cissie weren't any fault of yours."

"I left her, Ben." Tyler seemed to shrink back into the shadows of the porch, away from the stares of the people he had come to love and respect. "I walked out on her when she needed me. The babe was mine, and the fault was mine. Tell your mama I'm sorry, and I'm trying to be a better man."

Ben swung around to meet Evie's concerned gaze. "He was seventeen years old, Miss Evie. My sister kept after him, followed him everywhere. There ain't a boy that age can resist a willin' woman. Cissie was young, but she knew what she was doin', and she was more than willin'. Tyler was grievin' over his father's death, and she took advantage. She only told him they'd made a baby just afore he left to find his brother. There wasn't nothin' he could have done different if he'd stayed. She would have died birthin' that baby no matter what he done. It ain't any of his fault. Make him understand that, will you?"

Ben tried to hand the sheaf of papers to Evie, but she reached for Tyler instead, curling her fingers around his arm and standing close. "I'll do that, Ben. Will you be going back now?"

Looking slightly embarrassed, Daniel climbed up from the street to join them. "I told Ben about my family wanting to put me through college. I don't want to leave here. Ben's taught me a sight more than any college could, and Mr. Averill will teach me all I need to know about the newspaper business. So I thought those fancy lawyers your father hired to take care of your money could write my family's lawyers and have my money sent here. When my leg gets better, Ben can teach me to hunt and ride and fish, just like he taught Tyler. And I can pay him for his services, and he can send the money back to his family." He threw Ben an anxious look. "Unless you've changed your mind now that you own the Ridge?"

With the papers crumpling in his big hand, Ben looked down at the four-eyed cripple. "Boy, you askin' me to give you grief and get paid for it. Don't see how I can refuse. Besides"—he nodded at Evie and Tyler clinging to each other in the shade of the porch—"them two need lookin' after. They might have got all the looks, but they ain't much in the brains department."

Daniel whooped, bringing the men in the saloon crashing to their feet and running for the door.

Laughing, Evie threw Tyler a mischievous look, grabbed up her skirt, and began running for the church.

Tyler was off like a shot after her.

Not knowing what was going on, the men pouring out of the saloon took off after them.

Chapter 41

Tyler grabbed Evie's waist and swung her against him before she could burst into the church ahead of him. Holding her still, he wiped her face with his handkerchief, removing the dust and perspiration their chase had wrought. "You look beautiful," he murmured.

"There wasn't time to make a proper wedding dress." There wasn't an ounce of regret in her voice.

Tyler looked down at the midnight blue taffeta she had changed into. The cut of the bodice was relatively modest, but Evie filled it so well he had no difficulty imagining what lay beneath the slippery cloth. He had difficulty breathing just watching her trying to catch her breath. "That one's just fine," he assured her. "More than fine." His hands measured the slender span of her waist above the bustle of her skirt.

By this time, the rest of the wedding party had arrived, gasping and wiping their foreheads and glaring at the main participants.

Jason glowered at the two of them. "What in hell did you do that for? I thought someone was after you."

Donning a magnificent smile, Evie patted his arm tenderly. "You're going to make a lovely big brother. Thank you."

At the door, James Peyton looked out and harrumphed. "It's about time the lot of you got here. The guests are about to rebel. Have you seen José and Manuel?"

Tyler and Evie looked at each other and groaned.

Daniel came limping up in time to catch the question. "Don't worry. I know where they are. Let's get this

blamed thing over with so everyone knows what in hell
to call Evie."

"Daniel!" Evie reprimanded, but Tyler shoved her toward her father before she could launch into a full-
scale tirade.

Peyton grabbed her arm and pulled her into the church
while the men dashed around to the side door to take
their proper places up front.

Evie gasped as she entered the church. In the few
hours she had been preparing for her wedding, someone
had filled the interior with flowers. Huge baskets of red
and white and purple branches covered the altar. Hanging baskets of greenery adorned half the pews. And real
red roses covered nearly every available space between,
perfuming the air with their rich scents. Her head literally spun as she tried to take it all in.

It was then that a chorus of childish voices filled the
front of the room with song, and tears puddled in her
eyes.

She was clutching her father's arm and walking down
the aisle when Tyler's mellow voice cracked slightly, then
joined the chorus, taking over the harmony. The tears
rolled down her cheeks as she approached the altar and
saw Tyler standing with a hand on Carmen and Manuel's
shoulders while Maria and José stood between them,
holding hands. It didn't matter what the words to the
song were. They could have been singing "Silent Night"
for all she cared. What mattered was that Tyler was singing, singing and standing there with the children at the
same time, not running away. He had made his peace
with his past at last.

He really and truly meant to make this marriage real,
even if he'd never said the words she'd once dreamed of
hearing. Her smile was watery as Tyler reached out a
hand and pulled her toward him, this time in front of a
genuine preacher in a real church.

It wasn't exactly a traditional wedding, but nothing
they had ever done had been in keeping with tradition.
Daniel couldn't locate the ring. Her father had his hands
full keeping the two youngest in their seats and quiet
while pockets were being turned inside out. Carmen was

a little young to be maid of honor, but she helped Daniel locate the missing ring before Tyler could start turning the boys upside down to shake it out of them. And Ben stood off to one side, not quite one of the party or the family, but with them just the same. And when the final words were said, he was there to plant the first kiss on Evie's cheek, much to the shock of their audience.

"You're going to have to take care of him from now on," Ben whispered in her ear.

"I'll try." Evie sent her husband a misty look, but Tyler was busy glaring at the Hardings as they came down the aisle with determined looks on their faces.

Ben elbowed Tyler and nodded toward the side door. "My wedding gift to you. Get going."

Standing in the center of the aisle, arms crossed over his chest, Ben blocked access to the newly wedded couple. With a whistle and a jerk of his head, he was instantly surrounded by four eager young faces. Maria toddled to Kyle's leg and grabbed his trousers, tugging for attention. José and Manuel grabbed Jason's arms and dragged him toward the front door, shouting about the tunnel and the stolen goods still down there. And Carmen and Daniel politely stood on either side of Ben and Evie's father, greeting the guests as if this were their reception instead of a blatant blockade so the wedding couple could make their escape.

And as soon as Tyler understood their intent, escape they did.

Heads turned as the stylish young couple stepped onto the steamboat in Houston. Smiles appeared as it became obvious that the two had eyes for no one but each other. Elbows prodded sides and knowing smirks abounded as the couple immediately ascended to the staterooms, entered one, and closed the door.

Inside the luxuriously appointed cabin, Tyler pulled Evie into his arms and began unfastening her gown. "I'm not going to let you out of here until we reach New Orleans," he murmured as his lips made a path from her ear to the corner of her mouth.

"What will people think?" Evie asked before his

mouth could conquer hers, but she really wasn't concerned with the answer. She had been dying to do this for the entire frustrating stagecoach ride. Her hands went of their own volition to Tyler's hair as their lips met.

When they finally came up for air again, the rest of her bodice was undone and Tyler's cravat was lying on a chair. Lifting her meaningfully from the floor, Tyler carried her toward the bed. "People can think what they want. This time, they'll probably be right."

As he bent his head to kiss her, Evie gasped, "Tyler, what about babies?"

Tyler never hesitated, he simply moved from her lips to her cheeks, commenting casually as he went, "Anytime you want to present me with one is fine with me."

Evie felt the tingle all the way to her toes at this reply, and her arms slipped around her husband's neck. They would make beautiful babies together. But even as she arched into his seductive embrace, more objections rose to mind.

"The children? What about the children? Where will we live?"

Frustrated, Tyler rested on his elbows and gazed down into the beautiful worried eyes of his wife. "Why don't we get all of your questions out of the way right now so I can start this marriage out the way it's meant to be? The children have their uncle and Daniel and Ben with them. Your father is going to take them out to his ranch so they won't plague the town too much while we're gone. We can live any damn where that you want and take them with us if you wish. I can sell my half of the saloon to Starr and build a house in town. I can buy a herd and raise cattle. We can live on steamboats and travel the river. I don't care. I just want you with me wherever it is."

He saw the doubt and the little niggle of fear in the back of her eyes, and he groaned and wrapped his fingers in her hair. "Don't look at me that way, Evie. This is forever this time. You're not going to walk off and make me live in hell again. I'm sticking to your side like a burr. Have you got that?"

Eyes widening in astonishment at the sound of pain in

his voice, Evie touched Tyler's jaw and traced the line of his lips with her fingers. "I'm not ever going to leave you, Tyler," she whispered reassuringly. Realizing there were many ways of leaving, and he had suffered all of them, she poured her strength into her words. "Even if I die, I'll not leave you. I'll come back and haunt you. I'll be a ghost at your side forever or until you don't need me anymore. I love you, Tyler, and love never dies. Don't look at me like that, Tyler. I read a book about a ghost like that once."

His laughter caught like a sob in his throat as he saw the absolute sincerity in her eyes. Knowing Evie, she would do just that. Tyler pulled her into his arms and buried his kiss against her throat. He didn't ever want to think about life without Evie.

"I don't doubt that you have enough spirit to do just that, Evie. But if you don't mind, I want to make love to you for the rest of my life, so don't plan on being a ghost too soon." He was strangling on words he had never said before but needed to be said now. He didn't know how to get them out. Everyone he had ever loved had died, and he felt jinxed in thinking he could love again. But Tyler knew what he felt for Evie was way beyond lust, way beyond anything he had ever known as a callow youth. And he had to let her know, had to bind her to him as he had never done before.

With desperation, he muttered, "Do any of your books say how to tell someone you love them so much you'd die if they ever went away?"

Evie smothered his cheek in kisses. "I think they said you were supposed to tell them flat out," she answered between pecks.

With a sigh of relief, Tyler whispered, "Flat out," in her ear, before covering her laughing protests with his mouth and drowning them with his kiss.

And down on the main deck, two travel-weary strangers straggled on board carrying their saddles over their shoulders.

"I thought you was planning on catching that varmint

using your name, Pecos," one muttered as they headed for the main saloon.

The taller man shrugged his dust-covered shoulders. "I reckon he won't be doin' it again. I got my pleasure seein' that jumped-up lawyer rode out of town. He should have been hung with the rest of them, the way I see it."

His sidekick dropped his saddle at the bar and ordered a whiskey. "That ain't the way the stories in those books end. You're supposed to shoot them down yourself."

The man named Pecos contemplated his glass cheerfully before flinging the contents down his throat. Then wiping his mouth with his sleeve, he said, "I think I'll go after the writer of them damned books next."